Playing God

The evening might know what the morning never suspected.

Best wishes
Amelie Bullough

Amelie Bullough

AuthorHouse™ UK Ltd.
500 Avebury Boulevard
Central Milton Keynes, MK9 2BE
www.authorhouse.co.uk
Phone: 08001974150

This book is a work of fiction. People, places, events, and situations are the product of the author's imagination. Any resemblance to actual persons, living or dead, or historical events, is purely coincidental.

© 2009 Amelie Bullough. All rights reserved.

No part of this book may be reproduced, stored in a retrieval system, or transmitted by any means without the written permission of the author.

First published by AuthorHouse 12/23/2009

ISBN: 978-1-4490-4330-8 (sc)

This book is printed on acid-free paper.

For my grandchildren, Alvin and Freja Tyrland.

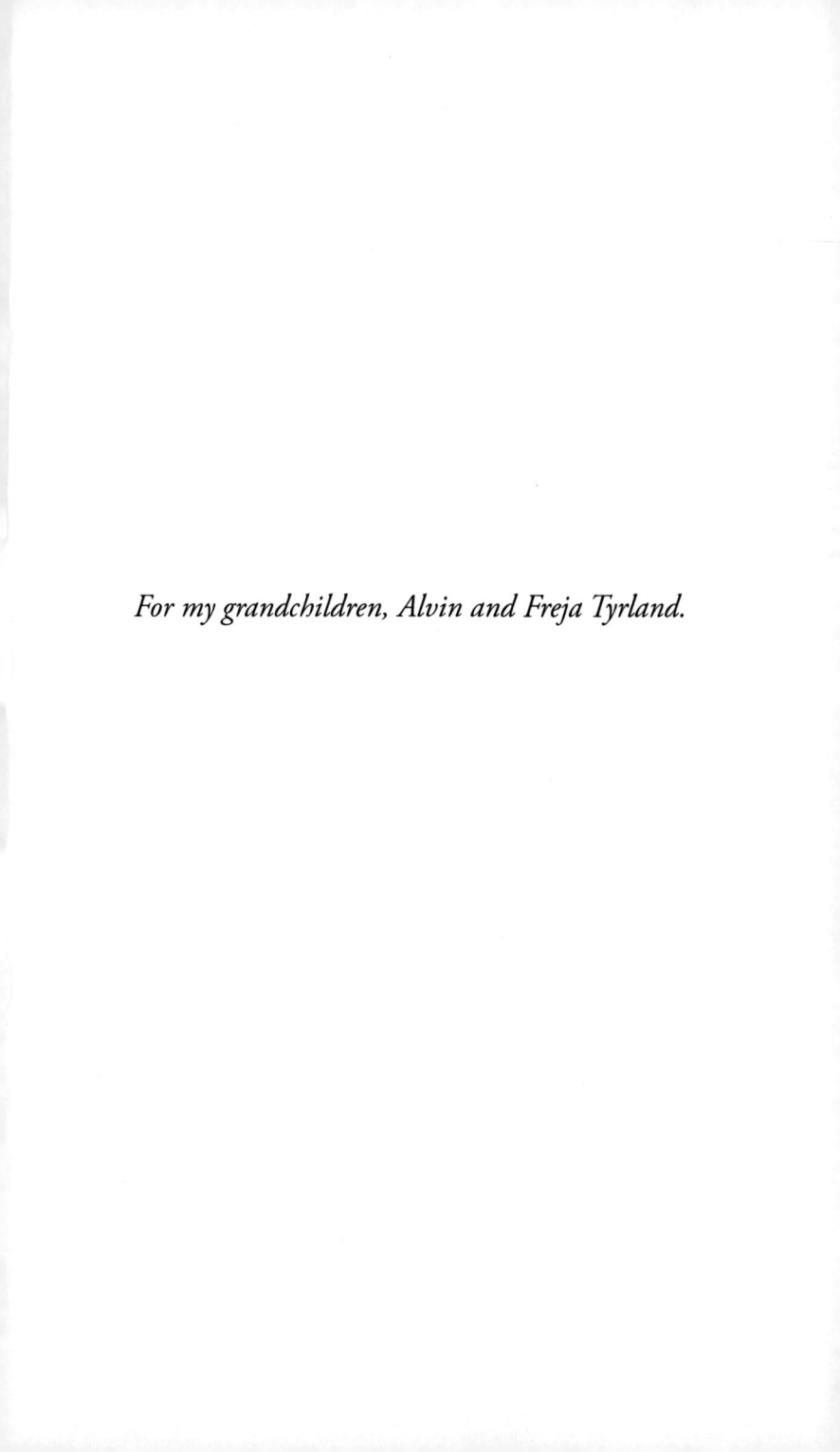

Acknowledgements

Coming to live in Scotland away from my native Sweden was not easy but thanks to my many new friends it has been a most enjoyable experience.

I would like to say a sincere thank you to the congregation at St. Cuthbert's Episcopal Church in Colinton for welcoming me into the comunity.

A big thank you to the ladies at Kingknowe Golf Club - all new friends - for putting up with my lack of concentration on my golf whilst my mind has been preoccupied with my writing.

To the members of the Book Group "Septima" for the regular guidance on good books to read and the encouragement their discussion engendered.

Thank you Frances Parsons and Malcolm Goldsmith for advice based on your own writing experiences.

To Pat Edwards a grateful acknowledgement for helping with the "translating" from "Swenglish" when reading the first draft.

To Peter Gibbons for helping me with my computer.

To my editors Christine Thomson and Will Dick for their enthusiasm, encouragement and speedy responces.

To my step son Jeremy (retired police officer) for helping me on police procedures.

To my sons Magnus, Mans, Olle and Anders Tyrland for keeping on telling me 'Yes you can'!

A huge hug for my darling husband Peter and grateful thanks for help, encouragement and always trying to answer my very odd questions. 'I know you must have felt neglected sometimes. So Sorry'.

CHAPTER 1

Rebecca was standing by the window. It was raining. Just drifting softly, almost like a silver, grey shining net curtain. It felt soothing. Thinking about it, she had loved the rain as a child and still did most of the time. She did not find it depressing.

The light was fading fast, and it was all but gone although it was only late afternoon. Dusk was descending.

Her thoughts were like the fluffy clouds, scurrying across the sky. Strange, as there did not seem to be any wind out there. It must be breezy further up.

She knew she would have to go home in a couple of hours, after another day had passed without any signs of Tom waking up from the coma he had been in, ever since that awful day of his accident.

She did not enjoy going home anymore. The house was so dreadfully quiet and empty with Tom in his hospital bed, and James at University, but she often wanted to be alone with her thoughts. In a way, this weather gave her a strange sense of peace and tranquility when she was tense. It gave her the courage and strength to go home for yet another evening on her own, even if she did not enjoy it.

She was lucky to have many good and supportive friends. James made the point of coming home to see her and his father every other weekend. Some marvellous friends from her golf club, the church, and the book club among others were keeping in touch with her. Rebecca was so pleased that she had started playing golf a couple of years ago. This had been Tom's wish, as he liked playing the game and wanted to play with her now that James had left home.

Tom was a member at another club, which meant that she often played with the ladies in her club and he with the men at his "men only" club. Rebecca and Tom had tried to play together once a week mostly on his course and of course weather permitting.

She loved playing golf, and the ladies had been friendly from the very beginning and numbered amongst her best friends. They did not ask too much, probably understanding that when there was anything to tell, Rebecca would let them know. They had showed great patience with her indifferent golf and lack of concentration lately.

Rebecca turned away from the window with a sigh, a heavy sigh, which would in better times have made Tom turn to her, asking what was the matter.

She looked at Tom and thought that he at least had been moved from the cold, glossy and brittle white world of intensive care, where she had felt claustrophobic surrounded by sterility and colourless shiny walls. This room gave her a shiver too, as it was painted in that so typical hospital green. It was almost too warm because of the central heating, but Rebecca felt cold from the inside.

She was pleased that Tom had been allocated a room to himself. Here there were no other people looking at her when she had a little cry or when she bent down over Tom and kissed his forehead. She had been promised that he would keep this room, even when he woke up. She appreciated this special treatment and consideration and the impeccable care.

Rebecca had built a shell around herself to retire into, trying hard to pretend everything was normal, that everything was going to be fine. It was not going to be the last time she would play hide and seek with her feelings.

Her friends told her that she had to open up and talk, but it was too difficult. It was only at night in her sleep, that she became defenseless and cried out in her hopelessness. The worries impaired her nights, and she had to fight during the daytime not to let the darker thoughts consume her life. She was tired most of the time. It was hard to watch Tom lying there in his hospital bed still attached to all kinds of machines, without being able to do anything about it.

He did breathe more easily now, and the doctors and nurses told her that he would wake up one day. They had warned her not to expect too much from him in the beginning. Nobody new what he would be like when he finally did wake up. Perhaps his memory would be blank and what would that mean? She might have to start teaching him to walk again never mind to talk.

Tom had survived an extremely severe head injury and extensive surgery and knowing that the brain regulates the entire body Rebecca was understandably worried. That was why it was difficult to predict the outcome of a head injury. This left her with so many questions unanswered. If only he would wake up so that she would know. This not knowing was the most terrifying feeling. To have to wait made her heart ache. She could not contemplate the rest of her life without Tom, and it occurred to her that even a long life could suddenly become terribly short. How foolish it would be to waste the time we have been given as a gift.

'Oh Tom, if you only could open your eyes. If you could stop wasting your life away',she said. She had to come to terms with whatever would be the future for them. It was frightening not knowing about Tom's future. Nobody ever knew what kind of a life fate would dealt to you. How would their life change? How would she ever be able to live with her sense of guilt? She felt as if she were walking on quicksand.

In only a few weeks time she would experience how "walking on quicksand" really felt.

She sat down in the armchair next to Tom's bed and held his limp hand in hers. What was the point? What was the use of her sitting here day after day with her thoughts? Rebecca had asked herself that question many times, but she had to go to the hospital to see Tom every day. She looked at his pale face, his closed eyes, and stroked her hand over his smooth cheek, grateful that he was so well looked after and nicely groomed every morning by the devoted staff.

When at home she longed to be back at Tom's bed side, but the staff had told her not to tire herself out, and that she should try to live outside the hospital as much as she could.

Rebecca turned down the music a little for Tom to be able to hear her voice clearly, if he could hear. Somebody had told her that a person in a coma might feel comfortable surrounded by favourite music, and that a person in a deep sleep needed stimulation through music and the voice of a loved one. Nobody knew for certain, but everything was worth a try. Every day she talked to Tom about James, their house and garden and the memories which they had shared together. In a way she spoke to him through her emotions, hoping he might be stimulated by sensing her love as she relived their tender moments together.

Mozart had to be played quietly but she left the music on as a back ground stimulant. It lifted her depression and made the room feel more tranquil, more homely.

She opened the book and continued reading aloud, for Tom to perhaps be able to sense her presence. Both the doctor and one of the nurses had told her that this might rouse Tom and that it would help him to remember her voice when he finally opened his eyes.

Reading a chapter each evening made Rebecca think of the story about the young beautiful girl, who had started telling a story for the King but was always saving the end till the following evening, and then start another one, all to keep herself alive for as long as possible. 1001 Arabian nights it had taken her for the King to ask her to marry him. Her life was then saved. Many were the girls who had been killed before she had started her story telling.

Rosemund Pilcher and Maeve Binchy were of course not authors that Tom would have chosen, but she had to have "easy reads" with happy endings. She had not read "Light a Penny Candle" by Maeve Binchy before, so why not? She had the wish to disappear into the story, looking forward to the next day's reading and another chapter for Tom.

She had started her readings with childhood memory books like Astrid Lindgren's "Pippi Longstocking". They had read these to James and had had great fun doing it together all three of them. "The Children of Noisy Village" and of course Milne's about Winnie the Pooh had been others which they had enjoyed.

Some evenings, when reading to Tom, she felt nothing

for the story. She could just hear her own voice filling the space in the room, not knowing what she was reading. Those times, the pages were just filled with ruffled words, crinkled like an unravelled woolly sweater. Rebecca knew this was not fair to the story. She did not give the book a chance. She had to ask Tom for forgiveness the next day and re-read the chapter.

When she was not reading for Tom, Rebecca tried to talk to him. She did this whilst she was doing some embroidery. Talking to Tom, she felt less alone, but a little afraid she would start talking to herself like a little old lady, wandering around the empty house on her own, more or less passing through room after room until she came back where she had started although their house was not big, it was like having had too much to drink and working her way through a labyrinth. The person who said "silence is golden" did not know what she or he was talking about. Silence was not happiness nor was it gold. It was just pure hell although she often valued being on her own and keeping the silence.

Rebecca knew that Tom loved her and she loved him. She knew that in no way did he mean to be cruel to her. It was not his wish to stay in his coma day after day, the nurse had told her, and yet Rebecca felt abandoned by him. Knowing about their love for one another made it even worse in a way. How could one leave a loved one, someone that loved you so much? How was this possible? She asked him, over and over again, almost accusing him of lying there wasting valuable time.

When the ambulance had brought them to the hospital Tom had almost stopped breathing, but with frantic attention from the medical staff and a myriad of life support machines, his survival had been hanging on a single thread. Another sigh from Rebecca. Despair must not win, must not take over. She sometimes did think that she needed help to move on, to get out of her protective shell, and yet she did not want to become dependent on that help. She would not admit that she needed someone else to make her independent. She needed help however, to move from within to outwith herself, and to start communicating her doubting faith would make her feel as if she had given up hope. Rebecca had to come to terms with the possibility that their future no longer would be what it used to mean to them. The fact that she was stubborn had become a strength.

She felt that time passed slowly. She was almost high, as if time was holding its breath, just like she herself did, waiting for something to happen, for signs that Tom was going to wake up soon, very soon. Sometimes she felt useless, as if there were no point in anything.

The thought of James kept her going more than the thought of Tom. Rebecca had to remember that James might have lost his father, so his mother had to keep her calm and keep her chin high in James' presence. A strange stillness touched her, wondering what was the use of her sitting here in her own rather selfish thoughts? What was the point of anything anymore? She found herself often repeating these thoughts to herself. She was in despair more and more as the days passed by.

Tomorrow James was coming home for the weekend so Rebecca whispered 'Please, please Tom open your eyes for him then.'

She affectionately stroked Tom's pale hand, picking it up and traced his unbroken life line in the palm. It was long. This line gave her hope that Tom was not going to die yet. He had been allocated a much longer lifespan. Rebecca bent down over his head on the pillow and kissed his forehead lightly. A tear rolled from her eye and passed her chin, before it slipped from her face to his. One single drop of salty water. She begged him to remain with her and told him that she loved him, and that she needed him.

To her no feeling was greater than the feeling of being close to Tom, and she just hoped that he also could sense her need.

'Tom, oh Tom, where are you now?' she pleaded.

Her question remained unanswered. She bid him good night and hesitatingly left Tom and the room.

The visit had been exhausting. It was dark outside. It had stopped raining when she went back to the car in the hospital car park. The tarmac was shining from the wet. Rebecca turned her face towards the sky and took a deep breath of the fresh air and sent a few words up to Him, hoping that He would find her there and comfort her. She prayed for Tom as she so often did these days.

Rebecca drove back home under the street lights, which were glowing in the dark like stars showing her the way, as if she were navigating an old sailing ship. It was like driving on glass with the lamps sparkling in the wet tarmac. Like glass without transparency.

Her thoughts were muddled with a mixture of feelings. She tried to bend them into the trail of what she had done during this day, which was about to bid her farewell at the beginning of the night. At the back of her eyes she kept the picture of Tom's pale face on the hospital pillow, and this image emerged out of her consciousness, even when she did not want it to. She had no power strong enough to stop his reflection popping up in her head. This disturbed her. She stopped the car, left the door open and the lights on, stepped out of the vehicle to open the gate so that she could drive up to the garage.

CHAPTER 2

Rebecca parked in front of the garage. She did not get out of the car immediately. She just sat there looking at the white painted part of the old stone building circa 1680. It didn't look that age. It was gleaming a welcome, trying its best to cheer her up.

She missed Heather. Now there was no dog greeting her through the kitchen door glass panes. The little Westie used to sit looking out of the bottom right end corner glass square.

Heather at only eleven had had to be put to sleep a couple of months before Tom had his accident. The vet told them that their beloved little dog was ill and was suffering too much. There was no help, no hope. They missed her terribly. Heather's little white face and upright tail waiting to be noticed and patted, stroked and scratched. She would have been excellent company for Rebecca now. Someone to talk to, someone who would quietly listen, looking up at Rebecca with devotion and trust, faithfully cocking her head from one side to the other when spoken to.

Tom had given away Heather's basket and blanket and told his broken-hearted wife that they would buy new things for their next companion, another dog. They had talked about getting a bigger dog, perhaps from a Dog Rescue Center. Tom had missed the dog as well.

Rebecca decided there and then, sitting in the car, that she would visit the Center with James the following day. A dog would be good for Tom when he returned home but why not for her now? Rebecca had spells of being afraid of the dark, so she told herself that a dog would not just be for company, but also to safe-guard her and the house. This was definitely a consideration, but could she buy a dog now without Tom?

Sitting in the car, gates wide open behind her, she pulled herself together with a determination she had not had for a long time. They would go to the Kennels together, mother and son, if James wanted to of course. Rebecca had something positive, something wonderful to look forward to.

She stepped out of the car, closed and locked the gates before she took the door key out of her handbag and let herself into the kitchen. She felt as if the car had wished her good night with a friendly smile twinkling its light at her as she had pressed the remote control to lock the vehicle. How pleased she was to have left some lights on in the house before she had gone out to visit Tom! It was quiet, the deep rural silence, though she was no further from Edinburgh than a ten minute drive. Wonderful to find herself in this oasis after having been surrounded by things and by people. The hospital was teeming, though Tom's room was quiet. Rebecca loved silence although she had to admit it could become oppressive. She was not fond of the radio being left on as background even for evening music. Luckily Tom thought the same. As it was, the only sound she could detect was the cuckoo clock in the snug telling her it was eight o'clock. A dog, she thought again. She had so much love to give and enjoyed going "walkies". Heather had been such a special little lady, but what dog owner did not think that about their pet? She had been trained to do a "widdle" on request before sleep at night or before longer car journeys. How many dogs were that clever?

Rebecca had to eat something. It was not often that she felt hungry these days, but she knew she had to eat. Rather, she had to make herself eat something. She knew that it was essential to eat properly to keep herself fit to be able to cope. She also knew that if she were not physically strong when Tom woke up, and was allowed to come back home, she would be of no use to him.

She locked the kitchen door behind her and put her keys back into her handbag, which she then placed on top of the worktop directly to her left. Rebecca went to the fridge which was built into the centre island together with the microwave and the ceramic hob. Never again would she have a kitchen with built in appliances. This fridge was far too small and old, but it was difficult to find a match and to get a bigger one into this kitchen, as it was architecturally designed by a man of course. They never seemed to put things in a position where they were most needed.

She took out a tomato, some lettuce, the rest of the spaghetti from yesterday's supper, the fresh mushrooms, butter and a clove of garlic. She turned round to take out a red onion from the larder. Next she lifted open the shining stainless steel lid of the bottle green Aga, exposing the heat under one of the two frying pans which she had taken from the corner cupboard. The pressed clove of garlic went into one pan together with the butter and the mushrooms, one by one as she cleaned and sliced them. She emptied the spaghetti over the olive oil into the other frying pan, adding some herb salt and stirring it when it started sizzling.

While the food on the Aga became hot and brownish

Rebecca mixed a salad straight on to her plate and finally, she spread chopped red onion on top. Strange as it might be, this was one of her favourite simple dishes. Rebecca just loved the crispy fried spaghetti with the garlic mushrooms mixture on top.

It was only Tom at the other side of the kitchen table and a glass of red wine that were missing to make her meal perfect. Rebecca served herself a large glass of cold tap water. Since Tom's accident, she had not dared to have even a single glass of wine, never mind a Campari or a gin and tonic. She wanted to keep a clear head and to be ready to take the car back to the hospital at any time if the phone rang. However, before she sat down to eat at the kitchen table, she switched on the outside lights at the front, the back and in the garden

The lights at the front of the building made such a difference to her when she was sitting at the kitchen table. It widened her view and scared away the black of the night further from her sitting at the table by the window.

From her seat she could see the climbing rose bush still in its dormancy. The thick beech hedge retained its rich brown covering.

It was a good hedge all year around and sheltered the house from the wind and protected it from the view of passers by. When the hedge was brown or in its spring green it was always beautiful. The only negative thing about it was that it was such hard work to trim. They had managed to get hold of a good gardener who removed this chore from the less enjoyable tasks in the otherwise rewarding garden. Rebecca looked out over the little stone wall across the flowerbed and the tiny lawn. This piece of grass was a pain when it needed to be mowed, as it sloped steeply from the hedge towards the flowerbed and the low stone wall. Rebecca was pleased that Tom had put down masses of yellow and blue crocuses and daffodils along this wall. There were lots of bright colours gleaming in the early spring, real wonders for her soul. She could just see them in the lamplight. It had been hard work and rather cold when they had been planted with lots of cups of both tea and coffee required for the worker.

The tulips were showing some tiny green leaves. They had had to put them into the ground deeper than normal in order to prevent them from becoming winter food for the squirrels. Rebecca had been surprised, that there were so many yellow crocuses on display. The squirrels must have had easier access to food somewhere else. Though it was only end of March, the garden looked alive with early daffodils nodding slightly to her in the night breeze. They were of course asleep now in the dark, and swaying, in the wind rather like a stream. The flowers provided some pleasant company whilst she ate her meal.

At the circular beech wood table by the window were three chairs. She had chosen Tom's chair, when she was on her own. It was facing the entire kitchen and the door into the dining room area. Sitting on his chair meant that she had her back to their bedroom door. To occupy Tom's chair took away some of her loneliness. By this choice she avoided looking at Tom's empty place at the table. That her own seat was left empty did not bother her.

Her thoughts went back to the daffodils. There were so many different varieties of these flowers. They ranged from white and yellow or with a pink middle to yellow,

yellow ones, single or more bushy and heavy doubles. Rebecca and Tom had bought all kinds of different species, tall and short and many miniatures. They resembled the sun. They were a joy and essential in the gardens during the spring. Daffodils were beautiful on the roundabouts and the roadsides. Surely they must put a smile on peoples faces but this spring, she had to admit, she hardly noticed them on her way to and from the hospital.

Tonight, while eating, she browsed through 'The Week', which had arrived for Tom with this morning mail. It was an excellent source of information, and for her, absolutely perfect now. She could get the reflective week's news with comments by reading just a few pages. There were articles about readable books, good and interesting exhibitions and films. She flipped through the pages about the stock market, as she could not concentrate enough to make any decisions. She and Tom always studied and discussed the market for their modest investment portfolio. Both of them had an interest in making the most of their savings and the market stimulated their small risk and gambling instincts.

Now being on her own she just loved their beechwood kitchen. It was probably her favourite room. She did everything possible around this table at the moment, but when Tom was there, it had been the cosy snug or the dining-living room with its big log fire place that took their favour. Rebecca had read quite a few books during her sleepless nights. She had browsed through magazines in the beginning of Tom's hospitalization, and had then gone from short stories to more satisfying novels. She lacked concentration, but with an easy exciting story, so-called "Page Turner", she found greater satisfaction. It was fantastic when a book drew her away from her dark thoughts of guilt and despair. It was a wonderful feeling to be absorbed by another person's words and feelings. It was comforting in a way to find a good book which made the time pass. Reading gave her the pleasure of disappearing into another world, another life and another place, particularly now when she could not go anywhere herself, as she had to be close to Tom. Some escapism must be good for her. A good book was an excellent conversation piece, something to share with her friends. To find something pleasant to read was like finding a good friend who did not ask too many questions, did not look at her feeling sorry for her. When people did that, she found it almost impossible not to cry. She did not want to sob and cry when looked upon. She had cried so much these last few months, but mostly on her own. She still had more than the odd spell when she let herself dissolve into waterfalls of tears.

Rebecca had always loved the feeling of a new book in her hands. To look at the cover, and then to open it gave such a promising sense of dreams and of company among the rows of black ink. Rebecca preferred the soft paper to the hard and glossy finish. She had always loved that very moment before starting to turn the pages over. Sometimes it was like knitting a sweater. She loved to start it, and she loved to finish it, but to make the second sleeve could be rather boring. as she had already seen what it was going to look like. When it came to reading a book however, closing the novel having read the end, she sometimes felt as if she had lost a friend. If a book had not totally caught her interest, her imagination, she thought it was wonderful when she could close it after the last page, and she could reach out for another one. The start and the finish produced a great feeling, but sometimes Rebecca felt slightly bored reading or "knitting" the middle bit.

Going to school she had longed for a fresh exercise book to write in, but when an empty page had been used, much of the magic disappeared.

Rebecca's best friend Anna had given her one of these empty but lined books when she had first visited Rebecca after having heard the sad news about Tom. Anna had told her to fill it with her thoughts, to clear her mind and perhaps be able to share it with Tom one day, like a comfort dairy.

'To write helps to keep a suffering person sane', Anna had told her. And yes, Rebecca did write in the book every so often. As a matter of fact she had to remember to buy a second one, as there were not many pages left in the original. Sometimes Rebecca had to remind herself that to live life was more important than to write about it.

She left her place at the table and put the dishes into the sink. She did not use the dishwasher when she was on her own. It was therapeutic to stand at the sink with the picture from outside the window in front of her. The sink faced the back garden, which was beautiful, the real garden with the weeping willow not yet weeping. Oh no, she must not think like that. It was much nicer to turn her eyes towards the daffodils around the tree trunk.

The Camellia at the outside corner of the terrace was only green but she knew it would be a splendid splash of deep pink soon. It always was, and people passing by stopped at the gate for a moment to admire this shrub each spring.

Rebecca longed for the roses to come out. They were climbing up the wall surrounding the kitchen door and the windows to the master bedroom and the kitchen.

She loved this house as much as Tom did, but they had started to talk about down sizing, as Tom was much older than her, and they had planned to do a lot of travelling together, now that both of them had retired and James no longer lived at home.. What would become of these plans, nobody knew of course. A smaller house with a smaller garden secluded and still in the village area was what they had decided to look for. This house sometimes felt like a tie. One had an awesome responsibility with an old house.

Rebecca went through the oldest part of the house to sit down in the snug and to watch the news. She had to keep up with the rest of the world in spite of everything. She started to think about the journeys they had made in the past. The most moving place she had ever visited was when they had been on a tour with their church group to Israel.

The Holocaust Museum in Jerusalem. Yad Vashem was situated on "The Mount of Remembrance" and " The Children's Memorial" there had been the most emotional place she had ever experienced. It was a powerful, and touching tribute to the one and a half million Jewish children who had lost their lives in the Holocaust. This memorial had been carved out into the underground cavern by the architect Moshe Safdie. It had given them a feeling of being suspended in space as she and Tom had walked through the enclosed interior in complete darkness, guided by an unseen handrail. The only sound came from recorded voices, softly reading the names, ages and the countries of origin of the murdered children, but in this darkness "there was light". Five candles were replaced every day to ensure that they were forever burning. They were reflected by hundreds of invisible mirrors into tens of thousands of twinkling stars like souls in the sky.

Rebecca had fought to suppress the grief that had wanted to escape from her into a torrent of tears. The grip of Tom's hand had increased for a moment, as they had experienced this deep emotion. She had felt the presence of these children and their spirits so strongly.

At the outskirts of this memorial site was a simple railway cattle truck, perched at the end of a track a striking reminder of a journey to death. This truck recovered from Germany, was an original, small and innocuous, and yet so evil. She remembered how she had almost been able to taste the fear, hear the horrors and the prayers. She had almost seen the shadows of the people that had been transported inside it. A desperate mother, who had left an unfinished inscription inside which read: "In this sealed car load I am Eve with Abel my son if you see my other son Cain son of man please tell him I........".

Rebecca could still today remember the exact words and tears were again filling her eyes. It must have been something on the News that had brought this back to her. She sat quite still for a minute or so in remembrance of this poor mother and of all the parents who had lost a child in that terrible war. Today as ever there are unsettled times in Israel with terrorist killings and more, which dissuade tourists from visiting this fascinating country.

With a sigh, her thoughts returned to Tom and to

James. She was lucky to have a son alive and living near by too.

It was much later, back in the kitchen for her late evening cup of coffee, that she noticed the fox dashing away among the bushes along the fence. There must be a hole somewhere for it to disappear like that. Rebecca let her thoughts float around and by the time she lifted her cup once again to finish her drink, the dregs were stone cold and she emptied the contents into the sink. She decided to go to bed to try to get some sleep. James would be with her by lunchtime the following day.

When she opened the bedroom door she remembered that she had forgotten to load the bread maker in order to be able to treat James to some fresh thick bread with the crunchy crust slices. He just loved her bread.

CHAPTER 3

After another restless night, Rebecca woke up with a start. It was the alarm on the bread making machine that awoke her. Never could she have dreamed that she would be fast asleep at nine in the morning when she had set the timer for the bread the previous night. It was a lovely morning but still fresh. She would have to wait till later in the day to have her coffee outside. Long may this weather last. James could help her in the garden at some stage of his weekend stay. He could mend the fence for her if there was a hole that had to be fixed to discourage the fox.

When James was at home, they always went to visit Tom before dinner, which meant that there surely would be an opportunity for James to help her with this and a few other tasks which Tom would have taken in his stride.

Of course Rebecca went at least twice daily to Tom's hospital bed, but during the weekends when James was visiting his mother, they had started to go just once a day, so that James could have the time to help her with things she had not been able to do herself.

Rebecca had a shower and contemplated having coffee and toast with cheese for breakfast and not her usual fruit salad and yogurt. She had looked at the bread and it was an aroma she could not resist. It was ages since she had had toast for breakfast. Tom could never understand why she toasted freshly baked bread but she enjoyed the overall crispness.

Before Tom had had his accident early in the year,

he had cooked himself bacon and egg for breakfast on Saturdays and for Rebecca he had boiled two eggs and always to perfection. 'Lion cooked' James had called it when he was a little boy. This was a runny yolk with a firm egg white. She still made herself the morning fruit salad as a daily ritual.

Saturdays were their days off and they used to sit for hours over breakfast, reading the two news papers they subscribed to specially for these mornings. The rest of the week they just had the Times delivered and no Sunday paper.

Pulling on her jeans and a warm shirt, she once again felt the fear creeping into her mind like a snake slowly slithering up to its victim. She had to shake her head to try and resist the weak tears getting further than her eyes. She shrugged away the feeling of despair. James would soon be arriving and she wanted to look cheerful for him.

Rebecca managed to pull herself together and sat down by the kitchen table and dialled her friend Anna's number. She wanted to talk to somebody about her wild idea of getting a dog before she discussed it with James. She had to talk it over with someone to know if it could be as lovely as she thought it might be. She did not always trust her own mind at the moment. Her judgment was like a creaking gate.

Rebecca prepared the soup for lunch so that it only needed to be heated when the time arrived for her and James to enjoy the freshly home made meal. One of James' favourites was his mother's bread of course, but her soup was yet another.

Rebecca phoned the Dog Rescue Centre asking if it

would be possible for them to visit and see the dogs and enquired about adoption. The staff said they would be delighted to meet her.

For the first time since early January she felt quite excited. Well, she had had this wonderful feeling that something good could be happening ever since her dog plans popped into her head the day before. She was well aware however, that James might not think it was something for her to commit herself to with Tom in a coma.

James arrived an hour earlier than usual so they decided to go to the hospital together to see Tom before lunch. Rebecca told James about her dog plans in the car. He was quiet for so long that she thought that he might not have been listening, but when she stopped the car in the hospital car park he turned to her and said 'Let's go to the Dog Centre after we have seen dad.' Her relief was genuine as it was only minutes since her question and thoughts had been put to James, although it had seemed like hours. No, he really thought this was a brilliant idea. He was sure it would mean a great deal to his mother, and perhaps make her go out and meet more people, other dog walkers. She would surely start a conversation with some of them which would take her out of her grief. His mother had always been such an outgoing "peoples person", and more often than not had a smile on her face. He had no doubt about his father's feelings about having a dog, and it would be good for him too, when restarting his life. All positive thinking, even if his parents might wish to travel in the future. James would be able to take the dog sometimes, and there were several reputable kennels not far away. He thought that his mother almost looked vibrant again, although she was awfully pale, but there was something in the air around her, something reflective a wish to start living again. James was worried about his mother, but he was full of admiration for her and how she had coped with such difficult times. He knew that she was often tearful, but she put a brave face on for him, when he came to see her and his father.

James hugged his mother as they went up in the lift to Tom's room.

Tom had suffered a restless night, but the nurse said she detected his eyelids fluttering for a moment, and hopefully this could mean that Tom was slowly showing some signs that he might be coming out of the coma he had been lost in for three months. The nurse told them not to get too excited just yet but it could be the beginning of the beginning.

Rebecca and James looked at one another with joy and revived hope, but Rebecca also sensed the fear creeping up on her as if she felt the premonition of approaching disaster. What would Tom be like? Would he be the loving father and husband he had been before his fall on the ice that dreadful day three months ago? Would he remember them? Would he be the same old wonderful Tom? With these questions in her head she half listened to James' one way conversation with his father. Rebecca told Tom that they were going to a Dog Rescue Centre to see if there was a suitable dog for her and Tom. She talked to him about his restless night, and how James and she were looking forward to having him home with them. She asked Tom to squeeze her hand if he could hear her, but Tom's hand stayed in hers, still and limp as she had become accustomed to during this time of no response, if one could ever get used to a situation like this that is. James, holding Tom's other hand in his, talked about his university studies and friends he had made. He begged his father to wake up before Easter. Tom was reminded that James was going away for a weeks skiing with friends for the Easter holiday. This Rebecca and Tom knew about, as it had been arranged before Christmas.

James did not want to leave his mother on her own over Easter if the situation had not improved, but Rebecca had told him to go. If Tom did wake up during James' absence, it could perhaps be less confusing for Tom to have only one member of his family to get used to. The doctor confirmed her opinion when they later went to see her for the regular formal update on Tom's progress. As he had been given daily physiotherapy for over two months now, his muscles had not wasted away altogether, but he would be very tired and would need a lot of sleep. It was not difficult to return quickly from France if James should be needed, and he would never be further away than a phone call even on the pistes with the miracles of the mobile and text messages.

With the prospect of Rebecca having a dog, a companion in the house, it would make it easier for James to leave his mother and go abroad for a week. She would be in good hands and Anna had promised James that she would see his mother every day even if Rebecca said that this was not necessary. Rebecca had also promised to go to Anna and Eric for dinner on Easter Sunday. She had already been invited. It would be Rebecca's first dinner out this year, as she had declined all evening activities up until now.

It was lunch time before they left the hospital, and

they decided to go home and eat before visiting the Dog Rescue Centre. One thing they did not want to do was to rush into things. James was afraid of what might happen if they did not find a suitable dog. If there was no dog that his mother liked enough to take home with her, would she be able to cope with such a disappointment? How would she react? She had looked as excited as a child at the prospect of getting a pet. Yes, James looked at his mother and realized what was different about her. His mother had more of a spring in her step. A very good sign, James thought. He was delighted, but also a shade apprehensive.

Rebecca considered herself to be a lucky woman, although with Tom in hospital after the accident, she felt guilty as if it were her fault that Tom had injured himself. Rebecca was lucky in so many ways. They had married late in life, though they had been acquainted when Tom had been studying at the University and she still at school. They had lost touch after Tom's parents and younger sister had died in an accident abroad. Tom had wanted to be on his own then, too young to share his grief with her. Rebecca had never had the chance to meet either of his parents.

It had been Tom who had found her, almost a decade after he had lost his family. He had told her then, that he had tried to trace her but she seemed to have disappeared from this earth completely.

After a few years Rebecca had married someone else and moved to Sweden with him. They had no children, and when Tom had finally found her, she was widowed after eight years of marriage. Rebecca had moved back to Edinburgh and had started working at the library close to her home.

Tom had suddenly turned up at her front door step one Sunday afternoon, and there had been no looking back from that day on.

It was sad not to have had more than one child, but Rebecca was almost forty and Tom several years older than her by the time James was born. The doctor had told them that another pregnancy could prove to be complex for Rebecca, so the decision had not been a difficult one at. It was just that Rebecca was an only child, and would have loved to have had a bigger family herself, at least one brother or sister for James. Tom was a loving husband and James a wonderful son. Rebecca had a good relationship with James and she felt that they could talk, really talk, about anything. Tom had the same relationship with his son, and now James had been a pillar of strength for her. He had told his mother that he had the strength to deal with this situation and still apply himself to his studies. The stubborn streak had certain advantages.

Tom and Rebecca had a wonderful marriage and were always taking care of one another, talking through every little problem that might occur. No quarrels really, but a few disputes, easy to resolve by discussions, respect and love.

When Rebecca and James got out of the car at the Dog Rescue Center, there was no doubt whatsoever that they had arrived at the right place. Dogs were barking everywhere.

Rebecca and James were met by a lovely lady and were first taken to an office for mutual questions and answers. Rebecca told her that she and her husband had had dogs before, even if they had always had Westies and never one from the Dog Centre. So why now? Rebecca explained that she felt that she would like to give an unfortunate dog a home and love. She wished for a bigger dog, more like a Labrador type, and not a puppy, but one which had received some form of training. A dog which could be a companion good for walking. One thing Rebecca said that she did not want was a dog that barked a lot, as her husband would be coming out of hospital soon. It had to be a younger dog but the sex did not matter and no, they did not work any longer. The dog would not be left alone every day and yes,they had a garden. The lady explained about her job with the dogs and the health checks. Every dog was thoroughly examined and vaccinated. It could be difficult to tell the exact age of the animal, of course. Some dogs were just left on their door step.

They were in the office for some time before going out to have a look around. The lady went round with them and other members of staff told Rebecca and James as much as they could about any dog they stopped to examine more closely. So many dogs met Rebecca's eyes, brown sad eyes asking her 'Choose me'. Lots of small dogs of all kinds and unknown mixtures.

They turned to see the bigger ones and the lady told Rebecca she thought she had just the right one for them, but wanted them to have a thorough look around, before she let them know which one she had in mind.

Rebecca and James noticed that there were some good looking dogs among the mongrels. Most of the dogs were lovely enough for Rebecca to love and take with her. In the end, she had found two dogs that she especially liked. They were both mostly black with shiny shorter coats. Rebecca would have difficulty in choosing. One of them was probably a Labrador cross, and looked like a long legged but sturdy Labrador, and the other more like a cross border collie which would need a great deal of exercise. Rebecca had always dreamed of having a border collie, but she felt that it would not be suitable for Tom and her at the moment, not as she did not know how much time it would take caring for Tom. Both dogs seemed to be delightful, friendly and loving animals, but when the black "Labrador" came running up to them Rebecca made up her mind. She looked up at James, who nodded and the lady told them that this was the dog she had had in mind for them.

His name was Mozart, and he was about two years old. He had been left a few weeks ago as his previous owner had suddenly died of a heart attack. Mozart had been found, by neighbours lying next to his master about 24 hours after he had died. Rebecca crouched in front of the dog, and cuddled his soft velvety ears. She looked into his eyes, lifting up his head and asked if he would like to come home with them, to a new home and a new family for a week's trial. After taking Mozart for a walk to see if he would like them, they got him into the car with a collar and a lead and enough food to last him a couple of days. He was a delight and looked so happy, said the lady. Rebecca gave her a contribution for the Dog Centre and thanked all the staff profusely. She promised to let them know how they were getting on. If Rebecca realized that Mozart was not for them or if he did not seem to be a happy dog in his new environment, she promised to come back with him. Rebecca was determined however, to give this dog a loving and caring home.

Mozart had obviously been well treated, and was a healthy young pet, but he must miss his old master. She felt that there was all the time in the world for them to become good friends. Rebecca was not going to change his name. She liked the name Mozart, and was sure that Tom would agree.

Rebecca sat in the back of the car with her new companion and James in the driving seat. The dog was restless, but Rebecca stroked his head repeatedly, telling him how lovely he was. She had become fond of him already, as though a void had been filled.

When they got home and had given Mozart his bowl of fresh water, they realized that they had spent most of the afternoon at the Dog Center. It was after 5 o'clock and Rebecca would have to start preparing their dinner. James said that he would go to visit his father on his own, if she did not mind. Rebecca could tend to the dog and just to be the two of them would be a good start for them. Mozart would have to be introduced to his new home, and Rebecca would give him his first meal with his new family. But first of all she was going to take him out into the back of the garden for him to have a sniff around. James reminded her not to let the dog into the back garden on his own, in case there was a big enough hole through which he might disappear.

'I'll tell dad about our day, and of course about Mozart,' James said before he left them.

The black Labrador look alike dog was running around the garden, but he often looked back at Rebecca, who was in the garden with him enjoying the spring air. They did not look at the same things. The dog was sniffing and marking his new territory, whereas Rebecca enjoyed looking at him and the daffodils.

She examined the Camellia and noticed there were hundreds of buds this year as every year.

It was dark, but there was a shimmering of cold light around the entire garden, because the moon had already taken its position in the sky. It was big and full, looking like a lit up round Dutch cheese. The man in the moon looked down on the two, and Rebecca had to lift her head up to greet him with a smile.

There was not a breath of wind. It was a clear chilly evening. The night would be drawing in. Rebecca wondered if there was going to be a frost. She hoped not. The magnolia tree by the terrace was already threatening to burst into flower. It always did this far too early and every year the frost would challenge the tree and often win. Every light pink flower would then be scarred. The early ones would have their edges burnt and miscoloured a light brown, all the way round each of the petals.

Rebecca saw Mozart by the fence happily wagging his tail. She called him back, but had to go up to him and she decided it was time for them to go back into the house. She cleaned up after him first however. This was one of the tasks she did not enjoy, but who did?

She gave him his meal which he gulped down as only a hungry dog could do.

When James came back later, just in time for dinner, he had bought a basket for Mozart. James had managed to be in time just before the pet shop had closed for the weekend.

At dinner Rebecca and James not only talked about Tom, but also about the new family member and his future with Rebecca and Tom. They discussed some rules for the dog and decided to teach him not to beg at the table, as he was doing now, although he had eaten his own meal. He would get the message soon enough, by not being presented with any nibbles from the table. Rebecca also wanted the dog to understand that the bedrooms and the furniture were no places for him. Mozart had obviously been used to having nibbles at the table at mealtimes. It was hard to resist him, his paw on their laps and his begging eyes. Rebecca had to avoid looking at him She put down his paw back on to the floor saying 'No', but it did not take him long to be back to her after a desperate visit to James going through the same procedure.

After dinner Rebecca softly fondled the dog's lovely ears.

Rebecca put all the used crockery into the dishwasher with help from James. When she started the machine, the poor dog jumped and, she showed him that there was no danger, talking to him and cuddling him time. Mosart would have to get used to this noise as his basket had been placed in the kitchen.

Earlier, just before James had returned, Rebecca had taken Mozart round the house. Not upstairs as there were just the two spare bedrooms and a bathroom for guests, which was a no go area for dogs.

James and Rebecca brought their mugs of coffee through to the snug to watch the 10 o'clock News. Mozart put his head first in Rebecca's lap and later on into James' lap. The dog did give up in the end realizing that there would not be any nibbles and with a big sigh he dropped down in front of the fire place. He looked so funny that both Rebecca and James burst out laughing. There this wonderful dog was, lying with his head on his crossed front legs. Yes, he had crossed his legs in front of him and it really did look funny. Poor Mozart looked up at them wondering why they were laughing. Rebecca simply had to get out of her armchair to cuddle him, even if it made

Mozart stand up again wagging his tail and licking her hands. He also tried to kiss her, but that was something she would never let him do. With a dog, you just knew where that nose surely had been.

After the News they took the dog out for a short walk, on the lead. It was a great pleasure to do so as he did not pull. Well, he tried to stop for a sniff and to mark his presence, but not often insisting too hard if they wanted to walk on. Tonight however, they let him stop everywhere so he would get used to the environment. Mozart was given a biscuit on their return. He was shown his new bed, the basket with a blanket. There had been no basket delivered from his old home, which made Rebecca wonder if he perhaps had been used to sleeping on his master's bed. Mozart did finally enter his basket and after having circled for quite some time, he put his body to rest with his legs once again,crossed in front of him. This was a special dog, thought Rebecca with a smile.

James went upstairs to his room and Rebecca left the kitchen to go to her bedroom.

It was a night of disturbance for Rebecca, but as she couldn't sleep well she often went to see to Mozart, who was sometimes whining presumably because he was on his own. He did not make a very loud noise, but it had been enough to wake Rebecca up from her light slumber. It was Mozart's first night in his new place, so of course she did understand his feelings. They were two lonely souls now together. The dog must miss his late master and Rebecca had a good cry missing Tom, tears streaming down her cheeks, cuddling the dog in his basket. It was the first time she had cried her heart out holding the dog close to her body sitting on the floor. It would not be the last.

CHAPTER 4

Rebecca woke up early on Sunday morning. Mozart had been trying his best to let her know that he was awake. She dragged herself out of the warmth of her cosy bed and wrapped herself in the bathrobe which Tom had given her for Christmas. 'Well', she thought 'as it is pure white it is not very practical when having a dog in the house, but it is soft and lovely.'

Rebecca wrapped her arms around herself in a simulated 'Tom's hug'. She could remember the feeling of his touch and of the smell of him. She could feel him and when she thought of Tom she could sense her guilt in what had happened. Rebecca thought over again how lucky she was having James and now Mozart. She felt utterly alone in spite of them both. The longing to be with Tom, or rather for Tom to once again be with her, would never die, and it did not get any easier as time passed. How did the one left alone in a loving relationship cope? How could one ever survive widowhood?. She felt the cold creeping up from the floor through her bare feet She untangled herself from the "Tom's hug", and went to the bathroom before she opened the door to the kitchen and the waiting dog. Mozart was wagging his tail and came up to her and licked her hand when she tapped him on his head, whispering her morning greeting into his ear.

Rebecca let him out into the back garden but she stayed indoors watching him through the glass. After some time she called him back to her, and he actually came for his biscuit. Rebecca wiped his paws as they were wet, before she returned to her bedroom leaving Mozart on his own in the kitchen. Rebecca looked longingly towards her unmade bed, but decided that she would get dressed instead, and after a shower she slipped into her jeans and pulled a warmer sweater over her head on top of her shirt.

It was cold in the house too this time of the day before the heating, kicked in and had spread some heat into the building. She prepared her fruit salad with Mozart following her every step. She laid the table for James. He would probably like to have bacon and egg for his breakfast. Coffee in hand, she sat down at the table and just stared out the window, watching the sun slowly rise and the night disappear in the ever brighter daylight. The sun was not the golden summer sun but a weak yellow. It did spread some warmth, now spring had arrived. She let her thoughts wander and suddenly she found herself meditating about how it had been when they had moved into this house. James had been a small boy then and Tom had helped Rebecca with the redecoration. They had loved doing this together and done it with joy and even bliss. James had been put to work too, like "helping" to paste the wall paper. So many years had passed since, and still it was almost as if it were only yesterday. Time had passed quickly then, but now when they were waiting for Tom to emerge from his coma, she felt as if time had stopped. Nothing developed. She started to feel melancholy when Mozart put his head into her lap. She bent down to him and thought that here at last was something good that had happened to her. She fondled his ears and left the table as she could hear James moving upstairs and Mozart clearly indicated that there was somebody else moving around.

When James came down and entered the kitchen, Mozart went straight up to him to get his morning cuddle. At breakfast the dog tried again to get them to notice him and begged for nibbles. Rebecca and James talked about the day ahead. James was going to come with his mother when she took the dog out for his morning walk before he had a good look at the fence. He would go back to St Andrews after lunch so when the fence had been attended to, they would go and visit Tom. Mozart would then be left on his own, for the first time since his arrival.

James noticed that his mother looked absolutely exhausted. These last months had ruffled her slightly. Her soft straight hair had turned into a mixture of black with more and more strands of grey. It suited her and he thought how lucky he was to have such a beautiful mum. His eyes followed the lines in her face around her mouth, signs of stress which made her look older than her years.

Rebecca had always been slim and had a super figure, but she was beginning to look almost thin. She was neat and smart and some of his friends had asked if she was French. James had always been proud of both his parents, his mother so much shorter than his father, she with her straight and very dark hair, whereas his father was fair with some curls around his ears and at his neck line. James had inherited his hair from his father although it was red but with the same curls.

The grey eyes however, were the same colour as his mother's. His father's were a deep clear blue', almost radiant.

James remembered when his mother once had told him that he should look up to his parents. James had then tapped her slightly on top of her head, telling her that he had been looking <u>down</u> on her for sometime now.

Rebecca had lifted her eyes meeting his and both of them had burst out laughing. James was taller than his father too.

After listening to the News on the radio they both left the table. Such a troubled world!. There was never one single day without so much tragedy, so many people that had been killed in fighting somewhere. There were always wars going on in the world. Why was it so hard for people to use words instead of using violence? Why did people use hatred when it was much easier and more pleasant to express love?

Rebecca and James had spent the morning up to lunch as they had planned to do. There <u>was</u> a hole in the fence which James had managed to repair. This would make it easier for his mother, as she could let Mozart out without being in the garden with him

There had been no apparent change in Tom's condition, but they talked to him holding on to one hand each. When James was talking to his father, he watched his mother as she sat in silence, head down looking at Tom, and James wondered how she managed to look so much at peace, when in reality she was torn to pieces with anxiety. He was too young to appreciate the meaning of true love, to have experienced the serenity by the bending of two souls.

After lunch James had to return to St Andrews. Rebecca begged him to drive safely. She was left to her thoughts again, but was pleased not to be on her own. Mozart was already great company.

Rebecca brought the phone to the kitchen table and dialed her friend Anna, while the dog was left to continue his solo exploration of the garden. He was hardly ever out of her sight. She told Anna all about Tom's restlessness a couple of nights ago, and of course their new pet and how they had chosen him.

In two weeks time Easter would be upon them and surely April would arrive with more warmth from a much brighter sun. Anna told her that she would love to see Mozart and perhaps they could meet halfway, and then walk back together to Rebecca's for continuing chat and coffee.

Later James phoned to tell her that he had arrived safely back at the university. He also said that he would come for a shorter visit before he left for France with his friends.

The following two weeks up to Easter went more quickly for Rebecca now when she had the dog to tend to and for company. Her golfing friends had told her that she looked much brighter. Rebecca had only played 9 holes. Now when she had Mozart at home on his own, she found it difficult to concentrate for longer, wondering what mischief he might get up to in her absence. He had done well, and they had also gone back to The Center to show the staff that Mozart was fine and that they had already found companionship in one another. The dog had given her some of her life back, produced a renewed focus. Some happiness had entered her life again, and spring had come upon them with sunshine, some early tulips and a warmer breeze. It was a delight, although Rebecca had always thought autumn with its fresh air to be the best of the four seasons. Nevertheless spring promised so much, but in autumn with the clear strong colours strengthened by the summer warmth she felt so much more active. Spring was also usually a time when she slowed down, perhaps exhausted by the trial of winter.

James had managed to arrange for his friends to pick him up at his parents' house, together with his skiing gear. It felt good seeing his mother and Mozart before he left for his holiday. It had been essential for him to have made it to the hospital to talk to his father, even though it was a one way communication.

James told his father that he found his mother so much more full of life lately because of Mozart. The dog had done wonders for her, no doubt about that.

When James left he received the usual advice from Rebecca. Mother's talk about not forgetting to put on his long johns, sun cream even if the sun was not out, and do not ever forget the sunglasses. James smiled down to her face and added 'Do take care, listen carefully to weather forecasts and never go out skiing without company and always tell someone where you intend to go.' They both laughed and Rebecca felt that he had obviously listened to her over the years.

She was standing in the middle of the drive, and kept waving until the two cars were out of sight round the bend. With tears in her eyes, she went back to the house with Mozart at her side. Did not mothers always worry when their children went away? Well, she had the Easter dinner at Anna's and Eric's house to look forward to. With James going on holiday and being so far away, she could not help feeling lonely and sorry for herself. She would never have let James know this and she did not want him to stay at home with her. James needed the respite from his parents and more than ever. To be out in the fresh air doing what he enjoyed in good company, and to take some time off his studies were important.

Rebecca liked his friends, and she knew most of them going with him for this week in France.

She decided to go for a walk. She could do the house work later. It was a blessing to have Mozart. He was now running around in the garden and lay down putting his head on his crossed legs looking at her on the other side of the kitchen glass door. She brought the coffee with her, and sat down on the door step, in the warm rays of sunshine. There had been a change in the air from the coolness early spring to the warmth of later spring.

Rebecca suddenly remembered what Eric had told her after the service in the church hall one Sunday. Anna had been away visiting her old mother. Poor Eric, he was devastated. He asked Rebecca, what to do when something got stuck to the iron. She had asked him with a smile what on earth he meant. What had got stuck to the iron? Had he forgotten the hot iron on some cloth perhaps and burnt it? Eric took some time before answering, in a half whisper, telling her that yes, he had tried to be a good husband wanting to help his dear wife. He had noticed this big pile of clean washing and thought that he might be able to help her with the ironing. The thing was that he had not managed many items before this unfortunate accident. A pair of Anna's favourite luxury satin briefs melted and got stuck on to the hot iron and he could not get them off. He had tried everything. Of course the briefs were ruined, but what could he do to save the iron?

Wonderful that Rebecca could sit here in the garden being sad and still be able to smile at the memory of that occasion She shook her head a little and burst out in a quiet sort of laughing. She could see Eric telling her so seriously about this incident. Mozart looked up wondering what had happened when Rebecca started to laugh.

The garden looked lovely. The earlier tulips were trying their best to make her happy. Oh, Tom you are missing all of this. We worked so hard at the bedding last year, all this colour showing now, and you are not here to see the fruits of our labour.

She knew that there were two more lots of tulips to come. So far there were only the early ones out. The last batch would flower at the end of May, and among those would be her favourites: the parrot ones, a light lime green and a soft pink.

The trees were dressed in different shades of emerald, but not the light green from the silver birch, which was stubborn and made everybody wait for its leaves a little longer. It had always been the same.

Rebecca had had to cut the grass a couple of times. She hated cutting the grass and the vacuum cleaning. You knew that after you had done it you had to do it all over again far too soon.

She picked up her cup and went indoors for the lead. Mozart followed her into the house and watched her as she put a few biscuits into her jacket pocket together with a couple of plastic bags. Returning to the garden and locking the kitchen door Mozart was excited, and he started to run to and from the gate. He knew that they were going "walkies.'

When they walked along the pavement, Rebecca thought of the almond and cherry blossom that would soon become a splash of delightful colours. It would be as if there were wonderful clouds encircling the trees, clouds of pink and white, another of the beauties of spring time. She knew, that within a week of the trees turning into bloom there would be a storm, a strong wind blowing it all off, covering the pavement and street in petals like wedding confetti. Every year had been the same as long as Rebecca could remember, and as a little girl she had danced around under the trees in a park with other little girls pretending that they were princesses in the dance hall of a castle, which was decorated in pink and white. 'Ah', she thought, that's probably why my favourite tulip has these colours.' Strange that she had never thought of that before today. The colours she preferred now when she had grown older were richer blue, red and she liked to dress in black. These colours suited her dark hair and were the colour scheme which was called "Winter", somebody had told her. Many of her friends called her "the lady in blue."

The days up to Easter Saturday and the dinner with Anna and Eric at their house were uneventful. James had phoned her twice daily and she had spent much time with Tom. Malcolm, Tom's best friend had phoned from Frankfurt where he and his wife Mary were visiting their son. Malcolm had been marvellous. He had visited Tom every week and when Rebecca for some reason had not been able to go to the hospital herself, he had stepped in, helping her out. The doctor had told Rebecca to keep the visiting within the family, but for Tom, Malcolm was closed to being a family member. They had been to school together and seen one another during their university years. Malcolm had studied law and was a well known solicitor until retirement. Tom on the other hand was the managing director at "Marsons" a chemical firm. Mary, Malcolm, Rebecca and Tom had met up for dinners or drinks over the years. They belonged to the same church as well as living close by.

Rebecca had finished reading "Light a Penny Candle"

and had read a few others to Tom since then. She had spent most of her days with the dog. He had behaved well outside Tesco when she had been shopping. She was proud of him. The first time Rebecca went shopping with Mozart, Anna had come with them and had been sitting in the car watching the dog standing by the shop entrance, his lead fastened to the dog parking pole. With his eyes he had followed every single person who had passed him, and he had stayed on his feet all the time refusing to sit down. His joy when Rebecca reappeared was wonderful to see. He must have been relieved. He got his reward biscuit when Anna had given Rebecca her report. They left together in Rebecca's car. The dog was used to sitting in the boot. They dropped Anna off at her house with her shopping and Rebecca and Mozart returned home.

Mozart was a dream of a dog. Of course he had the odd accidents on the kitchen floor when she had just introduced him to his new home. That had been expected. He barked if somebody came up to the house, which was a good thing. He loved chasing the rabbits, but had realized by now that he would get a biscuit when he returned to Rebecca after a good race, so this was improving. Disappearances were less frequent Mozart was a loving and faithful dog. She had heard that this was normal when a dog had been doctored, but he was still interested in the ladies!

On Easter Saturday Rebecca went to see Tom early in the morning and then again before she went to Anna and Eric for dinner. She had left the dog at home for the first evening since he had joined the family. She had promised him that she would not be too late back.

It was lovely to be out again for the evening, she had to admit this, and they had so much to talk about. They had talked about everything and nothing.

She missed the wine, especially that glass of delightful claret with the cheese. Not having anything to drink did mean that she had been able to drive with confidence and a clear conscience.

When Rebecca returned home, she stayed in the car for a minute. She had been looking at the house and the lights streaming out through the kitchen door glass panels. In the middle of that light stood the perceptible figure of a black dog standing there looking out. It felt welcoming to have a dog there again and how wonderful it was to get back to a house filled with some life in it. Rebecca had not felt as lonely as she would have done if Mozart had not shown up looking for her. She got out of the car, closed and locked the gate, before greeting him and letting him out into the garden, into the darkness of the night. He had gone absolutely mad when he spotted her and had whimpered with joy. Rebecca was extremely tired and had gone to bed as soon as the dog was back in the kitchen.

CHAPTER 5

Rebecca and Mozart were woken abruptly by the telephone. It was pitch dark and Rebecca glanced at her alarm to see what time it was before lifting the phone to her ear, heart pounding hard in her breast. She could hardly breathe. Her first thought was James. 'Oh please God, don't let anything have happened to him.'

At the other end of the line was a female voice telling her that her husband was showing signs of stirring and it was a possibility that he might emerge from his coma. Rebecca had asked the staff at the hospital to phone her whatever the time if there was any difference in Tom.

She sat up in bed, her mind a complete whirl after the shock of the nurse's wonderful news pronouncement. She untangled herself from the sheet and duvet. She could hear the dog moving in the kitchen. He was most certainly apprehensive after the phone had rung at such an unearthly hour. It was cold to have to get out of bed this early. Last time she had had to do it had been when she and Tom were going to Madeira for two weeks holiday last winter before Christmas. She had company then. Now she was on her own in the early hours of the darkness in the bedroom. Rebecca had a hot shower to wake her up and to warm up. She put on a pair of navy blue slacks and a short sleeve white blouse and finally the blue cardigan that Tom liked so much. She went out to the kitchen and talked to Mozart, opening the door for him, but he just looked at her and did not want to go out. She grabbed her handbag, and put in a banana. She gave the dog a biscuit out of bad conscience more than anything, bent down and cuddled him. She would be back as soon as she could.

On her way to the hospital she slowly became aware of the momentous implications of the phone call. She had been excited when she got out of bed, but now when she had settled down she started to think and become frantic. Fear penetrated her heart. Of course she was happy with the great news, but what was going to happen now? She was terrified. What would Tom be like? How would he react when he saw her? Would he recognize her? She was desperately excited and frighteningly nervous to be meeting Tom again. It could take some time for him to wake up completely and would give her some time to calm down.

Rebecca decided not to tell James until he was safely back from France. He could do nothing from where he was, so why disturb his lovely holiday. However, if James did ask her about Tom when he phoned her next time, she would let him know. She would perhaps tell Malcolm when Mary and he returned from their holiday.

Suddenly Rebecca realized that she could not let anybody know before James, or could she? It was getting complicated already, and that was before Tom had even regained consciousness.

She pulled into the hospital car park, applied the hand brake and turned off the ignition. Rebecca stayed in the car for a full minute to try and calm down, to take a few deep breaths. She got out of the car, locked it, then rushed into the hospital and went up to the ward. She stopped at the night nurse's desk. Rebecca, instantly recognized, was informed that two of the team who had performed the operation, were already at his bedside.

Doctor Smith would be at the hospital shortly. She was on her way. Before Rebecca went in to see Tom, she was handed a mug of hot and black coffee to bring with her.

Rebecca nervously approached Tom's room, restraining her desire to run instead of walk down the corridor. As she opened the door, Doctor Simpson, the neurologist put his finger to his lips, signaling to her to approach quietly.

The night light was on. It was not completely dark, more like entering a cave of sand. This light made the whole room look much softer, much more restful than the bright sterile white ceiling light. Tom did not look as pale as he had done the day before. He had acquired a pinkish hue. It was as if he was encapsulated in off white cotton wool. She stood at the foot of the bed for a few minutes examining the man in the bed, the man she loved. He had several electrodes attached to his head. Without doubt Tom's every little movement was being monitored on a computer screen somewhere outside this room.

Tom's hair had grown to a more normal length after his head had been shaved. The fair hair was more curly than she could remember, and he had also started getting a little grey around the temples.

Rebecca felt a difference and yes, his eyelids did flutter slightly. She had actually seen some movements indicating that at last there were signs of returning consciousness. She went up and sat down on the chair by the bed, the chair in which she had spent so many hours the last months. Here she had wept, slept, hoped, prayed and begged. She was sure it was now coming up to the time that she had longed for all those days; Tom to be with her again, not just in body but also in mind.

She had a bite of the banana which she had put into her handbag as she left home, but couldn't eat it. She was much too excited and apprehensive. The fear was back and her stomach and throat contracted with an almost cramp like sensation. She lifted the cup of coffee to her lips. The black scalding liquid did her good. The drink cleared her throat and made her swallow the piece of banana.

It was warm as always in this room, but Rebecca was shivering. She felt ice cold and had to warm her hand on the cup, before she took hold of Tom's hand. At the touch of her hand, Tom's moved slightly as if surprised, startled perhaps. It was not a visible movement, but one she had felt when putting her hand on top of his. She lifted it up slightly to hold it properly, before she started talking to him. Rebecca had to smile after a while as she realized that she had been whispering to this sleeping man, as if she did not want to wake him up and still, here she was talking to him hoping to do just that.

Tom looked more as if he were in a slumber than a coma. She could feel his hand in hers and could sense that the liflelessness had lifted. It was no longer a limp hand, but one that felt as if it belonged to a living person

Encouraged by the medical staff in attendance Rebecca talked to Tom about James being in France on a skiing holiday together with some of his friends for a week and that he would be back on Wednesday. Today, she explained was Sunday in fact Easter Sunday. She told him about the lovely evening she had spent with Anna and Eric having dinner at their house last night, and that Easter this year was late. She talked about the weather and the ungodly early hour of the phone call this morning. (Malcolm would also have sent his love if he had known about this happening). Then she started telling Tom about Mozart. She had of course told Tom most of this already, but now was the time for him to perhaps start listening and to take some of it in. Rebecca touched Tom's cheek telling him that she loved him as never before. She bent down and kissed his lips, before she let go of his hand to go to the bathroom.

Coming back into Tom's room she stopped at the window. She once again felt the growing tension bubbling up like the gas in a bottle of a sparkling drink after it had been shaken. It started from her feet, spread up through her legs through her stomach and she wondered if it was going to come out through the top of her head like a volcanic eruption. She took a deep breath and looked out recording what there was to see.

She felt the first rays of the morning sunshine as she looked through the window. She shook her head to shake off the rigidity of her body. She desperately wanted to feel only joy, the joy of a new beginning, a new day and it was going to be a lovely day too. She had been standing in silence for a while. She loved this sound of silence. She could hear Tom breathing. She was excited but also exhausted. She stifled a yawn. She continued talking to Tom telling him what she could see out there from where she was standing. She talked about the sun, the sky, the springtime with leaves on the trees. The silver birches were dressed in a soft green like lime velvet. She saw a couple of doves and quite a few small birds which probably had returned from winter migration.

Rebecca turned round at the sound of a sigh from Tom and she told him again how much she loved him, always had done and no doubt always would. She went back and stood over him. He was lying there, completely still, but his eyes, <u>his eyes were wide open</u>!

He seemed to look straight into hers. She gasped in surprise. Her heart missed a beat. Tom was completely still and Rebecca thought for a split second that he had died. She repeated his name in panic. She could hardly endure the pain, but then she saw Tom closing his eyes for another moment before he reopened them and tried to focus on her. She smiled and took his hand squeezing it gently. She bent down and kissed his cheek, tears of happiness and relief welling up in her eyes. She was trembling. They were both silent, but it was not an oppressive silence. The room was by now filled with the light from the rising sun, but the bed was positioned in the shadow, no doubt to protect Tom's eyes should he open them. Tom made a sound, a sort of dry croaking noise. He was trying to speak. The nurse rushed over from the corner of the room where she had been sitting observing. She pressed the buzzer to summon the doctor, guided Rebecca to the chair, reached over to the bedside table, picked up a moist wipe and gently brushed Tom's lips.

Doctor Smith arrived. She and the nurse gently slid an extra pillow under his head. The nurse let a few drops of liquid from a feeding cup pass on to his mouth. He spluttered, almost coughed. He turned his head to one side, took a deep breath, coughed again, more liquid, another deep breath, then a big sigh and the crackle became a discernible question.'"Where am I?' he squeaked.

The medical staff were reading the monitors. The doctor took her stethoscope and placed it on Tom's chest as if she did not believe what she was witnessing, what she was hearing.

Rebecca was beside herself with excitement gripping Tom's hand tightly.

Doctor Smith made a sign to the nurse who gently led Rebecca away and asked her to come with her and leave Tom to the doctor and her team for a short while. Rebecca was frantic, she did not want to leave him. Doctor Smith said that they needed Tom on his own for a few minutes. Tearful and reluctantly Rebecca left. The nurse guided her out of the room and they walked arm in arm along the corridor to the reception area.

It seemed like hours although it was only a short while before she was returned to the room and to Tom.

He was propped up on more pillows, tube removed from his nose, face shining as if it had been scrubbed, hair combed, sheet smoothed and smartly tucked in.

Ten minutes Mrs Chandler' said the doctor 'and then he must rest.'

'Rest!' Rebecca exclaimed. 'Tom has been resting for three months.'

She calmed down a little, sat in the chair, took Tom's hand, leaned over and kissed him lightly on the forehead. She fought away the tears and cried out 'Tom darling darling Tom, welcome back.'

Tom examined the woman sitting by his bedside. Her eyes were a lovely soft grey and smiling. He could see her eyes clearly although she was in semi shadow. She was slim and long-necked with short cut dark hair streaked with almost white. To him she was a strikingly beautiful woman and he was sure that she had said that she loved him. She must be somebody he loved. Rebecca confirmed her love yet again and told him her name. He smiled and softly, even hesitantly told her that he recognized her voice.

Tom mumbled that he felt woozy and that he was extremely tired. He closed his eyes once again. He had fallen asleep.

The nurse led her reluctantly away and told her to go home to get some rest and then return in a few hours.

Circumstances had changed dramatically.

Rebecca could start on the route to Tom's recovery. She knew they had to work together on this, and that it would be hard at times.

PART TWO

She was calmer now when she had exchanged a few words with him. At least he had said that he recognized her voice. The nurse was right to ask her to leave. She had to get a move on to go home to Mozart. Tom was probably going to sleep for a few hours which meant that she could absent herself to take care of the dog, and go for a short walk and try to eat brunch. 'Rest' the nurse had said. Rebecca was exhausted, but sleep she could do later.

Mozart went berserk when she got back home and into the kitchen. He rushed out into the garden as soon as he had licked her hands and made his greeting tour running round her legs. Rebecca was watching the dog, and then went into the kitchen, leaving the door open for him. She sat down at the table and hid her face in her hands, elbows on the tabletop, and cried. There did not seem to be any end to the flow and her entire body was shaking violently as she sobbed her heart out. All these days that had passed since she had made Tom come with her to the skating rink in Princes Street Gardens in early January. He had not felt like going but she had begged him to come with her as it had been such a lovely winters day. Surely it was her fault that he had fallen and hit his head so badly that the ambulance had to be called. The picture of Tom lying as if dead tied to all kinds of support machines was for ever etched in her mind. Would she be able to get rid of these images? Would she be able to rid herself of the guilt? She had told him to put on a helmet, but he had refused as he usually did when she asked him to look after himself. So why had it been so important to her to go skating that day? She had no recollection why she could not have gone skating by herself leaving Tom to "admire" her on the ice? Well, done was done and she had to live with this and now, she had to get a grip on herself again!. The poor dog was trying to get her attention by putting his paw into her lap. Rebecca moved down onto the floor, continuing crying but now into the fur of the dog. She did not know for how long they had been sitting together like this when the phone rang. She surfaced from her position on the floor and went to answer the call. Mozart came with her. He had tried so hard to comfort her, licking the tears from her cheeks.

It was the hospital telling her that Tom had woken up from his sleep. Rebecca looked at the time and realized that it was well past lunch time. She gave Mozart a couple of biscuits and went to splash cold water on her face. She made the mistake of looking at the face in the mirror. She looked awful. Her eyes were swollen with crying. Well, her entire face was swollen. She looked old. That was the result of lack of proper sleep and worrying. She had to put some make up on before she could face anybody. She brought her tooth brush and tooth paste. She would have to buy herself one of these unappetizing hospital sandwiches. She had to eat to get strong for Tom.

Guiltily, she took her leave of the dog once more. She gave him another biscuit. She had to start being more careful otherwise he would get fat from lack of exercise and too many bribes.

She rushed away without turning round to see the dog standing inside the door watching her go.

She had to get back into the routine of walking and spending time with Mozart and of visiting Tom regularly. How was she going to find the time to eat and sleep? Soon James would be back home. He was going to university after returning home. Rebecca hoped that it would be possible for James to continue to come home to see them regularly.

Arriving at the hospital Rebecca stopped and had a short update of Tom's condition from his doctor.

Tom was fully conscious. They would shortly start him on solid food, slowly so that his bodily functions could re-adjust. In a few days he would be out of bed and start physiotherapy to get him mobile and closer to coming home! They should take it slowly.

Doctor Smith gave her some advice to help Tom to get back on his feet. 'Take it gently. Answer his questions but don't pressure him. Give him time to find himself.'

Before going to Tom's room Rebecca ate her sandwich. She brushed her teeth and then went to his bedside. His eyes were closed and she thought that he was sleeping, but when Tom heard the noise of somebody entering the room he opened his eyes and smiled at her. She beamed back at him and sat down on the chair. She felt shy when she bent down to kiss him. He noticed that she obviously had been crying and wondered if that could have to do with him. Was he not going to be all right? Was there anything he should know about his recovery? Was he not improving? He had so many questions some he kept to himself for the moment. He asked Rebecca to tell him what had happened and why he was in this hospital bed.

He had asked for a mirror when he had woken up from

his nap. He could not say for certain that he recognized the pale face staring at him. The hair was rather different than he remembered and his face was lined and thin. Was this him, the man they called "Tom?"

He told Rebecca that he seemed to have lost a large part of his memory as he had no recollection whatsoever about them skating in Princes Street Gardens.

The name "Rebecca" sounded familiar, as did James and his own name, but it was at the back of his mind at the moment. They said that it would come with time. Tom had been in a coma for more than three months and the doctor told them that it was completely normal for him to be confused.

Rebecca told Tom about the dog and why she had decided to get one.

'He is called Mozart and I am sure you'll love him as much as I do. He is from a Dog Rescue Centre and looks almost like a black Labrador.'

Tom needed a great deal of rest and sleep, but if the test results were satisfactory he would be allowed to leave the hospital soon. He had to get stronger and to start moving as much as he could and of course to start eating solid food again He had lost a lot of weight during these last three months of being artificially fed.

Tom was grateful for the news about the dog. That was at least something he could not be expected to remember. He had never met this dog, although the strange thing was that he had a distinct feeling of recognition. What an odd sensation! He asked how the dog was getting on with the cat. Rebecca looked at Tom in surprise as they had never had a cat.

'Neither of us are particularly fond of cats, that's why

we have always had dogs, Westies actually. I'll bring some photos of James and our home when I come back to see you in the morning' she said bending down to kiss him. Tom thanked her for being patient with him. He felt a soft spot for her. 'Could that be love,' he asked himself?

After Rebecca had left him he closed his eyes and tried to relax, but there were so many questions with answers he did not understand. There were so many strange pictures in his head that worried him. And what about him being sure that they had a cat? He felt awkward. What on earth would Rebecca make of this? He was exhausted and fell asleep again.

Rebecca had a peculiar feeling about Tom too and his memories of things that did not exist. Strange about the cat. Good heavens, where did he get that from? She shook her head in disbelief and tried to convince herself that it was because he had been unconscious for so long. That was presumably all there was to it, but a cat?!

Driving back home it was already getting dark and a wet mist was creeping closer. However, she had to take a walk as soon as she arrived. It would do her good to clear her head and hopefully it would give her an appetite. She could not rid herself of the fear she carried around with her. A cat!! She could not fathom that Tom had asked how Mozart got on with the cat. She could not get this cat out of her mind.

Coming back she looked at Mozart standing inside the glass panel door. She was filled with tenderness and did not linger this time going straight inside after having parked and locked the gate. The phone rang as she entered the door and greeted the dog. She let him out and answered the call with her heart beating like mad. It was James on the line.

James said that they had had a super day on the pistes, but now it had started to snow with snowflakes as big as mittens and the wind had picked up. He described how beautiful it was with the lights glimmering from the village houses. The pine trees were covered with the new white snow. He told her to take care. ' See you in a few days.' he said.

Rebecca had to take a deep breath before she gave him the wonderful details of his father. James was overjoyed. She could sense the thrill as he called out the good news to his friends.

Rebecca begged him to be extremely careful the following day with this weather. Newly fallen snow on top of hard icy ground was dangerous. This was the precondition for an avalanche.

Rebecca put on her rain coat and grabbed the lead. She locked the kitchen door and let Mozart out of the front door this time and left the house with the alarm and the lights on. They had to do something about the alarm now they had a dog, as he was often left on his own in the kitchen. She wanted to be able to set the alarm when there was only Mozart in the house. He was a far too friendly dog to be an efficient guard dog. He would not scare any intruders away. He would probably bark, but undoubtably invite them in as friends!

She was absorbed in her own thoughts. She was exhausted but at the moment much calmer.

She realized that she had not been thinking about herself for a long time. She had to remember to phone one of the Tuesday ladies to inform them that she would not be playing golf for a while.

Rebecca and Mozart went for a long walk staying on

the pavement, as it was dark and wet. It had started to rain, but he needed a walk and as they were getting wet they might as well stay out.

The street lights were glittering on the wet tarmac and she enjoyed the walk almost as much as the dog. Not many people were out. There was some traffic although it was past supper time. She imagined that people were sitting in front of their televisions behind closed curtains.

The smell of rain was pleasant especially passing the big playing field where the scent from the wet grass was wonderful. A few of the trees were covered with leaves shimmering like pieces of foil. It was quiet enough for her to hear the rain bouncing off them. She stopped and took a deep breath, as the dog found one of the lampposts more interesting than the others. She was deep in her own thoughts. All she could hear was the rain, her own steps and the dog's claws on the tarmac. The cars passing them splashed water so that she sometimes had to move further from the road's edge

Returning home and indoors she dried the dog with one of his towels before she fed him. Then she went into the bedroom, undressed and immersed herself in a wonderful hot bubble bath. She fell asleep for a minute lying and relaxing with the bubbles' popping sound in her ears.

She towelled off and pulled on her soft raspberry coloured track suit and a pair of slippers, dried her hair and went into the kitchen to make herself something to eat. She fried a couple of pork sausages and sprinkled a little more grated cheese on to some left over cauliflower and popped it into the oven. She loved the smell of melting cheese and sat down at the table enjoying the feast. She wrote down Tom's progress and her own thoughts into her notebook. Rebecca wrote about the cat in big letters and underlined the word "cat" so she would find the place if she needed to come back to it one day. She made a list of people she had to phone the following day or two and what food to buy. The Reverend Marc and his wife Hilda had to be told about what had happened. She wanted the congregation to continue prayers for Tom in church each Sunday.

She went to bed early and slept through the night for the first time in months.

The next morning she phoned the hospital for a progress report. Tom had had a restless night with lots of dreams he had told the nurse in the morning, but he was doing fine.

First of all she phoned Anna and they had a long chat. Rebecca cried a little from pure happiness.

Returning to her list of important calls, to one of her golfing friends to tell her that she would not be able to play the next day. She said that she had work to do in the garden. Rebecca phoned Marc after some hesitation. She had a longer talk with him. He was given an update on Tom's progress, but was asked to keep it low key as James was away for another few days.

After breakfast she took Mozart for a longer walk, before leaving him on his own again whilst she made her first visit of the day to see Tom.

She was apprehensive, but when she entered his room he opened his eyes and turned towards her and smiled. What a wonderful feeling! Rebecca went up to him and kissed him. Tom took her hand, pulled her towards him and returned her kiss.

Rebecca had brought a few photographs which

she thought might be of some help for Tom to get his memory back into focus. First she sat down by his bed and they talked. He had not been told when he could be expected to get out. They both knew that he had to regain his strength and appetite and that his stomach would have to get used to normal solid food. He told her that he had had nightmares during the night but felt fine, weak perhaps, but fine. He was longing to get back home to see the dog and the garden. Oh yes, the magnolia had its flowers edged brown as the wind and frost had taken their toll as they did every year. The silver birch was covered in its lush, spring green jacket, as too was the weeping willow. The leaves were tiny but full of promise. The spring, gave rise to much enjoyment.

Some of the earliest dwarf tulips were opening already, and the daffodils were lovely. Hopefully he would be at home in time to see the apple trees in full bloom, all dressed up in pinkish white, and to catch the almond blossom.

Tom looked perplexed when Rebecca started talking about James, their son but she did not think much about it when he smiled back at her and asked where he was. She showed him a couple of photographs of them all three together and Tom was relieved to recognize his son.

'He knows that you are awake and back with us and he is relieved and excited, but I have told him not to break his trip as it would be very complicated and expensive for him. He is to come home as planned, but with the added joy of seeing his dad sitting up and sharing the wonderful re-union,' Rebecca said happily .

She told Tom that everyone at church sent their love and remembered him in their prayers each Sunday. He was visibly moved.

Tom looked at the photographs and with concentration acknowledged that he recognized their home and garden.

'Now, I have to get a move on getting fit to be able to leave here as soon as possible and to be able to help you around the garden.'

The nurse came in with Tom's light lunch, looking more like baby food than a meal for a man. She said to them that he ought to have a nap after eating. Oh, yes, he had to finish all of it. Rebecca left Tom as soon as he had swallowed the last spoonful, but promised to come back later in the day.

On her way back she stopped at the supermarket. She wanted to eat something special today and went for the smoked salmon for lunch, which with finely chopped red onions and a small salad would titillate her appetite. For dinner she selected a nice thick fillet steak.

The dog food aisle that she had passed before remembering Mozart, she now examined carefully and chose some special tit bits for him too. She did take her time today and was starving by the time she reached home. Mozart went straight out into the garden as Rebecca opened the door for him.

It was wet out there and the sky was grey, but spring was here to stay. Preparing her lunch, she was humming as she chopped the onion but soon the tears welled up and her eyes started to hurt. She could hardly ever deal with this chopping without the tears streaming down her face. She never did remember that her mother told her always to peel onions under a running cold water tap, an antidote which worked!.

James phoned earlier than usual as the weather was

not safe for skiing. They had been forced to stay indoors playing cards and reading. Luckily they had food to last them until the next day and some whisky. He said that it probably was a good thing to have a day off skiing as long as it was not going to be more than just one. They had only one more day left before returning home. He asked after Tom. Rebecca hesitated just long enough for James to feel puzzled. He of course could not wait to get back to see them both. She promised to tell Tom that James had asked after him and sent his love.

Back with Tom in the late afternoon he told her that he had been busy. First a visit from the physio then a nap and the doctors had been to see him. He had asked them many questions and had been told that he should be able to go home as soon as he could walk to the bathroom by himself. He was moving his somewhat heavy legs as much as he could whilst still in bed. He had been weighed and although they knew that he had lost weight, the three stone loss was alarming. What Tom did not reveal was that the many things and people that Rebecca talked about were familiar but his recall was woolly. So many images he could feel, still hiding at the back of his mind, but there were things he could remember with crystal clarity. He had told the doctors about this but had been reassured that all would come back to him with time. He could sense that if he told Rebecca about this it would probably upset her. Just think of her reaction when he had asked how the dog got on with the cat, and yet the cat was one of the crystal clear pictures in his head! It did not make any sense. Should he be apprehensive about this or let it pass? He did not know, and tried to put it back deep into a hidden corner of his mind. He wanted to forget about the cat, but he wished to solve this mystery, to understand why he had this memory. He should have left it in peace.

Rebecca had told James about the progress in Tom's health, so she had better get on with phoning some friends starting with Anna. Rebecca actually left the message on Malcolm's answering machine. The good news would be there waiting for their return from their holiday visiting their son Edward in Frankfurt.

CHAPTER 6

The following day when she entered Tom's room his bed was empty and the room deserted. She rushed out to ask a nurse what had happened. Nobody had bothered to inform Rebecca that Tom was having an MRI scan. They wanted to be sure that Tom was all right before even thinking of sending him home. The nurse was surprised that Rebecca had not been told. Rebecca was furious with Doctor Smith once more. Such lack of consideration for family was unacceptable and Rebecca told her so. The feeble excuse proferred by the doctor was that she had been busy. However, in the end she did say she was sorry.

Tom was exhausted when he returned and fell asleep shortly after he had been helped into his bed. Rebecca stayed for a while, his hand in hers. She noticed that his sleep was not relaxed. He was dreaming, fueled by his tormented memory or rather his alarming lack of recall.

It was lovely to see him without all the electrodes, wires and tubes. She tried to soothe him by talking quietly about James coming home the following day. She would come back later. Rebecca particularly wanted to get more information about his recovery and a possible date for the latest test results.

When Rebecca walked the dog, a thought, or perhaps more of a feeling, suddenly crept up inside her, making her feel uneasy. She had found Doctor Smith who had operated on Tom more aloof, even unfriendly, ever since Tom had come out of his coma. Why was this, Rebecca wondered? She felt that there was something she had not been told, something was not right but she could not put her finger on it. The fear which she had thought she had left behind was still there buried at the back of her mind. Would she be able to face up to it when the time came for it to surface? Would it ever surface? She sincerely hoped she would be able to cope and that the fear would manifest itself, surface, and emerge to be faced head on, because there was obviously more to it than she currently understood. Was Tom going to be all right? Could she trust his doctor to give her the facts however unpalatable? Once again, so many questions remained unanswered.

Ever since the accident Rebecca had been wearing the same perfume when she visited Tom. Somebody had told her that smell could be more evocative than anything else. She hoped that Tom would tell her that he remembered the smell of his favourite perfume, the one that he had bought her as her first Christmas present and which she had been wearing ever since. He had told her that he believed that her voice seemed to be known to him, but what about her perfume?

She entered his room and there he was, turning his clear blue eyes towards her, smiling. He kissed her as she leaned forward and asked about her afternoon.

Rebecca had brought more photographs, this time one of him as a boy with his parents and sister. He looked at it for a long time and then said that he thought that his mother's name had been Marlene, and that she had died relatively young, the same as his father and sister Elisabeth. Tom looked sad when he talked about them. He appeared to have some recollection of them. He had to think about his father's name, before Rebecca reminded him that they had christened their own son after him, - James Struan Chandler.

Tom then asked her about her parents.

'Did I ever meet your mother? Was her name Madelene perhaps? He had a faint memory about both their mother's first names beginning with the letter M. Didn't we have a laugh about that as we first met and started to talk about our parents? And your father's name was Jonathan, so both our father's first letter was J.'.

'We thought that it was such a coincidence, didn't we?'

Tom looked straight into her eyes and a tingle went through his body. He gave a sigh of relief. This was the woman he had loved before his accident, and he now knew that the feelings for Rebecca, his wife, were still there. He was sure that she loved him. Had she not been by his bedside every single day when he was in a coma? The nurse had told him so. She had described how Rebecca had been talking to him and even been reading to him. This could be why he recognized her voice so quickly.

He was looking forward to seeing James the following day. Tom was nervous about meeting his son but he was longing to have a father – son reunion and a proper chat. Rebecca told Tom that both of them had a good relationship with James.

Most of all Tom wanted to get out of the hospital and get back home. Everything was surely going to be much easier from home on recognizable secure ground. He did not want to miss any more of this year. He wanted to be able to go out for walks and to enjoy the springtime with his family. He hoped it would not take too long. He was becoming impatient. This was a good sign.

Tom had to admit that he was tired and that his legs

did not carry him for more than the few yards to the bathroom and back. The nurse was satisfied that he could do this walk unsupported. On the next day of sunshine, he had been promised a walk in the grounds of the hospital, even if it probably would be closely followed by a wheel chair. Change of air is what he needed and some sun on his pale face. He felt as white as a ghost. He was almost falling over himself telling Rebecca of this and asking her about the garden. Had she cut the grass herself or had James done this for her? 'Cutting the grass has always been my task hasn't it?' he enquired.

Rebecca surprised herself by her patience explaining everything and telling Tom as much as she could.

'The Camellia is more beautiful then ever before. You have to do your exercises and get your leg muscles back. I need you at home and Mozart will be so happy to go for walks with us both or with you on your own in due course. It is a good time of the year to be outdoors.'

Rebecca promised to bring some of the latest editions of the magazine "The Week" which had been his favourite regular Friday read. She was sure they would get him up to date with what had happened in the world since the beginning of the year. Books he could read later.

There were many friends who wished to come and visit, but the doctor had strongly advised them to take it slowly. Malcolm would see him after James had been, and the Reverent Marc. Others could hopefully wait until Tom was back home.

'I want my life back Rebecca, and I do hope you'll help me. I beg you to be patient with me. I am sure that I will be confused. My memory is a mess.' implored Tom.

Rebecca squeezed his hands and with a reassuring

smile told him that she would try her best. Hadn't she been waiting for just this since January?

'By the way, has James got a girlfriend?' Rebecca answered that as far as she knew he did not at the moment. He had not had a girlfriend since Susan broke up with him in December last year. 'Do you remember her Tom? Neither of us liked her much and how awful her table manners were? She couldn't hold a knife and fork properly and ate with her mouth wide open. We were never comfortable taking them out to a restaurant. We were surprised that James had fallen for this girl. Pretty and intelligent, but that had been about all we could say, although we never told James. We thought he could do better.'

Tom could remember some of what Rebecca told him, but no face appeared to match the name. Rebecca told him that she would bring a photograph of Susan for her next visit if she could find one.

Tom started to ask her about their holiday in Israel and their regular visits to Madeira. He had a clear picture of both these places, he was pleased to tell her.

'Oh yes, the Holocaust Museum " Yad Vashem" in Jerusalem. That was an experience so strong that nothing could make me forget that. I remember especially "the Children's Memorial. It moved us.'

Tom closed his eyes reliving the powerful emotion of the candles which were reflected by hundreds of invisible mirrors into twinkling stars. 'We both felt it was as if there were childrens' souls in the sky. I feel sadness thinking of this.

Here I am lying in a clean hospital bed having survived a dreadful head injury, and I am complaining about why it had to happen to me, to us? Isn't that awful? I am alive and have a darling loving supportive wife at my side. We are together and have a son who loves us and who is fit and well. I have nothing to complain about really.

Tom and Rebecca clung to one another now as they had done then in complete silence for what seemed an age, Tom with his eyes closed but traces of tears visible. Rebecca thought that he had overdone it and fallen asleep, when he opened his eyes and told her, that when they had been there he had promised himself never to forget what they had experienced. He was so pleased with himself that he had been able to at least keep this promise.

After all this sadness please let us talk about something that gave us pleasure, before I have to leave you for the dog. For instance' do you have any recollections of our visits to Norway and Sweden?.'

'Oh yes, we did the cruise on the ferry going North along the coast of Norway. What was it called again?' Rebecca told him that it had an odd name for them.

'It was the "Hurtigrutten". We brought the car with us and went by this working ferry all the way up to the North and disembarked in Kirkenes, I think it was, and then we drove South through Finland and Sweden to Gothenburg, where we took the ferry back home via Newcastle. Weren't we lucky with the weather to experience the midnight sun without a single cloud in the sky?'

'I can remember the wonderful lunches, but somewhat dull dinners. Am I right?' Tom asked her with slight concern in his voice, but he need not have been, as Rebecca told him that his recollection was correct.

Tom went quiet lost in his own thoughts, while

Rebecca went to the bathroom before she was leaving for the journey home. He sometimes had images in his head that he was not sure fitted in properly. It sometimes felt as if he had lived two very different lives. One life in his very strange dreams, but also the life he had with Rebecca and James. Had he had a secret life that his wife and son knew nothing about? There were some feelings and images which he could not fathom. Why did such contradictory thoughts pop up in his mind? It disturbed him. Tom knew he had been angry with somebody at some stage just before his accident, but it was in a haze. He had asked Rebecca about this, but she could not remember him having ever been that cross with anybody. She had told Tom this with her brows close together, expression in her worried face and questioning eyes. No, he would not bring this up again if he did not have to. He stretched out his hand towards hers when she returned from the bathroom. He wanted to hold her for one more moment before she left him on his own with his turbulent reflections.

It felt as if panic had struck him like a wild storm when he woke up abruptly from a bad dream. He became distressed and full of anguish. He could not recollect the dream. He did try hard to remember the nightmare which haunted him in his sleep. Little did he know about the problems that would soon follow. The slow measured return of his memory was fortunate for him at the moment.

'Hopefully James will be here tomorrow, but not before the evening. I'll try to remember to bring you the promised photo of Susan in the morning. It would not be a good idea to bring it when James comes with me.'

Rebecca felt as if she were going behind James' back, talking so much about his former girlfriend. She shook this feeling off and bent down to kiss Tom. She left him with a smile on her face. She turned round at the door, blew him another kiss and waved.

Tom rang for the nurse and asked if it would be possible to go for a walk along the corridor with her at some stage before nightfall. He wanted to get stronger and would love to surprise Rebecca. He wanted to walk as often and as much as possible without telling her. To keep busy was a way of escape from the torrent of his recall.

He went to the bathroom whilst the nurse was with him and then decided to sleep a little before improving his mind by browsing through "The Week" until she would have time for his walk. The nurse smiled at him when she left, promising to come back when everybody had been served their food and evening pills.

When she came back she had brought a zimmer with her for Tom to try. This would be a good thing for his confidence and to build up his strength until he felt steady enough on his own legs. With the zimmer he would be able to exercise by himself.

Tom did struggle. He was frustrated with his lack of balance on jelly-like legs. He was no doubt disappointed by his performance. He was exhausted after the walk and went to bed immediately falling asleep without even brushing his teeth, something that he rarely missed. Tomorrow he would see James.

It had been a lovely day. Rebecca thought it was like early summer now that it had become a little warmer. She went for a walk with Mozart and phoned Alice from the golf club to tell her that she would like to play with the group on Friday. Alice was delighted to hear this, and even more so to hear the good news about Tom. They talked for some time about everything, but mostly about Tom and golf.

The course was immaculate. They were back on summer greens on most holes. The dreadful par three first hole was going to be changed with a larger green and not such deep bunkers guarding the hole. That would be something to look forward to later on in the season.

Before Rebecca went to bed she loaded the bread maker and brought her cup of coffee through to the snug, dog at her heels. She sat down in front of television, but also had a book to read. It depended on the quality of the programmes. If there was nothing she wanted to watch, she would read for a little while.

She had to search through some albums of theirs to see if she could find any photo of Susan. She went for the camera as she wanted one of Mozart lying on the mat in front of the fireplace with his legs crossed in front of him.

Looking in the albums took time as she thought of the pictures and the memories when she turned the pages over. She realized how much she and Tom had done during these two last years. It had become quite late before she decided that enough was enough and concentrated on finding the picture of Susan. She did find a good one in the end and carefully took it out and put it in an envelope.

She opened the kitchen door for the dog and began getting ready for bed. The evenings were getting noticeably longer. It was going to be a summer this year too, she thought with a smile.

Rebecca set the alarm for early the next morning as she wanted to take Mozart for his walk, have breakfast and make her a shopping list to make sure that she had everything for the weekend and James' home-coming. She was going to buy a piece of ham and cook it tomorrow for dinner, and would make his favourite pizza with anchovies but without garlic for one lunch, and a fish pie for the evening meal.

Checking the wine they had in the larder, she made sure they had both red and dry white. She put one bottle of white into the fridge and a bottle of red Bordeaux on the worktop. It was a long time since she had enjoyed a glass of wine. She was looking forward to James' return and the red wine and cheese she had planned for the evening after they had been to visit Tom.

Her own mother had introduced her to this ritual and they often used to do this in the late evening to have a relaxed chat. Her mouth was watering and she was excited to hear about James' holiday.

The alarm woke her up like an early morning cockerel at 7am. She threw back the bedclothes, went over to the window and drew the curtains before realizing that the weather forecast from yesterday was going to come true. Not a cloud in the sky. It was such a delight to rise early on a promising day like this.

She let the dog out, leaving the kitchen door ajar for him. Rebecca did not need to wait for his return. She went to the bathroom to prepare for the early walk.

On their return the paper boy had been and the Times was available in time for a breakfast read. Rebecca sat down at the kitchen table with newspaper, pencil and rubber handy beside her plate. She always did one Su

Duko every morning while she had her fruit and big cup of strong black coffee. This had become another daily ritual. She was addicted to both coffee and the puzzle. Good for the brain and good for keeping Alzheimers at bay in an enjoyable way. After completing the shopping list she walked with Mozart, then she did some "dead heading"" and weeded the rose bed for another hour before the bread machine signalled that the bread was ready. She would go to the supermarket on her way back from hospital.

When Tom saw the photograph of Susan he said that she reminded him of someone, but Rebecca could not recollect anyone else she knew who resembled Susan. So many girls have long thick wavy blonde hair half shadowing their faces. Most of the girls tried to make their hair straight these days. Susan had not done this. Her hair had been beautiful and perfectly natural. She was a big girl and like so many others of her age, almost obese and messy in jeans, which were far too tight.

Rebecca could not recall anything special about her although she had a pretty face and was pleasant enough. 'She was studying languages or rather, one foreign language, wasn't it Japanese? She was into things Asian in a big way. No doubt the girl had talent, but she didn't seem to have a happy disposition. I could not remember James telling us anything about her family background, but her parents sounded pleasant and she did have an elder brother. James never talks about either of them so best forgotten I suppose. Can you make anything out of the photograph, Tom? I remember that we wondered what she was going to use her language for.'

Tom examined the photograph and told Rebecca

that he definitely had met this girl looking back at him, but there was more to it then he could explain. There was something, but he couldn't put his finger on it. Tom, shook his head slightly and handed the picture back to Rebecca saying that it could not be of any significance.

'As you say Rebecca, the big blonde girls today do look alike. Have you heard anything from James yet? When can you expect him to arrive?'

Rebecca confirmed that James had phoned when she was out walking the dog, and had left a message that he would probably be home in the early evening. 'We' ll visit you as soon as James has eaten she promised.

Tom did not tell Rebecca about the progress he was making with his walking. He was determined to make it home before the end of the month. That was his target. He had reached his first goal. He had been to the lavatory "properly". He had to smile about this. The joy he had felt, like a small boy showing his mother the result in his potty. The nurse had been pleased with him. Life is strange, so many twists and turns. One starts as a baby and he had been back almost where life started with potty training, baby food and struggling to walk.

Tom went for another zimmer walk along the corridor, and this time he was able to keep his balance much better. He was determined to walk even without the zimmer, and he managed to do that after his daily rest. He walked along the entire stretch of the corridor, keeping close to the wall , just in case. At the very end he sat down on a chair for a minute to get his breath back, before starting the return journey. Tomorrow he was going to walk outside, weather permitting, but now he had to get ready for a visit from Rebecca and James. Silly, he was feeling nervous about meeting his own son.

In the late afternoon he saw the physiotherapist, then he slept and read "The Week". He started with the current issue to learn what was happening in the world today. He had a shower and dressed in shirt and trousers for the first time. It was wonderful to get into other clothes and out of his pyjamas and dressing gown. He was grateful that Rebecca had thought of bringing him some of his own clothes before he met James. It felt much better even if he had to keep his trousers up with belt and braces. He had to put on some weight for them to fit.

Once more, Tom studied the photographs that Rebecca had left him. He knew that there were huge gaps in his memory, and he was fishing for his past with these images. He would put away the one of Susan before James' arrival. He couldn't get over his strange feeling looking at the photograph of this girl. Rebecca had made it very clear that neither of them had liked her and still, there was a peculiar feeling of something. It felt as if he had liked a girl resembling Susan. His eyes tried to tell him something but his mind could not understand what. He had to return the photograph to the envelope, as it made his heart ache as if from a strange sense of loss. If Tom had only left it at this, everything might have been all right, but naturally he did not know. We are a curious species. He had to get some answers of course. He could not leave the matter unsolved. Sadly he had no idea of the consequences. Later he would tell himself that he should have left it here. Some things are better forgotten and hidden, but there is also the proverb '"There is no secret time will not reveal.".

CHAPTER 7

James looked fantastic although tired. His face was sun tanned but, so typically for skiers, white around the eyes and with a white neck. His friends looked great and were sad to be returning to university to continue their studies. Rebecca told them that it was a good thing to leave when they were enjoying themselves. They agreed but laughingly told her that a few more days skiing would have been even better.

James unloaded his things from the car so that the others were able to go home to their respective families. They would travel together back to the university on Sunday, as James had his little car at St Andrews. They hugged Rebecca and told her to give their love to Tom.

The girls embraced James, and the young men tapped one another on the back. Rebecca watched them taking their farewells with a smile on her face.

She looked at these beautiful girls and handsome young men, all friends of James' most of whom had been together as a group for years now, ever since they had started university. Two of them went further back, to their school years. They obviously had great fun together.

James put his arm around his mother, walking towards the back door after having left his skiing gear in the garage. He wanted to hear about his father, have a shower and a bite to eat, before visiting him. 'I am absolutely starving,' he said..

Mozart was excited to see James again and had done the tour of James' friends for a tap and a greeting.

'Oh, it is good to be home mum, and I am looking forward to seeing dad again.'

James put his washing into the machine and Rebecca started it before she looked into the oven to see if the fish pie was ready. She was pleased that she had prepared the meal beforehand. The pizza could be for tomorrow.

James ate and talked enjoying the homemade meal and his mother's fresh bread. They had eaten mostly carry outs, pasta and rice in France.

'We didn't prepare one single meal with fish because of the smell,' he chuckled.

It was a delight to be home without anybody having been seriously hurt. Rebecca told him that she was relieved that he was fit and well and that the cars had been fine and had brought them back safely. Mozart sat for a while trying to get James' attention, begging for nibbles. The dog had more or less given up getting any from Rebecca, and of course had no luck with James either.

Rebecca told James about his father's health and memory, or rather his lack of it. However, she did not mention the cat. She had no idea why she kept this information from him. It must have been some feminine intuition.

'So when will dad be able to come home do you think?' James asked his mother between bites. Rebecca answered that she hoped to have Tom with her in about a fortnight's time. 'Are you going to be able to come home in two weeks time as arranged or have you too much studying to do? It could be that dad will be back home by your next visit.'

Rebecca told James that she had found the female Doctor Smith, who had supervised the operation, strange, and that the doctor had been almost unfriendly ever since Tom had come out of the coma. Rebecca could not explain this. James asked his mother if she wanted him to have a word with the Doctor. Rebecca thanked him but said that she would like to wait a little longer as Tom would be leaving the hospital shortly any way.

'Let's enjoy what we have and be the same family as before the accident.' she pleaded.

'Well, there have not been any problems only a feeling I have and lack of communication, as if they know something which she doesn't want me to know, like the MRI scan for example, and that she made me leave the room as soon as Tom had woken up from the coma.'

'When will we get the results from the scan, do you think?' James asked.

'That is one of the things I don't understand, because they are reluctant to reveal anything about this scan. They sidestep the question.' Rebecca answered.

'I agree that it sounds unfriendly, but let's hope that it is just that they cannot be specific.'

James asked his mother how she was sleeping and whether she was able to relax a little now that she was conversing with his father, knowing that things were going to work out.

'Yes, I do sleep better, thank you for asking, but I am still apprehensive. That will probably go away when Tom is back home. Nothing to worry about. Ready to go and see him or would you like another portion of the fish pie?'

'Two portions is more than even I should eat, but it was superb mum. As I said earlier, we didn't eat fish once, so this was a lovely treat. Thanks for the dinner. One more question about dad before we go. Do you find him much as he was before the accident or has he changed in any way? It might be too early to tell, I suppose. Stupid question, forget that I asked.'

In saying this James looked at his mother very carefully, as he did not want her to see that he was worried, and that he had been thinking lately as the weeks went by without his father making any progress.

Rebecca sat in silence, with her head down as if she were examining her plate, before with a sigh and with a smile she tried to reassure James that everything seemed to be fine. Her smile was not convincing.

'One never gets too tired for wine and cheese and we have a lot to talk about. I can sleep later. I can tell that you are not relaxed.' James said with concern.

Outside the hospital James put his arm around his mother's shoulders, as he had done so often during these last months. They had spotted Tom standing by his window looking out into the darkness of the evening. Rebecca and James waved excitedly to him but he did not see them. Tom was standing as if lost in his own thoughts, not seeing anything.

Rebecca shivered a little when she saw her husband standing like that. She had an experience of Mrs Danviers as in the film "Rebecca.' James had noticed that his mother was shivering and asked if she was cold.

CHAPTER 8

Tom turned round, away from the window, as Rebecca and James entered the room. He had a warm smile on his face, but James had to hold his breath not to let go of a gasp, when he saw how thin his father had become. He had not noticed that before, as Tom had been almost totally covered with blankets when he was unconscious.

Father and son hugged one another and Tom held James at arms length looking at him. Finally Tom opened his mouth and said that he was pleased to let them know that he did recognize him.

'Well, well, well, you are certainly a better colour than I am, but that'll soon change with some summer sunshine and a bit of fresh air. You must tell me what you have been up to during nearly four months which I have missed.'

Tom then turned to his smiling wife and as he let go of his son, he kissed Rebecca. Rebecca took hold of Tom's hand and with tears in her eyes she looked straight into Tom's. She felt happily relieved and was pleased that Tom had recognized James.

Tom went to his bed and half lying down propped up by pillows behind his back, he indicated that he was ready to hear about James' adventures and study results.

'I graduate early this summer in June, and after that I suppose it'll be the beginning of real life. I have started to ask around for a suitable job. I hope to be able to stay in Scotland. I have a good offer already, but that is down in Yorkshire. I might have to start working there as the most important thing is to get the first employment after graduation. Otherwise not much has happened. I have been coming home every other weekend since your accident and the holiday to France with my friends, some of them you have met, and some you haven't.

I have got some news for you. I am sorry that I have not told you this before mum, but I wanted to be sure of my feelings and how a very special young lady felt for me before telling you anything. I have met a girl and we have been going out for a few months. I will introduce her to you shortly. I am certain that you'll love her too. Her name is Gill, and she is different from Susan, who I don't think you liked much. Gill was also in France, but was delivered at her parents' house, before I arrived home, which is why you haven't met her.'

'We cannot wait to meet her.' said Tom. ' It is exciting. It is great news, isn't it, Rebecca?'

Rebecca did not have to answer. Her smile and the cuddle she gave James said more than words.

'So dad, how about you?' asked James.

Tom told them how he felt confused every now and then, but that he thought that his memory was getting better by the day.

'I have nightmares disturbing my sleep, which could have something to do with my accident or perhaps with some hallucinations from my time in the coma. Doctor Smith has told me that these things do happen. The dreams are not nice so I sincerely hope I will have an explanation for them or that they will leave me alone. I am weak and wobbly on my legs, and as you can see for yourself, pale and thin, but apart from this I feel great. Thanks to your mum, I think that my memory is recovering. I am longing to get back home and to meet Mozart and to be able to go for long walks and to be outside in the fresh air. To start living again.' He fell silent. When he suddenly started laughing, Rebecca and James exchanged glances. They were wondering what happened. Tom put his hand on one of his trouser legs and said with a big smile:

'Sorry I am laughing, but I just couldn't help myself looking at my trousers. If you examine them, you can tell that they have been pressed at least three times. Look at these creases along the legs and here are three visible lines. I remember that I used to say this and this made me laugh. Every little detail that I can remember is such a joy to me.'

Rebecca and James started laughing as well, but perhaps more from relief. James realized that he was looking at his father for signs of abnormality instead of enjoying him as he was. James did not think that there were any changes in his father which could not be explained. Tom was hesitant in his speech, but surely that must be normal for someone who had not spoken for over three months. James could not understand what his mother was worried about. She had scared the wits out of him when she had implied that his father might be different. It was going to be an interesting "cheese and wine" evening.

Tom brought him back from his contemplation 'A penny for your thoughts son.' James answered 'You know how it is when you are in love dad, don't you?' They laughed and Tom nodded, smiling up at his beloved wife sitting in her chair by his side, holding his hand in hers. He gave it a light squeeze. Rebecca blushed slightly.

A knock on the door and the nurse entered. It was the night shift nurse wanting to know if there was anything that Tom needed. With a lovely smile on her face, she told his visitors that it was time for them to let the patient get some beauty sleep.

'Good heavens, it is nine o'clock already. No wonder I am tired. I haven't slept much lately though I did manage to doze off in the car coming home!' James said as Rebecca kissed Tom good night. She told Tom that James would come on his own the following morning, as she had decided to play golf with the ladies, now that James would be able to help for a short while and was available to keep Mozart company. James had agreed to this earlier and she thought it would be a good idea to have a "father-and-son" talk for an hour or so, just the two of them. James felt the need for this because he would probably be more relaxed not having to watch his words and his mother's feelings.

'I think the nights are getting shorter and the days longer almost visibly by the day. I certainly noticed the difference after having been away for a week. Spring is here and we'll soon have summer.' James said.

There was not much traffic so they said simultaneously that there must be something going on, like a rugby or football match on television. Rebecca burst out laughing as they had said the same thing at the same time.

'Do you know what this means in Sweden? They say that we are going to the same wedding.'

'Oh mum, don't get carried away because of Gill. We have nothing planned. We haven't even discussed the matter yet.'

Rebecca had to reassure him that what she said about "going to the same wedding" was a proverb in Sweden and it only meant that they were going to the same wedding and not that one of them was getting married. She promised not to interfere.

' Do I ever do that?'

'Oh yes, all the time,' smiled James.

Mozart was standing behind the glass-panelled door when James drove through the gates which Rebecca had opened. James turned to her when exiting the vehicle, nodding towards the dog.

'I wonder if he has been standing there waiting ever since we left the house? He was looking out when we left too.'

'I sincerely hope not!' Rebecca exclaimed in horror.

'Don't worry. I was only joking.' laughed James.

Mozart greeted them and then rushed out into the garden to his favourite place, the gate post. Rebecca looked in surprise at the dog's behaviour.

'Surely we haven't been away for that long?'

James told her that he thought that the dog wanted to show them that he was not pleased with them for leaving him on his own again.

'This dog is a real character.' he said.

James opened the bottle of Bordeaux as soon as they got inside to let the wine breathe. The cheeses were already on the board waiting for them, apart from the cheddar, because Rebecca knew that Mozart liked it. It would not have been fair to tease him by leaving something which he loved on the kitchen unit when he was left on his own.

Rebecca went to the bathroom and put on her tracksuit before she uncovered the different cheeses and put the board on the table together with the basket of biscuits, her home made bread and butter. Her taste buds had already started working even before James came downstairs to join her.

They decided to have their "cheese and wine" at the kitchen table by candlelight.

Rebecca had managed to get his clean washing into the airing cupboard so that they could relax for the evening.

James served the wine and raised his glass 'Cheers mum, for the family.'

Rebecca closed her eyes for a second as the red velvet hit the back of her throat. How wonderful it was to be getting back to normal again. Tom would surely be coming home soon.

'Well, James, how about Gill? Such a lovely surprise you gave us. When can I meet her, or would you rather Tom and I met her together?'

'I have been thinking about this myself, as Gill has asked me when she could meet you, mum. I would like you to have met her before dad comes home. I don't know why, it is just a feeling I have about two women meeting before any involvement with the men, but at the same time, would that be fair to him? What do you think? Gill and I are early days yet and I don't want to rush things. I have met her parents as we went to Gill's folks first coming home from France.

I could on the other hand ask Sarah and Simon if they could collect Gill before coming here for me on their way back to St. Andrews. I would feel better if we did it that way, as this could have been something that just happened.'

'I can understand your feelings and I must say that I would be delighted to see her even if briefly. I am curious. Are the four of you together often?'

'Sarah is Gill's best friend and she is going out with Simon. We do see a lot of one another. I'll talk to them tomorrow.'

'Gill comes from North Berwick and is reading History of Art at St Andrews, the same as me. She also has a degree in Literature and in English, so there we differ as I will have my qualification in Architecture. She hopes to take up interior design. That's how we met, in the library trying to get hold of the same book at the beginning of the term. I have a photograph of her here. She is a golfer like myself and also likes skiing. As you can see, she is a brunette almost like you mum, but Gill has got some curls. Her hair is much shorter now than in the photograph. She has the most amazing eyes, which turn green when she is angry. Her father is a retired police superintendent and her mother keeps house. They are called Gordon and Helen Walker, and she has an older brother, Adam. She is the most wonderful thing that has happened to me. She is gorgeous. For me it was love at first sight and naturally I let her have the book before me. I instantly knew that this was the girl for me. You and dad met when you were students too, didn't you?"

Rebecca stretched across the table and squeezed James' hand. She was happy for him that he felt Gill was "The Girl."

'I do hope I'll soon meet her. I am sure dad and I will love her.'

'Of course you will and I think you'll get on well with her parents as well.'

Rebecca did not have to answer.

'What about dad? You seemed worried. Are you? Hopefully he will be back home soon to keep you company and to take turns walking Mozart. You were right, dad is awfully pale and will need a lot of fresh air and sunshine to get his colour back. He does seem to be my old dad and I am not worried. Everything looks normal to me. The only thing that I could say is that his way of talking is different from before the accident. His vocabulary doesn't seem to be as broad as it used to be. Please tell me about your feelings and thoughts. You do seem apprehensive, mum? Is there anything specific or just a feeling that you have?'

Rebecca did not want James to know how worried she was, as it could simply be her imagination. She thought about this for a moment and tried to think what was giving her this impression. She realized that it came back to Tom having asked about how the dog was getting on with the cat. It came back to this cat! She shook her head and told James that it had just been a feeling, a spur of the moment maybe. Of course this, with all the creases along Tom's trouser leg business proved that he was the old Tom. She felt a kind of relief.

'So how about your holiday? You have told me that it was fantastic, and the fact that Gill was there too must have made it more exciting. I do miss the snow after my years in Sweden. Especially the cross country skiing in an untouched landscape, with sun glistening on the snow covered pine trees. It's the silence and the smell of the snow as well as the beauty that I love. I find it so relaxing and peaceful and it made me feel happy, like in a dream in prose. Well, I don't think going downhill, like you do, can give you that same sensation, but you must have experienced the beauty surrounded by an infinity of white.'

'We did talk about going for a day's cross country

skiing. There were skis for hire, but that snowed off, or rather snowed in. The day we planned to do this was the only day of awful weather. I think it was pretty good only to miss one day skiing in the whole holiday. I feel happy on skis. It is the ability to reach the bottom without having any hiccups on the way down, and I suppose the sense of speed. Most of all, I think it has to do with the other happy people around experiencing the same feeling. And being on holiday of course. I have always loved the scenery of the mountains with snow on the peaks. It is beautiful and magnificent. I love the snowflakes falling on my face, though we did happen to have a little bit too much of it in one single go. By the way, there were avalanche warnings everywhere the next day. It is strange, that there are always some people who think that possible danger has nothing to do with them. Luckily there were no casualties, but some stupid people went down off piste and did start an avalanche. Fortunately it was a small one which didn't do any damage. I wonder if they were caught? I think that such inconsiderate selfishness should be punished. They could have ruined both lives and properties by not playing by the rules. However, nobody was hurt and that is the main thing.

We ate a lot of pasta and rice as you can guess, and we did have a pre dinner scotch each evening apart from the last night when we decided to keep off alcohol as we had to rise early and drive in conditions that might have been a bit tricky. We were fortunate in every way. The only thing that happened was that one of the boys, whom you haven't met, did break one of his skis on our last day, but nobody fell ill or suffered more than a little bruising. We did have brilliant weather except for one day, and we drove on well maintained-roads. I don't know what you do if the weather closes in on the day of departure. Never mind, here we are safely back home after a wonderful time. The flat was fine, but with eight of us in a flat for six it was bound to be a bit crowded and the kitchen could have been bigger, but we knew this before we set off. We took it in turns to do the cooking, two at a time, and we took turns with the cleaning – minimum of course. It worked out well, but mum, the scenery! You would have loved the view. We were looking out over the rooftops of a small village with the mountains as a backdrop. We didn't overlook the slopes, but you could have stayed indoors just looking out of the windows. I don't think that I could live there though, more or less in a hollow between these powerful mountains.

Oh, this Stilton is to die for.

Anyway, I think I would feel claustrophobic being vulnerable like that. A bit scary, thinking of the possible avalanches. The flat that we stayed in was higher up than the town, which we felt was safer. There was a terrible avalanche accident there some years ago, but that was before the security and warning systems. Today they go out on to the mountains and with controlled explosions blow the dangerous overhangs away before they get too bad and too big.'

'How is Edward doing? Asked Rebecca. He wasn't with you to France, was he? Is he still studying International Economics in Frankfurt? You haven't lost touch I hope.'

'No, we have not lost touch. We are communicating by email and through the chat rooms. He has settled down I think, and was going to introduce a certain young lady by the name of Rachel to his parents during the Easter holidays. Edward met her in Frankfurt, but she is an

American girl. You know that Malcolm and Mary have been visiting him during Easter, I suppose.'

'Yes and I have phoned them to tell them about Tom and left a message on their answering machine to phone me when they get back. First I thought I wouldn't as I felt I would rather tell them in person. In the end I changed my mind. This emailing is a real bliss. I communicate a lot with my Swedish friends through the computer.

This has been a wonderful day and evening. It is lovely to have you back in this country, but I think it is time for bed. It is almost midnight and you must be tired out after your travels. I have to get up at seven in the morning. Look at Mozart, even he is asleep and did you notice that he didn't beg as much?' Rebecca asked James.

She rose from the table as James had agreed that bed would be a good thing. It had been a super evening and she had enjoyed her two glasses of red wine. Rebecca realized how much she had missed it. They cleared the table as Mozart was let out and bid one another goodnight with hugs. Mozart got his usual cuddle before Rebecca went into her bedroom. It was with a delight after an eventful long day that she slipped between the sheets and she was soon asleep. .

CHAPTER 9

The alarm went off as planned and when Rebecca dragged herself out of the lovely warm bed, she went to the window and peeped between the curtains. Yes, it looked pretty good out there. It would be a lovely day. A good day for golf. A day without rain, and there did not seem to be much wind either.

Rebecca opened the kitchen door for Mozart and then she showered. She slipped into a pair of checked golf trousers. She felt brave enough for a short sleeved shirt but put on a wind cheater, just in case. Enjoying her breakfast, she admired the hedge now getting greener by the day. Suddenly one of the grey squirrels appeared. It jumped from the stone wall onto the roof of the empty bird table, which was no further than a few feet away from Rebecca and the kitchen window where she was sitting. She had never liked these grey animals, not since she had seen their lovely much smaller red cousins in Sweden. She looked at this one and was about to knock at the window to make it go away, when it suddenly turned towards her looking straight into her eyes and then at her breakfast on the table as if it was asking, 'So, what about me?' Rebecca laughed and then she did knock on the window and the squirrel shot away. Cheeky animal!

It was because of the squirrels that she had stopped feeding the birds. She was terrified that they were going to like it too much around the building and would nest and breed somewhere under the roof of the old house. It had happened before and they had closed that hole but it was not beyond the realms of possibility that the squirrels would find another way in. She recalled the time last year when they had put out a squirrel catcher. She had bought a squirrel proof bird feeder, which later on she had returned to the shop, as the squirrels just loved it. It didn't keep the squirrels off the bird food and she had succeeded in obtaining a refund. Tom had put this net tube filled with wonderful nuts for the birds hanging from the middle of a thin steel wire, one end had been fastened to the plum tree and the other tied to the house above the snug door. One late afternoon when Tom and Rebecca had been watching "The Open" golf on television, she had noticed one squirrel creeping out along the wire and on to the feeder, where it had started to eat. Rebecca was furious. She had jumped out of her chair to knock on the window. In doing so she not only scared the squirrel enough for it to fall off, but she also lost her balance, grabbed the curtain over the door behind the television, pulled it over the television and Tom missed seeing a match winning put!. Rebecca had managed to startle both Tom and the squirrel, and upset Tom enough for him to reach for the decanter and pour himself a stiff whiskey.

Rebecca went out and cut off the branches adjacent to the thin wire. First she cut some from the plum tree and later the same afternoon she almost demolished the lovely rose bush growing up the wall. Did it help? Not in the least. Squirrels are clever, she had to admit that. They must have been lining up on the roof, and then one after the other they jumped on to the feeder.

That was when she had decided enough is enough and managed to borrow a squirrel catcher from a friend. The cage was quite big and she had baited it and placed it under the feeder. What had happened? The squirrels were forming a queue for the feeder and the birds were flying in and out of the catcher pinching the bait. This had started off so badly it might have been organized by Railtrack!. Rebecca had been on the brink of giving up, when they finally did catch their first squirrel. One thing was sure. The squirrels did not use the bush telegraph. Rebecca and Tom caught seven all together. They could not bring themselves to kill them so in the end they put the catcher with a squirrel inside into the boot of the car. Under cover of darkness, they drove into the countryside following a narrow road with grass growing down the middle. Tom switched the lights off, hoping that nobody could see what they were doing, opened the cage and set their catch adrift. Rebecca did not like this, and had asked Tom what they would say if anyone came upon them in their car parked without lights along a dark country lane. Tom, with a wonderful smile on his face, had told her that he would tell whoever, that they were out courting. That had amused them enormously. When they returned home and found squirrels in their garden Tom said that the animals had probably hitched a lift.

Suddenly she was woken up from her thoughts by the dog scratching on the door for her to let him indoors. She became aware of the time and decided she had better get a move on.

Walking up the main road towards the golf club, she was surprised how warm the early sun was on her face. The traffic was awful at this time of the day with the school run and people leaving for work traveling by car.

The ladies were pleased to see her and she was greeted with great affection on her arrival at the clubhouse. There was quite a crowd this wonderful morning. One of the ladies gathered one ball from every player and threw them up into the air to decide who was playing with whom depending on the way the balls landed on the ground. This was a great way of ensuring a different pairing each time.

Three of the ladies went off directly, declaring that they were not going to play more than the first nine holes today.

Rebecca went out in the third game and played with Alice and Hazel so it had the makings of an excellent round.

It certainly felt wonderful to be out on the course for the entire eighteen holes again. She prayed that she would have the strength to concentrate. All the exercise she had done with Mozart must have done her a power of good, as she tried to walk quickly when out with him.

Alice had a bad tee shot on the fifth. The ball went more or less straight up into the air.

'Dear me, that ball will be covered in snow before it comes down into sight!' On the sixteenth Hazel had a good hit from the tee, but neither of them had seen it land as it was into the sun light. Hazel asked 'Where did that one go?' They laughed but never found her ball. Rebecca had a few hiccups, she had counted on that, but did not anticipate hitting three trees with three successive shots. Not even she could have dreamed that one up.

However, it caused a great deal of amusement. Rebecca played well apart from the disaster on the third "tree" hole and on the sixth she had to use no less than five shots to get out of <u>one</u> bunker. She visited several bunkers and managed to hit another tree or two before they were back in the clubhouse. She was tired and although she had not played within her buffer, she was not by any means disappointed.

When she entered the lounge to buy herself a drink, one of the men called out to her saying 'Rebecca, you disappoint me.' She looked straight at him and could see by his smile that this was going to be a joke, before she asked him what she had done wrong. 'Did I need three putts on the 18th?'

He answered no, but said it was much worse than that.

Rebecca had to beg him to tell her to what he was referring. He then asked how it was possible that she used an orange ball. 'A coloured ball is only for beginners, my dear!' he chortled.

She burst out laughing, as did the rest of the men around this table by the bow window over looking the eighteenth green. She responded by telling them that she had played like a beginner this morning. He smiled at her saying that she was a star and he did not believe her.

'By the way, it is lovely to see your rosy cheeks after a full round. Welcome back to us.'

Rebecca would be reminded of this conversation much later, when she played in a Texas scramble with three men. All four of them were using white balls. One of the men had asked her if she had run out of her orange balls. This man had been present when she had been told off.

She brought her usual Bitter Lemon into the sun lounge where the rest of the ladies were sitting. They had a lot to talk about and she explained about the progress Tom was making. When did ladies ever not have something to discuss or tell? It felt right to tell them about how Tom was when most of them were present.

Rebecca walked back along the road the way she had come and was greeted by one happy dog and a smiling son sitting in the garden. James had just finished cutting the grass. He had made the salad and the pizza would be ready in another ten minutes. James also told her that he had talked to Simon and to Gill about Sunday. They were coming here on their way to Uni.

'Gill was thrilled with the prospect of meeting you, mum, and she is looking forward to Sunday.'

Rebecca was delighted and told him so. She thanked him for having cut the grass, walked the dog and prepared their lunch. She told him about her round of golf. She said that it was great fun. She had had a "b and b" day, a bark and bunker round.

They ate their lunch and went to the hospital to see Tom. James told his mother that his morning visit had been fantastic. They had talked mostly about James' plans for the future, studies, work, and Gill of course.

'Dad is getting stronger. He had been out in the hospital grounds for a short walk with one of the nurses. He told me that he has lots of gaps in his memory and asked me about some of the photographs you had given him inquiring about the interior of this house. I "walked around it" with him telling him about the colours, our furniture and curtains for example. He wanted to know how you have coped, and asked if you had lost a lot of weight. I don't think you have lost that much, although you have certainly lost some, haven't you? I think you have done well and I told dad so. I am proud of you both.'

Rebecca was touched. She wondered how James could tell if Tom remembered their home. James said that he seemed to, but was often puzzled.

'I think he has lost some of his vocabulary. It sometimes feels as if he is lost for words - something he never used to be. Have you the same feeling?'

Rebecca had not thought about it. She had been so delighted to have Tom back in the land of the living.

'Now, that you mention it, I think you might be right. We have to help him. Hopefully it will be sorted with practice.' she said.

James had asked about the result of the MRI scan and had been reassured that everything was normal. No brain abnormality could be detected. This was indeed good news.

'Why they haven't bothered to let you know, I cannot imagine.'

Later in the early evening on their journey to the hospital, they noticed that the wind was picking up whistling through the branches, and the flowers were bending their heads. The wind felt mildish for the season, but if it became any stronger it could cause problems. It was not looking like rain but there was a distinct smell of rain in the air. The birds which had returned for the summer breeding would suffer. Rebecca had seen and heard some geese flying overhead when she was on the golf course earlier. There were masses of magpies, crows and seagulls. The seagulls, which should keep to the coast, had been lying flat on the grass anticipating a storm. Nobody liked any of these big and noisy birds and Rebecca had a clear view that if they were not killed off, there would soon be no small song birds.

The sky was an angry grey and looked rough like crepe paper, more like the sea with white horses than the sky with clouds.

Tom told Rebecca how much he had loved to be outside in the fresh air for his walk with the nurse in the morning. It had been wonderful to be able to listen to the birds. The dew on the grass had made it look fresh and clean. It was an odd feeling to have missed the winter and come straight into spring. It was almost a fairy tale, probably rather like in the "Sleeping Beauty." To fall asleep in the cold and dark to wake up in time for the spring, a terrible waste but one way of spending the cold weather away, hibernating like a hedgehog or a bear.

Tom had stopped in his tracks to take a deep breath of sheer joy and to examine the sky. The wind, which had hardly been noticeable then, had felt smooth on his face and had gently ruffled his wispy hair. He had felt so happy. All Tom wanted now was to get back home. He longed even more to join Rebecca and to do some gardening, see friends and play golf, if he remembered how to hit a ball that was.

His physiotherapist seemed to be pleased with his progress, and he was onto more normal adult food.

'If I were allowed to go home next week would that be convenient for you, darling? What I am trying to say is that I know it will be a strain for you, Rebecca, as I am not that mobile. Tell me your thoughts please, and do be honest with me. I will work hard to become your Tom again.' he pleaded.

Rebecca kissed him, told him she was thrilled and that she could wish for nothing better.

'If the staff are prepared to discharge you even temporarily, I am sure that we will be fine together and of course we will manage. I know that you will do your best. Do you really think that this is a possibility? I am surprised, as you were in a coma for so long, but I am looking forward to having you back home. It would please me enormously.'

When they left the hospital Rebecca and James were thrilled with the prospect of Tom coming home sooner than any of them had thought possible.

'Mum, don't read too much into this until you know the day Dad will be discharged. He has obviously not talked about this to anybody, but it is a wonderful prospect. It must mean that he feels well, which is in itself great news.' urged James.

They entered the house just before the rain started. There was a real storm brewing and it was much darker than yesterday evening. It was in fact almost pitch black out there.

Rebecca did not even want to let Mozart outside, as the rain lashed, and then streamed down the windows. The wind was roaring. It was indeed a fine evening to sit in front of the log fire in the living room, whiskey glass in hand, with some nuts and forbidden potato crisps to crunch on, whilst dinner was slowly cooking in the Aga. The pot roast looked wonderful and there were only the potatoes, Brussels sprouts and parsnips to cook. The vegetables were in their respective saucepans. Everything was more or less ready.

The malt went down Rebecca's throat like the best quality silk. Oh, it was enjoyable to sit here with James in silence looking into the burning logs, listening to the storm raging outside. On top of the mantelpiece Rebecca had lit the two candles. Mozart was lying by her feet. Only Tom was missing.

Rebecca was deep in thought. She had been thinking a lot about Mozart lately. Had it been unfair to the dog to bring him here? She had tried hard, and she did love him and enjoyed his company, but he had been left on his own much more often, than she had ever anticipated. She sighed and knew it had to get better. There was no way she was going to part from him. When Tom returns, it would be easier, wouldn't it? At least one of them could be at home, when the other one was out. Surely it would be alright for Tom to be left on his own with the dog sometimes? She longed for Tom's company, not to look after the dog, but for their life to be put together and for them to start living like the happy couple they had been. She missed him so much that it was unbearable at times. She had waited for so long. When she sighed both the dog and James looked at her, and he had to ask his mother what on earth was the matter. Rebecca smiled and told him how much she missed his father.

'Well, he will soon be here with you again.' James reassured her. ' I know how it feels to miss someone, when you are truly in love. Remember that I will be within "ear" shot if you have any problems. Please don't worry, mum. Try to be happy and patient for another few days.'

The storm did not seem to ease. The weather was just the same when they had finished their dinner and had brought their coffee back to their seats in front of the fire. Rebecca wondered how desperate Mozart would be to go outside before bed time. He would have to go, but although she loved the rain she would not put her nose outside tonight. Stormy weather was pleasant and relaxing if you were indoors, and your loved ones were safe.

She would try and read in bed for some time tonight, listening to the rain and the wind, which obviously tried its best to find gaps in the walls and windows.

Septima, her book group was reading "The Wall" by M. Haushofer for their next meeting. She would try to keep her concentration and to read this book on time. She had to load the bread maker and to plan dinner for the following evening. Pasta was out of the question, as James had had that for the entire week in France. She was craving pasta but would eat that for Sunday dinner, when she would be on her own again.

In the end she took out a beef casserole from the freezer. It was good that she had prepared plenty of meals some weeks ago even if it had been pure therapy.

The next morning when Rebecca woke up it was deathly quiet out there. She stretched lazily under the duvet in the wonderful warmth of the bed, wondering what state the garden would be in after the storm.

Poor Mozart must be desperate to go outside, as he had refused to face the weather last night. He was an intelligent dog, no doubt about that.

Rebecca surfaced from the bed. It was hard to leave her wonderful cocoon to let the dog out. She was surprised to see the time on her clock on the bedside table. It was early.

She was standing on the inside of the kitchen door looking at the dog running around marking. The garden had been badly battered. There were small branches, twigs, leaves and some flower heads all over the place, and several pots were turned on their sides. There did not seem to be any broken. Later on she would have to examine the roof to see if the tiles were in place.

She kept standing watching the sun rise and the night disappear. It looked as if they were going to be honoured with a good day. She would get dressed to go out as she liked the taste of the rain in the air. Everything smelled so fresh when the storm had passed.

Rebecca had not been able to read as much as she had planned to do. The weather last night had made her sleepy and she was tired. Her glass of whiskey and the red wine at dinner time helped her to fall asleep but disturbed her ability to concentrate on the book.

Mozart scratched the door to tell her that he wanted to come indoors. She left the kitchen door ajar and went into the bathroom to have her shower and to get dressed. It was not as warm out there this morning as it had been yesterday. The rain might have seen to that or perhaps it was too early in the morning.

The sun would do its best to take away the chill. She would let James sleep a little longer and wait for him so that they could enjoy breakfast together.

She left a note on the kitchen table for him in case he should wake up while she and Mozart were walking.

There was standing water on the playing field when Mozart was let free to run around. She herself avoided the wet grass and kept to the pavement. The debris, the fruit of the storm, was everywhere. Rebecca had to be careful where she put her feet so as not to fall over. One tree had blown across the road. The council people were busy cutting it up into pieces and moving it to the side. It was sad when a tree was gone. It took so long for it to grow and then only a storm, a saw and an axe to get rid of it.

It was the same, or even worse, to see a house being

neglected for the wind and nature turn it into a ruin. Rebecca thought of the hard working people who had struggled to put stone on top of stone to build a house to give shelter for a family, and the beautiful stone walls that criss-crossed the fields of this peaceful countryside. How could anybody let them fall to rubble? Whatever you did, in the end nature took back.

It was wonderful to be out early. It was completely quiet apart from the workmen moving the fallen trunk. There was not even any traffic. Only an odd car passed the lonely woman and her black dog trying to avoid the puddles.

Mozart was drenched and Rebecca had to give him a good rub down when they returned home. She had to change her shoes, socks and trousers as they were soaked.

James came downstairs and they prepared breakfast and sat down with the morning paper which had arrived, taking one part each. This paper boy was good being earlier than the previous one had been. Rebecca did the Su Duko to keep her mind active. It was lovely to take time over the meal. They did not have to rush. She had walked the dog and both lunch and dinner were prepared.

It was bright and delightful outside. The sun was shining and the sky was spring pale blue with small fluffy white clouds. The trees were covered with raindrops like glass beads reflecting the sun and the sky. Some drops of water were leaving their places on the leaves and fell to the ground with a small splash. It was vivid and lovely, and made Rebecca deliriously happy. Soon this magic would dry up and be gone.

James stifled a yawn and looked at his mother, noticed her smiling and hoped that everything was going to be fine. He could not get rid of that strange feeling of concern. He did not know where it came from nor why, but it was there lurking in the background. He was relieved to see her smiling and hoped that she would have more to smile about when his father was back where he belonged at home with her. He prayed for their future together. He knew that something was not quite right with Tom, but nothing he could talk about with anybody apart from the odd email to Edward, who had sworn not to reveal James' thoughts and opinions. He had promised not to tell either his parents nor Rachel, as James could not say other than expressing his creeping fear.

Mother and son went to see Tom before doing the shopping and went to the Gallery of Modern Art, which would be interesting and useful for James' studies.

During their hospital visit, the three of them walked around the grounds. Just a short walk as it was wet and slippery under foot. They had discussed Tom's homecoming. Rebecca asked if he would like to have his favourite dish for dinner his first day at home. Tom had looked happy and his face had broken into a smile.

'That would be fantastic. They don't serve fish and chips here. Please could I order mushy peas as well?'

Rebecca and James exchanged quick glances. They both knew that the good old Tom would not put fish and chips first on his list of desired meals. He had always wanted liver and bacon with potatoes and the Swedish lingon berry jam which they could buy in IKEA. Rebecca told Tom that he would get the mushy peas, but how about liver and bacon, wouldn't he like that?

'As you are asking me I suppose this could only mean

one thing, but did I really like liver? I cannot think of eating that at the moment. My taste buds must have changed.'

Tom smiled reassuringly and Rebecca answered that this must be the reason. She tried to put this to the back of her mind where the cat was already hidden. A cat and distaste for his favourite dish? She felt the tension returning. Where was this going to lead them? Something had definitely happened during his months away from them, away from real life.

She could tell by looking at James earlier that he was worried, or at least that it had given him something else to think about.

Rebecca had never been keen on modern art. She preferred contemporary art and loved the old buildings in Edinburgh and the galleries and museums. There were however, some exciting modern buildings and some art she liked for example some works painted by Anselm Kiefer. She thought that he was a master of light.

She remembered when Tom and she had seen works by this artist. They had been in a museum abroad and had had to sit down in front of a painting for a while to take it in. It was an image which would not have appealed to her if it had not been for this magic light. The subject had been completely empty of people as if all living things had been wiped out by some disaster and still it had seemed such a masterpiece to her.

There were obviously modern buildings that she liked too, and some which she had not even visited, just seen pictured in books. "La Sagrada Familia" by Gaudi in Barcelona was one that she had seen and in Vienna she had loved what Hundertwasser had created.

So far Dubai had been a favourite place for both her

and Tom. To them it had everything. They had been there twice and had stayed at Jebel Ali, a great hotel out of town away from all the building work going on closer to the centre. It seemed as if the entire city was one big building site. It was an amazing place, with exciting ultra modern buildings different from each other. Jebel Ali had its own superb nine hole golf course and a private beach, as well as several wonderful restaurants and a free shuttle bus into the city.

Last year they had visited the seven star hotel, Burj Al Arab, where they had had afternoon tea. Neither of them would have liked to stay there; although it was fantastic and splendid, it lacked the comfortable atmosphere they preferred.

They had talked about going back to Dubai when at least one of the artificial islands was finished, and to have a meal in the fish restaurant under water at the foot of 'epitaph to riches hotel' the Burj Al Arab. Rebecca had read somewhere that the way into this restaurant, which looked as if it is situated in the middle of an aquarium, was by a simulated ride in a submarine. It sounded exotic and exciting as well as awfully expensive. Rebecca hoped that they would be able to go one day. She had not made any enquires about travel insurance for Tom. She had to get the doctor's full report before she would know his post operative status. Perhaps she was too naive even to think about Tom traveling abroad again.

They had also talked about going back to Visby on the island of Gotland on the East coast of Sweden. There was so much to see and they had not been inside many of the over 700 old churches.

She became melancholy. They had planned to travel and there were many places they wished to see.

Rebecca was dreaming away, walking round amidst the modern sculptures. She started looking for James in the shop as he had wished to buy a book on architecture. They decided to go home for lunch and to Mozart. The desire to spend the rest of this gorgeous day in the garden was shared. Rebecca needed to do some dead heading and to tidy up after last night's storm. James would help her to tie up some of the roses which were desperately trying to cling to the walls.

Neither of them mentioned Tom's choice of food. Rebecca had made it clear that it was the last thing she wanted to talk about, not in actual words but through her body language. She wanted to leave the subject alone, at least for now. All she wanted was to get him home. Never mind the food!

The delight of working in the garden with James for company was wonderful. She could feel that this pleasure was mutual. They did not talk much. The conversation was kept to the necessities. It was a silent understanding between them to keep their conversation to a minimum, and their thoughts, especially about Tom, to themselves.

Back home they had let the dog out. As she left the door open for him, Rebecca felt as if it were an open door of opportunity. Present time was short and nobody could predict what will happen in the future. Rebecca felt the need of an open door in her own life.

They spent the entire afternoon, all three of them in the garden. First of all Rebecca and James had examined the roof. The tiles were intact. No trace of any broken ones on the ground. Then they did some work in the garden and later on they had coffee and scones with jam and butter but without cream. They had been sitting on the terrace for the first time this year.

Three pairs of eyes followed a big black beetle running across the crazy paving. It must have been woken up by the warmth of the sun. Suddenly Mozart made a go for it. A crunchy noise echoed and Rebecca shivered. She was happy she had swallowed the last bit of her scone and remembered why she did not let Mozart kiss her.

She turned a smiling face towards James and advised him that he had not been much better himself as a young lad. Rebecca told him that when he had been about four years old, he had been watching a beetle and finally he had put his little foot on it, making that same crunchy noise. 'You looked at the beetle that you had just tramped to death, and said in a soft voice. "Now you can go to Baby Jesus."'

Dad and I looked at one another then, trying hard not to show how close we were to bursting out laughing. We did laugh later on, asking one another what on earth Sunday School did teach you.' James smiled at his mother and told her that he had no recollection of this.

'Did I really do that? Did I talk a lot about God and Jesus?'

'I think it was the only time I heard you mention Jesus apart from at Christmas time and at Easter of course.' smiled Rebecca

Rebecca went in for a thicker jacket and to change her boots for a pair of warm shoes. She brought the book that she had started reading the previous evening. She was not sure that this was going to be a suitable story for her now as it obviously revolved around the strange life of a completely abandoned woman, although Rebecca did find it well written and was too curious to leave it unread. She would certainly call it a "page turner."

James read the book he had bought earlier before he went to visit his father on his own.

Later in the evening, after Mozart had had the treat of a second long walk in one day, Rebecca and James decided to continue reading. They sat in the snug and did not watch television.

Mosart had been hunting the fox when they were out before dinner. He came back to them when Rebecca called for him to return, but not at her first call, that had to be admitted. He got his reward. Hopefully he would learn to obey more quickly in the future.

There was standing water on the playing field, but most of the puddles along their route were gone. It was far too wet to walk through the Dell however, which Rebecca would have liked to have done. She never liked to cross it alone even when she had the dog with her. She had missed these Dell walks during Tom's convalescence but she hoped that he would soon be able to walk through this place of beauty with her and their new pet. When James was at home during the winter weekends there had been too much to do around the house, and the visits to the hospital and the weather had made them go into town museum visiting instead of walking in the countryside. Before Mozart, there had not been any need either.

Could it be possible that Tom would be coming home next week? It did not seem that long since he had regained consciousness and she had her doubts, but longed for him to join her at home nevertheless.

At the end of the weekend she was looking forward to the time when James was going to be picked up by Sarah and Simon. This Sunday was going to be special.

She was anticipating meeting James' fantastic girlfriend Gill and their friends Sarah and Simon, but first James took her to see Tom.

James' friends arrived early enough to stay with her for a cup of coffee in the afternoon. Rebecca did like Gill. She was different from Susan, indeed, not just in looks but also in the way she drank her coffee and ate the slice of apple cake that she was served. Gill was a true pleasure. Rebecca had felt it as soon as the girl appeared. When she first entered the room it was like a breath of fresh air. Rebecca envied her short cropped slightly curly hair and she had beautiful green eyes. She was much shorter than James not even as tall as Rebecca. No makeup on and smartly dressed in a pair of dark blue trousers, blue and white striped shirt and a navy sweater knitted in an Arran pattern. Gill did not wear many rings on her fingers, only a single one on her right hand. She was wearing earrings more like gold studs, not anything dangling. A sensible girl and she seemed to like James as much as he adored her. Rebecca was sure that this was an excellent match. Gill was a girl who Rebecca would like to get to know better. She hoped that James would bring her home for another visit soon, and hopefully by that time Tom would be there.

Sarah and Simon were a friendly couple, Sarah similar to her friend Gill although with longer hair. It was wonderful to see girls with the complexion nature had intended. Both of them looked clean and fresh and naturally slim.

Simon was a very polite young man, in fact, all three of them were. James had obviously made an excellent choice and Rebecca could relax. Her son was in good company.

The young ones left as they had arrived, with hugs and greetings. Rebecca wished them a safe journey, Mozart standing by her side. He had calmed down from this excitement with so many friendly people around. James promised to phone her as soon as they got to St Andrews.

CHAPTER 10

Tom was not discharged during the following week as they had hoped. He had been disappointed and cross with the doctor in charge. Rebecca had explained to Tom that it was better to be cautious and not to take any risks after he had made such good progress.

'Better to be safe than sorry.' she reminded him.

Rebecca was not upset. She had never thought that it would be possible for Tom to get home this early and therefore she had not put much expectations into his possible homecoming. She did find it hard to wait, but she had been waiting for so long that another week would hardly matter. It was strange that when she had a prospect of a more specific time for this to happen, this last week had felt longer than the previous months together. Hadn't it been like that when she was working? If she had been asked to stay overtime for only one hour, that hour felt like years. Her body clock had kicked in for the expected time and not for the overtime.

Anna and Rebecca had been to Dobbies Garden Centre one afternoon to have some shared laughter by the greeting cards display. They always found some funny ones and discussed who to send them to, which made them giggle even more. They did not buy many. The cards were often too rude for them.

Coffee and a shared cheese scone were on the agenda when they were visiting Dobbies and their chatter solved all kinds of problems.

Another day, she and Mozart walked to the village and met another friend for coffee at the tiny and cosy

"Cafe' Sugar Rush" Mozart had had to wait outside, but as they had been able to sit at the table in the window overlooking the pavement and the street, it felt fine to leave him there for the time it took them to finish their coffee, delicious cakes and conversation.

Oh it was dangerous to go there, but the atmosphere was special. To sit in the bow window and watch people walking past whilst enjoying coffee and their delicious apple tart was a real treat. .

First Mozart had been standing outside the window looking at them eating the homemade cakes, but finally he sat down. Rebecca was pleased to have some of his treats in her pocket.

Walking through the village did not take long if she did not meet friends. The dentist and the post office were on one side of the main road, along with an estate agent which she never had cause to visit. There was a recently built stone stairway which took visitors from the upper road straight to the post office.

The dentist was the one that both she and Tom used and the post office staff were always delightful, helpful and cheeky. The shop keepers in the village probably recognized everyone who lived in the area. On the pavement side of the road, where the cafe' was situated there were a travel agency and the village pub. No village, however small, lacked a pub or a gift shop.

There were a chemist, a video rental shop, an Italian bistro and Patsy's fruit and vegetables. With the optician, hairdresser, newsagent and the delicatessen there was only a book shop missing to make it perfect, Rebecca thought, walking back home after having stopped window shopping. Rebecca waved to Patsy, Bill, Tom and the other shopkeepers, before she retraced her way home, dog on lead.

At the top of the village was Rebecca and Tom's favourite restaurant. To have this within walking distance was a luxury – no need to drive there and back after a bottle of wine.

Down from the "Cafe' Sugar Rush" was the grocers' which stocked almost everything from home made fresh bread to washing powder and newspapers, but no books .

The village was more than 900 years old. The main road was narrow with most of the shops on the one side because the road followed a high stone wall on the other side. This stretched all the way to the bridge across the river and the Dell.

She ought to go to the library, but that would have been too much of a diversion, and Mozart was getting impatient. Perhaps he was getting hungry.

This week of waiting had passed dreadfully slowly, though she had made herself busy walking, talking, visiting Tom twice most days and playing golf. She had been writing regularly in her diary and often mentioned the cat and the fish and chips.

She was grateful for her email contacts, especially friends she kept in touch with in Sweden. How she had managed before she had joined AOL, she did not know. She had written many letters then, something she had always enjoyed doing.

James phoned more often during this week. Rebecca thought that he wanted to cheer her up. She was delighted to talk to him and to hear what he and Gill had been doing.

When she saw Tom and told him about her day, he was in great form and told her that he hoped to be discharged the following day before lunchtime, if everything went according to plan. Delighted with the news, Rebecca promised to be there with the car to collect him and the treasures that had rapidly piled up since he had come back to the land of living. He was like a small school boy full of sheer joy and excitement.

Tom went up to her standing by the window and put his arms around her in a lovely bear hug. Her head was resting on his chest and she felt him lightly kissing the hair on top of her head. It was such a wonderful feeling to rest in his arms like this again. He could feel her entire body relaxing and she could not help the tears of joy from running down her cheeks. She felt the tension from these months of fear and anxiety leave her and fly out of the window. Tom turned her round and started to stroke her hair. Smiling, he dried her tears and in a thick emotional voice, told her that he did understand what she had been through. He thanked her for her love and faith and let her know how much he cared and loved her.

Rebecca wiped the rest of her tears from her cheeks and turned her face up towards Tom's. Eyes meeting, he bent down and met her lips in a soft but intense kiss. It was a promising kiss, a kiss tasting of tooth paste, a kiss for the future. They stayed entwined for a long time enjoying the feeling of being together again, of being close in every respect.

Standing by the car in the hospital car park Rebecca looked up in search of Tom's window. He was standing there waving to her and blowing a kiss. She responded and on the way home she felt more relaxed than she had done for a long long time. She was lucky not to know then how soon it would change. This relaxed and happy feeling was destined to disappear into despair all over again. She would never ever forget the embrace and kiss which had just exchanged. This memory would stay with her for as long as she lived, a wonderful memory nobody and nothing could take away.

Rebecca started to tidy up and changed the sheets in the bedroom getting ready for the return of the master of the house. She managed to eat a normal dinner, hopefully the last one on her own.

She suddenly felt awful. The guilty feeling hit Rebecca. The guilt that had weighed her down when Tom had fallen on the ice. She had put it at the back of her mind, almost forgotten that experience, that sense of pain in her stomach and the horrible vision. She had managed to push it aside now that he was alive and well on the road to recovery.

Mozart and Rebecca were wet when they came back from yet another brisk walk. The dog had to be rubbed down and dried with his towel, and she had a wonderful hot foam bath.

Rebecca had her evening coffee in the snug in her dressing gown. She had even contemplated pouring herself a glass of brandy, but no, she was not going to get into the habit of drinking on her own.

The log fire was wonderful and Mozart had found his spot by her feet. He looked up at her with those faithful eyes of his before they closed, his head resting on his crossed front legs. He had been patted, and Rebecca had fondled his soft ears.

Then she switched on the television to watch a film.

Audrey Hepburn was one of Rebecca's favourite film stars. She had died like many others of that generation Rebecca enjoyed. David Niven, such an aristocrat, and Leslie Howard as the Scarlet Pimpernel. Danny Kay was another she had found amusing as a young girl. There was perhaps nothing wrong with the new generation of actors, but she was not taken with Catherine Zeta Jones and Hugh Grant, like Julia Roberts seemed to have fallen into the stereotype trap. To Rebecca they were always the same. Catherine Zeta Jones was a beautiful woman, but this was all.

PART THREE

The bed was in a real mess when the alarm woke her up. She had slept badly and had been restless. Tom and his fall had been transferred into images which entered her dreams as soon as she had closed her eyes. She had been reliving Tom's accident, how he had fallen so hard and she could hear that awful cracking noise as his head hit the ice. She had tried to cut it out. It had been such a violent and sudden incident. She saw him falling in front of her over and over again.

She brought back memories of a previous experience, when she had been driving up a snowy and slippery road in Sweden and had lost control. The car had started to spin around on the road surface, before it had slipped down a hillside and turned upside down at the bottom of somebody's garden. She could vividly remember how she had had time to think about her life and her dead husband. The incident had taken so long.

Half an hour later, Rebecca was still lying in her bed, being hugged by the duvet. She shook her head in disbelief and rapidly threw the bed clothes away from her body. She could feel the chilly morning air caressing her. She had to get up and move. She went into the bathroom for her shower. Rebecca took a long time applying the perfumed body lotion. To smell and feel soft, lovely and silky was exhilarating and extra special on a day like today, when Tom was coming home to her. The last day of solitude.

The rain was lashing down on the front of the windows. Mozart was shown the door but he did not stay in the wet garden for long. He would have to miss his walk, because there was no way Rebecca was going out in this weather. He had to wait to be exercised. Hopefully the weather would improve. She had only one thing on her mind at the moment. Tom was coming home.

Rebecca wanted everything to be perfect for his return. She had cleaned the house with extra care, and then tried to put everything back as it had been before the accident. She had taken great care not to remove anything. She thought that if everything was as before, it would be easier for Tom to recognize his surroundings.

She burnt her mouth trying to drink her coffee, which was too hot. She did not take long over her breakfast. Rebecca didn't even try to do the Su Duko in the paper. She only browsed through the pages of both the Telegraph and the Times, which were delivered on Saturdays. She thought Saturday must be an odd day to discharge a patient from the hospital, but with the savings to be made in the NHS perhaps it had become the norm.

By the time she arrived at the hospital, the weather had not changed. It was awful. The sky was literally weeping. Why did this have to happen today, which was so important to them both? Why wasn't the sun smiling instead? She was going to remember the weeping weather later, several weeks later in fact. The sky "crying" would haunt her. Did it have any specific meaning, a hint of what was to come maybe?

The wind had picked up and it was impossible to use an umbrella. Rebecca was grateful that Tom insisted on buying these long waterproofs last summer. She brought Tom's with her. Only snow could have made this weather worse. What a day to come home.

Doctor Smith, whom Rebecca had started to dislike, wanted to talk to them before Tom was discharged. She made it clear that she wanted to see Tom again in a few weeks, and she told them to call her if anything unusual occurred, or if they had any doubts or questions. She then said her goodbyes shaking their hands telling Tom to go easy, not to overdo things. The last remark she made to Tom but looked sternly at Rebecca, who took it as a warning. A warning about what? It made her feel uneasy and suddenly all she wanted was to get Tom away from this woman and this place, away and into the safety of their home.

Rebecca could not pin point what made her feel this way, that Tom was no longer safe in the care of this doctor. Her eyes had been cold and unfeeling. Rebecca shivered at the thought that this woman was hiding something from them.

One day she would be angry with herself that she had not asked to read Tom's records. Would things have turned out differently if she had? She was going to reprimand herself about this later, but for now she was totally obsessed with getting Tom back home. Home where he belonged. However, Rebecca would come to hate this doctor.

Tom was relieved to get into the car and to be driven home. He looked around as they passed vaguely familiar landmarks. He observed houses and trees and the waterlogged playing field close to their old house. Oh yes, he recognized the house and the garden. He experienced that wonderful feeling of coming home, as Rebecca drove through the gates that she had left open earlier because of the rain. Tom wanted to close them. He stopped for a minute, to breathe and to look around. He did not feel the rain soaking his head so that the wind was not able to ruffle his hair. Neither did he feel the water running down his face. The garden, though wet and battered, looked lovely. He turned his eyes towards Rebecca, who had stopped under the shelter of the porch. She was watching him, not looking at the garden.

They smiled when they noticed the dog waiting for them to enter.

Tom fell in love with Mozart at first sight. It would turn out to be a loving partnership between master and dog, as Rebecca had hoped. Mozart would always be her dog though. He turned to her and followed her every step. She was the one who fed him and the two of them had started their relationship being sad and lonely.

When they entered the house there were flowers in a vase on the kitchen table and a welcome home card. It was from Anna and Eric, who had let themselves in with their key. In the fridge was a home made chocolate mousse and some of Anna's wonderful fish pate'. How lovely and thoughtful of them!

Tom entered the house dripping wet. He was told to stay where he was standing on the door-mat. Rebecca helped him to take off the raincoat and put into the airing cupboard with her own. Both pairs of shoes went in too.

Tom was standing there trying to take it in. He was back. He was at home. He had left the hospital behind him and it felt absolutely wonderful. With a big sigh of pure delight he turned to Rebecca who with a smile said 'Welcome back home, darling.'

Tom went straight through their bedroom to get a towel out from the hot rail in their bathroom to dry his hair whilst looking around. He went up to the window on Rebecca's side of the bedroom and looked out. All he could see through the rain was the hedge that concealed the house from the road and the passers by. There were not going to be many walkers along their narrow road in this weather.

It was almost dark although it was only lunch time. He went to the window opposite, on his side of the bedroom overlooking the garden with the garage at the far right hand side. He could hear more of the wind which bent the weeping willow, than he could see anything in particular. He <u>knew</u> the tree was there, and that was more important to him than to see its beauty.

Tom walked slowly through the entire house memorizing every detail. He examined the pictures on the walls and picked up every single photograph from the shelves and the deep windowsills. He did not say anything, no questions, no comments, not a single syllable. He looked around every room, every corner of the house, in complete silence. Rebecca followed him with her eyes, but left him on his own. She did not follow him upstairs but stayed in the kitchen with Mozart and tossed a salad, cut the freshly made bread and prepared the plates with parma ham and melon.

She did not want fish and chips and mushy peas for dinner tonight, but would certainly eat the battered fish and some peas to go with it for Tom's sake. She wondered if they perhaps should eat her home made meat balls tonight and leave the fish and chips to the following evening. It would save her going out in this weather once more. Today would probably not be an evening to go out to "The Cod Father".

Doctor Smith had told them to go easy with alcohol, as nobody would know if he would show any symptoms to it in a negative way. If he had any negative reaction to anything, she wanted to know. This had been said more like an order. Anyway, Tom would have to wait a few more days before enjoying his favourite whiskey. They would start with a small glass of wine.

Lunch was ready by the time Tom came back downstairs. He was greeted by the dog whose tail was going from side to side at a precarious double speed. The dog had to be calmed down before he hit something off a side table.

Tom went up to Rebecca, put his arms around her and kissed her. He gave her a smile that said everything. He was so so happy to be at home.

Rebecca was used to sitting on Tom's side of the table that she did not think. She sat down and asked Tom why he was not joining her. He looked puzzled and she realized her mistake. She laughed at herself, and said she was sorry and took hold of her old chair. Tom watched her and she explained to him why she had automatically gone for the wrong one. He was relieved as he for a minute had thought that his memory was playing up. She reached for his hand across the table and squeezed it gently.

They did not talk much during the meal, both being deep in their own thoughts. They had been talking so much during her visits to the hospital. There was no need for either of them to speak. The only thing which could be heard was the rain against the windows and the sound of them eating. The clock on the kitchen wall ticked away and the big old one in the dining room chimed the hour.

They enjoyed the silence interrupted only by wind, rain and the clock. It was different to be in the quiet house when she was not on her own. She felt relaxed and it was great to be watching Tom on the opposite side of the table.

He looked tired and was pale and thin, but this was going to improve. It was going to be taken care of by her and not by any doctors. Good nourishing food, exercise, plenty of fresh air and sunshine were her recommendations and she had started by giving him the food he liked, or should she say used to like. She was still questioning Tom's wish for fish and chips and mushy peas for dinner! It must just be a craving after the bland hospital meals and of course the "baby" like food with which he had started his recovery.

Tom was the one to start their conversation by talking about plans for the immediate future. He would like to walk to the village as soon as the rain stopped. He wanted to have a real good look around. The Dell had to be postponed for several days. It was too wet.

These things were natural and easy to do but how about meeting all their friends? They did not want to overdo it. It would certainly be easier for Tom to remember people if he did not see all of them at the same time, although he would love to go to church the following day for the usual 10.30 service. There he would meet quite a few friends and it would be at the same time especially if they stayed for coffee afterwards. It should not be difficult in familiar surroundings.

'Couldn't we go to church tomorrow and if I realize it is going to be too much for me, we could skip the coffee and come straight back here? What do you think?'

'If you feel like going, of course we'll go and as you just said, we can sneak quietly away. Yes, let's try that if you still feel like going when we wake up in the morning.'

'If the weather is like this, we will have to take the car. You don't mind that do you?'

'I am certainly not walking in this and it would be too much for you anyway, and then to sit in the church with damp clothes would not be good for either of us. Did you ask anybody about you driving or was anything said about that?'

'It slipped my mind. I forgot to ask, but I must say I am pleased that I never did enquire about it. What a blow if I had been told not to..'

'Coffee dear?'

They cleared the table and put everything into the dish washer. Mozart followed their every step with his eyes. He probably wanted to know when he was going to have his daily walk. She opened the kitchen door for him but he just stood there in the opening with the wind and rain coming into the kitchen, even his ears were blown back by the wind. The dog shook the rain away from his face and turned his back to the door.

The kettle was boiling and coffee was made. Tom brought their cups on a tray through to the living room where the log fire was making it warm and cosy. It had become chilly in the house and the heating had been put on for the morning.

They sat with their coffee and relaxed in front of the fire, Mozart by Rebecca's feet as usual. Tom told her how much he had enjoyed seeing Malcolm the other day at the hospital.

'They had a wonderful time in Frankfurt with Edward, and were pleased to meet his Rachel. She is apparently a lovely girl. I must say that I am happy for them. When do you think we'll meet Gill, or rather when will I see her do you think? James, is he coming home next weekend? Do you know?'

'Yes, James is coming home on Friday. I am sure that we'll meet Gill on Sunday. James could go and collect her and then pass here on their way to St. Andrews. You'll like her. She is a great girl.'

They sat in the sofa close together listening to the fire and the weather, enjoying the beginning of their "together life" again. Tom put his arm around Rebecca and drew her near him. He put his face into her hair and took a deep breath. She smelled lovely and he remembered the scent of her perfume. He told her so and she rewarded him with a kiss

Tom fell asleep and Rebecca put the fire guard up in front of the fire before she also fell into a light slumber.

She woke up first. The dog had indicated that he wanted some attention. Rebecca tried to stand up without disturbing Tom, who seemed to be in a wonderful relaxed state, sound asleep. However, he did wake up with a start, not knowing where he was.

Mozart needed to go out, and as the wind had dropped they decided to go for a short walk, all three of them.

Pulling on their still damp raincoats and armed with an umbrella, they put the ecstatic Mozart on the lead and took a deep breath, laughing. Rebecca opened the kitchen door and they were soon out in the garden, entering the rain curtain. Tom was holding on to Rebecca's arm, for security, but with the umbrella in the other hand it was almost a Mary Poppins experience, though the wind had dropped. If the storm had been as strong as before he would not have been able to shelter them under any umbrella. He tried hard to keep it steady.

They walked arm in arm huddled together under the huge golf umbrella. Whatever the weather, he was back home and in the loving care of his wife. So much nicer to walk close to her, to be supported by her instead of walking with a walking stick or with a nurse.

The weeping willow was really weeping with tears of rainwater running from its leaves on to the grass. It was a suitable name for it in weather like this. There would be some flooding around if this weather continued for much longer.

Rebecca had noticed that there was a river of rain water cascading down the steps from the street towards their front kitchen door. She had been watching this flow for a while with concern, but the water disappeared into the ground in front of her. It simply vanished.

'We must have an underground swimming pool by now.' she thought. The house had no cellar which probably was just as well. They had never been flooded. She could not think of anything worse than having one's home ruined by flood water. The smell must be horrendous and it made the place impossible to sell. Stuck in a home that had been flooded! She often thought of the poor people who had had their homes ruined by water. What on earth would she do in a situation like that? The thought was not one to consider.

Their wellie boots smacked through the waterlogged path. To try and walk on the playing field was completely out of the question. Mozart went there however, after he had done what he came out to do. Rebecca never wanted to let him run freely in the field, before he had finished his "business", as it would have been impossible for her to pick up after him. It would not be fair to children and not to the mothers either. The dog had to do his business before being let off the lead. That was her responsibility.

They did not walk far, but were pleased with themselves for giving it a try. The dog was happy and they had had a change of air, a lot of air into their lungs.

Safely back in the warmth of the kitchen, she dried the dog first and then Tom's hair. The macs were put into the airing cupboard again, now with their wellie boots.

Tom ran the bath and offered it to Rebecca before using it himself. They were indeed cold and he remembered that Rebecca always felt the chill more than he did.

Tom was almost never cold, on the contrary, he used to suffer more from being too warm. This had changed since he had lost weight. Nowadays he experienced the cold that Rebecca felt.

While Tom was soaking in a hot foam bath, Rebecca fed the dog. She listened to the answering machine. Malcolm, Anna and the Reverend had called but not James. Well, he had not left any message anyway.

She dialed Anna and thanked her so much for the goodies.

'As you know I'll send you a card to say a proper thank you as we always do.' Anna had been concerned that nobody was in when she had phoned. She thought that something had happened at the last minute to prevent Tom from coming home. Never could she had imagined that they were out walking.

'You must be mad the two of you, or in love or probably both!'

Rebecca promised to phone to let them know as soon

as possible when she thought Tom was going to be ready for visits.

'Tom wants to go to church tomorrow morning. We'll probably see you there, but we might not go in for a coffee after the service. Has anything happened lately that we should know about? By the way Marc has phoned too. I'd better return his call as well.'

Tom was happy to save the fish and chips for the following day and eat her meat balls. Rebecca was going to offer Tom one small glass of red wine and also one of the dry white with the starter. They were going to have a good meal tonight with Anna's fish pate' and then Rebecca's meatballs. They had the chocolate mousse, which would make this first dinner together this spring a three course meal. With coffee in front of the log fire it would be perfect. She smiled when tossing the salad. That was one thing which they enjoyed, and this habit she had brought with her from her years in Sweden. They ate more salads than cooked vegetables, and loved it. They also liked to eat lingon berry jam with the meat balls. A traditionally Swedish treat.

Rebecca laid the dining-room table to make it extra special. It was wonderful with the log fire in the living room area. It made the entire living-dining room feel warm, welcoming and lighter.

She lit a couple of candles in the silver candle sticks on the table, and used the crystal glasses which had belonged to her grand mother. It was going to be a lovely celebratory meal.

Mozart was not begging this evening. For the first time he did not even make an attempt to ask for nibbles. Rebecca had to look to see if he was alright. He was gazing back at her but as she did not move or invite him to come, he kept looking at her from his place on the carpet beside the table, front legs crossed as usual.

She told Tom about the dog's bad habit of begging for food at their meal times, and how he seemed to have got the message that there were not to be any nibbles at a table. It could have something to do with them having the meal in the dining room of course. He had never experienced this. She had hardly had any meals at this table since Tom had his accident.

They ate slowly and to drink the wine was a delight in itself. To be able to enjoy a glass of wine together was a real bliss. Rebecca raised her glass and said 'Welcome home to Mozart and to me, darling.'

Rebecca served coffee together with the chocolate mousse. She always wanted coffee when having a sweet pudding, red wine with cheese, black coffee with anything sweet.

After having cleared the dining room, they went through to the living room and sat down close together in front of the sparkling and crackling fire. She had the mobile phone with her and asked Tom if he would like to phone Malcolm and Marc. Tom did not feel like talking to anybody, but he owed them a greeting from him personally. With a sigh he dialled Marc's number. He was going to try to cut that call short. He wanted to thank him for the prayers and thoughts and to let him know that he felt fine and might be coming to church tomorrow morning. Malcolm he could treat as the best friend he was, and tell him a little more how it felt to be back with Rebecca and Mozart, but he would phone James first.

As it happened that was a good decision, James had

tried several times to reach them, but no answer when he first called and then the line had been occupied. He welcomed his father back to normal life.

'I am looking forward to coming home in a week's time, probably arriving on Friday evening if suitable. Gill would like to meet you and I would like you to meet her, so that will be arranged somehow. How is it to be back where you belong?' asked James.

By the time Rebecca had undressed, washed and brushed her teeth, she realized that Tom had not moved. He was staring into the night outside the window being deep in thought. Dressed in her dressing gown, she went up to him and from behind put her arms around him with her chin leaning on to his shoulder. She could feel that she had startled him. No words were exchanged. She was holding him for a minute waiting for him to say something. She was the one to break the silence asking him if he was afraid of coming to bed with her? He sighed and whispered, 'Yes. Please, Rebecca I do love you so much.'

'Come on, I just want you to come to bed and to lie close to me. I have slept in our bed on my own for far too long, and I am longing to feel your body next to mine. It is getting late and you must be worn out, even though you had an afternoon nap.' urged Rebecca.

Tom turned round to face her. He bent his head and buried it on her shoulder telling her how grateful he was to have such a wonderful wife.

In bed they were naked between the sheets, and he moved close to her back, fitting his body to hers like a jigsaw. They fitted perfectly one against the other, although Rebecca could feel Tom's bones and cold feet. Yes, he had cold feet. There was a big sigh of relief from them both, when suddenly Tom whispered in her ear 'Thank you for getting rid of that painting that I always disliked.'

'Which one do you have in mind? I cannot remember taking any away. Darling, what painting are you missing?'

'Oh, the acrylic in bright colours. The one of a market place in front of that dreadful church building. The one I have asked you to get rid of for as long as I can remember!'

Rebecca was speechless. She knew that she had not taken down any pictures and definitely not one fitting Tom's description. They had never ever had anything like that on their walls. Where did he get that one from? She felt cold all over. The fear creeping into her mind once more. She would have liked to ask him more about this painting, but thought better of it. That would only upset him. It would ruin the homecoming. She simply could not do that to him. He was so happy being back. He had been pleased with himself remembering their home. They had loved every minute of this day. No, she couldn't ruin it for him. She felt her happiness slowly seeping out of her mind, out of her entire body vanishing between the sheets. She shivered from the cold she felt filling the space now left empty. Tom must have felt her slight movement and squeezed her tenderly. She would have to stop her mind going in the wrong direction, the negative thoughts. She would have to try harder to block the fear, to be happy and relaxed. Lying in bed, in her dear husband's arms, finally, after having been waiting so long for his company, she had to get a grip on herself. It was only one remark, for goodness sake, one single remark threatening to destroy her entire day. Would she let the fear win? Definitely not! She wanted to cry, feeling the tears gathering in her eyes. Lying still, she did not dare let the flow go. She didn't dare move. She did not want to disturb the man next to her. The man she loved. He needed her help and she would reach out to him, not push him away. What she was unable to do was to shut away the cold terror which she felt running down her spine. Where had he been during his time in the coma? Who was he now?

Tom kissed the back of her head, caressed her and turned over to go to sleep, tenderly whispering 'I love you. Thanks for everything.'

She could soon feel that Tom had fallen asleep. For her it took an age of different thoughts crossing through her mind, before she entered some kind of slumber. She would have liked to quietly slip out of the warm bed, to go to the dog and to cry into his fur, but she decided against it. Instead lying on her side, she bent her legs close to her stomach trying to stop the pain developing. She tried so hard to find any suitable explanation but she could not. Her fear was there and it would stay with her, sometimes surfacing, sometimes hidden, almost forgotten but never completely gone from her mind.

She woke up in the morning more tense and tired than when she had gone to bed the previous evening. Tom on the other hand seemed to be happy and relaxed after a dreamless night for a change. No nightmares had disturbed him. He felt great. It was lovely to be here with Rebecca again, at last.

Tom looked better, but Rebecca had shadows under her eyes. Tom asked her if she hadn't slept well and she smiled saying that she had been too excited having him back.

It was still raining. No wind whatsoever, and the rain was softer. The dark grey sky from yesterday had changed colour. It looked as if it might brighten up later on.

They took Mozart out for a shortish walk before having their breakfast. The ground was more like a huge shallow lake. The air felt fresh.

They took the car to church. After some discussion they had decided not to go in for coffee.

They were early and sat down on the left hand side of the aisle as always. People came up to them welcoming Tom back with kisses from the ladies, hand shakes or taps on his back from the men. Anna and Eric were early and managed to get the seats in the pew beside Rebecca and Tom. It was great to see them. Great to be together the four of them.

Rebecca had often been to church on her own while Tom was in the hospital and Anna and Eric were the friends who had taken her under their wings. Malcolm and Mary had done the same when Anna and Eric had been absent for some reason. Rebecca had felt the need of going to church then and still did.

The church had an important place in her and Tom's lives, although Rebecca hardly ever went to any of the services in Sweden. It was different here. She had felt at home from her first visit to this Episcopal church that Tom had introduced her to so many years ago. Rebecca told anybody asking what had been the most important factor for her. Her response was always the same. Tom had brought her there, the rector had made her return and the congregation had made her stay. She had never regretted this decision.

In this church among so many of their friends she felt a peace and a feeling that her prayers were heard. Wasn't Tom now by her side?

Marc started this morning service by wishing Tom a welcome back to church, and to any visitors and to the rest of the congregation. Somebody began to applaud and soon the entire church was filled with this sound. Tom's eyes were filled with tears of joy and thankfulness. He half stood, bowed his head as an expression of thanks for the support given to Rebecca, and for their prayers and concern.

The service began by singing a hymn. The sermon had to do with friendship and its importance to us. Almost everybody filed forwards pew by pew to take the communion. Rebecca dipped the oblat into the wine. No, she was not afraid of catching anything, but scared that the bread and wine would go down the wrong way. when swallowing it, if she drank the wine out of the goblet.

Tom was looking dazed by the attention of so many people waiting to welcome him back and telling him how much he had been missed.

He was overwhelmed by the babble of excited conversation. It was hard to get away afterwards. They stayed in the pew listening to the organist playing. Anna and Eric were coming with them for a short visit, a glass of wine and some smoked salmon which Rebecca had in the fridge.

At the church door Tom thanked Marc profusely and told him that he was determined to be back for good. Coming out of church the weather had improved. The rain had stopped, even if there was no sun showing.

Marc gave Rebecca a hug before the four friends left the church together but in different cars.

By their car Rebecca handed over the keys to Tom.

'You might as well get on with it.' she encouraged.

With not a little trepidation he switched on the ignition, backed the car a couple of feet without hitting anything, turned the wheel hard then, gently let out the clutch and carefully slid out of the parking space. He pulled the car round, put his foot on the accelerator, then he pulled away forward. He adjusted his bottom in the car seat, sped up and his face broke into a broad smile. Another first.

Rebecca relaxed, totally exhausted.

They arrived home without incident. Tom drove the car through the open gates and stepped out, full of himself. He felt fine driving. It came naturally as though it was only yesterday that he had been behind the wheel.

Tom wanted to see their garden properly and to start doing some work in it. He managed to see how green the lawn was and the beauty and colours of flowers and the trees. Spring was here to stay. Hopefully spring would soon turn into a gorgeous summer, like the one they had last year.

Eric and Tom sat down in the living room. Tom kindled the fire. It was damp and a bit chilly outside, although the heating was on so why not enjoy a log fire.

Both men had taken off their jackets and ties. Eric had worn a brown checked suit to church, whereas Tom had chosen his navy blazer and grey trousers. They never went to church without being properly dressed and this meant jacket and tie.

Anna came out to the kitchen to help Rebecca. She wanted to talk to her friend alone.

'It must be wonderful to have Tom at home again.'

she said. 'How did Mozart react? Does Tom like the dog? Tom looks just the same apart from being thin and pale. He is fine, isn't he? I am asking because you look tense and tired, Rebecca. There is nothing the matter, is there?' Rebecca opened the bottle of chilled dry white, listening to the torrent of questions. She put the corkscrew down, poured some wine into two of the glasses on the tray and offered Anna one of them, gripping the other one for herself. She looked into her friend's eyes, smiled and told her that she was delighted not to be on her own any longer.

'I do think that Tom is going to be fine, when he has got his strength back and has put on a stone or two. He comes up with some strange remarks and questions which I can't fathom. He has started to talk about watching football matches, even car races on television and he seems to love it. He was never ever interested in any of that before. He is my old Tom when it comes to our feelings for one another, but sometimes he is a different man. I cannot understand where he gets it from. Let's not talk about this today, Anna. Let's enjoy being together, the four of us, and the wine and the smoked salmon.

I would like to talk to you soon, but out of earshot, just the two of us. I think it has to wait a little until Tom starts moving outside the house on his own. Don't worry, Anna, everything is fine but different. It is great to be two in the house and on Friday James will be here for the weekend. It'll be wonderful for Tom to meet Gill. So how are things with your lot?'

'You are changing the subject here, but I do understand. You look as if you are going to burst into tears, so it must be something strange to upset you. We are fine. I don't mean to be unfriendly, but do talk about your problems, share them and cry on a shoulder if you feel like it. That's what friends are for, Rebecca, but as you said it'll have to wait until we are on our own, just the two of us. One question though, you don't think that Tom has been brain damaged, do you? To me he seems to be perfectly normal.'

'No, my fear, because it is pure fear I feel, has nothing to do with brain damage. It is as though he has been somewhere else. Ssssh, someone is coming. Could you carry the plate through for me please?'

Tom came into the kitchen and told them that he and Eric were dying of thirst, hungry and greatly missing their wives.

The two friends joined their husbands in the living room, and they raised their glasses to the home coming, friendship and love.

They talked about their children, and early memories they shared. Eric told Tom to lift the phone as soon as he felt like swinging a club. They could start by playing only a few holes and go on from there.

Anna wanted to invite them for dinner some time during the week after James had been home and introduced his Gill to Tom. It need not be a late evening, but she was dying to hear the news about this girlfriend of James'.

Rebecca looked at Anna and thought what a wonderful friend she had. She knew that she could confide in her. She knew that whatever she was told never went past her friend's lips.

Rebecca noticed that Anna must have put on some weight as she was broad over her hips, and her tummy showed a distinctive bulge through her soft blue roll neck. She was not a striking beauty as such, but always dressed well and colour coordinated, with matching navy skirt and jacket. The jacket she had taken off as soon as she had entered the house. It was neatly hung over the back of one of the kitchen chairs. Navy blue handbag on the floor beside her and matching shoes. Rebecca had not noticed her friend's broad hips before. It was a good figure for a woman and for bearing children. This may be the result of having given birth to five. Lucky woman to have more than one child, though five was perhaps a little too many for comfort.

Anna was a fraction shorter than herself and Eric was not much taller than Rebecca. There was almost the same age difference between them as between Tom and herself. Eric had only a ring of fluffy grey whisks of hair being more bald than a monk. It suited him well. So much better to accept age than to try to hide hair loss by combing the few remaining strands in all kinds of strange directions over the scalp. So many men did that and without exception they looked stupid. One day they would have to accept the way things were.

Anna on the contrary had a thick wavy white mane shortly cut and pulled back behind her ears. She had lovely brown eyes, bushy eyebrows for a woman, somewhat roundish face with a small nose. The mouth was just right, a bit heart shaped and always seemed ready for a friendly smile. She was one of these fortunate people whose mouth was turned up slightly at the edges giving the impression of a permanent smile.

Rebecca realized that she had never watched Anna as closely as this before during the years they had known one another. She smiled to herself. She was abruptly taken out of her daze by Eric who said 'A penny for your thoughts, my dear.' Rebecca laughed and managed to say something about her wearing a brown skirt and purple jacket to church today and Anna dressed in trousers. It was usually the other way round. Rebecca, who had taken off her jacket too, asked Anna if she was not roasting in her roll neck. They laughed when Anna responded 'Why do you think I have chosen the seat furthest away from the fire?'

After Anna and Eric had left, Tom and Rebecca had a light lunch and then Tom went for his afternoon nap. Rebecca went into the snug and sat at her computer to order some books from Amazon, but more important to answer emails, mostly from Sweden. She would have liked them to be able to take the ferry across to see her friends over there as they had done most every May. This ship did not operate anymore To return to Madeira, the Algarve and Dubai might be even more difficult.

The company of her husband and best friend felt like balm to Rebecca. She was tired, that was true, but perhaps she had overreacted last night. She felt lightheaded and desperate for sleep, but the time on her own felt like gold. Perhaps this was because she had been alone for such a long time and now she was surrounded by Tom and by people. She did feel ashamed thinking only of herself.

Rebecca switched off the computer, as her eyes were getting heavier by the minute. She needed some sleep to be able to get through this day. She put a rug around herself and stretched out on the sofa.

She was desperate for Tom, but knew that if she went into their bedroom she would only disturb him. She was only going to close her eyes for five minutes anyway, but as soon as her head hit the arm rest, she was asleep.

It was not until Tom kissed her lightly on her cheek that she woke up. She looked up into Tom's clear blue eyes and she smiled happily back to him. She had slept for almost an hour and it was high time for their walk with Mozart. Rebecca, still half asleep cast away the blanket shivering slightly. She laughed and told Tom that she should have had second thoughts before she took the cover away.

'It's cold isn't it?'

He shook his head and told her that this was only because she had been deeply asleep and far away. 'Coming with us for that walk, are you?'

The dog was standing there watching patiently, waiting for something to happen. Rebecca took Tom's outstretched hand and he slowly pulled her to her feet. She went into his arms for a hug and told her that she should have come to bed. 'To be disturbed by you entering the bed beside me could only be a treat.' he smiled.

CHAPTER 11

They went out of the kitchen door and Tom had a good look around their garden, taking his time. They talked about the hard work they had put into it the previous autumn.

'How many bulbs did we put down, can you remember that?' Tom asked his wife, walking around and admiring the daffodils and early tulips. The flowers, heavy with water from the rain, were bent towards the ground but they could tell the radiant colours of yellow, white, red and pink. They left through the gates holding hands with the dog on the lead

They had brought an umbrella as Tom said 'In this country you never know what the April weather will do.'

Rebecca stopped in her tracks, turned towards the man at her side and said

'Do you know what I have forgotten this year for the first time in my life? You'll never guess so I'll put you out of your misery. Your anxiety must be tormenting you.'

'What then?'

'I have completely and utterly missed the April the First. I wonder if I was fooled without even noticing?'

Laughing they continued their walk, their first together without rain since last year.

Tom was getting stronger almost by the hour, and today they walked much further. He had asked if they could walk through the Village so this was where they were heading.

'We can always get a taxi back home if you get too tired, Tom.' Rebecca reassured him.

Having passed the playing field, Mozart was put back on the lead, as it was too risky having him walking along the pavement, free to go anywhere.

The road was busy. It was more difficult to talk with the sound of traffic, but Tom and Rebecca walked comfortably holding on to one another, in a way as if each needed support from the other, even if it was for different reasons.

Rebecca felt so much more relaxed after having talked to Anna in the kitchen. She felt confident that when Anna was told the bits and pieces of Tom's odd remarks and questions, she would be able to see it from another angle and would come up with some explanations. Rebecca relied on her friend and at the moment she was happy. She felt almost drunk with happiness.

Passing the bridge that led into the Village Tom stopped for a moment, looking down on to the river and the Dell beneath them.

'Isn't it beautiful, Rebecca? Having you at my side and admiring this view makes me feel delirious. I know it was touch and go for some time. Thank you for never giving up on me. It must have been hard for you and for James. I cannot think of anything worse than to see your loved one being out of reach and perhaps suffering. I am so so grateful and realize that I owe my life to you.'

In saying this Tom bent down and kissed her lightly on the cheek. One car hooted and blinked its headlights, as it was passing the middle aged couple kissing. Tom and Rebecca waved back as the car turned the corner into the old village.

Tom wanted to stop and window shop in front of every window along the road. Only the small grocery shop, almost at the top, was open. Tom went in and bought a box of chocolate and some meringues which he suddenly remembered were one of his wife's passions. Rebecca and Mozart were waiting outside. She was touched, and thrilled with his memory and the goodies.

'How thoughtful of you, darling. Let's walk straight back for coffee and these goodies. I can hardly wait.' she laughed. She looked across at Tom and gave him one of her radiant smiles.

They quickened their pace and were soon at home, in the approaching dusk.

Rebecca put the kettle on and told Tom to relax in the living room. She found him there lying on the sofa fast asleep. He must have been exhausted.

She took the fire guard away and poked some life into the fire, feeding it with another two logs. Tomorrow it had to be cleaned out properly. She had her coffee and enjoyed the meringues. Rebecca could not stop herself, after having finished one, she helped herself to another two. She would let Tom sleep.

Rebecca watched Tom, noticing that he was moving his legs slightly and his fists. He must be dreaming, she thought. She left him and walked into the kitchen to put the kettle on again to make him a fresh cup of tea. He always loved his cup of tea in the afternoons and for breakfasts but she kept to her black coffee.

Rebecca did not know if she should leave Tom to sleep until he woke up by himself or if she ought to wake him. They would have to talk about this. Perhaps he would have difficulty sleeping at night if he slept too much during the day? Undecided she switched on the television for "Songs of Praise". Tom opened his eyes with a start. He looked frightened. Rebecca went up to him and stroking his hair away from his forehead, she offered him his cup of tea.

'Sorry to wake you up, darling. You must have been in a deep sleep. I think you have been dreaming.' she said soothingly.

They listened to Aled Jones and Katherine Jenkins singing. She went into the kitchen and tossed a small salad before she drove off to "The Cod Father" for Tom's special treat. She did phone first to order two fish, one chips and one mushy peas. Tom put the plates in the Aga so that they would be warm by the time Rebecca returned.

He laid the kitchen table for the two of them with wine glasses and a side plate for Rebecca's salad. Oh, how he was looking forward to this! It was mouth watering. Ketchup and salt were placed on a dish in the middle of the table. White wine and tomato ketchup put a smile on his face

He served the wine, a bottle of Chablis, and lit the candles. They sat down to eat.

Rebecca was surprised that she had managed to eat not only the delicious white fish, but also the batter, greasy though it was. She was grateful for the salad she had made for herself. Tom had finished his fish and his peas, but had left at least half a portion of the chips, complaining that they were soggy.

They went through to the snug to watch the recorded "Antiques Road Show" enjoying coffee and two pieces of chocolate each. It was a clear but chilly evening. The moon was full and spread a cold, ghostly glimmer around the garden. It was not really dark, more like a grey mist enveloping everything. However, when a cloud floated in between the moon and the earth it went completely black and made Rebecca shudder. All at once it looked unfriendly.

Tom, in his baggy old corduroys and a thick roll neck sweater came up to her, put his hands on her shoulders and told her that she did not need to come with him and Mozart for the evening walk. He could walk the dog alone. He was not going to take long just up to the playing field 'I promise not to let him off the lead tonight.' he said.

It was a tempting offer and she turned her face up to him saying 'If you are absolutely sure I think I'll take you up on this one. But don't be longer than quarter of an hour please, or I will start to worry.'

Tom did not have to call for the dog. Mozart was standing by his feet as soon as the lead was touched. Tom put on a jacket and with his walking stick in one hand and the dog's lead in the other, he went out into the night.

Rebecca did not get undressed in case she would have to go out looking for them. The thought of it made her feel uneasy. She sat down at the kitchen table after having switched off the dishwasher. She wrote in her diary that they had been to church, and about having had wine and the fish and chips. She could not relax and watched the clock on the kitchen wall as every minute passed. After fifteen minutes with still no sign of the two walkers, she went to the kitchen door and waited staring out into the garden. The moon was clear again so she could see the gates flung open and there they were. Rebecca heaved a big sigh of relief and they waved to one another.

'I told Mozart that I bet Rebecca will be standing in his place behind that door watching out for us.' Tom laughed.

He smiled happily, bent down and patted the dog. 'I was right, wasn't I? You were worried and couldn't relax until you spotted us by the gate, could you? I have to do more and more on my own for me to get my confidence back and for you dear, to get used to me being out there in the big wild world without you at my side. We have to get back into orbit, to the way it was and was always meant to be. You do agree with me, don't you? You wouldn't like either of us to be completely dependent on the other any more than I would, I am sure.'

'I know but it's hard to let go,' Rebecca said. It feels similar to when James started going out in the evenings, remember how restless we were then. Of course you need to get out, and to walk the dog on your own is a good start, a beginning for both of us, as you correctly say. I was worried all the time, but I am proud of you.'

They went to bed more relaxed than they had been the previous night. They fell asleep as soon as Tom had kissed her goodnight and moved away to his side of the huge king size bed.

Rebecca was awakened with a start by Tom sitting up breathing hard and unevenly. She switched her bedside light on and looked at him. He was wet from perspiration and looked scared with wild eyes staring in front of him. When she had been so abruptly woken up, her first thought had been that Tom had been taken ill. She thought that his breathing difficulties were symptomatic of a heart attack. Her heart madly pounding, she put her arms around Tom talking to him soothingly, and she could feel his body slowly but surely relaxing in her embrace. 'Sorry, I had a terrible nightmare. The thing is that I think I have had the same dream before, in the hospital. There is a big tractor coming straight at me and it is about to crush into me, when I wake up. It is scary to see this monstrous thing coming closer and with such speed too.' gasped Tom.

Rebecca did not say much. She held onto him rocking him as if he were a child who needed comfort. In the end she asked Tom if he thought he could go back to sleep or perhaps he would like to get out of bed for a cup of tea.

'Let's try to go back to sleep. We are both tired and need our beauty sleep.'

'Oh, thank you very much!'

They laughed and he said sorry once more. He did not feel that this was a laughing matter. 'But I suppose if we can't laugh we will go mad.' he said. With this in mind and after a few playful kisses they fell asleep.

They woke up the next morning without any further disturbances. Neither of them talked about Tom's nightmare, although Rebecca was sure that they had the night's experience fresh in their respective minds.

The following day she wrote about Tom's dream in her book. Little did she know how important this bad dream would prove to be.

The sun was shining and it was going to be a wonderful day. After walking the dog they decided to relax in the garden, but not before they had done some weeding and dead-heading. Rebecca started the boring job of knotting the dead headed daffodils' leaves together. They were delighted that they had put down so many bulbs during last autumn, and with many different varieties, shades and some flowering later than others.

She stretched her back standing up and looked around her. There were still some daffodils in flower, some not yet out, and of course the earlier ones she had just dead-headed. Soon it would be the glorious time for the tulips, her favourites.

It was wonderful to be working side by side and Tom even cut the back lawn. The smell of freshly cut grass mixed with the damp earth and the coffee that she brought for them to enjoy sitting on the terrace, where Tom had put the seats out for them to sit and read or simply to admire the day's work.

It was getting warmer. The April sun was doing a super job. The spring was early this year with a couple of warm days even in March, although after a rainy day it became chilly for a day or two.

The birds had been coming back after spending the winter abroad. Rebecca had listened to the geese flying overhead a week or so ago, remembering how Tom and she had been walking close to the sea front talking about autumn, happily listening to the geese leaving. Now Tom sat relaxed leaning back in his chair and as if he had read her thoughts said ' I think that most of the migrating birds have returned, like me. It is truly a lovely, warm and relaxing day.'

'James and I sat outside once when he was at home. We saw this year's first big beetle then. Poor creature, it didn't live long. Mozart spotted it.'

They were wearing jackets. April was not a month to trust when it came to the weather and the heat from the weak sun. Tom fell asleep later, whilst Rebecca read a book.

At dinner time Tom asked her if she would mind if

Marc came to see him for morning coffee and a chat the following day. She could play golf with her lady friends, if he had company.

'I'll have lunch ready for you by the time you get back, and before you ask, I'll promise not to overdo it. Mozart and I will stay here or in the garden. I think it's an excellent idea. I have an appointment with the doctor at the surgery on Wednesday morning; you could come with me. I would like you to. Malcolm will probably come here after my appointment, but I thought I would ask you first. I imagine that you would love to have another girly chat with Anna.'

'Lovely. I could walk to her place with Mozart and of course I'll come with you to hear what the doctor has to say. Have you listed any questions to ask the doctor when you see him?'

'Such as?'

'Well, I would like to know what to tell the travel insurance people. We have to decide if we are likely to go to Sweden as we have done every May so far. I would like to know about flying if we wish to go to Madeira later on in the year we have to know about these things. If you are asked to avoid flying I suggest that we book something in UK for the autumn.

'I had thought about the flying, but that I might have problems getting travel insurance never occurred to me. As you are coming with me, please feel free to ask or to comment on anything. I would appreciate that.'

Rebecca phoned Anna to ask if she would be free on Wednesday morning. 'It'll not be that early as Tom has got a doctor's appointment at 9 am. Do you mind if I bring Mozart?'

'It'll be lovely to have you and Mozart too.' replied Anna. ' If you phone me when you are about to leave home, I could walk down to meet you halfway. I need some exercise. Somehow I don't think that gardening is enough.'

Rebecca and Tom had a lazy afternoon and evening. She sat in front of the computer emailing for a while and then went on to write some letters. Tom started to write thank you notes in response to the cards, notes and letters that he had received during his convalescence. This would take him a day or two at least.

CHAPTER 12

The night passed and they woke up feeling refreshed. They woke before the alarm went off. Tom left the bed and got dressed without having his shower, not even shaving. He wanted to take Mozart out for his morning walk first of all, which meant that they could have breakfast together later.

Rebecca was pleased with this arrangement. She would be able to relax more, knowing that master and dog had been out for their walk and would stay at home in the company of Reverend Marc.

The weather looked promising. By the time the two walkers returned Rebecca had packed her things into her little golden "Daewoo Matiz", put Tom's tea to brew, made her own coffee and their fruit salad.

She was about to sit down to the part two of the Times when she heard the gate. Tom was all smiles and asked her if she would mind sitting opposite an unshaven tramp.

'I am ravenously hungry, so if you think you can stand it, I could eat first and have my shower afterwards?'

Rebecca laughed and showed him to his chair.

'Of course I don't mind. What time is Marc coming? I have taken out some scones from the freezer and the jam is in the fridge.'

'Marc! Oh dear, I had almost forgotten about him. He asked if 10 o'clock would be all right. Scones! Jammie! You really shouldn't. Marc ought not to eat that kind of food. He is as heavily built as a bulldozer. He does love your scones though.'

'If you put the scones in the Aga oven around quarter to, you can serve him them "butter melting warm".

They kissed at the door when she was leaving. She tasted of toothpaste. He didn't.

'Have a good game darling, and keep those eyes of yours on the ball.'

Laughing, she promised to try to follow his instructions and sent her love to Marc.

'I'll be back for lunch, say two o'clock.' She cuddled Mozart and left.

When she returned, Tom had made onion soup. He had been roaming around the freezer and successfully too. He managed to serve a couple of cheese scones with the soup. Rebecca sat down at the table after her shower and a change of clothes. They had much to tell one another after having been apart for several hours.

'I was teeing off wonderfully and was pleased with myself until I found a bunker on the seventeenth and couldn't get out. My putting was appalling, but we had a super time. There were quite a few ladies this morning. How about your morning with Marc?'

'We talked a lot about you and how well you had coped. I thanked him for his wonderful support and the congregation for their cards and prayers. Small talk about the future of the church and more about the church garden. They have a few volunteers but need one or two more for planning the summer planting, weeding and well, the lot, apart from cutting the lawn. I am afraid I did say that I would help as much as I could. Do you mind that? I should have talked this over with you first, but the word just slipped out. I did tell Marc that I didn't feel strong enough yet, but he said he needed me more for the planning, to be the coordinator in other words. To be honest with you, I felt delighted that he consider me up to it.'

'I am happy for you as long as you don't overdo it.' answered Rebecca. 'This soup is delicious! You are an excellent soup maker, Tom. These scones must surely be the last ones, because I couldn't find any the other day. It is wonderful to come to a house with somebody there. I don't want to experience an empty house ever again. It is such a delight to have you back and a treat to have the food made for me. Thank you, Tom.'

After lunch Tom slept for an hour, or rather until Rebecca woke him up with a cup of tea. He had asked her not to let him sleep for too long. He did not want to have his tea in bed but unfolded the blanket and put on a pair of trousers and the same roll neck as he had been wearing before his rest. Rebecca had found some time to read. She found 'The Wall' a great book.

They looked through their dairies to see what they had planned, and to discuss what they wanted to do or wished to do, anticipating that everything would be all clear after Tom's chat with the doctor.

Both of them had put Sweden and Madeira on their lists, as well as Loch Melfort.

They had already booked to go to Madeira for the two first weeks of December in their timeshare When would they go to Sweden and to Loch Melfort?

'Well, I think we should save Sweden till September when we know more about fitness and insurance prospect. We have to think about who to ask to take care of Mozart when we go away.' said Rebecca.

I would like to stay at home and enjoy our garden this spring and summer.' suggested Tom.

He took Mozart out for an evening stroll. Rebecca tidied up the house and started getting ready for bed.

Tom came up to her when they were almost undressed and caressed her gently the way he had done before his fall. Rebecca could feel life was indeed returning to normal and gasped in anticipation. Was it going to happen tonight? She had been longing for him for some time and her entire body was burning. In Tom's breathing she could clearly make out that he wanted her just as much.

He caressed her tenderly and slowly slid his fingers through her short hair. Neither of them said a word. It was magic. It felt as if they had never made love before, as if it was their first time. fumbling tenderly. Tom stroked her shoulders and followed her spine down to her rounded but firm buttocks. His hands touched the line between her thighs and her heart shaped bottom, feeling their way, tracing the contour of her figure.

He kissed the nape of her neck. He bent down and liberated her from her panties, then kissed his way back to her neck and shoulder blades. He reached for the clasp of her bra and removed it meaningfully. Rebecca could not hold back her sighs of desire anymore. Her firm breasts fell out of the bra and Tom took her hand and steered her towards the bed. She lay down facing him as he slid beside her, both completely naked.

His hand followed the line of her face, down the slope from her chin, along her neck, teasingly stopped for a second before he felt the wonderful curves of her breasts. He took her right dark brown nipple between his thumb and finger delicately as if he was touching a drop of water on a rose petal. Rebecca could hardly breathe and her body arched towards him. She was whimpering like a small child. She stroked his cheek, ran the tips of her fingers down and slid her hand between his thighs. She found his erect manhood. It was firm and hot. A few gentle strokes and she could not wait any longer. She didn't dare to wait.

Rebecca rolled her body on top of him, putting one leg on either side of his thighs. In her sitting position, she put her right hand behind her and helped him to find the way.

She started to move her body in a slow motion rhythm, but soon she quickened the pace, trying to squeeze him every time she moved away. He almost fell out of her. She moved her body not only up and down but also slightly from side to side. They made love as if in a fever, Tom's hands moving from her back to her breasts.

It was soon over. Far too soon. The excitement was like the first time, but with the confident mutual feeling of experience.

Rebecca lay down by his side. It had been quick but, oh so wonderful.

At the moment Tom's climaxed with his eyes closed, he had an image of another woman sitting on top of him. It lasted not even for a second. It had only been a flash, but he had had the time to see her clearly. She had reddish hair with a much heavier body than Rebecca, someone he sensed that he did not like. Somebody he was cross with. Oh, how absolutely horrible. Who could she have been?

He had never ever dreamed of making love to anyone other than Rebecca. Tom did not tell her about this vision. He had to keep this image to himself and he hoped that this other woman was never going to appear in his dreams, or in his fantasies. Tom buried his face in the space between Rebecca's head and shoulder hiding like an ostrich.

Their bodies were glowing in the darkness in the rays from her bedside light. They were both breathless. Tom whispered in her ear, when he had got his breath back. 'Darling are you ok?'

Rebecca simply nodded. Tom went on holding her tight into his own body. They rested like that. Rebecca had her eyes closed and there was a happy smile on her face. Tom was wide awake with his brain working full time, his thoughts turning around like water disappearing down a plughole in whirling circles.

He pulled the sheet and blanket over them so that Rebecca would not get cold. He stroked her hair, caressed her whole body. He was delirious with pleasure.

'Thank you my darling, darling Rebecca. Thank you for your patience and your help to get me back to life. I am so happy. I feel fulfilled at last. Life can begin again.'

Rebecca opened her eyes and he saw them glowing with love. She was watching him with tearful gratitude. She loved him so much.

She went to the bathroom for a quick wash and to brush her teeth. To have a shower or bath would have to wait until the following morning. She felt exhausted and tumbled back to bed where she pulled the sheet and duvet high up to her chin. She had almost fallen asleep by the time Tom came back to bed and they put the two jigsaw pieces perfectly together.

She slept with a smile on her face, whereas it was a long time before Tom joined her in the land of dreams. He could not work out who this big red haired woman was. He tossed and turned, thinking. The worst was, that this image had flashed passed his brain at the actual time when he was about to climax. He disliked having secrets from Rebecca, but this one he had to keep to himself.

When she woke up relaxed the following morning, he still felt tired. Rebecca was concerned about him, when she realized that he was tired and not exhilarated. She hoped he had not overdone it. He assured her that he was fine. He hoped they would be able to make love soon again and perhaps less like a couple of oversexed teenagers, but taking their time for greater fulfillment.

There was a clear blue sky and hardly any clouds. Lovely day for her walk to meet Anna.

Tom had his shower and Rebecca had a bath before breakfast and walking the dog. There was no time this morning for Su Doku as Tom was due at the surgery for his appointment.

They went in when Tom's name was called. It felt good to be back to his own doctor. Dr MacNeal might be able to tell them something and to give them advice.

'Tom, how are you getting on? How do you feel? No head aches I hope?'

'I feel fine, but I am tired and have a nap every afternoon, but no headaches. No problems that I can think of.'

'Do you manage to do any exercise? I think you should take it easy for some time. You haven't started to play golf, have you? Do some walking and keep up the exercises that the physio gave you. You have had major head surgery. You mustn't forget that. You know that you are special, don't you? I mean you are the first patient ever to survive this particular operation. I suppose that's why they kept you in the induced coma for so long. They wanted to make sure that your brain would have a complete rest for some time before wakeing you up.'

'Did you know this, Rebecca? Nobody told me anything.' gasped Tom.

'This is completely new to me too. Doctor Smith, who operated on Tom was not forthcoming. She had been, but that stopped from the moment Tom came back to life. Well, that was the impression she gave me. I felt as if she didn't want Tom to leave hospital. I was upset that nobody told me that Tom was having the MRI scan for example.

The main thing though is that you seem to be fine and that you are getting stronger by the day, Tom. And to answer your question about exercise. We have a dog to walk and are out twice daily and we have been gardening.'

'That is excellent. I am sorry that you didn't feel that Doctor Smith was informative. She and her entire team saved your life Tom, remember that, both of you. Your heart is behaving normally and so is your blood pressure. I cannot find anything wrong with you. Eat proper food, keep on walking the dog and you'll be fit as a fiddle in no time. Any questions?"

'May I travel? I mean not tomorrow but in the not too distant future - flying for instance?' asked Tom.

'I can't see any reason why not, but you know insurance may be difficult. Your surgery was unique but entirely successful. I'll write a short version of it and also that I consider you fit to travel in another month or two. You may collect this at the reception from Monday afternoon. It is a delight to see you looking so well, Tom. I would like to see you in around four weeks' time just to make another check. All right? Don't hesitate to come and see me if you have any problems whatsoever.'

On the way home in the car they discussed the news they had been given - the news that Tom had been deliberately kept in the coma. Why had Rebecca not been told? It would have made her life so much easier if she had known not to expect Tom to wake up during all these weeks she had been living on hope, praying and waiting. Neither of them could understand this, but agreed that there was no point in raising the matter or questioning Doctor Smith.

'Let's just get on with our lives and enjoy it now that we are together again. Life is too short and they did save your life, Tom.'

He was preparing himself to meet Malcolm, and Rebecca phoned Anna to tell her that she would start walking from home in another five minutes.

'Are you sure you don't mind me bringing Mozart?' Rebecca was looking forward to this morning with her friend and Mozart would get another walk. She changed into a pair of light blue jeans and a sweater with blue, red and white stripes. On top of this she put her blue windproof jacket and blue shoes and handbag to match.

The sun was warm enough for her to open up the front of her lightweight jacket.

The two friends met half way. It was a bliss to be out in this warm spring sunshine.

They decided to try to stay outside in the sheltered corner between the summer house and close to the house in Anna's garden. Mozart could be let off the lead and everybody was happy.

The garden was a mass of colour, tulips planted in clumps of about 25 of the same variety. Their were patches of orange then yellow to white, dark purple almost black, red and pink. They were mostly in bud but showing colour. The hundreds of daffodils and narcissis spanning from white to bright orange were fighting against the polyanthus and primroses to see which could attract the most attention. The planting scattered around the flowerbeds looked like boiled sweets in a bag, covering the soil, and the taller bulbs gave a lift to produce a cacophony of colour up to two feet high. It was beautiful. In a few weeks when the tulips came into their own season, the whole area would be magnificent.

The trees foliage and the different shrubs in varying shades of green provided the perfect backdrop. It was clearly a well-maintained and much loved garden. The wisteria clinging to the house looked promising too.

Anna prepared the coffee and had made meringues especially for the occasion.

'I am so pleased that Tom is progressing. That is the best news I have heard since you told me that he had regained consciousness. Although the hospital staff treated you the way they did, I think both of you are wise not to let it get to you. Do you have anything you want to discuss with me or has that other problem you were talking about last Sunday been resolved?'

'It hasn't Anna, and it is a long and complicated story but I would love to talk to you about it. I would appreciate your opinion.'

Rebecca told Anna her own thoughts about the cat, the painting, and the fish and chips. She told her that Tom had terrible nightmares. It seemed to be the same one, which involved him crashing a car head on into a big tractor.

Anna listened to what Rebecca was telling her, and

when she had finished talking Anna sat quietly for a little while before speaking.

'I can understand your worries and concern, but let's try and think of some possible explanations for these matters. This recurring nightmare which he has will have to be solved by himself. Don't you think it must originate from an experience in the past? It could be something he has read or seen on television. The best thing would be if he could remember where it happened and then go to that place with you. We don't know if he had any dreams when he was in this coma, do we? Does it interfere with your sleep? If it continues, he should seek psychiatric help and talk it through with a professional.

The fish and chips episode could be a throwback to hospital food. He might have had a craving for some unhealthy but tasty meal. I do that myself sometimes. I find myself craving for odd food sometimes.'

'I would like to believe that this could be the reason for him wanting fish and chips so you might well be right.' said Rebecca. ' He asked specifically for his favourite meal and I ask you, mushy peas?!. Liver and bacon has always been his favourite dish, but when I asked him about that he said that he couldn't believe that he had ever liked liver and he didn't think he could face it. Let's hope you are correct, Anna, can we leave this one and go on to the next problem The cat? Tom's question about how Mozart got on with the cat.'

'It is more puzzling. Perhaps Tom has had a lot of odd dreams whilst in his coma? Did you meet Tom's parents and sister or have you heard anything about his grandparents? Perhaps one of them had a cat or owned that awful painting he was so happy not to have in the house? Or could it be related to a childhood experience? I agree that it is confusing, but I am sure given time, something will occur and provide an answer. It might be that not even Tom will be able to pinpoint whatever triggered these memories. Unless you are absolutely desperate to get to the bottom of the matter, I think you should leave it alone for the time being. Tom has so many things on his mind without adding to his frustration. Nobody has implied any brain damage, and he acts perfectly normally as Eric and I have observed. You have had the "all clear" from the doctors and they would never give Tom the thumb up if there were any doubts. He has been told that not even flying should be a problem. I do understand your being apprehensive, but it doesn't seem to me to be a major problem, apart from his nightmares keeping you awake at night.

As I said, he might have to seek help for that. When it comes to the strange remarks, take them as part of the healing process and get on with your lives. A friend's advice is leave it even if we can't come up with any logical explanation. I am sure as time passes it will sort itself out.'

Anna did not know then how right she was. The two friends would remember how happy and lighthearted they had been before it turned nasty, really nasty.

'My problem is that I have difficulty in ignoring it, but I will try to follow your advice and cast it out of my mind. Thank you for listening, Anna. I do appreciate it. To sit down to talk helps a lot. It is such a relief to be able to talk to somebody. Do you know what we learned today at the surgery? Tom was not in the coma because of his injury but was kept in a comatose state deliberately! I cannot understand why they did not tell me. It would have made life easier for James and myself. How could the staff keep us in the dark? To be secretive about this and the MRI scan, I think is so awful that I would have liked to tell them off, but I can't go on about it. You must admit that not informing me about this is odd and badly handled. The communication between myself and Doctor Smith was non existent towards the end of Tom's stay there. We still have not been told the result of his MRI scan other than that he is fine.'

'Rebecca! You must be joking! I always thought that the family was told of any special treatment, and to be kept in a coma as part of his treatment most definitely comes under that heading to me. It is unbelievable. What does Tom think?'

'Tom was as upset as I was when we were told this morning. Let's talk about something else. How about your children and their studies? Are they getting on well with their lives? And how about you? I recall how you panicked when Sandy left for University. Your "baby" leaving home and this big house with just Eric and yourself to rattle around in.'

'They are fine and I think we have got used to being on our own far too quickly. We talked about it at breakfast the other morning, and we feel guilty enjoying being on our own.'

The two friends chatted with Mozart by Rebecca's feet. He had a bowl of water, but Rebecca did not want him to run around marking his territory against the shrubs and trees. He would get the chance on their walk back.

When Eric returned home from his golf, Rebecca left with Mozart after exchanging a few pleasantries as she made her exit. It was warm and Rebecca had to take her jacket off and tie it around her waist. She was carrying two books which Anna had read. One was written by Robert Goddard and had been a thrilling page turner according to Anna. The other one was by Salley Vickers. It was great to swap books the way they did. Whenever either purchased a new book they let the other one know to ensure that they did not buy the same title.

On the way home she went into Patsy's to buy some fruit. Rebecca was the morning's last customer. Patsy changed the notice from "Open" to "Closed" and locked the door after Rebecca left.

Rebecca felt happy and there was a bounce in her step. Her spirits were high after having seen Anna. Rebecca did not realize that this very day was later going to be remembered as a high point before more trouble surfaced. Nor did she know that she had left her friend worried. Rebecca transferred some of her worries from herself to her best friend. Anna had tried her best to comfort Rebecca, but was nowhere near as convinced herself about the possible explanations. Anna's problem was that she could not talk this over with anybody without compromising a confidence.

Tom greeted her with his home made vegetable soup and her freshly baked bread. He had had a delightful morning with Malcolm. They had talked about his visit to Frankfurt and Edward and his girlfriend Rachel. A stunning girl apparently. Mary and Malcolm hoped that this girl would become Edward's wife.

'It was wonderful to exchange news of our children

and their girlfriends, but we also talked about times gone by. So much I remember but some things I wonder if I would have remembered if it hadn't been for my fall. So darling, how about your morning? Did you tell Anna about the surprise revelations at the surgery today? What did she think about it?'

They discussed their morning before Tom became tired and decided to have his nap. He managed to have shorter afternoon sleeps, which they thought was good. He had put on some weight and was much stronger than when he had been discharged from the hospital. However, he still needed his sleep as the body was healing from having been non functional for so long. One of the best medicines was rest.

Rebecca sat outside in the garden and started to read one of Anna's books. She had made herself a cup of coffee but before she settled down to relax and to have a lazy afternoon, she put the books which she had read and enjoyed into a bag in the hall, to give to Anna at their next meeting.

Tom had his nap before he joined Rebecca. He went through more back issues of "The Week" saved for him to catch up on current affairs. James phoned and wanted to hear about the visit to the surgery and to confirm that he would be coming home on Friday.

Although the days were warming up, the nights were a bit chilly, especially when the sky was clear. Since Tom's return Rebecca had made their bed with the summer duvet on top of the mattress but the thick winter one under the bottom sheet. It made the bed more comfortable to lie on without being too soft for their backs.

Rebecca and Tom walked Mozart this bright and clear evening. They walked hand in hand in silence listening to the light breeze ruffling the leaves..

There were obviously memories that Tom did not understand, some he did not even want to remember, such as the woman sitting on top of him flashing through his mind. He tried to push these images away. Memories like these usually came back to him during the night in his sleep, as part of his nightmares. There seemed to be nothing he could do to stop them, disturbing his much needed rest.

CHAPTER 13

When Rebecca suddenly woke up, her heart was jumping wildly in her chest. At first she did not know what had happened. Had she been dreaming? She could see nothing in the darkness of their bedroom. The silence was intense and oppressive. Mozart was not moving so there couldn't be any intruder. What had woken her up so suddenly? She didn't move. She didn't want to disturb Tom. She started to listen for his breathing and soon realized that he was not having a relaxed sleep. Then he kicked her. His foot went more or less into spasm and he flung out his arm, only just missing Rebecca's face. She turned over on to her side and switched on the bedside light. She sat up looking at Tom. He opened his eyes with a start. He exclaimed repeatedly, in a husky voice, the word "NO!" He was having another of his nightmares.

Tom was wet from fear and he did not seem to notice her. He shuddered, but calmed down when Rebecca talked to him soothingly, hugged him and let her fingers find their way through his hair, which was standing straight up. After some time he started to talk.

'I cannot understand what is happening to me, Rebecca. I seem to have the same nightmare night after night.' he gabbled.

'Tell me about it, Tom.' implored Rebecca

'I am leaving someone because I am furious. I cannot work out why I am so angry or with whom, but I drive off following this narrow country lane. I don't know where I am or where I am going, only that I am speeding, too fast for that narrow lane. The car is green I think. Have we ever had any green car? Going round a sharp bend I suddenly see a monster, a tractor appearing straight in front of me. I know I am going to crash, when I manage to wake up. It is at the same time in the dream and at the very moment when the huge fork in front of this gigantic farm vehicle is piercing the bonnet of my car. I can even hear the screeching noise when the fork hits my car head on. No way would I have any chance of surviving.'

'As far as I know, you have never had a green car, but perhaps you have rented one or driven one belonging to somebody else. I wouldn't know that, Tom. You are not the kind of man who gets as angry as the person you describe, and certainly not one who would drive in such a condition. You have never liked speeding. Could the explanation be in something you have read or seen in a film? Let's write your dream down in details in the morning and see if it is the same every time, because as you say you have had this nightmare a few times. It seems as if you could have been trying to hit the brakes to stop this car in time. You were saying 'no' and lashing out your arm and kicking. I am sorry I can't be of any help. I do know that I didn't read anything like this to you when you were in your coma. It could be something that happened to you when you were younger.'

'Let's try to get back to sleep. I feel scared like a small child. Please could we cuddle up. Let me hold you tight in my arms. I think that what I am experiencing must be similar to the torment soldiers coming home from a war might suffer. The image is dreadfully clear and vivid. I am sorry to have frightened you.'

'I am fine and I am going to get one of these children's night lights tomorrow so as not to leave this room in complete darkness. It might scare your dreams away. Good night my darling.'

This time neither of them could fall asleep. Tom was afraid to close his eyes, scared that the dream might return to him as soon as his body relaxed into a slumber. He would write down every detail of this nightmare the following day to see if he could make any sense of it.

Rebecca knew that Tom had difficulty in relaxing. The nightmare remained in their minds. What was it about? Rebecca felt that they were leading Tom and herself towards disaster. She shivered although the bed was warm and cosy, and it was such a comfort to be close to Tom. It was wonderful to nestle up to him. She finally fell into a deep sleep as dawn was breaking. She missed the first daylight seeping through the gap between the curtains. She was tense and exhausted.

Tom woke up before she did. He carefully disentangled himself from the sheets and slipped out of bed. He grabbed his clothes and quietly left the room. He used the upstairs bathroom and slipped into his dark brown corduroys and a new beige sweater, his heavy shoes and green jacket. He left a note for Rebecca on the kitchen table and put Mozart on the lead. They were going for a walk before breakfast.

It was a magical morning but it probably would not last. The birds were singing, which reminded him of the nesting box which he had forgotten to secure. He hoped he had not left it too late. There was no wind. The trees and even the leaves were absolutely still.

The daffodils stretched their proud heads towards the bright red sky. Tom tried to remember the saying forecasting the weather. He had to think hard. 'Red sky in the morning – shepherd's warning. Red sky at night – shepherd's delight.' They were going to have another storm later on. That this morning's weather in a way, resembled his own life, he never could have imagined. They were mostly tranquil, but with a feeling of calm before the storm.

If Tom had been vigilant he might have recalled that he came out of the coma on Easter Sunday, and that the weather on his homecoming had been unsettled. The sky had been crying and another storm was definitely closing in so what was to be expected in the near future?

Whilst walking he was deep in thoughts. He could not let go of last night's nightmare. He sensed that something was wrong, terribly wrong.

He had left the house to be away from Rebecca and her sad tearful eyes filled with questions to which he had no answers. Walking the dog gave him the excuse he needed. He wandered through this beautiful spring landscape unseeingly. He did not notice how green the grass was on the playing field nor the daffodils around the tree trunks, nothing but how red the sky was. Strangely enough he heard the birdsong around him and the doves cooing. He could hear but was oblivious to his surroundings.

He called the dog and they walked back. He stopped at the gate, as he had done so often recently and was amazed at the beauty of the garden. 'This is our creation.' he thought. 'We have created this. What an achievement!' He suddenly felt happy and his worries disappeared like water down a drain.

At once he was determined not to let this nightmare pull him down. There must be a reason for it. He missed his parents and his sister, and he needed his father and mother to talk to, to ask about his childhood. He must have had "a near death experience" during his youth. He was convinced that this nightmare must come from memories surfacing after his time away in the coma. Memories he had wanted to forget.

He entered the house and met his darling wife with a relaxed smile on his face.

Rebecca was taken aback by Tom looking so cheerful, but was happy to see it. Tom went up to her and drew her close to him, kissing her tenderly.

'I think I have come up with an explanation for my nightmare. It must be an early well hidden and forgotten memory from my youth. Something during my time in the coma must have triggered it, as I never had this dream before.'

Rebecca looked up into his eyes and said that she would love to be as certain as he was, but she was not sure it would fit. 'Didn't you say that you had a feeling of being angry with somebody and that you were driving too fast, speeding down a country lane? You always say that it is _you_ driving Tom.'

Tom turned his eyes away from hers and looked up at the ceiling, sighing.

'I was so relieved to come up with a solution that I forgot about the anger and that it is me in the driving seat. No, it doesn't fit. I have to agree. Sorry.'

They decided to walk to the village through the Dell before lunch, and to take advantage of it being dry under foot, before making notes about Tom's nightmare. It felt like rain coming on so the earlier they managed to get away the better.

Breakfasted and dressed for the woodland walk along

the river, umbrella and dog lead in hand, they left the house.

Mozart was delighted to be allowed to run wherever he wished. He sometimes ran ahead and stopped and waited for Rebecca and Tom to appear round a corner. Other times he was so far behind that he had to run at full speed to catch up with them.

Rebecca and Tom walked arm in arm and they too stopped here and there to look around and enjoy the beauty. On the little stone bridge across the river they watched the water moving at a rapid pace beneath. It was murky, probably from the peat up on the hills.

There was still no wind.

They followed the footpath along the water's edge. It was like walking through a tunnel of vegetation as the trees on both sides stretched towards one another, branches touching across the foot path above their heads. It was deeply green with the moss and ivy clinging on to the tree trunks and the leaves taking away some of the light from above. If the ivy climbing up the trees was not removed the trees would soon be dead. Sad but true, but who would be able to see to that?

Rebecca would never walk here on her own. She sometimes felt as if the branches tried to reach out to her and not in a comforting way. It is an enchanted wood. To come here with the dog and with Tom gave her a sense of relief from her hectic and unsettling life. The moss covered not only the trees but also the stones. It gave an impression of softness. Wild garlic grew mixed with carpet of bluebells just out. During the summer it was lovely to come here and pick brambles and wild raspberries.

They stopped and admired the little waterfall before entering the old railway tunnel. It was dark in there for the first few steps as the tunnel turned. There was no chance to see the end of it until one actually arrived. It was as dark as pitch and she held on to Tom's arm. Usually there was a light, but the bulb must have gone. A few steps forward and they could see the light at the end of the tunnel. It wasn't far, but far enough for her to feel uncomfortable. Good to have a man and a dog as company.

In the village they met friends and decided to go down to "The Swing" together and have a bowl of soup. Mozart had to wait outside, but he was tired and lay down looking at them at the other side of the church hall window.

'Tom, did I see you in ASDA the other day? Were you both there, or did you do the shopping on your own?' one of the ladies asked him.

Tom told her that she must have spotted him when he was there by himself for the first time. He was proud to tell them that he had not only done the shopping on his own but had also been driving. He had felt quite at home in the supermarket

'But why didn't you come up to me to say hello? I never saw you.' Tom asked the lady.

Tom told Rebecca on their way back home that he would go shopping again this afternoon, before his nap, to get the few things on their list, and to see if he could find one of the night light bulbs which Rebecca had talked about. He wanted to go out and about in the car on his own to get confidence.

They chose the path on the other side of the river for

their return. No tunnel but it was rather wet under foot.

Tom went shopping, while Rebecca prepared their afternoon tea.

This time when Tom was in ASDA he was more observant of other people and of what was going on around him. He was people-watching. As he was going to exit the car park he stopped so suddenly that the car behind him nearly bumped into him. Tom had seen a plump woman with reddish hair walking towards another car. His heart almost stopped in its tracks. This Rubens like female resembled the woman who had flashed by in his mind when he had made love to Rebecca. It could have been her. Blast!! By the time he had turned round to re-enter the car park, this woman had disappeared without a trace. He had not been clever enough to notice what kind of car she had been driving. 'How stupid can you get?' he muttered to himself.

He had to find out who she was. He had to. Tom had taken the first decision that would lead them into trouble, of that he was happily unaware.

He sat in the car park for a short while to calm down. He sensed that he should know this woman's name, but his memory failed him. He couldn't tell if she was known to Rebecca.

What were these secretive images about? He had to pull himself together. The red haired woman was gone. He hoped to see her again soon. He would talk to her and she might solve his problems, by telling him who she was and why he thought he knew her.

He left the car park and drove home. It had started to rain by the time he left the supermarket. Big heavy drops fell from the sky and broke against the windscreen with a splash. It did not take long for the tarmac to look slippery and wet, and soon the wind picked up. They were lucky to have been out walking through the Dell earlier. Tomorrow the tracks through the woods would be too muddy for comfort.

He unloaded the car. He had not bought much, only two bags with fruit and vegetables and some cheeses for them later in the evening. It was dark and the trees creaked in the wind which was building up. He was glad to get home without being soaked.

' Am I glad to have you back. The weather has turned nasty, hasn't it?' was Rebecca's greeting.

' I suddenly saw a woman that I am sure we know. I sat in the car for a while trying to remember her name. I saw her briefly as I was about to leave the car park and it is so annoying not to be able to remember who she is.

She is a big lady, with red hair. She looked ordinary, not somebody with style. I cannot recall where I have seen her before or why I even think I recognized her . Do you know anybody fitting her description? Have we had a cleaning lady or any other helper in our house-hold that you can think of? I didn't particularly take to her.'

'Was it by any chance Rosa, who works in the laundry? She has reddish hair. I cannot think of any other woman with red hair.'

'The name is not right.' said Tom shaking his head. 'I have to leave it for a while and see if my recall improves, probably in the middle of the night.'

'Please, don't wake me up if it does.' Rebecca smiled and went up to Tom and gave him a hug.

The storm was howling. ' Who would have thought that this weather was coming after we had that wonderful walk this morning? How about another log fire?' Rebecca suggested. 'I do hope it'll be the last fire we'll need before autumn. The climate has changed, hasn't it? We never used to have storms like this in the spring, certainly not as frequently. I do hope the roof will be ok. How are you Tom? You look a bit pale.'

'I feel fine but I think a lot about my nightmare. I have come to the point when I feel scared of falling asleep. I am afraid of the nightmare taunting me.' Tom said.

'I brought pen and paper. Let's try and sort out your dream. You told me that you are angry and are driving too fast, when suddenly there is a tractor in front of you.?' Rebecca said.

'Yes, I am in a real state. Somebody must have upset me.' answered Tom.

'I am driving down this narrow country lane and then crash head on into a huge tractor. Where this lane is, I don't know. It must be a winter's day, because there is some snow on the ground around me. If it had been dark, I am sure that I would have noticed the oncoming vehicle. I would have seen the head lights. It has to take place during daytime.' Tom paused, collecting his thoughts. 'Why I am angry, I don't know. I suppose I am speeding, because I am furious, and that accounts for why I am where I am, in my dream.' he said helplessly.

'Tom, it seems to come down to who has upset you.'

'The only thing is that I remember that I do love driving this car. My first thought is about my lovely car which is about to be ruined. I know that I am going to die but, I am more concerned about the car. Isn't that odd?' Tom looked at his wife.

Rebecca answered Tom after a minute in silence. 'Perhaps this concern about the car indicates that you are driving somebody else's car, and that's why your main thought is about the car.'

'Well, that still leaves me with the questions of why I am angry and with whom. I get more and more confused. I think we have to let this go for the time being. I can't recall any event leading me to have my nightmare.'

'How about talking to James about this? He might have some ideas. If it continues to haunt you I think you ought to talk to the doctor about an appointment with a psychologist. To have someone completely detached to talk to might not be a bad idea.' Rebecca said.

'If I don't sleep I will have to do something, but I would like to leave James out of this, at least for the time being. Please.'

' Tom, I have been thinking.'

'Oh dear, how much is it going to cost me?'

'Nothing like that. I had a thought about this red haired woman you think you recognize.

Doesn't she work at the checkout? Could she have upset you at some stage before your accident? This could be a reason for you to think you recognize her.' Rebecca suggested.

'It would be wonderful to eliminate her and leave us with one less problem. Thank you, my darling. You are brilliant, although I don't want to say that. It might give you some ideas above your station. You could become a big head.' Tom chuckled.

He fell asleep. It was not as relaxing as Rebecca would have wished for him. He was tossing and she wondered what was going through his mind. She watched him for a while before she continued reading the last pages of her book. She finish it and would be able to start reading another one. Anna had lent her one by Margaret Forster called 'The Memory Box'. It looked promising especially as her friend had told her how much she had enjoyed it. 'A clever plot.' she had told Rebecca.

The weather was still awful by the time Tom woke up in time for their evening drink.

The crackling and hissing of the log fire from the fireplace was a contrast to the storm. It was April but more like autumn. Everybody knows that the weather in April is not to be trusted, but this was completely out of the ordinary.

Ever since they had made love and he had that awful experience seeing this red haired woman in his mind, he had been apprehensive. He had not dared to make any further advances. He was scared of it happening again. He longed for Rebecca and could sense that she longed for him He had to get on with it like he tried to get on with his sleep. It was ruining their love life too!

'I sincerely hope this will be the last spring storm for this year. It's not doing the garden much good and what it is doing to the roof doesn't bear thinking about. I do hope it will subside before James has to drive from St Andrews tomorrow afternoon.' Rebecca said sounding worried.

'I wonder if Gill is going to come with him, or if she will be coming here on Sunday before they return to St Andrews? I guess we'll just have to wait and see. If the weather is like this, I don't think they will be coming home.'

Tom fancied a brandy in front of the fire. 'Would you like to join me?' he asked.

After her enthusiastic response they went back to the sofa and sat down close to one another. With brandy cup in hand, eyes on the fire, ears to the wind outside Rebecca leaned her head on to Tom's shoulder with a sigh of content. She could easily have fallen asleep like this, if it had not been for the glass in her hand.

Tom felt relaxed, and the brandy slipped down his throat like silk. It had been so long since he last had a brandy. It must have been Christmas. After what seemed like an age Tom gathered both glasses, and Rebecca put up the fireguard and let the dog out

Mozart went to his basket, got a cuddle and licked their hands. They were such a happy family.

Rebecca put the bread maker on the worktop so she would not forget to load it in the morning. Tom put the night light in one of the bedroom sockets.

Rebecca remembered how they had walked for miles in and out of shops to find the curtain and bed cover material for their bedroom. She loved it, with the birds and flowers on a creamy white background. It went well with the carpet that picked up one of the colours from the material.

The bed was king size, made from oak with matching bedside tables, dressing table, varnished in a natural shade. They had managed to find good reading lights reaching out from each side of this heavenly bed. To have good lights was important as she liked to read in bed.

She looked around in admiration. Rebecca loved this room and felt comfortable in it with the off white wallpaper with an unobtrusive leaf pattern. Water colours on the walls carefully blended with the room's colour scheme. They were mostly landscapes reminding them of happy times spent in Kent.

Rebecca brought her book with her and put it beside the lamp to read a little before falling asleep. She prepared herself for bed and pulled her white cotton nightdress over her head. It was one of her pretty ones with lovely lace across the front. She removed the bed cover, folded it into a square and lifted it off. She put it on the floor by her window then grabbed her book.

Tom, on the other hand, had other intentions, other anticipations and was soon out of the bathroom. He came into the bedroom and went up to where Rebecca was standing, book in hand. He pulled her close to him and kissed her hungrily. She responded with full lips. His embrace was firm as he caressed her lower back and whispered into her ear, ' Do you need to wear your nightdress?'

With his teeth he nibbled tenderly at her ear lobe. Rebecca put her book down and turned until she was facing him. Her left arm around his neck indicated that she was happy to play along, and ready for him. She slid her hand down his back and inside his pyjamas trousers pulling him towards her. He was hard against her and and she caught her breath. Sensing her enthusiastic response, he detached himself from their embrace and removed his trousers. In the same moment he took hold of her nightie and pulled it over her head, dropping it onto the floor by their feet. He held Rebecca at arm's length, letting his eyes caress her body beginning with his eyes meeting hers, then tracing down wards, stopping for a second, when reaching her parted lips before continuing South. His eyes devouring her lovely breasts he brushed his tongue over her brown erect nipples. When his eyes reached her firm tummy with the small and beautiful navel he could hear her sighing with delight. Still holding her at arm's length, he finally stopped his gaze at her secret place. She tried to pull him close, but he had become stronger and managed to keep her at the distance far enough away from him to feel the joy of her nakedness. This woman with skin white as milk after long winter months. Her skin was as smooth and firm as ivory.

The silence in the room was not oppressive, on the contrary there was an understanding between them. A bond of trust and of expectation. The only sound was the wind rushing round the corners outside and in the room the breathing and sighing from the two lovers. They were standing opposite one another in the pool of white cotton and lace. The curtains were drawn and the dimmed light from the single ceiling lamp cast a slightly yellowish warm glow, which gave life to the birds on the curtains. The pillows and the duvet on the bed looked crisp and inviting.

Tom removed his hands from Rebecca's shoulders, but did not let her get any closer to him. He was teasing her. He wanted to take his time. He wanted her to become completely aroused. He lifted his right hand to her cheek and stroked it at the same time as his left hand touched her nipple so lightly that it was as if his fingers had brushed past, nearly missing her. He noticed her breath quickening. She threw herself towards him, desperate for his arms to enclose her. She could stand it no longer. She had to feel the touch of his body.

Her hands moved down his back and stopped for a split second just above the cleft in his bottom before she let them slip below his waist and suddenly firmly caressed his buttocks. Tom made a slight move towards the bed and with one hand succeeded in throwing a corner of the duvet to one side before they toppled, pulling her gently beneath the covers.

His hands found her smooth body and slowly and gently explored each contour. As he slid his fingers between her parted legs, still toying with her, he kissed her nipples one by one and with his tongue he felt them harden with excitement. By this time she was whimpering. Her hands moved on to his manhood and she felt it moist to the touch. His fingers were parting the hair of her vagina and he gently parted her legs before sliding his body on top of her. She held him whilst he slid inside her.

Their bodies adjusted to the union as she moved her thighs towards him. Tom kept as still as he could bear to be. He was too close to ejaculation and he wanted Rebecca to climax before him or in the best of worlds simultaneously. He managed to start the long thrust deep inside her withdrawing at the maximum stroke. He kept his eyes wide open watching her expressions as she absorbed him. The were in joint ecstasy and drew the maximum pleasure from one another.

He could both hear and feel Rebecca's climax and then with a few faster movement let his sperm flee into her body. He stayed inside her whilst they relaxed, before he withdrew and slipped to one side of her. He covered them with the duvet.

It was unlike anything she had ever experienced before. He had become the complete lover, a different man with his gentle dominance.

She whispered into his ear 'I love you. Thank you. You are fantastic. I thought for a moment that I might die. You managed to tease me into desperation.'

'I absolutely adore you, Rebecca.' breathed Tom.

He relaxed at her side then made the mistake of closing his eyes too soon after climax.

The woman was back! He jerked slightly and drew a short but sudden breath. Rebecca noticed this and asked if he was alright. With horror, Tom realized that he had had the experience of the strange woman's face and red hair appearing before him several times since the shock, when they had made love for the first time after his homecoming.

Tom and Rebecca fell into a deep and satisfying sleep in one another's embrace. Even Tom slept until Rebecca carefully moved away and slipped out of the bed to go to the bathroom.

She washed herself and she was about to turn off the light when she realized that she had woken Tom. He gave her a warm smile and left the bed to give her a cuddle on his way to the bathroom. He switched off the light when he returned. The night light enveloped them in a blanket of soft colour. It was just light enough for him to find his way back into their bed.

He kissed her before they turned away from one another to sleep.

The wind had dropped by the time Tom woke in a sweat. His nightmare had visited him again. He felt like crying and wanted to sob. He felt helpless. He was completely still as he didn't want to disturb his darling Rebecca. He felt a cramp invading his stomach but tried hard to keep his breathing as normal and even as possible.

Still working on cause and reason he came to the conclusion that he must have had a quarrel with someone.

In his dream he is rushing out of a building and into a sports car driving off with a wheel spin. Where is he going? And this enormous tractor forking into the car must have killed him? Tom was ready to believe in a life before the one he was living, but why this dream now? His unconsciousness was over. It must relate back to those three months. It simply had to.

Tom turned onto his side, trying to fall into a relaxing sleep, when he started to think of this other woman again. He had seen her, hadn't he? It wasn't imagination. The sighting had given it a mysterious presence. He would go back to ASDA as often as he possibly could to try to pick her out a second time, then not let her disappear. He had to approach her. He would walk there with Mozart tomorrow. Rebecca was playing golf in the morning if the course was open. He could hear that it was still raining.

In spite of the problems he was experiencing, Tom considered himself a lucky man.

He had the most wonderful wife. A wife whom he loved more than anything and whom he knew loved him. He had a marvellous son. They were the owners of this beautiful home and garden and on top of everything they had many friends, and a faithful new found companion in Mozart. Living in a peaceful country and with adequate finances he lacked nothing but his own peace of mind.

When he finally fell into a slumber, it was more out of exhaustion. Oh God, he who badly needed his sleep. He categorically refused to take sleeping pills. He had had enough of pills to last him a life time.

When the alarm went off Tom was startled, his heart pounding hard in his chest. The sound had frightened him. Rebecca did not fail to notice his reaction. She cuddled him to calm him down.

'You must have been dreaming darling, but everything is fine now. You are at home in your own bed with me at your side. You have nothing to worry about. Nothing will hurt you, just relax.'

Little did she know, how much her words of comfort helped Tom. She told him to stay in bed for a little while. She would get up and attend to the morning chores. If it was still raining she would phone one of her lady friends to see if they would meet up at the club for a coffee and chat later on if there was no golf. By that time she would know how Tom was feeling.

She opened the door for Mozart. It was raining sheets out there, but the wind had subsided. No hope of golf. She wished for some sunshine during the weekend when James would be with them. Rebecca dressed before letting the dog back in. She put on the kettle and brought a lovely cup of tea for Tom. She found him sound asleep. When the phone rang she rushed to the kitchen to answer it, before the signal would disturb the sleeping beauty.

Coffee at the club was arranged for about ten o'clock.

Rebecca prepared the breakfast, but first she loaded the bread maker to have a fresh loaf for lunch.

Tom was moving. She returned to the bedroom with a freshly made cup of tea. He looked tired but greeted her with a smile, telling her that he was fine.

'Nothing that wouldn't come right with a proper night of undisturbed sleep. My nightmare was back, and I ended up having great difficulty falling asleep again. I am worrying too much about this and am trying so hard to come up with a reason that I can hardly keep a clear mind. My head spins round and round in circles, not making any sense.

Last night was magic. I gather that you are not playing golf this morning. Rained off, are you?'

'Yes, rained off indeed, but I would like to go there for a coffee and a chat at ten if you don't mind.'

'I'll be fine. I might take Mozart for a walk if it eases up a little. Do we need anything?' No time given from James as usual? Well, "children are fun, children are fun", as my mother used to say, bless her.'

'I'll be back in about two hours. Are you sure you don't mind my leaving you?' Rebecca asked.

CHAPTER 14

When Rebecca and Tom had had breakfast and she had left for the golf club, he looked out of the window. It was raining, but not as hard as before. Still too much to walk all the way with Mozart to his planned destination. He decided to leave the dog behind and take the car.

He wanted to be alone for a little while and to concentrate on his past, whatever that was, although that was exactly what he had tried to work out during most of the night.

He wanted to go to ASDA, but at the same time he dreaded it. It was like an electro- magnetic field, anything which could trigger his thoughts. He felt as if he was trying to grasp a shadow instead of the substance of his real life.

He looked at the man reflected in the bathroom mirror. He was no longer as sickly pale as before. The cheeks were still rather hollow, although he felt much better. Lack of sleep was taking a great deal out of him, but he was getting better.

Tom started the car and drove off. He knew that it might take several weeks before he spotted the red haired woman again, but if he did not try he would go mad. He would return on the same week day and at about the same time he had first spotted her, but he needed to try before then. He could not sit and wait for a week, doing nothing about it.

He went inside and had a look at the checkout staff on duty before he selected two large bunches of yellow tulips for Rebecca. He also bought some blueberries and strawberries and the latest copy of "Hello" magazine. He walked around the shop for ages before he realized that one of the security staff was keeping an eye on him. He must be acting in a strange way. He checked out and went to his car, looking around but there was no trace of the woman he was seeking. It probably was lucky that James was coming. That would make him concentrate more on his family.

He put the tulips in a vase on top of the magazine for Rebecca to see as soon as she came home. Then he went for the lead. Mozart was as happy as Larry to get some attention and a walk. The rain had nearly stopped but Tom took his umbrella anyway and used it as a walking stick. It was not cold and it gave them pleasure to be out in the fresh air and to be moving, both of them getting some exercise.

By the time they came back to the house Rebecca was inside. She was standing motionless by the tulips, holding the magazine in her hands looking at the front cover.

'Hi, darling. Did you have a great time?'

Rebecca turned towards Tom, holding "Hello" in both hands. She asked Tom why he had bought her this magazine.

Tom went up to her after releasing his feet from the muddy wet shoes and dried Mozart. He looked at her in puzzlement.

'You do love yellow tulips, don't you, but I couldn't remember if it is "OK" or "Hello"' you prefer. Did I buy the wrong one?' he asked.

'The tulips are wonderful, but what I don't understand is this magazine. I have never liked either of them. I don't think any of our friends read them. It was thoughtful of you Tom and thank you for the tulips though. You couldn't have made a better choice of flowers.'

Tom's brain was working overtime. Why had he been so certain that "Hello" or "OK" were her favourite magazine? Now, when looking at his wife he knew perfectly well that it was not "her scene." It didn't fit, but why had he, without thinking about it in the shop, been so sure? It had been natural for him to grab this one. So often these days he came back to this little word "<u>why</u>?"

He shook his head holding on to Rebecca for a long time as he told her that his memory was obviously playing up.

'At least I remembered your favourite flowers.'

Rebecca kissed him and smilingly stroke his cheek. 'I love you Tom.' she whispered.

They drew apart when the beeping told them that the bread was ready.

'Hungry?'

'Starving. This bread smells like heaven. Soup, bread and cheese is it?'

At the kitchen table they talked about the ladies at the golf club. Tom told Rebecca that he had returned to ASDA by car this time, but no sight of "the lady." The walk with Mozart had been wet, and slippery under foot, but Tom felt much the better of the fresh air and the exercise.

'Do you mind if I have my snooze now as James will be arriving this afternoon?' Tom asked. 'I would like to be fit and wide awake when he arrives.'

'I'll prepare dinner and I will make some of the Swedish sweet oatcakes for our afternoon tea.' Rebecca responded.

Oh, fresh bread for lunch and home made cakes later. What a treat!.'

'Look, it has stopped raining. I can spot a patch of blue sky. Soon we'll have some sunshine. When you have your afternoon nap Tom, I'll take Mozart for a walk. I am looking forward to getting to know Gill better.' said Rebecca. 'You'll like her.'

The bread is superb, and this Brie is to die for. We can have our wine and cheese this evening with James. We never had our planned evening last night. It sort of slipped my mind. I wonder why?!!' laughed Tom.

Rebecca walked along with the dog on the lead for a while before she let him free. He sprinted off across the field chasing some poor rabbit. When she was about to leave the playing field behind, she called him back. For a minute or so, she thought she would have to cross the waterlogged grass to get him, when he gave up on the rabbit and came rushing back to her side. She gave him his reward, before putting him back on the lead to walk briskly along the pavement. She wanted to go back to make an apple spongecake too.

Mozart had at least had his exercise and fresh air. He was muddy, but nothing that some water and his towel would not take care of.

She tried to be quiet cleaning the dog and then looked for her Swedish recipe book. She would wake Tom using the electric whisk. The apple sponge had to wait. She prepared the oat biscuits first.

Rebecca made Tom a cup of tea.

She entered the bedroom cup in hand, realizing that Tom was awake. He looked at her, smiling.

'You did sleep, didn't you? Are you all right?' she inquired.

'Yes I am fine, thank you. A cup of tea in bed! Lovely. I'll get up to enjoy my tea with you.'

'I am making a cake before I have my coffee but it'll not take long.'

While Rebecca whisked the ingredients together Tom went to the bathroom. Before she made his tea, she had prepared two apples, cut them into smaller chunks and turned them in the cinnamon and sugar she had mixed in a dish. Once the oven was hot enough, she put the tin inside and set the timer. The oat dough would have to rest for a while in the fridge.

Tom and Rebecca relaxed, reading their mail and enjoying the hot drinks. Tom had cleaned out the fireplace in the living room and prepared another log fire in case they wanted one this evening. They would eat dinner in the dining room at some time during the weekend.

Tom could not sit still. He went out to rake up the twigs from the lawn and walked round the house looking for fallen tiles. They had been lucky, he told Rebecca when he came in to get changed for the big occasion. By that time, the apple sponge had been taken out of the oven and was out of the baking tin. Rebecca turned it the correct way up. It looked and smelled delicious.

The small balls of oat dough were spread onto baking trays and were ready to go into the oven when the phone rang. James informed them that Gill was with him and they were ten minutes away.

'Gill will stop for coffee with us, before she'll take my car down to North Berwick.'

Gill had an essay to finish and of course she wanted to see her parents. She would be coming back on Sunday for lunch after church, to pick James up on her way North.

How pleased Rebecca was to have made the different kinds of cakes! There was the fresh bread and some cheese as well if the children were hungry.

Mozart heard the gate before anybody else. He barked wagging his tail madly. As soon as the gate was closed behind Gill and James, Rebecca let go of the dog, who went straight up first to James and then to Gill, licking their hands and whirling around them.

Tom went into the garden to greet them.

'I have heard so much about you. It is a delight to see for myself that you are even more beautiful than I have been told.' He went up to James and gave him a huge hug, but left the kissing for Rebecca.

'Tea or coffee or something else?' asked Rebecca.

They sat down in the kitchen. Gill was over the moon about the bread and the rest of the treats.

'Absolutely wonderful. Please would you mind giving me the recipe for your apple cake? I would love to make one for my parents for tomorrow's tea.'

'But of course, my dear, it would be a pleasure. Here, you have pen and paper and I'll translate from the Swedish.'

When Gill had left, Rebecca asked if dinner in the kitchen would be fine. They would dine more formally on Saturday evening.

They were having baked fish with a dill sauce topped with a layer of mashed potatoes serving it with a dry white wine and a mixed green salad made it perfect.

'I am getting hungry.' said James.' Oh, look at the colours in the garden! Your tulips are fantastic, mum. What a wonderful display!'.

Mozart was happy running around their feet.

Tom served scotch for James and himself, but Rebecca asked for a "thin" gin and tonic.

It felt good to sit in the snug in front of the cosy fire, and to be together.

James told them, that he had accepted a job in Yorkshire and would start working in July. Gill was hoping to go there too. It looked promising for her. They had started to look for somewhere to live in the Harrogate area, but it was frightfully expensive.

'I take it that you are planing to move in together.' said Tom.

'If you are going to live together, does this mean that you are considering marriage? I know it is none of my business, but you are our only child and as a mother I am hopeful and curious.' asked Rebecca.

I have not yet asked her to marry me, but I am confident enough to do this when I feel it is the right moment. We do love one another. I know that we haven't been going out for long, but I am sure of what I want.

Mum, and of course you too dad will be the first to know.'

'Your happiness is the most important thing to us. It always has been and always will be.' said Rebecca.

Mum and I are delighted at the prospect of you starting your adult life. Yorkshire sounds ideal.'

'We promise to come and visit you often, or perhaps that is more like a threat. We'll miss having you close by.' said Rebecca

'Oh mum, I'll miss you too. The two of you are the best parents in the whole world. I have said this before and I'll say it over and over again. I have been proud of being your son all my life.'

Later father and son took Mozart for his evening's walk after the superb fish dinner. James needed to do some work on a conservatory plan for a client and Rebecca and Tom were reading before the sports programme started.

It was a clear night. Tom woke up during the dark hours. He did not have a chance to conceal his nightmare from Rebecca. He had been kicking and shouting. He was soaking wet and shaking. It took Rebecca some time to calm him down.

This time neither Tom nor Rebecca could get back to sleep. In dressing gowns and slippers they went into the kitchen for a cup of hot tea. Mozart was delighted to see them. They sat at the kitchen table while Rebecca poured them the milk and tea. Tom talked all the time about his nightmare and kept on saying how sorry he was to have woken her up like this. Rebecca held his hand in hers. Tom promised her that he would contact the surgery first thing Monday morning. They could not go on like this.

'I am afraid that I can't help you. If talking to a psychiatrist does not help, I am sure we'll find a way out of this somehow.'

Rebecca only wished that she was as certain about this as she tried to make out.

'Please don't tell James. I feel afraid and ashamed.' said Tom.

'Let's try and get some more sleep, shall we?' suggested Rebecca.' At least we have to try to get some rest. In case we look worn out tomorrow James will get worried.'

'He might think that we have made love all night long and get excited for us.' laughed Tom. God, I am pleased I am still able to make jokes in spite of our present situation.'

Rebecca was much more worried about Tom than she had let on. She managed to fall into a deep sleep, almost like unconsciousness.

When she woke up in the morning, the sun was high

above the horizon. She turned her head towards Tom's side of their bed. He was still asleep. Looking at the alarm she noticed that much of the morning was gone.

Rebecca moved herself slowly towards the end of the bed and managed to untangle from the sheets without Tom stirring.

She left him looking almost as he had done in his hospital bed not that long ago. It was hard to resist giving him a kiss on the forehead but she only smiled at him on her way into the bathroom.

The shower had to wait until he was awake. She slipped into her tracksuit and went into the kitchen to find a much awake dog. She softly closed the bedroom door behind her and whispered words of love into Mozart's ears before she let him out into the garden. He would have to wait a little longer for his morning walk.

As Mozart was desperate to be let out she realized that James must still be upstairs, and perhaps they had all slept in this Saturday morning.

It was sunny and the grass shone from the dew, or was it from yesterday's rain?

Rebecca put the kettle on before she stepped outside. It was going to be a gorgeous day. It was warm and the birdsong was deafening. She stretched and moved her body slowly in a few gentle, relaxing movements.

It was like this that James found his mother when gazing out of the window, looking at the weather and the garden. He watched her with a smile on his face. He found his mother beautiful and she had a wonderful figure. He could tell this even though she was dressed in a tracksuit and slippers. His mother was out in the garden wearing her slippers!?

James had a shower and then went downstairs in the hope of finding some breakfast. He made two cups of black coffee and brought a biscuit for his mother. He kissed her good morning and was rewarded with a smile.

'I gather dad is still in bed? Is he all right?' James inquired.

'Yes, I think he is fine, but tired so I let him be. Did you work late last night?' asked his mother.

'I got my second wind and just kept on working. I have to do some writing today, if you don't mind.'

It is lovely to be out here in the morning, listening to the birds and admiring the colours..'

'Tell me the truth mum - is dad as he was before the accident or has he changed?' asked James with concern.

'What makes you ask that, James?'

"Well, he started to talk a lot about football matches when you were preparing our dinner last night. I was so surprised that I didn't manage to say much myself, but he has never showed any interest in the game, has he? It wasn't only football which seems to have caught his interest lately, but also car racing.'

'Well, there are some differences from my old Tom. He is as loving and caring as he has ever been. This interest in sports could have started with him watching a lot of television in the hospital. I would prefer him to keep up his pre accident interests for golf and art.

Let's prepare breakfast. I am getting hungry aren't you? Would you like to eat out here, or indoors?' asked Rebecca wanting to change the subject.

By the time James had clattered with the breakfast pans and Rebecca had begun making more coffee and a pot of tea, Tom appeared in the kitchen.

'Morning! There is a lot going on in here. My word, you were chatting like a couple of noisy magpies.'

'Sorry to have woken you up. We are discussing where to have today's first meal, in the garden or in here in the kitchen. You as the head of this household, please make up our mind for us,' Rebecca begged.

As the papers had arrived Tom decided that it would be difficult to eat egg and bacon outside , and impossible to read.

Rebecca had her usual Saturday morning fruit salad, low fat natural yogurt and two soft boiled eggs.

'Lion cooked?' James asked with a happy smile on his face.

They talked about their plans for the day. Tom and Rebecca decided to take the car off towards the coast somewhere, with Mozart, and the picnic basket with coffee and scones.

James, on the other hand, would sit in the garden and do some writing on his laptop.

'We'll be back in time for afternoon tea, but if you want to eat something for lunch there is onion soup and cheese in the fridge and freshly made bread?'

Tom drove telling Rebecca merely that he was going to take her to the coast. They had a lovely run to Dirleton, although the traffic was busy.

'These week-enders are leaving the city like us. Next time we want to go to the coast, please remind me that it is much better during the week and not when everybody else has the same plan. We are able to go whenever we like, so why did we have to choose a Saturday?'

Tom entered a roundabout and suddenly there was a policeman beside them with his hand raced indicating that Tom should pull over. He drove from the roundabout and stopped past the corner. The constable noticed that he had stopped and walked up to the car. Rebecca opened her window. The officer leaned forward and asked 'Morning Ma'am. How can I help you ?'

Tom and Rebecca looked at one another.

' Well officer,' Tom replied, you indicated that you wanted us to pull over so I did.' The policeman shook his head and looked surprised, before he put his hand to his mouth and with a smile said 'Terribly sorry about that. I was waving to my mum!

The car park was not crowded. Mozart was kept on the lead for some time then let off to run freely after a short walk along the woodland path. All they could hear when strolling among the trees was the light breeze that slowly rustled through the leaves. After a brisk walk hand in hand, they turned towards the beach. Tom took off his shoes, carrying them in one hand and soon Rebecca followed his example. The sand was not hot but "spring warm". The grains spread between toes.

The smell of seaweed was strong. They filled their lungs with salty sea air.

The sand looked clean and bright. Tom grew still' listening to the water breaking onto the edge of the beach. The music of the small waves meeting the sand and then retreating was relaxing. He was bemused as they stood watching the gulls pecking at the pebbles and turning them over looking for food.

The sea was not clear blue but looked inviting although he knew how cold it must be. He woke from his trance when Rebecca's voice asked him if he was contemplating a swim.

After walking along first the path and then the beach,

Mozart went off on his own adventure, tail wagging. It looked so funny when he met another dog. They started chasing one another, but both dogs often went back to their masters for support, as the chase became more exciting. The animals paid the humans a short visit, usually hiding behind them, before starting to run after one another again. They continued like this for some time, until one of them suddenly turned and went straight for the water. Mozart was shy to begin with jumping back as the small waves licked his feet. He made some friends and when one of the other dogs dived into the sea to fetch a stick thrown out there, Mozart did not hesitate before he went for a swim too. Tom and Rebecca smilingly admired his efforts to reach the stick first. The dogs enjoyed themselves, turning and jumping with acrobatic movements.

There was a small crowd on the beach watching the dogs swimming and retrieving the sticks. Often the sticks were too long for them so they had a struggle to get ashore. People around them were laughing at the spectacle by the water's edge and in the shallow bay.

Some smaller children tried to wriggle free from firm adult arms. Others were restrained in an effort to avoid confrontation.

Tom made Rebecca aware of an elderly couple walking past. The old man was dressed in a pair of shorts. His legs looked like two hairy sticks of bone ending in a pair of white socks and a pair of brown sandals.

'Look at that couple! One of his shorts' legs has been caught up in something and the old lady at his side looks as if she has had a bad night. Somehow I don't think she is his mistress.' he whispered.

'Oh Tom, you are awful. They are probably a sweet old couple. We'll soon be there ourselves remember. I have to agree though, they do look funny. I am surprised that he doesn't appear to feel the cold, but those chalky white legs do need some exposure to the sun.'

Two boys in their early teens braved the cold water and hitching their jeans up as far as possible, they tried to throw some pieces of driftwood for the dogs even further out to sea.

'I am pleased you brought a towel to dry Mozart I suppose if we walk higher up the beach to enjoy our coffee, he might keep closer to us and away from the water long enough to dry off'. Said Rebecca.

'I would like that coffee now, darling. Did you say something about cheese scones earlier?'

Tom whistled for Mozart. He came back out of the water and Tom managed to catch his attention before another stick hit the water. Mozart looked at him and then turned towards the sea, and hesitating for a split second. When he heard another whistle and realized that Tom and Rebecca were walking away from him, he took off in pursuit. The dog came up to them and Rebecca gave him his treat. Mozart swallowed it, and then started to shake off the water beginning from his head ending up with his tail. Tom and Rebecca screamed and stopped dead to avoid the drenching. They laughed together with others watching it.

"Tom, how clever you were to get him up here away from the water's edge. I have never heard you whistle like that. Next time will you please tell the dog not to shake himself so close to us. I am wet through.'

'I think Mozart had had enough playing by the time

I called him back. I'll go up to the car for your sweater, the blanket and basket if you wait here.'

Tom walked up to the car park and fished the things he wanted out of the car. He locked it and was turning around to walk back to the beach when he stopped dead. There was that woman with the red hair! She was about to leave in the company of a big chap with tattoos on his arms. Tom smiled and walked up to them as they were about to enter their car.

'Vallie!' he exclaimed.

The woman stopped half way into the car, one leg on the floor at the passenger seat and the other outside. She turned round quickly towards Tom and nearly lost her balance. She would probably have done so if Tom had not caught her arm. She wriggled free from him and stood fixed with both feet on the ground holding on to the car door frame. She looked at Tom and asked him firmly but not too politely.

'And who are you? What do you want? How do you know my name?'

Tom watched her in surprise. He recognized this voice. She asked him again who he was. Tom could not believe that she had not recognized him. Was she pretending because the brute who was with her and was in the car's driving seat? He shouted to Vallie.

'Hey woman, get a move on. We need to get back home!'

His voice did not sound pleasant, Tom thought watching the couple. No, he didn't think that he could say that he recognized this man. Tom turned to the woman again and asked her if she was absolutely sure that she did not recognize him.

She looked at him, shaking her head.

Tom asked her who she was and where she worked. 'I am sure I recognize you.'

She looked at him and said she thought he was mad. 'I have never seen you before in my entire life. How do you know my name? What do you want from me?' she cried.

The man had stepped out of the car. He was standing on his side of the vehicle telling Tom to piss off.

'The likes of you just bring problems and we are leaving here right now, at this very minute. Val, get in the car so we can get away from this lunatic.'

'I am <u>not</u> mad,' Tom started to say but the redhead was quickly inside the car, door shut, and off they went, wheels spinning the gravel high in the air. Tom noticed that the woman did not take her eyes off him.

Tom was certain that she knew more than she wanted her companion to hear. He had managed to get the car registration number plate and opened his own car to reach for pen and paper before he forgot it. The car was a silver Honda.

When Tom got back to Rebecca, she looked at him enquiring why it had taken him so long.

'Couldn't you find the car key?' she asked

'I am sorry to have kept you. Here is your sweater. While we have our coffee and scones I'll tell you what happened in the car park.'

Rebecca watched him for a second and then without another word slipped into her lovely dry warm sweater. She sat down on the blanket which Tom had spread out for them.

She gave Mozart some fresh water. The poor dog was thirsty after his prancing around.

She opened the basket and poured hot water on the instant coffee. Without saying anything, she handed the cup over to Tom and gave him a buttered cheese scone. He sat down beside her sipping the hot drink, looking at her and then turned his expressionless eyes towards the sea and beyond, starting to tell Rebecca about the meeting with this red haired female ghost.

'I am sure she must have recognized me, though she said that she had never seen me before in her life. It might be that she had never noticed me, or that she did recognize me but for one reason or another did not want her partner to know. Rebecca, I called her by her name!. I knew her name!!! When I called it, she almost fell over. She was half way inside the car, when she heard me calling "Vallie." She looked surprised, well, almost scared now that I think about it. She turned towards me so abruptly when she heard my voice. That was why she nearly lost her balance. She would have fallen if I hadn't managed to get hold of her arm. I knew her well enough to call her by name.'

'Are you sure that you did call her by her correct name?' asked Rebecca.

Tom turned, watching Rebecca. 'No doubt about that. She even asked me how I knew it. Her name is Valerie and her nick name is Vallie, though I think her partner called her Val. It is an extraordinary feeling to have seen her again and to realize that I even know that her nickname is Vallie. I cannot get over it. Sorry darling, what did you say?'

'Oh nothing important, but look at Mozart loping around like a lovesick sheep, when knowing that that kind of pleasure is denied him.

What I did say was if you have any recollection why this woman seems to play an important part in your past? You have recovered most of your lost memories by now, don't you think? So where does this female fit in? You certainly have got your life with James and me back on track. There doesn't seem to be any gaps in our "together life," To me this red haired female friend of yours or whatever she has been to you, doesn't sound as if she could have been any of your past girlfriends. Try and explain to me how you feel seeing her.'

'The first time I saw her when shopping was like a shock. I instantly felt that I knew her and strangely enough that I didn't like her. Seeing her again today, I was thrilled to bits at first, because I thought that she was going to tell me why I remember her and more about where from and in what capacity. I had hoped that seeing her and talking to her would explain so much and give me a clue to my nightmares. I don't know. Perhaps that man of hers was right in saying that they didn't want anything to do with a sick man? Perhaps I am going mad? Perhaps I am a lunatic? Do I act like a person going mad, Rebecca? At the moment, I certainly feel as if I am. You see, I had been so certain that if I could only talk to Vallie my problems and nightmares would fall into perspective and vanish. This thought has kept me going and has helped me. Now however, I am not sure of anything, apart from that I have always loved you. You don't doubt that, do you?'

'No, I can feel that you do love me as I love you, but please Tom please, tell me the truth. Have you ever been unfaithful to me?'

Tom turned his head in horror and looked at his wife.

Rebecca could tell that he was hurt and frightened. He searched her eyes, looking straight into them. Tom was getting scared. Did he act as mad as that? He bent forward and took her hand in his grasping it tight, holding her gaze he told her that he had never been unfaithful to her. He had never had the slightest interest in any other woman other than her.

'Oh darling, please, this red-haired woman isn't my type. I instantly felt that I didn't like her. I can only give you my word and hope that you trust me. I do need your help solving this nightmare and I think at the back of my head that somehow this Vallie is a key to the problem. I'll have to see if I meet her again, and hopefully without a man at her side. I may have heard somebody calling her by name. I recognized her angry voice. I don't remember the man she was with. Rebecca please, don't let this come between us. You have to believe me. Oh, this is horrible, but I am trying so hard to explain and to find a solution, without knowing what I am trying to say to you.'

Rebecca looked down to the sand by her feet. She watched some ants trying to drag bigger insect with them, but they were not coordinated. They seemed to be pulling in different directions. Rebecca watched this going on, and she suddenly thought that if they didn't work together here, pulling this problem they had in the same direction, they would never find anything out. She was sure that Tom was telling the truth, but there was a hint of a seed of doubt planted in her thoughts, a fragment of suspicion or whatever. Something was there and she tried to shake it off without great success. Oh, she thought, this is dangerous.

'We have to get to the bottom of this, Tom. I do believe what you are saying. I don't think you are lying to me, but there's no smoke without fire. Something must be hidden at the back of your mind.'

They looked out over the sea. The sunshine had all but disappeared behind some clouds. Rebecca shivered slightly. She did not know if it was getting chilly, or if she shivered because of the shock of this woman. The sea looked uninviting and colder than before, reflecting the colour of the grey sky. Tom leaned forward and burying his face into the soft part of her neck, he kissed her and asked if it wasn't high time for them to start thinking of going home.

'I think you are getting cold. We cannot solve this problem, sitting here playing table tennis throwing thoughts back and forwards. I think the joy of being here is gone.'

Rebecca nodded and Tom stood up and whistled for Mozart.

CHAPTER 15

The tide was out, just as their moods were. Rebecca stood up and they started to fold the blanket and clear up after their coffee. Now after lunchtime the beach had become more crowded although the sun was gone. Their day was ruined, but Rebecca decided there and then, that she was going to suppress her suspicions. She would try to help Tom. If Tom had in fact been unfaithful to her before his accident, he had forgotten about it. She knew that Tom was telling the truth when he said that he never had been with another woman, and trust would be restored. She looked up at her husband, walking hand in hand carrying the basket and keeping the dog on the lead. He could feel that she was looking at him and he looked back at her with sad eyes. She returned his smile. She was not going to let today's event get to her.

Tom smiled back with relief and told her that he was fine as long as Mozart did not pull. He kissed her on her cheek telling her that he adored her.

They rubbed Mozart off with his towel before letting him into the car. Not that he was particularly wet. It was more an attempt to get rid of the sand from his paws and under his belly. Rebecca saw the note with the scribbled registration number and the words "Silver Honda." She notched it into her memory. She didn't know why, but she knew she would never forget that number. From now on she would examine every silver car's number plate for a match. She could not tell what use that would be or what she would do or gain from doing anything if ever that car did come her way. Oh yes, she would have a close look at this Vallie woman, of that she was determined. 'Aren't we women always curious?' she asked herself in defense of her thoughts.

At a red light Rebecca was aware of Tom's eyes examining her. She turned her face up to him as the light turned green and said 'Darling, it is green.' They laughed, as this was far from the first time she had told him the colour of the lights. 'Would you like to go to that little place for a hot cup of something on our way home? Our favourite place up on the hillside?'

'Why not. We do need something to cheer us up.'

They went off the main road and went into the small pub for a hot chocolate. There were not many people in the place as it was almost closing time. The fading log fire was giving out some heat.

They went to the car red cheeked and feeling so much the better for the hot drink. Mozart needed to get out for a short walk. On their return Tom opened the boot, put his jacket away and closed the boot. He then went to the driver's door and stopped dead, realizing that he had locked them out of the car. Rebecca laughed at first and told him to tell her another joke. Tom had put the car key into his jacket pocket, which now was safely in the closed boot. They looked at one another. The pub was closed and Tom had his mobile under the front seat inside the car.

They started to discuss what to do. Tom would soon get cold without his jacket.

Suddenly there were two other cars coming up the hill towards them and stopped next to them, obviously not knowing that the pub was closed for the afternoon. The newcomers were going for a walk in the area and nobody had brought a mobile. The family's eldest daughter of about ten, rushed back into one of the cars returning with her own phone. Fantastic! What a clever girl.

They could phone and ask Directory enquiries for the telephone number for "Green Flag."

Tom made the call to tell them what had happened and ask for help. "Green Flag" would send somebody out, but it would take around an hour before anybody appeared on the scene.

The other visitors would go for their walk. They had a Dalmation called Disney. She belonged to a friend who had not been able to come with them. Before they left they lent Tom a wind cheater jacket so he would not catch cold and told them that they would be back shortly. Off they went and Rebecca and Tom were left on their own again with Mozart.

Tom took Rebecca's arm and they walked around looking at trees and other plants. They did not stray far from the car so that they could keep an eye on it. They walked in circles to keep warm. It was lucky for them that it was not raining.

They could hear the walkers coming back and there was help coming up the hill. Tom returned their jacket and thanked the walkers for their help. He had no money on him as his wallet was in his jacket pocket in the boot.

The families and Disney left and the rescuer started the procedure to get into the car. It took him less than half an hour and without even a scratch.

Tom kissed Rebecca and gave her the key asking her to drive.

Rebecca took the driver's seat with Tom beside her. After a little while he asked if she could stop the car for a second. He was desperate.

She stopped at a roadside pub, and they went inside. Rebecca asked for the menu and the price list, while Tom went to the gents. Rebecca started to get worried as Tom was away for such a long time, but when she was about to ask another man to go into the gents to see if Tom was all right, he reappeared all smiles. He took her hand and they left. Back in the car Tom told her that the door bolt was faulty. He had been locked in and could not get out of his cubicle. No other men were around. He had had to shout through an half open window standing on the lavatory seat to attract attention and get a member of staff to come and let him out.

They decided to go straight home and relax before something else happened.

'It surely hasn't been your day, Tom.' said Rebecca.

They took to the road in silence.

'A penny for your thoughts, Tom. You are extremely quiet.'

'Sorry, but I was thinking of how important you, James and Mozart are to me. I don't want to lose you. I couldn't bear it. I love you too much, Rebecca. I am scared about what on earth is going to happen or rather what is already happening to us. You do believe me, don't you, when I say that I have never been unfaithful to you? I cannot get it out of my mind, what happened by the beach today. It was unpleasant and I don't think either of us will be able to forget it'

Rebecca loved Tom just as much as before this "Vallie" story. She would like to confront this woman herself, if she dared. She was apprehensive of what she might find out in the process. Was she prepared for anything that might come out into the open?

They arrived back home and let themselves in.

'Let's have a drink.' said Tom. We are in a sort of limbo after the shock. What can I get you?'

'Thanks, Tom. I am sorry I suddenly feel confused. You are the one who has more reason to feel as I do. I think I would like a Campari, please. What do we say to James? He is bound to notice that something is the matter?'

'Leave James to me. Don't worry. I'll tell him that I was rudely told off by another beach visitor in the car park. Campari is coming up, neat with a slice of orange and ice only, as usual?'

'Please.'

Tom entered the kitchen, the dog at his heels and went to the stairs calling out 'Hello' to James. 'We are back home and are going to have a drink in the garden. Would you like to join us?'

'Yes please, sounds good. Whiskey and water please. I'll be down in a sec.'

Tom fed the hungry dog and returned to Rebecca with a shawl and a tray of drinks. He looked at her and thought she looked pale. He told her so and that after a day on the beach, the idea was to look suntanned not paler. Rebecca smiled and said that she was going to be fine. She was surprised that she felt almost sick.

Rebecca had been through so much these last months that she had begun to think of herself as a strong woman who could deal with anything. However, this wasn't anything but something, and her mind and body had had enough.

'Tom, how are _you_ feeling?'

'To be honest, I feel drained and as pale as you look. I

am shattered and scared. I have to try to keep my cool for James' sake and for yours. First thing Monday morning I'll phone the surgery and make an appointment.'

At this James joined them on the terrace and grabbed his glass of whiskey.

'Are you nearly finished or have you had some kind of 'writer's block?' asked Tom.

'If I am able to get on with it after this drink I'll have it on my laptop in another couple of hours. How about you? Was the beach crowded, it being a Saturday and a sunny one too? Did Mozart go into the sea for a swim or was he too much of a coward?'

Rebecca told him about Mozart's adventures and said that they would go to the coast on a week day next time to avoid the crowds.

'It wasn't too bad when we first arrived. However, before we left there were many families around. It was lovely to stroll along both through the woodland park paths and to follow the water's edge on the beach. This was our first picnic by the coast this year. It'll certainly not be our last.'

Tom admired his wife playing it calmly. James obviously did not suspect nor notice anything special. Let sleeping dogs lie, he thought.

'I have spoken to Gill. Nothing would keep me from that - definitely not an essay. She made the apple cake last night using your recipe, mum. It is gone already. She sends her love. They had been walking along the seaside, but Gill found it a bit too chilly for comfort. If there is anything in this supposed global warming business, we'll have a nice summer coming up. Last year was great and I must say I do like the prospect. We could do with some warmer temperatures in this country.

Rebecca had got some colour back in her cheeks. However, Tom could not tell if she was relaxing because the glass of Campari was half empty or if she did felt better. After having met Vallie and even confronting her, Tom was more lost than ever. He did not feel anything other than anger at the sight of this woman but she had clearly appeared in his mind. Would he ever be able to get rid of Vallie?'

Rebecca and Tom had never kept secrets from each other during their marriage. Had so much been changed by his accident and the time he had spent "away from life"? All he wanted was to get their "together-life" back to what it had been. Before he could dream of this happening, he had to find out more about Vallie. He was going to try to trace the silvery Honda, but how to do this he had not decided. He thought that he would walk Mozart and examine the cars he saw, and to go to ASDA to see if any of the cars parked there fitted the description. His problem, was that Vallie and her man knew him by sight.

The maddening thing was that nothing explained why he had seen her when he made love to Rebecca. 'Vallie did appear to me before I had seen her for the first time, before I spotted her in the supermarket car park.'

'So where are you now dad?' James' voice interrupted his thoughts.

'Thinking deep thoughts. This global warming is much more frightening than we imagine. I remember when the first men fell ill with AIDS. The female Swedish health minister at that time told everybody that this was never going to become a problem, as it only affected men who were gay. She didn't know what she was talking about. The same happened with BSE and a minister let his grandchild eat a hamburger in front of the press to prove what? So now we have another problem around our necks. Politicians are all talk, and they don't appear to have a clue how to deal with it.'

James looked at his father in such a worried way that Rebecca had to smile.

'We know that it is no laughing matter, but a sense of humour in our "luggage" is good to have and if we cannot laugh when we make funny faces, what will we have then to make our sorrows disappear?' said Rebecca.

Tom blew her a kiss.

'By the way, what's for dinner tonight? I am getting hungry.' James asked.

'Haven't you had anything to eat since breakfast? It'll be another hour at least. How about you, Tom, are you starving as well? I have some of that smoked salmon. We could have an open smoked salmon sandwich with red onion for starters. How about that?'

'Then I am hungry too. I'll make them. The two of you may stay here and discuss me as I am out of earshot.'

'Dad, do you need any help? No? Thank goodness for that.'

Rebecca and James talked about Gill and as she had enjoyed the apple cake so much Rebecca wandered if he might like to bring one to St .Andrews.

Mozart was tired after his swim and lay on the terrace by Rebecca's feet.

'Tom, do you realize that today is the first day that you haven't had a nap? Aren't you tired?'

I'll probably fall asleep in front of the television after dinner.' Tom said

James asked why they had not had any lunch. 'Didn't you bring the basket? Don't tell me it was empty.'

'Of course it wasn't empty but we only had cheese scones and coffee as we did have a late breakfast. I think we could have called it brunch.'

As Tom had predicted, he fell asleep straight after they had eaten having sat down in his easy chair in front of the television. When Rebecca came to join him, he was sound asleep, mouth wide open. She sat down in the chair next to him, enjoying her cup of black coffee. She put down his glass of milk on the small table at his side. She switched the programme over and when golf started she bent over towards Tom and gently woke him up.

Tom was startled although she had tried to be gentle, only whispering in his ear and stroking his cheek softly. He sat up suddenly, looking around as if he could not remember where he was, but as soon as he got his bearings he looked up into Rebecca's grey eyes and let out a huge sigh of relief.

'Sorry, I must have had a bad dream again. I didn't know where I was when I woke up. I am pleased to see you sitting next to me.'

'You have slept for more than an hour, and I honestly didn't want you to sleep any longer, as it's getting late and I know you would like a relaxing sleep tonight. You said that you were dreaming again. Do you remember what it was about?'

'I had an argument with somebody.' Tom did not want to tell Rebecca that he thought that this could have been with Vallie, but he did not want to lie to her either. The balance was difficult. How he wished that he had been born a female! The female sex seemed to be able to share their problems with each other, unlike men. He could not talk about this even to his best friend.

Rebecca watched him closely and asked him if he was feeling all right.

'I feel fine, but confused, Rebecca. Everything that has to do with my health is great. It is my mind which doesn't seem to work. I didn't use to suffer from bad dreams, did I? Please, could you tell me exactly what happened that day of my accident?'

'Of course, if you think there could be something hidden to reveal to us about your recurring nightmare.

It was a sunny day with a clear blue sky. The air was crisp and there was some snow on the ground. The snow had fallen during the night. I wanted to go skating and I begged you to come with me to the ice rink in Princes Street Gardens, but you were not keen. I asked you to please do it for me as a special favour. I suppose you were irritated by the way I asked you to, because I didn't give you any chance to refuse. You were cross as we left. I tried to cheer you up but I don't think that I succeeded.

We parked at the multi story car park and walked to the ice with our skates. I more or less ordered you to put a helmet on, knowing that you never were confident on ice. I don't think you enjoyed it either. Anyway, you were not going to look stupid as well as not being a good skater. So no helmet. That was some daft Swedish rule. I used one.

You were furious having this day spoiled, and flew out on to the ice at full speed, a speed you couldn't master. You did this, I am sure, to make a point. I had only time to get on to the ice to follow you when I saw you tripping over something. I think it must have been a stone or something. You didn't only fall but with the speed you had accumulated, your entire body made a loop in the air before you hit the ice. Your head took most of the fall. It was a terrible crashing sound. I remember thinking that I hoped it was an arm or a leg that you had broken, but I knew that it came from your head. It made a sickening noise.

Some people screamed in horror when this happened. I don't think I did. I think I went into a kind of shock. So many things appeared in my head from the time you made this acrobatic jump up into the air until you actually hit the ice. To me it was as if it happened in slow motion.

You were lying there on the ice without any sign of life. There was blood.

An ambulance was called. I took my jacket off and put it over you trying to keep you warm. I felt your pulse and knew that you were alive but your pulse was weak. We were taken to the hospital. You were attached to some machine straight away. At some stage they asked me to sign some papers to allow them to operate on you. The operation in itself took hours and it was dark by the time I started to think of getting my car back home. Anna called James who came home that same evening. Anna and Eric brought me home. Eric drove our car back here. Oh Tom, it was frightening and I had nightmares about your acrobatics and the noise when your head hit the ice. I have a bad conscience about making you skate with me that day. If I hadn't forced you, none of this would have happened. I am grateful to have you here by my side Tom, and I find it extraordinary that you don't suffer from any headaches. There were no other people involved in your accident. Nobody but yourself, a stone or similar and of course me.'

'Thanks. I hope that you're not going to have your nightmare any more and please don't feel guilty. I should obviously have listened to your expert advice and put that helmet on my head. I have to remember that the Swedes are clever with their safety rules. Listening to what you have told me doesn't shed any light on why I have my nightmare, more than I have the feeling of being cross. I don't think it is the same kind of anger that I must have felt towards you. I never feel any anger towards you in my nightmare. Never! When I am cross with you it is a different sort of fury. I absolutely adore you, remember.'

'I love you too Tom. I can't stop saying how sorry I am about that day.

I think it has come up to bed time by now. I thought we were going to watch some golf but are we in the mood for that?'

'Not really, but I think it would be stupid to go to bed straight away. We have far too much to think about. Too much to keep us awake into the small hours of the morning. How about some cheese and wine? Let's ask James if he would like to join us.'

Tom went out for a short walk with Mozart while Rebecca went upstairs to James' room to ask if he fancied anything before bedtime. James had finished his essay and was sitting reading it through.

Rebecca cleared the table and loaded the bread machine. She brought out the ingredients for the oat biscuits that James had asked her to make for him. She prepared the baking tray for them and the baking tin for the apple cake, everything she could possibly do this evening to save time the following morning. She was pleased that she had made the onion soup.

Rebecca made herself ready for bed, but first she wrote several pages about the day's happenings, and her own thoughts on the matter. She underlined the name Valerie alias Vallie or Val. Rebecca was not comfortable sitting on the bed with the book on her lap but she did not want Tom to know about her note taking. She did not want him to read what she was thinking. This was like keeping a diary, as she had done as a young girl.

With a heavy sigh and a sense of guilt, she closed the book and put it back at the bottom of her linen drawer. The stupid thing was that she was sure that Tom would understand her writing this down, but would he be hurt to know that she felt the need to do it? What would he make of her thoughts about the cat, fish and chips, the awful painting, his new interests in foot ball and motor sports, the nightmares, and now there was this "Vallie" too. This red haired "other woman" as Rebecca had started calling her, although she did not deep down even consider that Tom had been unfaithful. Surely she would have noticed. Wouldn't she?

When Tom came back from the bathroom Rebecca switched off her bedside light and curled up to go to sleep. Tom mumbled in his sleep but had a dreamless night as far as Rebecca could tell, or perhaps she had been too tired by the time she finally fell asleep for anything to wake her up. She did ask Tom in the morning if he had slept well and he said he had indeed. He drew her close to him.

After breakfast Tom and James went for a walk. Mozart was as happy as ever. The weather promised another day of warm sunshine. The air was as a hot summer's day and everywhere looked fresh and colourful. The different shades of green made the surroundings shimmer like a Thai silk dress slowly wafting in the breeze. It shifted and rustled, and the smell ... It was one of these beautiful days when life was easy. It put a smile on Tom's face and a light into his eyes.

James took a sidelong glance at his father and was pleased with what he could see. Tom seemed happy and relaxed and apart from the improvement in his colour, he had a noticeable spring in his step. He had put on weight. James told him that he looked well. Tom said that it was because of Rebecca. 'She has taken such good care of me, James. Please promise me, that if anything should happen to me you'll take good care of her.'

'Good heavens, what makes you ask that, dad? Of course I will, and I will take care of you if anything should happen to mum. Why do you ask? Are you keeping something from us?'

'I am feeling fine. I am feeling sentimental that's all. We should have gone to church, but mum had too much to do with all your requests, plus it was Matins today and neither of us are keen on that' as you well know. What time will Gill be with us?'

'Dad, look at that dog playing with Mozart! Hasn't it got its lead trailing along after it? Odd, isn't it? I mean, you don't let go of the lead, you take it off. We'd better keep our eyes open for the owner. Perhaps this dog has escaped.'

'Mozart, come here, have a treat! Be careful, James. Let's see what it says on the collar of his new friend. Can you make it out? Is there a telephone number?

Did you bring your mobile?'

'I always bring my mobile. I can't go anywhere without it.' James answered looking at the collar of the estranged dog.

'I could only manage to get the dog's name. Her name is Disney.' continued James, before the dog broke loose.

She started to get ahead of them along the path and ran some twenty yards in front of them and then stopped, as if she wanted to make sure that they were following, before starting off again. After a little while, the dog stopped long enough for Tom to manage to get hold of the lead. They were walking with two dogs both on leads. They walked along the path and called out to see if they would get any answer. This lonely dog tried to make them pay attention, and indicated that it wanted to show them the way. When they had been walking for some time, Disney got impatient. Tom let her go and she disappeared down the slope towards the edge of the river.

Some twigs had recently been disturbed. There was a walking stick lying on the slope.

They called for Disney. The dog answered from below their feet. Further down, in the undergrowth they saw the old man. He was lying on his side, not visible from the path. James phoned immediately emergency service, while Tom talked to the man who said that he was bruised and had hit his head on the way down. It did not look too bad and was not bleeding but he had a large bump on his forehead. He was wearing an old overcoat which had probably saved him from getting too chilled. The coat was an old well worn tweed. His trousers were "old men's" brown. He had lost one shoe in the fall and they could see that one leg was at a strange angle. He was thin but not tall and was probably in his eighties. His cheeks had prominent veins showing almost like a spider's web on a white pale face similar to waxwork at Madame Tussaud's.

His small pepper corn eyes looked up at the two strangers absently patting his companion. He had a distinguished look about him with only a slight wisp of white hair surrounding his head at the edges. His nose was big for such a little face. It was blueish probably from cold although the weather was lovely and warm. The ground where the man had ended up was damp. He told them his name was Angus Anderson. He had slipped and had rolled down the bank. He thought that he had tripped over something, and with the dog pulling, it had not made things any easier. Tom took off his lightweight jacket. It was not much, but at least gave Angus something to rest his sore head on. He was shivering and told them that he was sure that he had broken his leg in the fall. He appeared to be in a state of mild shock. Angus told them this himself.

'I practiced as a GP in my day, so I should be able to tell. Disney is my best friend and partner since my wife died two years ago.

Tom looked at the dog and thought that he did recognize her. There were unlikely to be two Dalmations living around the area named Disney.

'My voice is no longer strong, I am afraid. Nobody would have heard me calling. I am lucky to be alive and to have the dog. She is lovely and faithful, as you can tell.'

'Are you in much pain, Mr Anderson?' asked Tom.

'I was in pain, but cannot feel anything at the

moment. It'll get worse when I move, I know that. I feel cold and I am tired. This is why I keep on talking. I don't dare fall asleep. I want to have a clear head when the ambulance arrives. Will they be able to get as far as this, I wonder? Please call me Angus.'

'My son has gone to meet them. You'll be fine. Is there anything I can do to help you in any way? I don't dare move you.'

'No, please don't touch my leg! In my breast pocket, you'll find a plastic envelope. Do you think you can get that out for me, please?' asked the man.

'Have you anybody who could take care of the dog for you? '

'Well, it is written inside this folder. Could you read it to me and I'll tell you what you need to know. That first name is my daughter who lives in Glasgow. If you could be so kind as to phone the second name please. That is my neighbour and she will be happy to take care of Disney. She loves the dog and helps me if needed. We support one another. She will phone my daughter. Keep the piece of paper with the name and number of this lady. The rest I would appreciate if you could hand over to the ambulance staff. They have the information they need there about me.

'Don't you worry about anything. We'll take Disney home with us and will look after her until your friend can pick her up.'

Tom could tell that Angus was tiring fast. His voice was getting weaker and his eyes becoming unfocused. He wanted to tell him to stop talking and save his strength, but thought that a GP would know how to handle a situation like this even if it was himself that needed treatment, and Angus was happy to be talking.

James had run ahead to show the ambulance people how to reach the victim. He was constantly on his mobile helping them to locate where he could be found.

The ambulance took ages, or perhaps it just felt like a long time, before three men came down the slope with a stretcher. One of them recognized Angus and asked him what he had been up to. They talked for a minute or so while he gave Angus an injection to ease the pain and to calm him down. He first of all examined the suspect leg. It was indeed broken.

Tom got hold of Disney's lead. She was not happy to let these men lift her master on to the stretcher as the old man called out in pure pain before he finally lost consciousness.

Tom was asked how they came across him and was told that Mr Anderson would be taken to the Royal. They left the way they had arrived with Angus Anderson on the stretcher, well wrapped in blankets. James, holding on to Disney, had great difficulty keeping her calm. She wanted to go with Angus. Tom was pleased to have some of Mozart's treats in his jacket pocket, as the two men with the dogs started to walk back to their house, where Rebecca was waiting for them. James had given her a call.

'She might have seen the ambulance driving down to the Dell as it must have passed our house. Knowing her she would have been worried sick.'

When they returned home, Gill had arrived.

CHAPTER 16

James made another phone call. This time it was to Angus' lady friend. She was horrified to hear what had happened to her neighbour.

Gill met Tom and James at the door. Rebecca kissed them with relief.

'Thank goodness that you are well. I immediately took it more or less for granted that something terrible had happened to you. I am sorry to hear about the old man. How is he, and where did you find him? What had happened?'

'Mum, calm down and we'll be able to tell you the whole story. But one thing at the time. This is Disney and a lady is coming any minute to collect her.'

James was a proud young man. He had kissed Gill when he entered the house and he had his arm around her shoulders in a manly protective way.

Tom looked tired, but he brightened up meeting this important young lady again. He stepped forward kissing Gill on her cheek telling her how wonderful it was to see her.

'If you two adventurers could wash your hands please. We can sit up at table and talk while we eat. Lunch is ready. I am sure that we are all hungry and you two probably need something hot and a drink. Or do you think we should wait for Disney to be picked up first?

Mozart seemed to settle down, but Disney was running from door to door looking out. She was whining, but made happy signs of recognition when being stroked by the lady who was going to look after her. They knew one another that was obvious. As they were about to depart the lady looked back at Rebecca and asked if they had met before. 'I know, you were locked out of your car, weren't you?' she exclaimed.

'I thought I recognized you. I am sorry that I didn't know you straight away. I should have done. How terribly ignorant of me.' said Rebecca apologetically.

'Not at all. We were pleased to be able to help.'

When the kind lady had disappeared with Disney, the family sat up at table in the dining room. They had so little time left to talk about so much before the young couple had to leave for St Andrews. Poor Gill, she had to answer many questions, mainly asked by Tom. He even asked her what her parents did when they were working.

Gill's father still kept in touch with the police force where he had been employed for many years. When there was something big going on or a tricky death he was asked to help, and he loved it too much to give it up.

The lunch was much appreciated, but after coffee it was time to say the usual departure pieces that James was so familiar with. Gill was probably used to hearing the same things from her own mother.

'Mothers that care are the same I guess.' said James, with a big smile on his face. Gill laughed and said that it surely would be noticed if her mother suddenly decided to stop and only said ' bye see you soon.'

'Dad, please let me know how Angus Anderson is getting on when you find out.' asked James.

Later, Tom sat down with a big sigh. He was exhausted after this morning's events. He immediately fell asleep. They had the house to themselves once more.

Rebecca opened the French door windows to the

garden. The afternoon sun warmed up the parquet floor and the curtains danced slightly in the breeze. Mozart followed her out on to the terrace and after his normal tour around the bushes and the trees, he settled down at her feet. She had brought herself another cup of coffee and the last meringue and one of her oat biscuits. She had saved a few for Tom and herself, but most of them were on their way to St Andrews, together with an apple sponge cake and a fresh loaf of bread. Gill had told them that this would be superb with her mother's homemade marmalade. Their dinner was going to be a lasagne, which was secure in the boot of their car.

The house was quiet and with Tom fast asleep, it did not take long before Rebecca closed the book she was reading and she nodded off.

Later when the garden seats were back in the summer house and the shadows were lengthening, Rebecca took Mozart for his walk. She left a note for Tom on the kitchen table. It had to be a short walk as she wanted to be back for some of her favourite television programmes and to prepare the dinner. It would have to be served and eaten on their laps in front of the box as they did most Sundays. Terrible as it was, she enjoyed it, although to eat on a tray limited the kind of dinner she could serve. To eat soup or pasta for instance was not possible and a luxury meal was definitely not on.

CHAPTER 17

She had learned the silver Honda number plate by heart. Rebecca watched the cars passing by. . She did not expect any to match and it was getting dark and therefore difficult to read the plates. She only managed to decipher odd numbers, which were enough for her to know that no car was the one she was looking for. Did she really want to find this vehicle? She was not sure, but she was certain that she did want to solve the mysterious "Vallie," this red-haired woman who Tom said that he knew. He seemed to be sure that she was keeping vital information from him. 'She is the key.' Hadn't he said so earlier?

What Rebecca had not thought through or rather had not managed to find an answer for, was what she would do if or when she did find this silver Honda and its owner. It was not only for Tom's sake that she wanted to find out the truth. It was the sake of her own sanity too.

She walked along deep in thought. She had never realized that most cars seemed to be silver. If it was a Honda or Volvo or something else however, she had no means of knowing. She had never been interested in cars.

By the way Tom had described Vallie and her husband, Rebecca never thought that she was going to spot their car close to the village or on this side of the supermarket. They were probably more likely to live in a not so upmarket part of the city.

Rebecca could sense that it was not only herself who kept secrets, but that he was holding back information from her. There must be more to it than he had let on. It made her sad that they no longer could talk through thoughts or problems, as they had done before his accident. Their marriage had been built on their love for one another, and on their ability and willingness to discuss everything in complete trust. Now that seemed to be diluted. Would it be possible to go on living in a happy relationship without trust? Would it be possible to continue to be happy together, without sharing thoughts and problems? She shivered as she realized what her answer to these questions would be.

She felt depressed and her steps had once more become heavy. The happy bounce of only a few days ago had disappeared. Her guilt flared up. She had to accept her guilt, and not to blame Tom, but herself.

She opened the gate for the dog and stopped for a minute looking at the garden and the old house. How happy the whole family had been here! How happy the couple who lived here had been only a few months previously and then again only a week or so ago. Rebecca sighed heavily and went up to the kitchen door. She knew as soon as she opened the door and took a step forward over the threshold into the house that something was wrong. Terribly wrong. She called out for Tom. He was screaming.

Rebecca rushed into the living room where Tom had fallen asleep on the sofa. As she went into that part of the house she pushed Mozart in front of her. What she did not notice was that Mozart did not indicate that there was anyone else in the house. She was too scared of who she was going to meet, of what she would find and what could have happened for Tom to be screaming like that. It had been a sound made by someone in pain.

Mozart went running up to greet Tom, who was sitting up straight as a poker with hair disheveled. He had had a shock of some kind. He was staring into space. Tom did not see her. He looked past her, straight through her, having another image in front of him. He was gasping for air and his face was wet from cold sweat. Rebecca tried to make him focus on her. Tried to make him leave what was on his mind, and to come back to Mozart and herself, to come back to the living. The way his eyes stared at something unseen were not the gaze of a sane person, but more like a stare from a madman. Rebecca felt the rapid pacing of her own heart. She felt her pulse in her entire body and she could hear her heart beat in her ears. Was Tom going mad or was she perhaps? Whatever, she had to do something and do it now.

She started talking to Tom, but her voice was so husky that it did not make any sound. Nothing passed her lips. She had to take another deep breath and start all over. She talked soothingly to the stranger in front of her, because the man she had known by the name Tom was more like a ghost. This man she did not know and she did not want to know, but Rebecca knew instinctively that it was up to her, to make Tom return to her, to make him her own Tom and husband. 'Everything would be fine.' she told herself. She was here and so was Mozart. When talking like this to the man on the sofa, she prayed that everything was going to be fine.

Tom did calm down eventually and Rebecca went for a glass of water and sat down by his side touching his wet cheek. He started sobbing like a small child, leaning on to her shoulder. She could feel how he was crying and shaking. She held the big man in her arms and stroked the back of his neck. She let her fingers brush through his hair until he stopped crying. He told her how sorry he was, how ashamed he felt of his weakness and behaviour.

'Rebecca, I am so terrified not to understand what is happening to me. It must have to do with my head. Perhaps I was brain damaged after all,? Why would I have this awful nightmare if I wasn't?'

'Tom I don't know what to say or what I do think any longer, but something is the matter. However, you can't blame any damage to your head for the fact that you recognize a woman not only by sight but also by name.' Rebecca said.

If Tom could get rid of the problem, they would have come a long way. She was terrified of what Tom experienced in that nightmare which he obviously had just awakened from as she and the dog had entered the house.

She started to think about any noise she might have made when she entered. There was the sound of her opening the door. It must have been this that had frightened him. If one has a dream, noise around is included in it. She had thought of this several times. She could remember when Tom had a cold once and she had fallen asleep in her armchair. She had dreamed of a fire engine and woken up startled only to realize that there was no fire, only Tom who had blown his nose. They had laughed then, but now she hoped that this past experience could be of some use in putting the matter into perspective.

She asked him about his dream and he told her what he could recall. He had had an argument with somebody and rushed out of a building. He entered his green sports car and turned at high speed into the country, where he suddenly met a big heavy tractor with a fork at the front. Tom drove round a bend and there it was. There was no way he could have survived this collision, which was imminent as there was nowhere to go, no escape from it. He had heard the crash in today's version of his dream. It had been such an awful sound of metal grating against metal. He told her that he did not think that he had dreamt that far in the dream before. He had woken up just as the two vehicles were converted into one big heap of crumpled metal.

Discreetly withdrawing into the comparative calm of the kitchen, Rebecca occupied herself with food preparation.

It was too late for one of her favourite Sunday programmes, but she came into the snug with Tom's dinner on a tray with it a glass of wine. She thought that some food and the distraction of television would do them good.

They were surprised that they managed to eat and not only that, they enjoyed the meal and the wine. Rebecca served coffee and even asked Tom for a brandy.

They watched "The Antiques Road Show" and later on flicking through the channels Tom was lucky to find out that there was going to be a repeat of the splendid programme "To the Manor Born" with Penelope Keith. It fitted their requirement. A laugh before it was time for them to let the dog out and to go to bed.

Tom was holding his wife's hand, repeating how he loved her and how he needed her by his side more than ever. They had found happiness in one another all over again.

Rebecca wanted to have a bath and so did Tom. He filled the bath for her with lots of foam to soak in. He lit some candles around the tub's edge to soothe her mind. He had his bath after she had enjoyed hers. The candles were still there for him, and the smell of lavender was lingering.

They went to bed close together as their usual jigsaw pieces. They were exhausted.

The last thing Rebecca thought before night overcame her was that tomorrow was another day, hopefully a day of promise. Little did she know, that the Monday was certainly going to be a day to remember, but not for reasons she would have preferred.

They slept through the night. Tom had not been woken up by his dream. He still felt tired. It was as if his entire body had been working and not relaxed during his sleep. His legs felt heavy and he had a headache for the first time since he had come back home. He went to the bathroom and had his morning shower to wake up properly. It worked with a cold shower. His headache he put down to what had happened the previous day. It had been a hard day, in fact a very tiring one. He was nevertheless happy to have met Gill again. Rebecca was right as she so often was. He did like Gill. She was a different girl entirely to James' ex Susan. Tom could understand what he saw in Gill. He had never understood his choice of Susan.

Finding Mr Angus Anderson in the Dell had been emotional for Tom. He wondered if Mozart would have been clever enough to look for help and to make somebody react. When he was waiting for the ambulance and listened to Angus talking, he had asked himself if it had been like that for Rebecca when he had <u>his</u> accident, <u>his</u> fall. Had she been waiting for help to arrive for as long as Tom had in the Dell? He was pleased to learn that Angus would not need surgery on his leg. They would keep him in hospital for a short time because of his age. Angus could not have been in a better place, being looked after properly and with help with the pain he surely must be suffering. Disney, his dog was also well looked after. In the end all was well or at least as well as could be expected.

But his own mental state did worry him and he could feel that Rebecca was concerned too. He would have been surprised and disappointed if she had not been.

He dressed to take Mozart out. Weatherwise it looked likely to be another lovely day. Some small white cotton buds clouds were scattered in the sky but they did not look threatening. Cotton buds were the first thing that came into his mind, but when he examined them again, it was more like some child had thrown hard whisked egg whites around. Whatever, it was beautiful and the dew on the grass looked fresh glistening like diamonds spread on a green table cloth.

He kissed his wife good morning before he left the house, Mozart on the lead. She promised to have breakfast ready by the time of their return.

Tom walked fast. The air smelled of the wet grass mixed with the scents from different flowers.

He liked to get his limbs working and the blood in his body circulating. His headache had lifted and he felt clear in mind by the time he turned round.

He knew he had some important phone calls to make, sooner rather than later, and he would find time to go to ASDA.

Rebecca was frightened, a state she was becoming used to. She wondered what this day would bring them. She did not know if she would be able to take anymore. She was worried sick for Tom and for their relationship. She felt as if her whole life had not only been put on hold as she had sensed when Tom was lying motionless in the coma, but this time there were more things happening than she would be strong enough to cope with. That Tom had scared her yesterday was an awful experience. They had to sit down after breakfast for another talking session. She felt stronger from having made a decision. She would phone Anna, as she had asked them to come for a meal some time during the week. Before this she hoped that Tom would keep his promise to contact the surgery for an appointment. He looked worn out. He needed his sleep, but had his nights torn to pieces by his nightmare. Tom and Mozart entered the kitchen and they sat down to breakfast.

Mozart did not beg at the table any more. He watched for any signs of them asking him to join in before he gave up and lay down to rest in his basket. This morning Rebecca and Tom turned and watched him as he let out a big sigh of pure dejection. They looked at one another and laughed.

They read the Times and Rebecca did one Su DoKu, but she had done something wrong and gave up. She could not concentrate enough on what she was doing. She was disappointed in herself. It was not often that she did not manage to solve the puzzle.

They listened to the radio news. There had been another young girl found strangled in Edinburgh. This made it three girls that had been found in a month.

They talked about how awful it was to have a serial killer running wild. Tom asked Rebecca not to go out without Mozart and definitely not to take the short cut through the Dell.

It seemed that this man might have killed before, and now something had triggered him to kill again. He did not sexually assault the girls, but they had been naked when found. Handbags, mobile phones, jewelery, shoes, nothing had been found near the victims. One thing that the police did reveal was that they had been strangled and on the spot where they had been found. There would be another postmortem of course but the police had little hope of finding anything new.

A killer always makes a mistake in the end and some even want to be found. What the police asked for was any information about anybody behaving strangely.

The victims were young, one only 17 years old and the oldest girl, so far had been 24, all with blonde hair, natural blonde in two of the cases but the latest girl had had her hair bleached.

Rebecca said that she was pleased that they had James with Gill at St Andrews so they did not have to worry about her.

'I know it is selfish, but I cannot help it. Parents with daughters must be at their wits end, with this happening. Many parents work and these girls were students at schools or at universities around the city. Tom, it is a tragedy and awful. I cannot even bear to think of the poor relatives. How would one survive if your child was killed in this way?'

'I cannot imagine anyone being able to commit such crimes, murdering a young beautiful girl? I am worried about you. Promise me that you'll be careful.' Tom begged.

'I promise though I don't think myself as a young blonde student. I must say that I am amazed that the girls do tend to think that it cannot happen to them. This latest victim, apparently missed the last bus and started walking back home in the dark. Why do this? Surely everybody must have heard about the two girls having been strangled? Or didn't she know about them? Young people seem to be so carefree and not reading the papers or listening to the news.

Whatever, it is to the poor parents my thoughts turn. I hope they'll catch the killer soon.'

CHAPTER 18

Tom put the paper to the side and as he poured himself a second cup of tea, he told Rebecca of his plans. Before he did anything he was going to phone the Royal to see if he could find out if Angus had a reasonable night.

He phoned and made an appointment at the surgery for himself. He would have to see his own doctor before he was allocated to a consultant. He knew this but it did not make him less frustrated when told so. Tom was well aware of the possibility of a much faster procedure if he had contacted the hospital and asked for a consultation as an ex patient, but he did not feel like going back and he did not fancy seeing Doctor Smith ever again. Rebecca was of the same opinion. Somehow they did not trust her.

Then Tom made another phone call which he had not told Rebecca about. He should have done this last week, but his courage had failed him. He was nervous about the outcome of this conversation. He phoned his travel insurance company to ask them if he was covered.

He had a long discussion with a young lady and with the manager. Tom was told that it was unlikely that they could offer him cover. Tom had told the young lady what he had gone through, and despite the medical advice that there was no objection for him to travelling, the insurance company said that they could not cover him for at least another year. Everything had changed. Tom had to admit to himself that he was not surprised but he was disappointed.

Tom put the receiver back with a heavy sigh. This

information was a major set back and he realized the serious complication for their travel plans. Their yearly visit to Sweden was out of the question, out of reach. He was staring into space thinking how it would feel if he never was going to be able to travel abroad again. He was devastated. He felt numb. When he hit his head on the ice, that fall had changed his life. People would say if he complained, that he should be happy to be alive without being brain damaged, and was lucky to have a caring wife and wonderful son. Yes, he knew that he <u>was</u> a lucky man, but he was going to have to miss out on so much. He felt great, but he might never visit Venice, not be able to go back to his favourite hotel Jebel Ali in Dubai, and how about Sweden? Rebecca would have to go on her own to see her friends. He would have to stay put and eat Swedish pickled herring bought in IKEA in Edinburgh. This was as far as he could think at the moment. How was he going to break this bad news to Rebecca?

He felt awful. He was scared to have to give her more bad news.

He phoned the police department to ask where to get details of the owner of a specific car when he knew the numberplate, colour and make of the vehicle. The answer to this question was another let down, as there was no way for him as a private person to obtain information. Any such information had to go through police channels and they would not tell him. So what was the problem? Tom made something up about a scratch on his car. He only wanted to talk to the owner of the car parked next to his when it had happened. No, he wasn't going to make any complaint as he thought the police had more important matters to deal with.

He kept sitting by the phone feeling sorry for himself.

He thought of the places they had talked about and now Barcelona with it's fantastic 'Sagrada Familia' went out of the window like some sea mist untouchable as did the planned visit to St Petersburgh. He stayed by the phone for so long that Rebecca came for him with a mug of hot black coffee in hand and a piece of her apple cake. He had to put on some more weight. She was envious that he could enjoy food that she should keep away from.

Rebecca was worried about him, he could see that in her eyes filled with unasked questions. He tried to give her a smile of reassurance, thanked her for the coffee and cake and stood up to come with her into the garden, Mozart in tow. Tom looked down into the faithful brown eyes of this wonderful dog. Of course he knew that at this moment the dog was more interested in the piece of cake on the plate in Tom's hand than in him as a person, but he was pleased that Rebecca had brought Mozart into the family. He was special and became more and more important to Tom. And now when he would have to stay behind this animal felt like a real friend.

Tom asked Rebecca to sit down with him on the terrace. Of course that was the reason why she had come for him in the first place.

The sun was shining and the garden now filled with tulips in various colours made it a joy.

Rebecca searched for the gaze of her husband.

'So Tom, what bad news are you going to tell me, or are you leaving me in the dark. I can tell in the way you don't want to meet my eyes, that it cannot be anything but bad news. Has it anything to do with your doctor's appointment? It must be something tormenting you. Please trust me, it is much better to let me know.'

'It has nothing to do with my appointment. I have received one for later on today. I was lucky that there was a cancellation. No my darling, I phoned about my travel insurance. I am afraid that there was disappointing news. I was told that everything has changed and that my insurance is no longer valid. After an argument they said that they could no longer cover me, but told me that I could apply again in about a year. I am devastated, Rebecca. I am so so sorry thinking of our plans for the future. I cannot even come with you to Sweden this year.'

Rebecca was quiet for so long that Tom had to beg her to say something.

'I must say I am not surprised. It is disappointing, but it is not the end of the world.' she said comfortingly.

'I haven't been able to think. I must admit I feel sorry for myself. I cannot come up with any ideas other than that you have to go to Sweden to see your friends on your own and I'll stay here with Mozart. We will look after one another and keep each other company. Won't we, Mozart?' Tom was touched by the way his friend looked up when he mentioned his name, wagging his tail.

'The best thing you did was to get this lovely dog, Rebecca.'

When we know how you are. When we know more about your nightmare, you'll get rid of it and we are sleeping better, we could start talking about where we would like to go. If it isn't too far away we could take the risk of you travelling without insurance cover, but not yet. The most important thing is to get to the bottom of the problem with Vallie. Don't let this get you down, please.'

'You are a gem, Rebecca. Thanks. Do you honestly think that we'll ever be able to solve my problems?'

Rebecca shook her head and told him to have some faith.

'Back to our present life. I am going to phone Anna as they want to invite us for dinner one evening this week. How do you feel about that? It'll be only the four of us.

Would you mind if I have a game of golf with the ladies tomorrow?"'

'As you just said, let's start living. I am looking forward to seeing Anna and Eric and of course you must play golf tomorrow morning. I'll go to the surgery on my own this afternoon if you don't mind.

Rebecca assured him that it probably was going to be easier for him to talk freely if she was not there. It would be helpful if he could do the shopping for her on his way home..

When things got better Rebecca hoped that they would not miss church as often as she had done recently. Church was comforting not only for her faith but also for the friendship she felt from the congregation. To go to church had always been an important part of their lives ever since they had married there. She wanted this to continue and she was certain that Tom felt the same.

They did not have their meal outside but sat opposite one another at the kitchen table. He told her that he was nervous at the prospect of seeing a doctor and talking about his problems. He felt ashamed in a way he could not explain. He had always been in good health both bodily and mentally. He was not happy about feeling in need of therapy or whatever it would be called.

Rebecca tried to tell him that everybody needed help sometimes whether it was with solving legal matters or problems with health. 'You happen to need help to solve a nightmare to get some sleep.' she said. 'I suppose that this will be like a poor soldier coming back from horrible war experience. It happens to be another kind of sufferance in your case, but it is certainly a near death one.'

Sitting in the waiting room Tom looked around him at other patients. Some were sniffling, others moving stiffly towards the doctor when their names were called. Tom was deep in thought when his name was called, and the doctor had to repeat his name twice before he reacted and stood up.

After more than the eight minutes allocated for every patient nowadays, Tom was told that some kind of counseling might be the best solution for him. He was fit and well apart from having difficulty sleeping because of one recurring bad dream. He would be put on the waiting list to see a consultant. He was warned that it could be weeks before a slot for him could be found. Everything possible would be done to pull the right strings. The doctor asked him whether he had headaches, which Tom was happy to answer in the negative. His blood pressure and heartbeat were normal so he was ordered not to worry.

What Tom had thought about in the waiting room before his appointment was what he was going to do the following morning while Rebecca was out playing golf. He had decided to use his bus pass for more or less the first time and travel around to see if he could figure out where Vallie lived. To be honest with himself, he wanted to see if he could spot the silver Honda. He had felt good about this decision and was surprised that he had not thought of it before. He might not find any answers, but at least it would keep him busy. He would be doing something positive, not just walking with the dog or going shopping.

The next time he saw Eric, Tom would take him up on his offer to play a few holes. The more exercise he had the better it would be, and he wanted to get out of the house more and away from Rebecca. Not that he did not enjoy her company; on the contrary he loved being with her, but was scared that she would get fed up with him and his problems. They had always done things together, and this is what he wanted to do in the future too, but at the moment he felt she needed space.

His heart was beating as if it wanted to jump out of his chest as he neared ASDA. He had Rebecca's shopping list in his pocket and his wallet in his back trouser pocket securely fastened with a button. He tapped and felt for both to make sure that he had everything he needed.

He grabbed the scribbled note with the a car registration number on it and examined it once more to learn it by heart. He left his car in the car park.

He went round the entire car park looking at all silver cars. There was no match. He was disappointed but entered the shop, list in hand, and filled his trolley. He added meringues and some pink tulips for Rebecca

Tom asked the girl at the check-out, if she could tell him if she had a colleague called Valerie. She smiled and looked up at him telling him that she could not say as she had not worked there for long, but suggested he enquired at the information desk?

Tom steered his trolley with the two plastic carrier

bags across to the lady behind the information counter and asked her the same question. Tom was examined from top to toe with a suspicious glare but he got the answer he wanted. There were two cashiers named Valerie but the lady did not know if either of them had red hair or any nicknames. Tom thanked her and left the shop. He opened the boot of his car put the food away and marched the trolley back to where it belonged before making another tour of the car park. He had not been able to ask when these two "Valeries" were on duty. Tom had felt like a dirty old man in front of the information desk.

When he came back to the car and stopped in front of it making a last glance, he realized that he was being followed. One of the security guards was watching him and probably had been for some time. Tom felt like a criminal. He opened the car and drove off to hide in his own house, needing the company of Rebecca. What was he putting himself through? Why was it that he was concerned about what other people thought of him and his actions, but he had not done anything wrong. He did not mean to upset anybody so why did he feel guilty?

Tom was pleased to get back home. Rebecca was told of the visit to the surgery. He did not tell her everything, but he did tell her how awful he had felt when asking for Valerie at the information desk in the supermarket. Tom let her know that there were no less than two checkout cashiers called that name working there. That was at least something.

Rebecca told him that he had looked so upset when he came into the kitchen with the shopping and the lovely flowers that she had thought that he had bad news from the doctor.

'Tom, when you look for this Vallie, you have to be discreet. You have to be careful not to be taken for a mad man or a sex maniac. There are so many odd people out there that we don't need another one walking around.' In saying this Rebecca smilingly gave him a hug.

'While you were out there chasing other women I talked to Anna and we are invited to dinner tomorrow night.'

Tom kept the secret about examining the cars in the park from Rebecca nor did he tell her that he was going on a bus tour the following day.

Rebecca did not tell Tom that she had had a long discussion on the phone with Anna, who was given full details of Tom's recurrent nightmare. In the end Anna became silent and now when Rebecca returned to their conversation she recalled that Anna had said something about this nightmare. Hadn't she absentmindedly said that it was "vaguely familiar"? Anna had said that although she couldn't pin point why, she had heard something similar or perhaps read about something like the nightmare. Rebecca became excited thinking about what her friend had told her. If she had heard or read something, Tom might have heard or read the same thing. He could have become upset and therefore dreamed about it. This was not too far fetched, was it? Rebecca had not been with him 24 hours a day when he was in hospital. A nurse might have talked about something that had penetrated Tom's mind. This could be the solution. She had to talk to Anna about it later on.

Tom had his usual afternoon nap, then they took Mozart out for a walk before 'drinkies' time, news and dinner. It had been a splendid day and it was still warm.

It had been a day of many things happening. Mostly bad news, Rebecca thought, but perhaps not that bad when she reflected on their day. Tom was healthy. He had managed to find out that there were two ladies working at ASDA named Valerie and she had Anna's remarks to keep her spirits up.

They had enjoyed the chicken cooked in a curry sauce served with wild rice and the usual mixed salad on the side with a glass of red wine. The vanilla ice cream sprinkled with ordinary instant coffee granules had been a success too. It was a delight to cook for one another. They liked their food. To eat was not only about good food. To them it was a festive ritual.

Before bedtime, Tom opened the kitchen door to let the dog out but in so doing he stepped outside, looking up at the stars in the black silky sky, like the rice they had just eaten. He knew that if he concentrated a little he would make out the pattern of these twinkling lights but he could not be bothered. Instead he lowered his gaze towards the grounds and walked out to the middle of the well manicured lawn.

To breathe the fresh night air was a good way of ending a tiring day. He turned around, whistled softly for the dog and they re-entered the house for the night.

Rebecca woke up with a start. She felt helpless seeing Tom drenched with perspiration night after night, his eyes staring past her into infinity, eyes that did not see. The dream was obviously cold and terribly real to him. She could almost sense his despair.

Her heart was pounding, nearly pacing out of her chest.

She stroked his forehead, talking to him in a soothing

voice, before she left the bed to fetch a towel to wipe his back.

Before he was aware of her being there with him, and that he had not been crushed by this monstrous tractor he had a tightness to his mouth. It was not only despair she could see but also determination, a sort of tense anticipation. She watched his face and his eyes and tried to read his body language. She was able to do this as she knew the pattern by now. Tom was not going to give up that easily.. The line around his mouth and the creases round

his eyes were there but he held his fists tight. He was going to fight this dream.

The next morning was another sunny day. It was perfect weather for golf.

Tom looked tired, with dark half moon shaped shadows under his eyes. 'Perhaps I look as worn out as Tom,' she thought, but he had been through much more than she had. Both of them worried but his sleep was disturbed for longer. In his nightmare he probably fought. That in itself was tiring and she did not know for how long he was awake after they had switched off the light.

They got out of bed at the same time. Tom did his daily exercises. He walked the dog and Rebecca prepared their fruit salad with the natural yogurt, tea and coffee. The Times had arrived and they sat down at the table, he reading and she doing Su DoKu. They had never talked much over breakfast. It was wonderful to eat in silence. A good way to begin a day.

Rebecca rose from the table and returned to the bathroom to make herself ready to leave for her game of golf. Tom stood up and gave his wife one of his bear hugs and promised her that he would have lunch ready when she returned. He told her to keep her eye on the ball.

Tom cleared the kitchen and made minestrone soup for lunch before he bid Mozart farewell for a few hours. He grabbed his wallet and checked once again that he had the bus pass with him before leaving the house. It was good to know that Rebecca had taken her own set of keys. He told himself that he could relax, but he was as tight as a rubber band stretched to bursting point.

He got on the first bus that came along and chose a window seat upstairs to give himself a good view. There were mostly older people travelling at this time of day with school children already in school. He was on his own for quite some time on the upper level. He watched the people getting on and off and those on the pavement and on the roadside. From where he was he carefully examined the areas they passed and made notes. When he saw something he recognized but did not know anything about, he wrote a reminder to ask somebody for information.

Suddenly he straightened up in his seat. He saw two girls on the opposite side of the road queuing to get on another bus going in the opposite direction. He stared at these two "bomb- shells": Blond long hair, straight as straw. Without doubt they were identical twins. They were dressed in black from top to toe, as if they were in mourning Tom thought, but nowadays girls often did dress in black. There was something sad about these girls wearing black shirts and jackets, black tight trousers- too tight - and high heeled shoes with bags to match, big bulky black handbags. One of the girls had put a black ribbon in her hair. Yes, that was what had made Tom thinking of mourning! This black ribbon in the blond hair!

He was cross with himself that he had chosen to sit upstairs in the bus. He had not had a chance to get off and catch the bus the girls were taking. The only thing he could do was to get off at the next stop and take a bus back and try following these girls. He stood up to go downstairs when he thought better of it. Instead he wrote down at which bus stop this had taken place and the number of the bus the girls had taken. He would have to come back another day and try to catch up with them. He looked around but did not think he had been here before.

The twins were heavily built and in their late teens. He felt that he knew them well. They looked like the photo of Susan that Rebecca had brought to him at the hospital. Tom was thinking hard trying to place them. He could feel that they were special to him and his heart had jumped almost into his mouth when he had spotted them. He felt strongly about them in a strange way. It was a bond of love for them. But how on earth could that be? He did not understand the pang that had hit him at the sighting.

He could not get the girls out of his mind. Who were they and why did he have such feelings for them? Could he talk about them to Rebecca? What was he going to do? He closed his eyes for a second, but was startled by a young man with a rucksack on one shoulder asking him in a friendly way if he was feeling all right. Tom smiled up to the stranger standing in the aisle next to him and said that he was fine. He realized that he must have looked pale and with his eyes closed unwell.

Tom persisted with his tour all the way around the circular bus route and got off where he had started. The bus driver looked him up and down. He shook his head slightly as Tom left. Tom did not notice this which was lucky. If he had seen the driver examining him, Tom would have felt embarrassed.

Why did these girls touch a sensitive spot in his heart? He could not say that he was enamoured by their appearance. He was sure that they would never have attracted his attention if he had not recognized them.

Returning home, he sat down with a glass of water, closing his eyes. He remembered that they were wearing contact lenses. There was no way he could have seen that from where he was sitting on the bus. He could not tell if anybody was using lenses even if he was standing close enough to have a conversation and staring straight into somebody's eyes. Furthermore he was certain that they had straightened their hair. Their natural hair was thick and softly waved in the way he had always liked to see it. Where were his thoughts taking him? He stood up abruptly, looked at his watch and took the lead from its place and told Mozart that it was time for "walkies."

Absentmindedly, Tom walked the dog. He could sense that he knew the girl's names but this information was hidden further back in his mind. It would come eventually, but now when he tried to find it, it did not emerge. He would probably wake up in the middle of the night remembering.

When Tom and the dog returned to the house, it was time to get lunch ready as he had promised.

He laid the table, heated the soup, and prepared a salad. The cheese was already on a plate in the middle of the table, warming to room temperature to enhance its creamy texture. It was Gorgonzola.

By the time Tom heard the gate and the car, he had not made up his mind how much to tell Rebecca If he told her about the bus journey, he would have to explain why he had made it and if he told her about the two girls, he had to tell her the rest. He was not ready to let her know how he had felt when he had seen the twins. It might hurt her and he did not know why he knew them.

'Rebecca, how was your game today? Played well did you? Who did you play with?' he asked cheerily.

Rebecca burst out laughing and told him that he had to ask her one question at a time.

She had not made a fool of herself. She confessed to great difficulty getting out one bunker. Tom was taken hole by hole round the course. Rebecca had so much to tell him and she was full of it.

'So what have you been doing?' Rebecca enquired.

'I have taken Mozart for a walk and prepared your lunch. The weather has been fantastic hasn't it?'

Nothing more was said about the morning. Tom was pleased with himself for getting out of the dilemma without having had to lie. The more he thought about his morning experience the less he understood. He had felt sheer panic for a short while on the bus. How was it possible for him to have warm feelings for those twins? His heart had jumped with joy when he had seen them. What on earth was the matter with him? They were only young girls, for heaven's sake. What had happened to him during his time in the coma? He had never turned his head when he saw blonde girls. Well, that was not quite true. Of course he had admired good looking well dressed, slim, beautiful or pretty girls but that was normal for a man. What he had felt for these plump twins however could not be explained as normal, not even to himself. He was terrified by his own feelings.

Tom went into the bathroom after they had cleared the kitchen. He looked at his reflection in the mirror. He took his time, noticing the tense lines around his mouth. He thought of himself as an old man, something he had never done before. He was not as pale as he had been when he had been discharged from the hospital and not as thin either, but with the dark half moons under each eye and with more creases than he could remember, he did look old. He told the man looking back into his eyes that he hoped that he had not become a dirty old man.

'Are you all right Tom? You were in the bathroom for such a long time,' Rebecca asked when Tom reappeared in front of her.

'I was contemplating in front of the mirror. I have grown old lately, haven't I? To be as thin as this doesn't become me and my hair has gone grey.'

Rebecca looked up from her book and told him that they had both aged a lot since his fall.

'Worries do that to people, Tom. Don't tell me that you are becoming a peacock. You look distinguished, and I love you, so stop worrying.'

Tom bent down and kissed her. He told her that if she did not mind he would like to put his feet up for half an hour.

It was easier to tell somebody else not to worry. She herself was worried sick but she tried to suppress her feelings. She was lucky to have Anna to confide in. It was a female thing to be able to talk things through with a friend, a trustworthy friend, to unburden her racing thoughts and to share her fears. She needed her friend to help her to cope with the emotional impact she went through every night when Tom woke her up with his nightmare. She did not want Tom, or James for that matter, to become aware of how worried she was. Sometimes she thought that what she was going through now was even worse than what she had endured when Tom was lying in his hospital bed. The difference she told herself, was that she was not in charge then. She had put everything in other people's hands. She had not been in charge and therefore was more relaxed than she was now.

Today, when she should be able to change things for the better, to be of more help to Tom, she could not do it. People said about her then, that she was a strong woman but what would they have to say if they knew how much she had cried and how much she still did? No, she did not consider herself to be anything but stubborn. Today she had sensed in Tom that something had happened to him, something he did not want to tell her and she had not had the courage to ask him. Was he scared of how she would have reacted if he had told her more? Why was he holding back? Did he not trust her anymore? This was too terrible to even consider. She hoped he did not do anything foolish behind her back because if he did she was not sure she could cope with yet another situation. So why did not she put him against the wall and ask him to tell her the truth and nothing but the truth? She must be frightened of what he might have to tell her or even worse, scared of realizing that he was lying straight into her face. Why did life have to be so complicated? Why did love have to be so complicated?

She remembered when James and Edward had been about ten years old and had made a short video film. It had been about a vehicle, a banana with satsumas as wheels, and this "thing" was driving around killing people, smashing clay figures flat into the ground. She had asked James why they had to make a film with so much killing in it, could they not make it a nice love story instead?

James had smiled saying 'But mum, love has to be explained and it is complicated. You see everybody understand violence. That is easy.'

How right he had been. Love is complicated. We make it complicated.

What was she going to do? Was she going to leave it and pretend that everything was all right like Tom was obviously doing or was she going to do something about it?

What could she do, and when? She could hide behind a book and let the written word take over her life. She could continue to escape into other people's fantasy and let the author take her for a ride. However, she had to remember that not taking action could be fatal for their "together-life" and for their future. She sighed and knew the answer. She had known the answer all the time, but she did not want to admit it. The only thing was when and how?

She looked at the sleeping man on the sofa. There was a tiny smile on his face. 'What was he dreaming of? Whom was he thinking of?' she wondered. It most certainly was nothing to do with his night terrors. Was she becoming a jealous woman? Oh not that, and not because of those stupid dreams. She decided there and then, that she would give Tom the chance to tell her. She would give him a few more days before talking seriously to him A few days for him to sort himself out. She was a coward.

She got up and went into the kitchen. The dog followed her. The kettle was already filled so the only thing she had to do was to press the switch. Tom was going to be woken up to a nice cup of tea and she would have a cup of coffee to keep him company.

He was awake when she returned to the living room, cups in hand and dog on tow. She looked at Tom and asked if he had had a good nap. He told her that he had.

'Rebecca, I had an extraordinary dream. About children in a pink bedroom. Strange, but it was so clear to me. I realize that I do dream in colours. Somebody asked me that once if my dreams were in black and white or in colours. I remember that I did not know then, but I do now. That room was a soft pink.'

'Yes? Well, James' room has never been pink, that's for sure. Whose children do we know who have had a pink bedroom? It must be a room belonging to a girl.' Rebecca said.

Tom could not think straight. He wondered if his sister had been sleeping in a pink room. He could not remember. That would be a possible solution. Too easy may be, but he had to ask his friends if their children had had pink bedrooms. Why? Did it really matter? He had never been able to find out what his dreams had been about before his accident, so why bother now? Why take it so seriously?

He looked at Rebecca with eyebrows lifted. She agreed with him. Why had everything after his accident have to be explained? She smiled back to him and they finished their drinks.

'Are you coming with me and the dog or have you had enough of walking on the golf course this morning?'

'I am coming with you, but surely if you and Mozart had a good walk this morning he doesn't need a long one this afternoon. Let's get moving. We are out for dinner tonight, remember.'

Tom had to admit that he had forgotten about this evening.

As predicted Mozart did not get a long walk. Rebecca was in good spirits and talked a lot. Tom tried to relax. There was nothing he could do at the moment, so why get all uptight?

Before they left for dinner Tom let Mozart out into the garden. Tom also went out there and once again he looked up into the sky as if the solution to his problems could be found there.

The sunset was beautiful. Tom was amazed how colourful the sky was made by the aftermath of the sun. The sun was no longer there to be seen but the mixture of pink and orange was radiant. It made him happy to see such a wonderful splash of colours. He admired this mixture. 'Whenever did orange and pink go together? Never, so what made a sunset or a sunrise look so fantastic. The mixture of these two tints would not be seen anywhere other than at dawn and at dusk. Rebecca would not wear a pink blouse and an orange pair of trousers or skirt, would she? Of course not, because these colours did not go together and yet, here he was standing admiring the sky, breath taken by its beauty. Strange. This meant that they were going to have another gorgeous day tomorrow."Red sky at night, shepherds delight."

The shadows were getting longer. They would soon disappear and the darkness of the night would take over. He thought of the book "Daddy Long-Legs" and saw the little girl's imagination in front of him. He turned round with a smile on his face, whistled for the dog and entered the house, but not before he had noticed that the garden needed attention. He had to do something tomorrow about the dead heading and tidying the daffodils, otherwise this garden would look abandoned and unloved.

CHAPTER 19

Tom and Rebecca took the car to Anna and Eric as they were late. Tom would drive back and therefore keep to only one glass of wine.

He was wearing a shirt and a sweater in navy blue to match his new pair of jeans. Rebecca, on the other hand had chosen a pair of brown slacks and an orange roll neck. Her hair was brushed and shiny. Tom looked at her and told her how lucky he was to have such a beautiful wife.

As they had left the house, Rebecca had looked back closing the gate behind the car. She noticed Mozart standing there on the other side of the glass kitchen door watching her. He looked so lonely that she felt a prick of conscience. She lifted her hand and waved to him. She smiled realizing that the dog would not understand the gesture.

Anna greeted them dressed in jeans and a pink sweater Eric was dressed in the same navy blue as Tom. Anna had come out from the kitchen when she heard them talking to Eric. Her pinafore was one with jokes on it. Tom commented on it. A good way to start an evening.

With drinks in hand, they looked out through the dining room french doors into the lovely garden. They had dead-headed their daffodils and the tulips which had already performed their ritual colour dance. This garden showed no signs of neglect. It was indeed neat and tidy. It had a small pond with water running into it and some goldfish were darting around the lilies. He remembered that they had to put some strings and some netting over it to keep the heron away. Tom told Eric that the sound of water running into the pond made him needing the gents.

Tom had to get organized. He enjoyed his tonic with lemon. It did not matter whether there was gin in his drink or not. He did prefer a whisky but tonight was Rebecca's evening and he had promised her that he would drive her home.

Tom and Eric sat down and started talking about golf, agreeing to play together.

'We could play a few holes and see how you are getting on Tom, and then have lunch at the club.' Eric suggested.

They decided to give it a try. They could make up their minds when the weather forecast indicated that it was going to be a good day for it.

Anna was in the kitchen preparing the meal or rather putting the finishing touches to the food. She had decided to make it easy so as a starter she served melon and Parma ham. For the main course grilled salmon fillets and an orange sauce, boiled potatoes and vegetables.

Rebecca helped Anna to put the starter on the table, but most of all she kept her company. The orange sauce smelled delicious The two friends talked about everything that was on their minds. Anna wanted to know if Rebecca felt more relaxed.

She was told about Tom's latest strange dream.

'A pink bedroom! Have you heard anything as absurd as that, Anna? I mean, he is a man and has got a son - neither of them is likely to have been brought up in a pink room. I know that James certainly wasn't. Did any of your children sleep in a pink bedroom?' Rebecca asked.

'No. Their bedrooms had off white walls with colourful pictures on the walls and curtains, bed covers and cushions with bright patterns. How about Tom's sister? He did have a sister, didn't he? It wouldn't be surprising if he had dreams about her, would it? I think you make too much of Tom's behaviour. You don't mind me saying this? I understand that you are worried after all you two have been through. Tom must have had strange dreams before his accident but didn't talk about them. We have strange and horrible nightmares sometimes. Try to relax Rebecca. I don't mean to patronize you but I worry because you worry too much. You'll make yourself ill.' Anna went up to her friend and hugged her.

'I believe every word you say Rebecca, but it isn't that. I think you might be over protective. I think you are scared and <u>look</u> for changes. You have become over sensitive. How shall I put it for you to understand what I mean? You are frightened that there could be something wrong with Tom because of his head injury or as a consequence of having been in a coma for so long. I have a feeling that you are looking for odd and strange things about him because you love him and care about him. If I am wrong please tell me.' Anna continued.

'You are probably right,' agreed Rebecca ' but there are things about Tom that I don't recognize, or as I have told you before, strange remarks or questions which I wish I could find explanations for. I promise you that I'll try to relax.'

The four of them had the most wonderful evening together. After the main course they enjoyed the cheese board with the remains of the claret, and then finally the pudding. Rebecca knew that in Scotland the pudding was usually served before the cheese, but she could not adapt to this drinking red wine after a sweet dish.

They left the dining room to sit in more comfortable chairs to have their coffee and After Eight Mints.

Anna and Rebecca sat next to one another on the settee. Eric looked up and told them that they had obviously not discussed what to wear. The girls looked surprised. Anna asked what he meant by this remark.

Eric laughed and told them that they did not match. They clashed. 'One pink girl sitting next to brigh orange doesn't go.'

Anna and Rebecca examined one another. Eric was right. They did not match.

Tom told them about his thoughts of tonight's sunset and the beautiful mixture of orange and pink and this discussion carried them through different memories.

In the end it became high time for bed and Rebecca and Tom bid their friends good night. More than four hours of conversation about children, gardening, food, colour scheme and the troubled world they were living in had made them tired, but it had raised their spirits and put them in a good mood.

It was dark but as they said the nights were getting shorter, leaving the days to be longer and longer. Summer was quickly approaching and if they were not careful they would miss the whole spring season with a blink of an eye.

Tom turned to his wife and asked her what she had thought of the salmon and the orange sauce. 'Wasn't that absolutely divine?' Tom said.

Tom was going to take Mozart out for a short walk. Rebecca wanted to come with them as it was such a lovely night. They walked arm in arm in silence. There was hardly any wind and a strange feeling enveloped the couple. Rebecca felt such a tenderness towards Tom and was so happy. A wave of love for him swept her off her feet and through her body. She felt warm and cosy.

They made passionate love that night going about it carefully and slowly. Everything was perfect and lying in their bed close to one another Tom turned towards his wife kissing her gently.

'Thank you for this evening. I didn't think I was going to be able to make love tonight being tired but you made it possible. You are a clever girl and a good lover. You have always been splendid in bed. I must have done something good in my life to deserve you.'

'Tom what on earth are you talking about? Such nonsense. To make love you have to be two. You are an extremely good lover yourself.' she responded.

She noticed the untidy pile of clothes as she later returned from the bathroom. Rebecca smiled and thought it was lucky that James was not living at home anymore. Tonight, she could leave the pile as it was till the following morning. A bliss to be allowed to go straight back to bed. Not that she did not miss James, but everything has its time and place and children should never stay living with parents for too long.

Tom woke up a couple of hours later. He was yet again gasping for air, looking terrified and bathed in sweat. His body was cold and shone as if he were made of marble. He sat up straight and stiff as a poker. Tom could have been mistaken for a statue until he slowly moved his head looking at the woman next to him. He started to shiver.

Rebecca comforted him and when he had calmed

down she made him put his arms up in the air to take his soaked pyjamas jacket off. She collected a few towels from the linen cupboard, wiped him dry and then spread out a clean and dry bath towel on top of the wet sheet so that he would not catch a cold.

After this terrible dream, he was like a child wanting to keep close to her for some time until he fell asleep again. She usually got too warm as Tom felt like a hot water bottle as soon as he got his normal body temperature back. She listened for his even breathing and when she knew he was fast asleep, she turned away from him to regain her own side of the bed. She tried to follow him into the night but had to count masses of sheep. Once she had started to think about these sheep jumping over a fence. They were all white, but then she started wondering where they were going and where could they come from? After that she could get no peace counting them. She started to count Tom's breathing instead. Tonight he had been breathing naturally for a long time before she finally relaxed and fell into a merciful sleep.

In the morning Rebecca woke up with a start. She had heard Tom letting out a frightful scream. It had not been a loud scream, but it had woken her up. She rushed into the bathroom prepared to see him splashed out on the floor. He was standing up with both hands leaning heavily on the washbasin looking awful.

He was staring into the mirror. Rebecca looked at his reflection and saw a pale face with big frightened eyes looking back at them.

Tom's hair was standing up as if he had seen a ghost. She thought he was feeling sick as he looked it, and asked how he was. His eyes turned from watching his own face to looking into her face through the mirror's reflection.

He told her that he was not ill, although he felt slightly sick because he had just seen a ghost in this mirror. He looked back into the glass examining his own face and then at hers. He shook his head, before he turned away from the mirror to face Rebecca in person.

'Darling, it was terrible. I swear to God that I saw somebody in this mirror and that person wasn't me, but another man. Have you ever had a similar experience?'

She looked back at him, stroking his hair back from his face to flatten it slightly. She caressed his face with both hands on either side of his stricken face, and talked soothingly to him as she did every night.

'Tom, my dear, dear Tom. We all see other faces when we get out of bed too early and half asleep. Sometimes looking at my reflection in this mirror I see exactly what I look like and that could scare me to death. I wonder sometimes seeing myself wrinkled like a prune, hair on end and looking as if I had had a bad night, and I ask myself what on earth can you possibly see in me?'

Tom started to explain what he had seen, but soon let it go because nobody would understand, not even Rebecca. And when she had told him about her own experience from looking at reflections in the mirror, he was not sure what he had seen and why it had scared him half to death. He smiled back at her face, kissed her on her lips and said how sorry he was to have woken her up from her sweet dreams.

Rebecca took off the night's sheets from the bed to be washed and she left the mattress bare to be properly aired. She would wash their towels and sheets with the white underwear from the laundry basket.

She watched Tom and noticed that he could not help himself looking in the mirror more often than usual. She smiled at him and told him how attractive he was. Tom smiled back and gave her a bear cuddle telling her that she was awful to him. He leaned over her and placed a tender kiss on her neck. Rebecca pushed him away with a smile and told him that he had better let her go otherwise there would be no breakfast.

Tom opened the curtains and let out a disappointed. 'Oh no!'

Rebecca came over to where he was standing by the window. It was milky white out there. Everything was gone. There was nothing to be seen but soft, wet, white mist.

'What a sad sight. I had hoped for another sunny day. Last night's sky was so promising. There is much to do in the garden. I have been looking at these dead daffodils for a few days now and had decided to take care of them today. A haar usually stays for two to three days. Well, well cannot be helped, the dog will have to have his walk anyway. I'll let him out in the garden this morning to take him out for a walk later on as this mist might have lifted a little by then. I am looking forward to that promised breakfast. I'll put the kettle on and let Mozart out.'

Rebecca heard the kettle boiling but no sign of Tom. She could not see anything in the garden but she supposed the dog and master were out there somewhere. It felt chilly. She was not worried. Tom was probably not quite awake. What a silly thing to think that he had seen a ghost in the bathroom mirror when all there was his own face. She shook her head smiling at the thought. A grown up man afraid of ghosts.

Tom was in the garden. He was enveloped by the

white mist and by his thoughts. He tried to get the image from the mirror back into his mind but the only reflection he could get was that of his own face. He thought that he must be going mad. Of course there could be no other image there than of the person looking into it. He started walking back to the kitchen door when he stopped dead. That was it! He had seen his own face in the mirror! It had been his reflection in it, but of course. The thing was that he had <u>expected</u> to see another face in that mirror. That was what had scared him. He thought he had seen a ghost but it had been the face of himself in it and not a face, which he had <u>expected</u> it to be. That was why he thought he had seen somebody else, a stranger. Oh God, this was getting too complicated. He closed his eyes standing motionless. He tried to recollect the detail of the face he had thought should have been meeting his eyes. He was certain that this image had been of another man. It could have had something to do with his nightmare. He decided not to tell Rebecca. It had scared him at the time.

He walked on towards the kitchen door. He could hear Rebecca preparing their breakfast. He was often starving after a good evening with lots of food.

The mist could not have been lingering for too long as the paper arrived in the letterbox with a thump and the milk was on their doorstep.

He opened the front door and brought the bottles back in and put them into the fridge after having wiped them with a piece of kitchen towel. The Times he put on the table and helped Rebecca to serve their breakfast. He reached out and squeezed his wife's hand on the table top. She looked lovely and he told her so.

Tom had planned to do so much during the day, but

this weather put a stop to it. He had wanted to go on a bus tour again, and to do some work in the garden. When he had been to Anna and Eric's last night and saw how neat and tidy everything was around their beautiful garden, he had longed to get cracking with the daffodils. The edges around the lawn had to be cut properly too.

He had to be patient and wait until Rebecca had a golfing morning, a lunch out or something else away from home and when the mist had gone. He could not play golf with Eric either with this haar lingering.

After having read the paper, listened to the news and finished his breakfast, he went for a walk with Mozart. Rebecca was happy to stay at home with the washing and to make up their bed with fresh sheets. She had a few letters to write and emails to send and the thank you note to Anna and Eric.

Tom decided to take Mozart out and to walk somewhere different. He turned to the right directly out of the gate instead of his usual left. It was not as good walking or as peaceful along this stretch but a change would cheer him up.

There was no traffic on a morning like this, or was it because he had started out later today? He did not know, but the school run was over by this time. This mist did not only put everything away out of sight, but it muffled the noise from the cars. It was nearly as if there was snow on the ground and still snowing. That made everything much quieter too.

As there was not much else he could do he had told Rebecca that he would go for a slightly longer walk. It would do both dog and master good to exercise. In any case they ended up in the big parking area outside ASDA.

Tom walked around checking the number plates of the silver Hondas he could see. He walked the parking from row to row until he realized that he was followed by the same attendant that had been looking at him the other day. Tom felt uncomfortable and had to leave out the last row of cars. It was lucky that there were not many shoppers. He had been watched and recognized, which was not what he wished for. He would have done anything to have gone unnoticed, but the damage was done and he had to be more careful in the future. Perhaps he should not walk around the parked cars, but only drive through one or two rows to pretend he was looking for a suitable space. He could then later on walk through another row going into the shop, and to choose another way back to his car. This way he would not be able to look through all the cars, but it could not be helped. He turned around to start walking back the way he had come. He did not even enter the supermarket.

When they left he did not turn towards home but walked in the opposite direction. The village was getting further away but a more neglected looking area soon appeared.

If it had not been for the mist this morning, Tom might have seen the twins walking on the other side of the road. As it was, they have followed the same road in the same direction but on the opposite pavement. This went on for a while until Tom decided that it must be high time to turn round and walk back home. It was lunchtime and if they did not get a move on and step up the pace Rebecca would be worried.

If Tom had been able to see clearly across the road he would have seen the girls turning away from the main road up a footpath. He had been so close in this mist. In a way it was lucky that he did not know. What could he have done, if he had seen them?

Mozart and Tom could smell the onion soup as they entered the gate. He realized that he was starving. This walk had taken them further away then they had walked before.

Rebecca commented on the timing when Tom kissed her. Lunch was ready.

She had put the sheets in the drier and asked Tom to help her to fold them so she would be able to iron them later.

By the time they had eaten, the mist had lifted a little and Tom said that he wanted to do some dead-heading before he had his daily nap, although he was exhausted after his walk.

Rebecca joined him, and they knotted the daffodils foliage together. It was wonderful to work side by side in the garden and in spite of the weather they enjoyed what they were doing.

They talked about the time in the autumn when they had put down these daffodils and tulips and how beautiful it was this spring.

Mozart stayed inside the kitchen door which was left ajar for him to make his own choice. The damp mist was chilly and Rebecca and Tom were properly dressed for gardening. She was wearing her woolly hat to keep warm. How different the temperature and the weather was living in the UK! It was never boring living in a country with four seasons in a day.

Rebecca stood up trying to stretch out her back from the bent position and said to Tom that they must be mad gardening in this kind of weather. There had been so many lovely days without either of them having lifted any green fingers. Tom had cut the grass but that was all. 'This is what happens when you are lazy and leave for tomorrow what you could do today.' she scolded

'We are not leaving work that we can do today for tomorrow, but I think it's time to pack it in and swop this work for a nice cup of tea or coffee. I have had enough, at least my back has.' complained Tom.

After tea and coffee Tom had his nap. Rebecca did the ironing before she allowed herself to sit down in a comfy chair to read. She has always loved this time of the day. When James was little he had been asleep in the afternoons. Now Tom was her baby.

The house was quiet and peaceful.

Before she had settled down to read, it occurred to her, that she had not written anything in her diary for days. She took it out from its hiding place and wrote about Tom's experience this morning and the ghost in the bathroom mirror and how scared he had been. If it had not been such a strange thing to happen to a man, it could have been funny.

Rebecca sat for a little while by the kitchen table, pen in hand and the writing book in front of her, only staring into space thinking about what Anna had told her last night. Perhaps she did overreact? Perhaps she was over protective? She knew that she had been with James and still was, so if she was over protective with Tom she would not be surprised. He did make odd remarks which were disturbing. She could not get over either "the cat"' nor "the awful missing painting", which he had talked about. Tom was a changed man. What about his choice of sport he wished to watch on television and even in the middle of the day? She shook her head and thought that most things could be explained by his hospital experiences. She told herself to relax and to leave things. She left the table and went back into their bedroom where she hid her diary. Would she ever be able to show Tom what she had written?

Rebecca went back to her reading. She was pleased to have found a good book to take her away somewhere else, to make her forget and disappear to other places and to meet other people. This book was taking her to Australia. They had been there a few years ago. Sydney was great and so was Port Douglas. In Port Douglas they met a couple who were about to get married, and invited Tom and Rebecca to join the newly weds for dinner in a restaurant on the eve of their wedding day. It was a splendid evening with a lot to drink, whiskey, champagne and wine. Luckily Tom had said no thanks to the offered brandy with the coffee.

Tom told the bride and groom that as they stayed in the same hotel he would take the four of them home. It was just down the road. As they turned down towards the entrance of the hotel car park, the police emerged from a lay by and stopped them. Tom had to answer questions about the car. Had he had anything to drink, and when did he have his last drink? He had to blow into a breathalyser and when the policeman saw the result he went off to his colleague and they were discussing for such a long time that the four in the car became worried. Tom had told the policeman that he was driving a bride and groom back to the hotel. The constable then looked into the back of the car and saw the couple sitting there with a bouquet of flowers in the bride's lap.

They were holding their breath – as if it would make the slightest bit of difference.

Rebecca feared that Tom would have to spend the night in jail for drink driving. Tom had been honest though. He had told the police that he had been drinking, and that he had his last drink about an hour and a half ago which was true. After what seemed to be an age the policeman returned to the car and leaning through the driver's window said, that as Tom was close to the limit would he please drive straight to the hotel and not have another drink before he was back inside. He bid them good night and congratulated the couple in the backseat.

They had been lucky. Not another car in sight. Tom parked the car and they went into the bar and ordered coffee and brandy. What would life be without memories?

They had liked Port Douglas though she had preferred Sydney. Thinking of Australia and the travels she had made with Tom put her in a sad mood. Perhaps they would not be able to do such things anymore. Anyway, she straightened up and told herself that she was silly and selfish. How many couples had done as much as they had been able to do? 'Stop these thoughts, get a grip on yourself and do whatever is needed to get everything out of the life we are living now. Live in the present time and be grateful for what you have!' In a determined frame of mind she put her bookmark in the book she was reading, put the book away on the side table, stood up, put a smile on her face and went into the kitchen to put the kettle on.

She made tea for Tom and coffee for herself and tray in hand she returned to the living room to wake her husband. She was about to put the tray down, when Tom said 'hello darling'. She almost dropped the cups. She managed not to spill anything which must be considered as clever.

She turned her face towards Tom who met her with such a broad grin that it felt as if he was laughing at her. He looked like a schoolboy.

'Proud of yourself are you? You nearly scared me to death! Did you have a relaxed nap? As you can tell tea is ready.'

'Sorry darling. You know I don't try to frighten you deliberately. I seem to have had a relaxed sleep and for far too long. What have you been doing?'

'I have been reading and then I started to think about our experiences in Port Douglas, as the plot in this book takes place in Australia.' Rebecca answered.

'That was something I don't intend to do again, drink and drive I mean. We were lucky that time. Do we hear anything from the newly weds by the way? It was his second time around and they were in their early fifties weren't they?'

'We do get a Christmas card from them and they seem to be fine. It is wonderful to have these memories with you, Tom.'

Tom looked out of the French windows and realized that not only was it getting dark but it was still milky white out there. The weeping willow looked like a shadow in a dream world and with leaves wet from the dampness of the mist it looked ghostly.

'Anything worth watching on the television tonight? Do you know?'

'I could watch "Judy and Richard". It starts now, I

think. Wednesday is the day they discuss books, Anna told me. Do you mind?'

Tom became restless after he had finished his cup of tea and went into the kitchen, opened the door for the dog and examined the contents of the fridge. He asked Rebecca what she had planned for their dinner as he would like to start preparing their evening meal.

The chicken was already in the oven, well wrapped in foil to be roasted but she would love him to prepare the vegetables to go with it.

Rebecca finished watching her programme. Anna had been correct. It was about books. She was pleased to have remembered and been able to see it. She would get their list from Amazon and would try to read some of the proposed titles. Ten books seemed to be on their list. After dinner enjoyed in the dining room, wine with the meal, Tom phoned Eric to say that there would obviously not be any golf the following day.

Rebecca continued reading the book she had started earlier on and Tom watched some football.

They did not take Mozart out. It was dark and like the "London Pea Soup" out there - the foggy description in the detective stories with Sherlock Holmes. It was unpleasant in other words, and not the weather for walking. They let Mozart into the garden and had an early night.

They went through the same procedure every night following Tom's nightmare. Rebecca had to put dry sheets on the bed. She decided that she would stop ironing the top sheet.

Tom had gone to the bathroom. She stopped in the middle of what she was doing, as she realized that he was staring into the mirror again. She could see his reflection in the glass and the look of terror in his face. She had been frightened last night but she was not scared this time. Curiosity had taken over.

When they went back to bed neither mentioning the incident.

Tonight Rebecca went off to sleep long before Tom was relaxed enough to follow. His thoughts were everywhere. He had seen his own face, Tom's face, staring back at him in the mirror but he had expected another man's face to be there. Furthermore it was a man that he did not think he knew. He had jumped when he had met the reflection of himself, clean shaven and not a man with a beard. A man with a black beard! Tom had never been able to grow a beard as he did not have enough growth. He must have met this man somewhere and he must have made an impact on Tom or perhaps threatened him.

Tom thought that it might be this man who figured in his dream, although he never saw the man in this recurrent nightmare.

The next morning, Rebecca told Tom that she had forgotten about the ladies lunch she was planning to attend. It was in town so she would take the bus there around eleven and be back no later than four o'clock. So how would he spend his day she wondered? It was not the weather for golf, although the mist had lifted dramatically.

Tom told her he would pay a visit to ASDA to do some shopping and would take Mozart for his walk later. For lunch he would enjoy a quiche and a salad.

CHAPTER 20

Shortly after Rebecca left the house for the bus to town, Tom followed. He told the dog to jump into the car and off they went. Tom went along the same route as the bus and stopped for a minute to look at the bus stop, where he had seen the twin girls the other day. He had no feeling of recollection of the place more than that he had seen the two girls there.

He found a parking space not too far away and put money in the meter for two hours to be on the safe side. He opened the door for Mozart. Dog on the lead they walked down the street. He chose to walk up the main road following the bus route out of town in the opposite direction from where Rebecca's bus was going. He wanted to see where the girls could have come from when he suddenly spotted them.

His heart missed a beat. He had been passed by a silver Honda and he was fairly certain that it was the one he had been seeking.

The car was travelling fast and Tom had been taken by surprise. The car had appeared quickly and disappeared before Tom had noted the turn off where it had vanished. In fact Tom did not even know if it had turned off. He was excited but as he continued walking along the road, he had to admit that the car was gone and there was nothing he could do about it. He turned around and dog and master traced their way back along the pavement towards his own car.

He started to think about the silver Honda as he walked back. Perhaps the driver had been to the supermarket or had dropped Vallie off? It could be that this car belonged in this area, which would indicate that Vallie or her partner lived somewhere in the vicinity.

He quickly made it back to the car and turned his vehicle round to go shopping.

He remained sitting in the supermarket car park for a while contemplating what to do next. Should he leave Mozart where he was and go shopping or ought he to take the dog with him and leave him outside the entrance? As it was not a hot summer day he opted for the first choice. Tom opened the window slightly and left the dog locked in.

Tom did not have to walk along the rows of parked cars as he knew the Honda would not be there. It was with a sense of relief that he entered the store. He was nervous, but it felt good not to have given any reason for the guards to follow him.

He walked along the checkouts before he started shopping. He walked along between the shelves, stopping here and there to put something from his list into the trolley. Tom watched the staff. He did not think that he had missed any department. He finally went to the end of a queue to pay and pack what he had bought, and went back to Mozart who was waiting for him.

The dog was so pleased to see him that Tom was afraid he was going to injure himself as he was jumping up and down with his tail working overtime.

He hurriedly opened the car door and let the dog out to greet him. Tom bent down, cuddled and talked softly to Mozart before he put the carrier bags into the boot and Mozart into the back seat and drove off.

What Tom had failed to notice was that one of the guards had kept his eyes on "the man with a black dog."

Tom's presence would be noted whenever he went to the store. His persona had been observed. It could prove unlucky for Tom that he had spotted the silver Honda this particular morning and therefore would return more frequently. He toyed with the idea of confiding properly in Rebecca, but did not think anybody would be able to understand him. Not even his dear wife. How could anyone see things the way he did when he did not know what he was seeking? He was looking for answers to questions he did not know how to ask so how would it be possible for anyone else to understand?

Tom did not know how he felt or what he wanted. How could it be that he became frightened looking into mirrors and seeing himself but thinking that his face should have been somebody else's? Never mind seeing ghosts! It was as he himself was the ghost.

To be honest he was scared of who he had become. Perhaps he was like Doctor Jekyll and Mr Hyde? Was that what had happened to him or had he developed a split mind like a schizophrenic?

'Mozart, what the hell is wrong with me? What happened to me during the time I was in that hospital?' he shouted in frustration.

Tom drove the car home and through the gates. Closing them behind him he let the dog out before he walked up to the kitchen door to let himself in. Why did he not trust Doctor Smith, the doctor who had saved his life? What was it about her that made him not wish to talk to her? Was it because she had been abrupt with Rebecca rather than informative, and communicative? What was it that put him off her? He knew that he would have to go back and get some straight answers. He was going to try to work out his personal problems by himself. He had to get to the bottom of the story about Vallie. He wanted to know about these twin girls too. Who were they? Why did he feel an attachment to them? A recognition of closeness, of fondness? Surely it could not have anything to do with Susan? All these odd and strange questions and feelings. Would he ever get the answers he wanted? Did he wish to know the truth? He shuddered at the prospect of his last thought.

He put the quiche into the Aga, tossed a salad and looked through the mail.

As often there were a couple of letters from Sweden addressed to Rebecca. A pang of irrational jealousy hit him when he looked at these handwritten envelopes. Women had friends to talk to and they always seemed to be able to open their hearts easily. Not that he minded, but he wished he could do the same. He had a best friend in Malcolm but to tell him about what was going on in his head was impossible. No, he couldn't talk to anyone.

He felt distressed about his problems, and thought that he had to be careful not to turn into a frightened and miserable old man. He had to cheer up, at least in other people's company and especially for his family. He had become an unbalanced, over sensitive person. If he was lucky, his worries would turn out to be pure nonsense.

Tom heard the egg-timer bleeping. His lunch was ready. He told himself to take one day at a time and live for the present. Impossible he knew, as he had this horrible dream to solve, but he could always try his best.

He enjoyed his salad of fresh leaves, tomatoes, olives and mixed fresh vegetables sprinkled with olive oil, balsamic vinegar and some garlic. He sometimes liked to be alone at home. It was peaceful not to have any obligations, and to be able to eat whenever and whatever he fancied although he always missed having Rebecca around.

After lunch, Tom took the car and parked slightly further along the main road than he had done earlier. He was walking the dog again, but this time he turned off from his path into another small road lined with flats and smaller semi detached houses in a council estate. He walked for nearly two hours before they were back at the car. Tom had not noticed anything of interest. What a waste of parking meter money and time. He had however, saved up other areas to explore the following day. Mozart had a good brisk walk although he had to be kept on the lead.

Tom returned home. As he came closer he felt the warmth and sense of homecoming, which succeeded in making him happy. It was a wonderful feeling. Thinking of this, his problems seemed to evaporate and fly out through the back window, left slightly open to give Mozart some air.

Tom entered the house through the back door as usual. This door opened directly into the kitchen He was relieved to be at home in time for his afternoon cup of tea. He would drink it whilst watching football on the box.

Rebecca came home about an hour later. On her way into the snug she put the kettle on. She could hear the noise from the television.

Although she detested how Tom had started to watch football and become an almost obsessive fan, she silently pushed the door open and tenderly looked at the man asleep in the armchair. The match could not have been exciting then, she thought. She turned the television down little by little until she finally dared to switch it off completely without disturbing him. She returned to the boiling kettle. Rebecca brought her coffee with her into the living room and stopped in front of the French windows which were overlooking the garden. They had made a good job of tidying up in the mist.

It was wonderful to rest for a minute and feel the stillness entering her body. Soon the shadows would grow longer in the predicted twilight, and the dusk would turn day into evening and finally into night. She loved this garden and their home. The big stone house with its sheltered walled terrace was a fantastic feature. She knew that they had to start taking steps to move to a smaller property. It was a responsibility to have a house as old as this building and to maintain it would soon become more of a burden than a pleasure. It was with a sense of sadness she turned her back to it. Rebecca went into the snug to wake up Tom. It was a shame, but better for him not to let him sleep for too long during the day.

Rebecca had made Tom another cup of tea before she stroked his chin and started talking to him. It was lucky that she did not keep any cup in her hands. She had learned from previous mistakes. As she touched Tom he flung out his arm against her, and kicked one leg into the air. He had been in a deep sleep and had difficulty in waking up properly. His dream started to slip away from his mind although he tried to stop the images from leaving him completely. He muttered to himself as he came back to life again. Tom thought that he had seen something important in his dream, but it was gone before he could figure out what it was. He was absent minded for a while, trying to surface from his slumber but smiled up to Rebecca when he noticed her presence. He stretched out his hand to touch her with love when he realized that there were traces of tears in her eyes.

He sat up in the chair, took her hands in his and tried to focus, but she looked away.

'Rebecca, why have you been crying? Have I said something hurtful in my dream or didn't you have a good time with the church ladies' lunch today?'

'I am sorry Tom, but as you looked so peaceful in your sleep it came as a shock when you suddenly flung arms and legs into the air. I was startled, that's all. Did you have your nightmare?'

'No, I tried to hold on to something at the same time as I have a feeling that I tried hard to get rid of something else. I thought I had found an interesting information, but it vanished before I could get a grip on what it was. Did I hurt you?'

'I managed to keep out of reach after touching your chin. I only had a fright. Can you remember anything from your sleep?'

'The only thing I can remember is what I've just told you. It left me with a strange feeling of something important. Let's forget it for the time being Sometimes dreams surface again if you leave them alone. I am sorry that I scared you. You know I love you too much to ever want to hurt you.

Rebecca sat down in her armchair and told Tom about her time in town and Tom told her that he had been shopping, made lunch and walked the dog.

It is wonderful to have you back home and as dusk is closing in, how about a drink? What would you like?'

They sat in silence having their evening drink. It was

a lovely time of the day sitting together like this and to be able to relax in the company of one another.

On his way to bed after they had their dinner Tom opened the door to let the dog out. It was a lovely evening and he looked up at the stars wishing once again that he could remember their patterns, and the stories about them. He thought about how different the sky had looked when they had visited Australia with the constellations the opposite way around.

He left the kitchen and went out on to the lawn and took a deep breath.

He was pleased to be wearing his baggy corduroys. There was a nip in the air in the evenings. How he loved this garden. How could it ever be possible to leave it and to move? Tom knew that it had to be done sooner rather than later. If anything happened to him he could not leave Rebecca in this house on her own. He would not relax until they had moved and settled down in an other property.

Tom turned round with a big sigh and headed for the door which he had left ajar to let the evening air enter the kitchen. He did not have to whistle for Mozart. After having had a drink of water the dog went for his basket and settled down for the night. Tom bid the dog good night and wished that he could settle down as easily. Tom had begun to dread the nights because of the nightmare. He knew it would soon be haunting him in his sleep. He longed to have a dreamless night, an undisturbed sleep. He would give anything to leave his restless nights behind. Tom felt guilty each time he woke Rebecca up. He had to get rid of his recurrent black dream.

To be able to sleep peacefully through the night had

become a dream in itself. Tom hugged the dog and went into the bedroom to join his wife. Rebecca was already in bed reading whilst waiting for Tom to join her. She looked so relaxed and beautiful. The night passed as every night, but this time he was able to keep still in order not to wake Rebecca.

His side of the bed was soaked with his perspiration, but when he had calmed down he went into the bathroom, took off his pyjamas and slipped back into the bed naked. On top of the wet sheet he managed to put a dry towel.

Tom was pleased to wake up in the morning when the first rays of sun tried to enter the room between the curtains. Rebecca was fast asleep, when Tom got out of bed. He brought his clothes through to the kitchen where he dressed in order not to disturb her.

The kitchen looked pleasant in the sun and with the rays creeping into the room. He made himself a nice cup of tea and sat down at the table watching the sunbeam moving slowly but away across the floor. Summer was near. It gave him a great feeling of hope for the future. What was it that his mother so often had said to him when he had been troubled? He thought about it for a second, before he could recall her voice and her smile as she told him that there was always another spring, another summer. He felt a pang of sadness missing her and at once the silence around him became oppressive. Here he was, a grown up, soon to be an elderly man, missing his mother. It was pathetic.

His father had been strict but Tom missed him as well but not in the same way. He also wished his sister had been around.

Tom sighed, stood up and made a cup of coffee for

Rebecca. He brought it to her with her usual biscuit. He needed company.

Mozart looked at the scene in front of him. He stayed at the threshold waiting with anticipation for his morning walk. Tom had let him out into the garden, but that was not the same as a walk.

Tom talked to his wife and bent over her placing a kiss on her cheek. Her skin was warm, and relaxed from the sleep. She smelled of the Rebecca he adored. She was gorgeous with her hair framing the beautiful face and when she opened her grey eyes and saw him she gave him a smile to die for. He very nearly crept back into the warmth of the bed and her body, but resisted it.

Tom took Mozart out for a short walk while Rebecca prepared the breakfast. It was a pleasant day. When he had been out earlier in the morning he had noticed that the wisteria framing the French windows facing the terrace was starting to show its lavender blue. He loved this, but he knew that he would soon have to clear the terrace floor from the fallen petals. They did litter. He had made a point of admiring the polyanthus he had seen from the kitchen window earlier. The colours were breathtaking. He walked along the path into the Dell as it was fairly dry. What a difference it made to be able to do this walk from along the playing field.

He reached the little stone bridge. He walked on to it and stopped at its peak looking down at the peaty coloured water. He stared down watching it passing under his feet. Where he was standing, he thought of the days when they had played "Pooh Sticks" . James had been a small boy then and always won.

Tom knew how much Rebecca loved this old bridge.

She loved bridges, gates, window, doors and trees, most of which could be opened or closed. As she used to say to him, "open to opportunity".

Trees were different but to think of how long a tree had been growing to reach up into the sky, and what it had experienced on its way up there? What tales a tree could tell! It was a sin to chop one down, according to her.

This morning he lingered longer than he had anticipated. The weather was good and it was wonderful to wander along the muddy path through the Dell wood. He felt at peace. Perhaps he was soothed by the sound of the running water when he was walking along the river side or maybe it was because of the weather.

The insects loved this morning as well. There were clouds of them dancing in the beams of the sun. The bluebells covered the grounds with their heavenly colour.

He reluctantly whistled for the dog and walked back up the hill leaving the Dell behind and entered the gate to rejoin Rebecca. She had laid the table on the terrace and they enjoyed listening to the birdsong. It was a fantastic day to be alive. He kissed her on the mouth and squeezed her hand, still not breaking the spell by talking but smiling into one another's eyes.

They watched the blue tits examining one of the bird boxes. Then they lifted their eyes towards the Dell. There was the first spring cuckoo. It came from the North, which meant sorrow. They sat in silence.

To read the paper at this small table was a problem. In the end they left the table and brought the dirty dishes in to the dishwasher. The spell was gone.

Tom was going out to walk the dog to examine the

rest of the small roads where he had been the previous day. He did not tell Rebecca exactly what he was up to apart from walking the dog in the sunshine.

Rebecca had a lot to do in the house and some letters she could write sitting outside. She was going to play golf the following morning in a competition. Tom phoned Eric and they decided to play a few holes on Monday, weather permitting.

Tom took the car and drove further along the road before letting the dog out and starting their walk. He had decided to see if he could take Mozart along some of the side roads before turning back home.

It was warm with no wind. A perfect day for walking and for golf too if he had arranged to play.

Tom looked at the semi detached properties he passed. Some had lovely but small front gardens with colourful flowerpots, well maintained patches of lawn, flower beds and a painted front door, showed that in that house, there lived someone with green fingers, who loved and cared for their property.

A couple of garden gnomes half hidden behind a bush put a smile on his face although he had never liked ornaments in the garden. They look like toys but today these two fellows behind this bush had made him smile.

Mozart greeted dogs that stood behind closed gates barking. The dogs put their noses between the iron bars saying hello to one another but cats were everywhere and quickly ran off at the sight of them.

There were gardens that looked as if nobody had touched them for years. Grass and weeds were all that could be detected and the usual bins and even litter.

Tom and Mozart returned to the car without any success but as Tom was about to open the car for Mozart, he spotted the twins again. This time they had come off the bus and started to walk away from him. They were crossing the road.

He felt his excitement mounting. He locked the car and started to follow them at a respectable distance. He crossed the road and continued to walk, turning off the main road into a smaller side road following the path the girls were taking. Tom had not been here in his search for them or for Vallie, but he recognized a building he and the dog passed.

It had a strange extension and a square bow window upstairs. He remembered that he had thought it odd when it was added on. It was built almost as a covered balcony with a patio underneath it. He could not afford to stop to look more closely at the semi detached house now. He was too conscious of the girls in front of him and he did not want to lose sight of them.

The girls were dressed in identical denim skirts which were much too short, with black tops showing their midriffs. From where he was, he could see that if the tops had been cut any lower, the contents of their bras would have escaped.

The black high heeled boots were indoor boots, he guessed. Their blonde hair were not as straight as when he had first seen them. They carried a denim jacket over the straps of their black shoulder bags.

They were chatting as they walked along. Suddenly one of them turned round and looked straight at Tom. Tom smiled at them but did not get any smile back. The girls hesitated in front of one of the houses. Tom watched them as they opened the gate, stopping after they had closed it behind them.

Tom did not know what he wanted to do, or what he ought to do or say. It was his turn to hesitate slightly. The twins had not made any signs that they recognized him. Yet they did not walk up to the house but waited inside the closed gate pretending not to look at him. They only watched one another, One of them pretended not to be watching him. She kept an eye on him although she tried to conceal that she was observing him. Tom felt uncomfortable. He was pleased to have Mozart by his side.

Tom slowed down, but in the end he decided to walk on. He walked past another house before he stopped. In front of him was a cul de sac. The house at the bottom was a small detached white painted Scottish bungalow with an upstairs room. He turned towards it. He knew this building well! He must have known somebody living there. Tom remembered having planted the pine tree in that front garden. He knew he had. He had painted the house brilliant white although he would have preferred it in a softer off white. Tom kept staring at it and felt weak when he could recollect that it was called 'Number Thirteen'. It stood out from the other detached and semi detached properties as it was brilliant white and most of the others were boring grey.

There was no car in the front of the house. It looked as if nobody was at home. It seemed to be empty. He decided to be brave and opened the gate. He walked slowly up to the front door and pressed the bell. He could hear the signal echoing inside the house. Nobody answered the door as he had predicted. Standing on the doorstep, he was unsure of his feelings except for the certainty that he knew this house. He could tell any passers by about the indoor layout and colour scheme.

He turned round and noticed that the twins were back on the pavement and had been watching him but when they saw him looking at them they quickly passed the gate and walked on. He knew it then. They lived in this house! This was their home!

Tom returned to the gate and once more he and Mozart were standing on the pavement with the black painted wrought iron gate closed behind him. It needed another coat of paint, he observed, touching the rough part of it.

He looked towards the two girls and started walking up to them. They looked agitated and frightened.

He stopped in front of them and asked them if they recognized him. They denied having seen him before. He stared at them.

'I hear what you are saying but I can't understand why you refuse to acknowledge that we have met before.' Tom said. 'I planted the pine tree in front of the house when you were little. It was for you to be able to enjoy Christmas lights. Do you still put lights in it every year?' Tom continued.

'Piss off!' one of the girls spitted out. ' You are mad. Our father planted that tree for us.'

Tom became apprehensive and the uncertainty increased when he remembered their names. He looked at them for a minute or so before he told them that he was disappointed in them. He did not understand why they had to pretend that they had never met him before.

'Well, you haven't met Mozart, my dog before but I know the pair of you from somewhere and that you live here in this very house.'

Tom became cross with them as they did not answer

him. He examined the two of them carefully before he told them their names.

'I know you are Amy and that your name is Kate. I hope to see you again soon, and I do wish, that by then you will have changed your minds and tell me where we have met. I have always liked the pair of you. Goodbye!'

Amy then turned to him and said that he must be mad, but she was curious enough to ask him how he could be sure of their names. Even their best friends had difficulty in telling the difference. Tom just said that he could but would not tell them exactly how he knew who was Amy and who was Kate.

Tom turned round and walked back the way he had come. He walked quickly as he was frustrated almost to tears and did not want anybody to see his suffering. He was furious. Why did people say that they did not know him? Had he done something terrible? Would Rebecca know and would she be able to tell him? He was not sure that Rebecca knew anything about this. He was not in an area where their friends lived, so what on earth had he been doing here?

What Tom did not know was that he had scared the girls. They looked at one another in horror. How could this man have known their names and put the correct name on each of them. Had that been pure luck or had he been able to tell them apart? Not many knew their secret.

They ran into their house, making sure they closed the door properly before they put the kettle on. They talked about this man. He had not told them his name. No, they were going to tell their mother about this stranger when she came back from work later. This must be a madman

- what else could he have been? No normal person would insist that he had planted that tree and they realized that he had been following them from the bus. If he was a man with bad intentions he knew where they lived!

The girls looked at one another and shivered. They considered themselves to be in danger.

Tom returned to the car. This time he let the dog inside and drove off. What he was in great need of now was a drink but that would have to wait until six. He longed for Rebecca.

He was frightened but of what he did not know. He was upset and had to calm down before he could face Rebecca.

Why was it that the girls had looked scared? They did not want to admit that they had met before. They had responded to him as Vallie had when he had met her. Had he done something which had made them frightened of him or had they done something to him that they were ashamed of? In any case Rebecca would have known about it but she had made it clear that she had never heard of anyone called Vallie.

He had to stop the car at the roadside as he realized that Vallie must be the mother of the twins. Vallie lived in that house too, so why did he know it and the inhabitants? He tried to think about the husband, but the man that had been present when Tom had talked to Vallie at the beach parking the other day was not someone he had met before - or had he? He was sure he was not the father of the twins and not Vallie's husband either.

What was happening to him?

There were so many things that he did not understand. He wished he could talk to Rebecca, but he knew that it would only upset her. She would not know these people. She certainly did not know Vallie.

When Tom returned home Rebecca was out. There was a note on the kitchen table but he was disappointed anyway. He felt a great need for her company. He had been looking forward to seeing her. He wanted to feel the security and reassurance of being at home and with her where there were no mysteries, although nowadays some secrets.

When Rebecca did come back she told him that she had had coffee with Anna in the village's "Sugar Rush".

They had talked about the serial killer as there were now five girls around the city who had been strangled. Anna had bought an afternoon paper. Apparently there was one girl who had survived. She had been able to give some clues. She was found alive although naked. A dog and its owner had come across the naked girl in a parkland late in the evening. Probably the killer had been scared off by the dog. The dog owner had heard something running off from the bushy area, but at first he had put it down to a deer. He had not seen anybody around and there were no traces of clothing to be detected.

'Have the police no idea who this killer might be? Five beautiful young girls. How was it possible with CCTV cameras everywhere? This man must know where he is safe and cannot be picked up on camera. What did you and Anna talk about other than these murders?' Tom asked.

'What did we talk about? I cannot remember. We talked about everything and nothing. The usual girlie talk about our husbands, children, our thoughts and books. Oh yes, she promised me the recipe for her rich chocolate cake, and for the orange sauce.'

I am looking forward to Anna's cake. What would you like for dinner tomorrow ? Wouldn't crispy duck be great?' asked Tom with a smile on his face. Rebecca laughed at him and told him that it would be lovely, obviously not believing his suggestion.

Tom told her that he was going to have a soak in a hot bath before "drinkies time." He felt the need to relax.

Rebecca sat by the computer for a while and emailed James, which they did more or less every other day.

James did not come home as often now that his father was back with his mother and they seemed to be fit and healthy. Rebecca missed him more than she was prepared to let anybody know, apart from Anna.

Rebecca also emailed her friends in Sweden, as exchanging news with them was important.

Meanwhile Tom was soaking in his hot bath with some aromatic oils in the water. He was recalling memories which seemed to crop up unexpectedly. He was not pleased about this but could not do anything to stop them from entering his mind - memories that he would have liked to have been without.

He had come to terms with the face staring back at him occasionally when he looked into a mirror. Sometimes he wondered if he had lived another life and that was why he recognized places which he did not think he had visited before, or recognized people who did not want to admit that they had met him.

When he got out of the bath, the tepid water had made him wide awake. He had relaxed lying in the hot water. He fell in sleep. It was a wonderful feeling to disappear into nothing for a short time. He slipped into his velvety bathrobe for now and to get dressed for dinner.

It had been a warm day but when the sun was sinking behind the houses it felt cool. Tom, warm after his bath decided to put on a short sleeved shirt and a pair of jeans. He combed his hair and returned to the bathroom to hang up the robe on its place behind the bathroom door next to Rebecca's white gown. It smelled so much of her that he could not resist burying his face into it for a second and taking a deep breath.

Tom asked Rebecca what she would like to drink, poured himself a whiskey and water and sank into his armchair. Rebecca switched on the News and sat down next to him. Mozart shifted to the rug in front of them and put his head down and crossed front legs. With a sigh he closed his eyes to fall asleep.

After dinner they sat talking for some time before settling down for a relaxed read. Later they went out hand in hand for a walk closely followed by the dog.

Walking along the path between the trees, Tom felt a tingling sensation in his entire body as he observed Rebecca when they stopped to wait for Mozart

The moon was shining and he could clearly see Rebecca's cheekbones like triangles. It was magical in the grey light of the moon. He looked into her eyes which were twinkling like stars and bowed his head over hers. Holding her tenderly in his arms, he kissed her. She tasted of coffee and the After Eight Mints. As they embraced, the trees were the only witnesses.

Walking back Tom told her that when he had looked into her shining eyes he thought of the Disney film "Lady and the Tramp". They laughed at the thought of washing on lines between the trees.

TWO WEEKS LATER

May had started with some rain but then sorted itself out to become lovely and warm. Summer was on its way.

They were getting extremely tired as there was never a fully relaxed night's sleep. Tom had his nightmare. He had stopped sleeping during the daytime but often sat down after lunch to read the paper or a book.

The grass was soft and green and the wisteria around the terrace door was bright blue with the grape-like clusters.

The tulips were mostly gone and leaving only the stalks from the dead headed flowers and the foliage to tell a tale of more colourful days. The proud ones still standing were the last.

The rose trees were covered with a mass of swollen buds. Around the kitchen door and window there would soon be pink flowers against the white washed walls. The pink and yellow Masquerade clung to the trellace all the way up on to the roof. The bedroom window was surrounded by soft colours. The terrace was the place for the dark velvety red roses, clematis and honeysuckles.

The wallflowers had been taken out to leave space for the begonias and the geraniums and other bedding plants which would spread joy during the entire summer season and well into autumn. Tom and Rebecca had a spell of pure bliss sitting in the warmth reading, planning the garden, discussing what to plant where, before they had ordered from David at the local nursery.

The Forget-me-nots' blue stars looked beautiful before the blackflies would get to them. It was the same with the roses and their annual problem with the greenfly. The primroses, the pansies and a few odd late daffodils were in colour. The whole garden looked alive and in expectation of even warmer weather.

This morning there was a balmy westerly breeze. The days had lengthened into weeks and gave more light with shorter nights. The light was brighter and the bees and bumblebees were humming from flower to flower to the chorus of singing birds. In another week or so more insects would join in to give the small birds lots of feed for their babies. The bright yellow beaked black bird and his wife went into the flowerbeds looking for worms and other "goodies." They were a proud couple.

The two apple trees were draped in pink and would soon spread their colour around the lawn like confetti, but when the blossom was gone, it would be taken over by the climbing honeysuckles planted alongside the tree trunks. This had been one of Tom's brilliant ideas.

There were bird nesting boxes up in the trees and Rebecca had been watching some blue tits house hunting. There was so much happening. One just had to know what to look for.

It was a pity not to be able to feed the smaller birds, but if they did there would be a lot of squirrels and unwanted big and noisy magpies around. Sometimes there were choices that had to be made.

It was wonderful in the Dell. It was lovely to wander with the dog along the paths even if they were sometimes muddy. The woods had always given Rebecca and Tom strange feelings of peace soothed by the running water and, the murmur of the river flowing between two of the paths.

The smell of wild garlic, damp moss and peaty water

was pleasant. The banks were covered with bluebells shining as if mirrored by bright and cloudless summer's sky. They were beautiful here, but in the garden a big nuisance. Every year Rebecca tried hard to get rid of bluebells and the wild garlic. There was a place for everything, and garlic and bluebells were for the wild.

The tree trunks were rough, scarred and furrowed by the wind, but sometimes Rebecca had a feeling it was from sorrow. She interpreted the nature around her according to her own needs or mood; the tree's branches stretching towards the sky one day from joy and happiness, another from desperation or mockingly pointing to the sky for help, sometimes the trunks and branches were slowly strangled by ivy. How beauty could conceal the truth - of sorrow and disaster in this case, as the ivy was slowly killing its host.

This morning Tom had woken up at dawn. It was only six o'clock when he slid out of bed putting on his morning gown and leaving the bedroom quietly so as not to wake up his sleeping wife. It had been another of these horrible nights when he had been screaming and kicking in order to try to stop the speeding car, to get it to stop in front of the tractor and not against it. He had been weeping in Rebecca's arms. He felt humiliated about his actions! He had tried to persuade her that it would be better for her to sleep in their bed on her own and he would start sleeping upstairs in the guest room. It would be better for him too but he did not tell her that. He was tense when they went to bed, because he was scared of falling asleep and having to deal with these dark horror dreams, and as he knew he would wake her up with a start. This had become a nightmare in itself.

Rebecca did not want to hear about this silliness of

sleeping in separate rooms or different beds.

This morning he was pleased to wake up before her. He needed some time to himself and Mozart gave him a good excuse to flee away from his loved one in bed.

'Oh you stupid, stupid man. You have forgotten the slippers. They are in the bedroom.' He told himself off knowing that he was not going to walk back into the room where Rebecca was asleep as she must be in serious need of a rest.

He opened the door to let Mozart out into the garden. Tom stepped out into the bright warm morning sun and walked barefoot on the grass. It felt cool and wet from the heavy dew but gave him a wonderful sensation when the grass tickled him between his toes. He stopped, looked down on his feet and the green carpet he was standing on and realized that the grass needed a haircut. At the moment it felt more like a burden than a joyful task. He usually did not mind mowing the lawns. He liked doing it as much as Rebecca hated it.

This morning he had planned to go out for a ride on his bike. He would go back to the twins' house to see if he could see them or Vallie. He had not been back to the actual road since the day when he had confronted the twins. He had been shopping of course, but no sighting of any of them nor the silver car.

Today was going to be the day. Rebecca was blissfully unaware of this. The opportunity for him had arisen as she was going to town to meet friends for lunch. Tomorrow she was going to be out all day first to play golf and after lunch she was having the book group ladies. She hoped that they would be able to sit outside for their coffee and book discussion.

Tom was getting more and more unhappy and confused as night after night passed with the same torment. A small voice whispered to him to let Vallie and the twins go but he ignored it stoically or stupidly. Nothing was going to stop him. He had made up his mind to find out, if not the truth, at least more. He was not certain about the outcome, far from it. He even had a premonition of disaster waiting around the corner, but he was obsessed. He did not know if he would have the energy for much longer to cope with what-ever he was going to find. He knew that he failed Rebecca and their marriage in not telling her everything. He kept things from her because he did not want to upset her. He did not want to hurt her although this was a meagre excuse. Secrets made things worse and could be more hurtful than sharing them.

Tom went in and dried his feet on Mozart's towel. He would have a shower when Rebecca was awake, but not until he had cut the grass. He would do this as early as possible after breakfast to convince himself that he had done something meaningful.

Tom waited for the kettle to come to the boil before making Rebecca a cup of coffee and a steaming cup of tea for himself. He went back into the bedroom, tray with the cups and some biscuits in hands he woke her up by singing 'The hills are alive with the sound of music.'. Rebecca smiled and blew him a kiss.

They had breakfast and Tom cut the grass before Rebecca caught the bus to town, Tom walked the dog and husband and wife had time for their cup of morning coffee on the terrace in the sunshine. They listened to the wildlife of their garden. The smell of the freshly cut grass was soothing. Rebecca asked him when he and Eric were going to play golf again as Rebecca wanted to play with Tom too.

'How about phoning him today to make a date?'

Tom promised to phone later in the day.

As soon as Rebecca had left for town, Tom went into the garage and brought in the promised dinner from the big freezer. He had found it in the supermarket and was looking forward to the "crispy duck."

CHAPTER 21

He took out the bike, checked and inflated the tyres. It was an old "Hermes" bought in Sweden years ago. It was black with no gears, a convention foot-brake, lights back and front conforming to the traffic rules of its home country. There was a cross bar and a big luggage carrier at the back above the back wheel. This last particular detail was a useful one. He did not want to leave anything to chance. It would not have been fair to Rebecca, although he looked a complete idiot dressed in it. He put on the helmet and secured it with the strap under his chin. He was pleased not to have a mirror handy.

He closed the gate behind him and went out on his first bike ride since his accident. He was pleased that the weather was lovely and no rain forecast.

Initially he felt somewhat uncertain. He did not know if his balance would be all right but after having pedalled for a minute or two, he realized how much he had missed biking. There was the sense of pure freedom. If it had not been for the headgear he would have felt the wind blowing through his hair. He could only remember and imagine that feeling.

There seemed to be much more traffic and he wished he could have used the pavement or that there were better paths for bikers as in Sweden. He would become more brave by the time he was on his return journey. He was pleased to have told Rebecca that he was going to try his bike. It felt as if he had told her what he was up to. There was no car hooting at him so he could not be doing too badly, or perhaps he looked so unsteady that they did not dare disturb this funny creature on an old cycle in case he fell off. He smiled to himself as he turned the corner after the traffic lights with ASDA in full view. He decided to go there first to buy himself a bottle of water and some fruit pastilles.

He took his helmet off and put it into the shopping basket and went round the store. He came out with what he had gone in for plus a banana. He thought to himself how impossible it was to enter a supermarket and come out without having bought something other than the items intended, but he was hungry.

He put the bag on the luggage carrier after having eaten the banana and had a drink from the bottle he continued his ride.

This time he examined the house with the odd bow window. He closed his eyes and could see how he had been there on the opposite side of the road watching the builders at work. He could remember, and even feel, one little child's hand in each of his. The twins!!! It had to be the twins! He could see them so clearly dressed in pink track suits with a Barbie picture on their front. Both girls had white ribbons on top of their heads in an ambitious attempt to keep there blond wavy hair out of their eyes.

Sandals, yes they had been wearing white sandals and pink socks. It must have been during the summer. The girls had been only a few years old then. How strange that he remembered this occasion so clearly! He wondered why. It must have meant a lot to him to stand there with the girls holding his hands. Why had he been there? What was he doing with the girls and where were their parents? He sighed as he could not find the answers to these questions.

He did not sit up on the bike but walked slowly to the end of the road looking into the gardens as he passed by. He could reflect on much more this morning as he knew where he was going. He did not have to listen for somebody else's footsteps and he took his time.

He stopped outside the "neighbour's" gate and looked for the sandpit that he knew in his memory had been visible from where he was standing. There was no sandpit but a rockery and by the look of it, it had been there for some considerable time. He searched for the swing, which should have been hanging from the apple tree in Vallie's garden. The swing was gone as well. The girls were too old for that sort of thing now. It made him sad. With his eyes closed the image of this was as clear as tap water.

When had this happened? It must have been at least fifteen years ago. He hesitated before opening the gate in front of him leading up to Vallie's house. Where had Rebecca been when he had been here? It did not fit and he became frightened. His heart was beating fast. What on earth was going on in his poor head?

He felt weak and nearly turned round, to retrace his footsteps, but he had to go on. He had to pretend to be strong and get to the bottom of this. He parked the bike outside the gate and was bending down to lock it when he heard the girls coming towards him. He kept his head down still dressed in the crash helmet and let the girls pass him through the gate. Why he had not wanted them to recognize him, he did not know. He bent down more out of instinct.

He let the girls enter the house giggling. They probably thought that there was an odd fellow with his old bike.

The bike itself, was old and a strange looking thing quite out of place. He could see more than one head turning as he passed. Rebecca had offered him a new bike for his last birthday but he had declined. He loved this old thing. It felt like a friend and when he had told Rebecca, she had smiled understandingly, telling him that when she was a child she had had a blue bike which she had named Figaro. Her bike had been a proud, wild, Arab stallion.

He took off the crash helmet but did not want to leave it by the bike. He stopped once again by the gate, turned round and lifted up the back wheel of the bike and rolled the cycle through into the garden leaning it against the hedge and out of sight from the road.

He knew he was not going to be made welcome, but there were things that had to be done, had to be dealt with even if it was not going to be pleasant. This was one of those occasions and he did not particularly look forward to what was in prospect.

The gravel on the path was noisy. He wished he had chosen to walk on the grass instead, but it would have looked suspicious if anyone had by chance been looking out of a window and spotted him. He did notice that there were a lot of weeds and the grass edges were not properly trimmed. It had obviously not been tended to this spring. How he managed to think of trivial things when there was so much at stake he could not understand.

He quickly pressed the bell before he had any chance to change his mind and sneak away to safety. Later on he would ask himself why he had not sneaked away. He ought to have played this whole matter in a different way. What was going to happen to him soon was to be the worst experience of his life. What is done cannot easily be undone. The door was opened by one of the twins. Tom looked at her closely before she backed off slightly at his greeting 'Hello Amy.' Kate had been standing close behind her sister as the door was opened and Tom was in full view. She shouted for her mother to come to the door even before Tom asked if Vallie was at home.

As both girls were in a state of panic and backed off from the open front door, Tom took advantage of this and crossed the threshold. He stepped into the hall helmet in hand closing the front door behind him.

He could tell that the girls were upset. This was an understatement listening to the high pitched voices coming from the kitchen. Vallie came rushing into the hall and as she recognized the man in front of her, she asked in a barely audible snake like hiss, what he wanted from her daughters. She held out her hands shielding the two girls behind her like a hen.

'What do you want?' she repeated in a more normal voice this time.

Tom said he was sorry if he scared them, but he was not going to move from there until she had talked to him.

'Please Vallie, and you too Amy and Kate. Please talk to me. I am not going to harm you. I only want some answers. Please at least hear me out.'

He looked at the girls smiled at them and said it was clever of them to keep in the shadow of the room as he then could not tell them apart.

One of the girls, was braver than her sister as she was the one to open her mouth first, asking Tom why he was stalking them.

'Mister, you are not going to ask any questions before

you have answered ours. I would like to know how you can tell us apart, or may be you cannot. Perhaps it was pure luck when you told us our names last time we met. Tom had to smile as Amy had disclosed herself as being the braver one or the more confident of the two.

Her attitude was not pleasant. It felt like a threat. They were three against one and she was hiding behind her mother's plump body. Tom answered her question by saying that she must be the elder of the two and therefore her name was Amy.

He then told her that when he had seen them in the street in the outdoor light he had looked for her freckle.

'I know that Amy has a freckle in her right eye's iris and this is the only thing that can tell you apart. I don't know why I have this knowledge.'

Vallie stepped forward, only half a step but a fraction closer to where Tom was standing and asked him why he called her Vallie.

'Your name is Valerie, isn't it?' He felt anger for this woman in front of him. He did not know why, but it was clearly there and he had to suppress his desire to shout at her. Vallie was on guard, and she repeated her question of why he called her Vallie, why by this nickname?

'I don't know, but as I know you by this name I call you Vallie. Do you object to this?' Tom asked.

Vallie did not answer only repeated her inquiry what he wanted from her and her daughters.

Tom hesitated for a second and he hoped that they had not noticed. He suddenly decided to ask some other questions, and he did not want to start with why they pretended that they had never met him before. His next question had to be about the pine tree in the front garden and who planted it. Amy told him that their father had planted this tree. She said it in a way that made him understand that there would be nothing to gain by this statement. He had told them earlier that <u>he</u> had planted this tree and remembered how upset they had been. He could smell a rat a mile away but did not know how to react so he continued asking questions.

'Did he plant it for the pair of you so that there would be a tree outside in your front garden to hold the Christmas lights?'

'Yes he did.' Amy told him in an angry voice before she thought better of it. Perhaps she realized that she might have given him more information than she had intended to.

'What about the swing that used to hang from one of the big branches of the old apple tree? Who put that up for you and when was it taken down again?'

Vallie asked him why he wanted this information.

'Fourth birthday wasn't it?' Tom said and noticed how this information startled Vallie. She looked uncomfortable and nervous and surprised when he had filled her in with this statement. She raised her eye brows slightly and the wrinkles around her mouth became tighter. She was getting more uneasy by the minute, whereas the girls became more and more obstinate and brave.

'It was for the twins fourth birthday, wasn't it?' Tom insisted.

Vallie watched Tom with knife sharp eyes but when she finally answered him it was in a hoarse whisper. She cleared her throat and made another attempt and said her 'yes' in a loud voice.

Tom had had the time to look around the hall where they were standing only feet apart. It was almost dark without any windows but four doors opened up to the rest of the building, not including the staircase to the first floor. He pointed to the doors and told them which one went into the kitchen, sitting room, dining room and the downstairs bathroom. Vallie put her chin forward in defiance and told him that these kind of houses were so alike that it was not difficult. This was information that he could have guessed or worked out and did not prove that he had been in their home when they were living in it.

Tom turned his face from the cheap brown hollow doors and asked her what proof she needed. He could tell her that they had moved here before the twins had been born and that she had been five months pregnant at the time.

He looked up at the ceiling and asked her where the crystal lamp was. There had been one small lamp with glass beads in the hall ceiling.

He could tell her that the table just in front of him had been her mother's and the red velvety armchair at its side her uncle's. When she had first moved in it had been the place where they kept the pram. The coat pegs had been where they could be seen now, to the right of the front door.

He stretched his neck as far as he possibly could and looked round the corner into the sitting room and had the shock of the day. There was a big cat lying on the rug by the window. The cat was basking in the rays of the sun. The grey and black striped cat was lazily stretched out on the sheep skin rug. It was not any farm cat but one of a better breed. Tom stared at the sleeping animal.

Vallie reacted and took another step forward closer to Tom, who began to feel threatened and not as confident as one minute ago. He had a sense of weakness in his knees when he had first rung the bell and been confronted by three women. However, he had quickly regained confidence in their uncertainty. Now he could feel it changing and it was not to his benefit. He took a step back towards the front door and stood up straight almost in defiance, telling them that he knew that the cat was 19 years old. He was a castrated tom cat and had been in the family for about 18 years, as he had been a rescue cat. His name was Buddy. He had come into her home as Vallie had thought that there would not be any children. The cat had been taken in a few months before she had realized that she was pregnant.

He was aware that he knew so much about them. Scared about what he knew, what he had told her, he at once wished that he had asked more questions before making statements. He wanted answers and it occurred to him that he might have blown this opportunity by being too confident. How stupid of him!

He turned away from where his eyes had been fixed on the cat. He could no longer see it as he he had taken a step back. He examined Vallie and in a softer voice asked her how he knew this.

'Why do the three of you repeatedly say that you have never met me before? What can possibly be so horrible that you don't want to admit that we know one another? Please tell me and I'll leave you alone not ever to bother you again. Please tell me, I recognized you when I first set eyes on each of you.'

The twins looked surprised at what Tom was telling them, and then looked simultaneously at their mother. The girls had moved forward and were standing at either side of Vallie examining her reactions to Tom's words. Again Amy was the one to break the oppressive silence in the entrance hall with a single almost accusing word. 'Mum!?'

Vallie did not move. She made the situation worse by not reacting immediately. Her hesitation kindled her daughters' suspicion.

Kate repeated what Amy had just said, looking expectantly at her mother, waiting for an answer. It was obvious to Tom that the girls wanted their mother to tell them the truth and he took the opportunity which had presented itself as he at once picked up that the girls did not recognize him. He could not understand this but now they were watching Vallie and they wanted an explanation and some answers from Vallie.

The atmosphere in the hallway had changed again and Tom thought for a second that it was to his advantage. How wrong he was. If he had bade farewell at that moment, he might have got away with it. He could have slipped out of this house without answers, but Tom was determined to get what he came for. Answers! He was obstinate and could not see what was happening in front of him.

He had managed to sow seeds of doubt. It had not been his intention to do this and to turn these two girls against their own mother. He had not wanted this reaction although he was not going to do anything to help Vallie out of the corner, not until he had heard what she had to say. Help could come later.

He had not understood that Vallie was in a state of shock. She needed to think to decide what to say and how to behave. She had been frightened into speechlessness, but not because, what her daughters thought, but what this man in front of her knew about her life and about her family. The walls exuded the smell of fear of the four people in the hall. The fear was of a different kind and for different reasons. Tom was scared because of his memories and was now frightened of what was going to materialize. Vallie was horrified of what she had learned from this mad man. She was scared of him and terrified when she realized that her beloved daughters thought that <u>she</u> had a hidden secret. The girls had started to disbelieve their own mother. The rock in their life had suddenly become unsteady.

When Vallie finally spoke, her voice was croaky but resonance soon returned and she nervously but callously answered Tom.

'I don't know who you are. I had never ever seen you before that day by the beach. I am pleased that Bruce was with me, as your behaviour cannot be normal. You ought to see someone. This is my first piece of advice to you. My second is not anything less than an order and that is to leave this house now, at once! Leave us alone! I don't ever want to set eyes on you again. I'm telling you! I don't want to hear from either of my daughters that you have tried to talk to them. Don't you dare bother us with your ridiculous statements, silly information and accusations, your stupid questions and tales. Just leave!!'

Tom looked at the women, noticing that the twins were crying and slowly turning away from their mother. His glare was met by ice cold green eyes and he felt he had been subjected to this piercing stare many times before this morning. He shivered and knew that he was close to understanding everything but it was blocked in the back of his mind. He was furious and had to hold back as he told Vallie that he would leave but not before she had answered the question as to why he knew her and the girls.

'Just explain to me how I can be in the possession of such knowledge of your family?'

Vallie gave him a mocking hard laugh and told him that he must have got it from the girls' father.

Tom wanted to know the name of this man and where he could be found. Vallie told him under her breath that if he did not leave this very instant he would meet him earlier than he would wish to. She shook her head as she said this obviously feeling triumphant.

Tom could not get any more information out of her. She was agitated, pointing towards the front door positively hissing the words 'Get out!'

Tom backed off. He opened the door and left the house. He followed the path back the way he had come. He grabbed the key to the bike padlock, unlocked it and manouvered it back through the iron gate which needed a coat of paint. He stopped on the pavement in front of the house to put his crash helmet on. His hands were shaking. He was angry, frustrated and upset. If the father of the girls was the key to his problems and memories, who was he? Why did Vallie not want to tell him where he could be found? The father must be the key to his questions and it was <u>not</u> the man called Bruce. There must have been a divorce.

Mounting his bike, he started to ride back home making a point to look at the gate. "The Simmons' Cottage" was readable through the rust . How could he have missed this earlier?

He was soon back on the main road proceeding in the direction of home passing by the supermarket when a police car appeared in front of him. The car stopped and one huge policeman opened the passenger seat door next to the driver and stepped out on to the pavement. The thought rushed through Tom's mind that this must be the father of the girls and that was what Vallie had meant when she had told him that he would meet him "earlier than he anticipated."

The officer stopped Tom who was scared stiff. The policeman restrained his progress by putting his hand on the handlebar. Tom was pleased that there were others around. There would be plenty of witnesses to whatever was going to happen next. Soon enough Tom would wish that there had not been anyone there apart from himself and this policeman and his partner.

The policeman asked Tom to get off the bike. Tom was shivering and felt cold although it was a warm afternoon. Cold sweat had began to run down his back and forehead. The lack of food did not exactly make him feel any better.

He was in trouble, he could read this in the other man's face although he acted in a friendly manner.

Tom was subjected to a barrage of questions. He had to give the two men his name and address, where he was going and where he had been. Tom thought to himself that surely they knew the answer to their last question. He asked why they had stopped him and what they wanted from him, what they were after.

'We have had a report of a man fitting your description stalking two young girls and who has been to their house leaving them and their mother upset. We would like you to come with us to the station for more questioning.'

Tom was formally detained by the officers on suspicion

of acting in a manner likely to cause a breach of the peace. He was warned that everything he said would be noted and might be given in evidence. Tom said nothing.

The old Hermes bicycle was put in the back of the marked police van and the back passenger door opened for Tom.

Tom did not want to enter the police car but had no choice. He was frightened. Perhaps the father wanted to have him in the van to transfer him to some remote place where there were fewer witnesses. Tom was apprehensive. Should he refuse to enter? He felt sick! He was terrified. He could no longer tell where this new nightmare began and reality ended. His thoughts went to Rebecca, and he decided to do what these men ordered him to do. The sooner he was attended to the quicker he would get it behind him and be back home. He had already decided not to tell Rebecca about this incident if he did not have to. He climbed into the van without understanding why he had to.

At the police station the bike was taken out of the van and propped up against the garage wall. Questions started to enter his head. The first thing he had asked them was what he had done wrong, telling them that he had never intended to make the three ladies upset.

Escorted to the custody area and entrusted to the duty custody officer who entered Tom's details into their computer system. It was a desk with four computers boxed in and the officer in charge behind it.

Tom was asked if he wanted a lawyer.

'No?'

He was then asked if he wished any other named person notified of his detention. He immediately thought of Rebecca but he did not want her to know where he was. He thought that he was going to be let out shortly and therefore she would never have to get this information. He felt such shame and wanted no one to know. He tried to swallow but there was a lump in his throat.

He had to take his belt and his belongings off at the desk. He felt naked without his wedding ring.

Shown to an interview room he realized that this was not going to be as quickly dealt with as he first had thought.

The room was small, no more than ten feet by eight, with a table and three chairs. On the table was some recording equipment. No decorations, and painted in an uninteresting colour that made the room look much used. Tom fell exposed and lonely.

The officer in the room made it clear that the interview would be recorded and then he switched on the machine as a grey haired man entered. His name and title were recorded together with the date and time. It was 3.47pm as superintendent Walker registered.

Tom was reminded that he was under caution and that anything said could be given in evidence. It was four o'clock as he was served a paper cup of water.

Tom was asked a lot of strange questions mostly about his whereabouts at certain days and times. He did not understand why, but gave them the answers he could remember. One of the days and times he had been on the golf course with Eric Gown, so that was easy enough. Tom could tell them almost the exact time and of course the name and telephone number as they wanted Eric to confirm this.

Tom wanted to know what these days had to do with

what had happened earlier the same morning at Number Thirteen? He told them that he had only been there twice and inside the house for the first time this very day. He knew that he had been there years ago but not why.

Why he had been taken to the station was that Mrs Simmons had phoned them and she had reported Tom for behaving strangely. Tom asked them for another glass of water when they told him that he was where he was because of his behaviour and they had a serial killer to catch.

Tom stared across the table, absolutely speechless. His whole world stopped. It was now about him and the two men across this table. He felt sick again and a cold sweat broke out all over. The entire room must have smelt of fear and perspiration. Tom shuddered when he was asked if he wanted a lawyer.

'I don't need any lawyer. I have not done anything wrong. I have been with my wife at home most of the time, or I have been out walking our dog.'

'What kind of dog do you have sir?'

'Mozart is a rescue dog and a mixed breed, but mostly a black Labrador. He is big for that kind of animal.'

'When you walk your dog where do you usually take him?'

'I walk from home down through the Dell once or twice but most of the time we walk along the playing field on the main road. Mozart is off the lead running as he wishes on this playing field not far from our house. I have taken the car shopping and sometimes brought the dog with me. I cannot recall that the dog and I have been elsewhere.'

The recorder was switched off after a third man

suddenly appeared at the door asking the men to leave. All three left the room together, probably to talk things through in private. They obviously did not want Tom to hear what they were discussing. He was nervous. He felt weak. He longed for Rebecca. The comfort of her next to him. To be able to hold her tight in his embrace. He was leaning forward and let his heavy head rest on to the table. Forehead on the surface, he prayed for his life. He could no longer think clearly. He wanted to cry but that would have been humiliating. He tried to swallow the lump he had in his throat. He drank some water from the glass he had been given. It helped him not to actually be sick. He must be white as a sheet and probably looked guilty. His thoughts went to Rebecca again and he closed his eyes to be able to see her comforting face. He wanted to drown in her lovely, clear grey eyes enclosed by thick black eyelashes. He wanted to feel her skin which felt like satin under his fingers. He knew that he had let her down.

He stood up, staggering unsteady in the state of shock. He paced the floor knowing that he was being watched. Tom could not have cared less. He was feeling so, so tired .

There was no window in this room, only the light in the ceiling casting ghostly shadows like at dusk, shadows that surrounded him when he stopped under the light, grotesquely distorting the corners of the room.

All he could hear was his own breathing.

He was standing there pensively, in the middle of the room under the lamp, shoulders hanging, when the men returned. They were quiet until they had the recorder back on, and asked Tom to please sit down.

Tom asked them if they had all the answers from him so he could be on his way back home.

The two men glanced at one another and told him that they had not been able to get hold of his golf partner, but there had been yet another girl found murdered.

As Tom had been in Mrs Simmon's house at the probable time of this girl's death in another part of the city he was no longer a main suspect, but was asked not to leave town without letting them know. He was lucky however that Mrs Simmons was not going to press charges for stalking her daughters. Tom was advised to stay away from that family.

Tom's mouth fell open and he could only stare at the men from one to the other. He was relieved to be able to go back home, but that this was only made possible because of another poor girl having been found dead was absurd! It was unbelievable. It was so awful. No words could explain his feelings. He was disgusted with himself.

Having been taken by the police because of stalking was going to ruin his life, a life that doctors had saved from certain death only months ago.

Tom was in shock. He felt terrible. He felt listless. His guilt was an enormous burden to carry. Why had he not told Rebecca what he was up to?

He knew the answer. He wished he was dead. If there was any mercy, God would let him fall asleep never to wake up again. It would be the best for Rebecca and for James as well. He felt sorry for them, but most of all he was frightened and filled with self pity. He was exhausted.

He was too tired to work out how best to tackle this

mess he had put himself in. He had to work out how to deal with his problem.

As Tom was told he was free to go, he was offered a sandwich and a cup of tea. He had to eat so he slowly put the food into his mouth and chewed it well. He managed to swallow with the help of a sip of the hot tea. He did not know what he was eating. He was too tired and scared to care.

He dreaded meeting the eyes of Rebecca after this. His thoughts jumped back and forwards from deepest despair to a slim ray of hope.

The thoughts of Rebecca electrified him. She gave him strength. She was too good for him. He loved her. She must feel betrayed by him and he felt awful having let her down, although he had done what he had done thinking this might solve the nightmare. He had done what he had done for the sake of them both. They desperately needed the rest and good nights sleep. At the moment they were not getting either.

Tom was not their serial killer.

He left the station on weak legs and was given his bike back. He was told to go easy and to have a safe return home.

As he entered the house head down he was met by a red eyed furious wife.

Rebecca asked him if he was alright.

'Where have you been Tom? I have been worried sick about you. You have been away for hours. What have you been up to? You look tired out?'

Rebecca was in shock. She had obviously been crying. She had tried to get a grip on the world tumbling down around her and to keep on trying to clear her mind. She did not understand what was happening to them as a family.

Tom couldn't get a word in. He poured himself a whiskey and then he poured one for Rebecca as well before he asked her to sit down and handed her the drink.

He told her what had happened to him and how sorry he was to put her through so much pain. He tried to explain why he had visited Vallie and the girls. He talked for a long time without Rebecca interrupting him. When he had finished she looked at him and in taking his hand she only said that she needed to be on her own for a while to try to come to terms with what he had told her. She would take Mozart for a short walk whilst Tom had a shower and then they would eat the dinner that she had prepared.

Now that Tom was back home, back with her, released, she must make an appointment for him to see Doctor Smith. They had to talk things through with her. Something must have gone wrong as he was having these hallucinations and nightmares.

She took Mozart for a short walk relaxing a fraction whilst admiring the pale pink sky. The early evening air felt light in spite of her heavy mood. She walked as though in a trance and staying within her deep thoughts. She could not understand it. Why did the police suspect Tom who was the kindest man in the world? Could they not see that he would not be able to hurt a fly?

She was livid that Tom had gone behind her back to see Vallie. She felt betrayed.

Returning home she told Tom that she loved him but was sad that he had acted behind her back, but continued by telling him that they had to get a grip on their lives and to have no more secrets. With a smile she turned her eyes on his face lifted her hand and stroke his cheek.

'Let's have something to eat. I am sure we will feel better on a full stomach. I would also like to see the news, please'.

After they had eaten she still felt cold. Tom lit the gas fire in the snug. They had to try and keep calm and to be strong for whatever would come upon them in the near future. They were frightened.

Rebecca loved Tom. How was he coping? It was absurd to think that Tom was this killer. The police were desperate to find the guilty person but Tom!!??

Rebecca was tired, exhausted in fact. Until now, she had thought that they had a life in front of them but the improvement had only brought new, even worse problems.

She had seen her own face staring back at her from the bath-room mirror as she washed her hands before dinner and the sight had given her another shock. She looked old and pale. She looked completely washed out and with red rims around her swollen eyes.

When Tom had regained consciousness and had come back to her she had been so happy. She thought that this was going to be the end of their worries. Little had she known. She felt as if life was a fraud. <u>She</u> was a fraud. Had she failed the man she loved? She had thought that love and tenderness would be enough but obviously she had been mistaken.

Love did not solve everything even though it helped. Answers to questions were needed in Tom's case and in hers too.

Rebecca made herself a cup of coffee and went into the snug. Tom had declined a glass of milk. Tom switched the television on. The breaking news came at the end of the news programme. The police had been able to identify the murdered girl who had been found earlier the same afternoon.

It was Susan!!!

Tom and Rebecca gasped for air and looked at the screen not wanting to believe what they had just heard.

Tom was the first one to break the silence. He took a deep breath and said that he was going to phone James.

James answered the phone directly and after some pleasantries Tom told him about Susan. James became quiet and Tom had to ask him if he was still there.

'Yes dad, I am still here but I had to sit down. Are you sure? Can't it be a huge mistake? It must be! This is such awful news. Who would do a thing like this? What do you know about it?'

Tom told him that it was most likely this serial killer's job and that it had been a jogger who had made this ghastly find. No clues!

Tom didn't tell James about his own experiences with the police. This information he was going to keep and Rebecca had promised not to tell a living sole.

Tom looked awful. He was nearly as pale as he had been when he had first been discharged from hospital. His eyes were tired and the body language told Rebecca more than words ever could. Tom was close to a collapse. She had to do something about this and fast.

She put him to bed and then undressed to carefully slip close to him. She had to try to keep her mind off things.

Finally Tom fell into a heavy sleep. Rebecca left their bed and went into the kitchen.

Sitting on the cold floor embracing Mozart she hid

her face deep in his fur and cried and cried and cried. What a sad sight. A crying woman desperately holding on to a dog. Rebecca's mind was completely washed out by the time she returned to the bed. It felt warm under the cover.

The night was interrupted by Tom's nightmare as every night. He was exhausted and so was she. It was later than usually when she finally woke up the following day. Poor Mozart, he must be in great need of the trees.

Tom was fast asleep. Rebecca tiptoed out of the room let the dog out and then phoned the hospital. She dialled the number they had been asked to call if there were any questions or problems with Tom's wellbeing after his operation. Rebecca managed to make an urgent appointment with Doctor Smith for the following week but meantime they would ask his own doctor too. That was when it dawned on Rebecca that Tom was indeed considered to be an important patient. It hit Rebecca, that there could be something radically wrong with the surgical treatment Tom had received. Why else would the doctor have agreed to see Tom in only a few days time? NHS queues were miles long and usually a waiting time stretching into months could be expected. To be taken on in just a few days meant that Tom was jumping the queue.

She shivered although it was not cold. There were too many "buts" and "ifs" for her liking.

She tried to talk herself out of this scary mood, to gloss over it. Rebecca tried to convince herself that she was only finding it difficult to adjust to how Tom was now, how everything turned out to be after his operation. This secrecy between them had to stop. She and Tom had to have a serious talk.

She stood up from where she had been sitting, and opened the fridge to get the cheeses out to take the chill of them. She was pleased that they had some biscuits left and a bottle of claret was put to warm to room temperature. Then she prepared their breakfast. She cheated and was going to serve Tom bacon and eggs and thought she better have the same as it was nearly lunchtime. They were going to have brunch, but first she had to talk to Anna. Rebecca had to share the awful news about Susan.

Tom came into the kitchen and kissed her. He had difficulty meeting her eyes. He knew how much pain he had caused her and was filled with shame.

'It smells fantastic. I am not worthy of this treat. What time is it anyway? The alarm said 11.52, but surely it can't be correct.?'

Tom shook his head in disbelief but sat down to eat when asked to take his seat. He did not touch his food but started to talk. He had to let the pressure of guilt out of his head. He once more told Rebecca about his visit to Vallie and the twins. Rebecca listened and told him that she had prepared for a cheese and wine talk that evening.

'I am hurt, Tom. I do not understand why you had to visit this woman and I feel betrayed. Let's go for a walk this afternoon and leave the talking for later. I still love you, so please eat up.' Rebecca told him with tears in her eyes.

She was not looking forward to this evening talk but it had to come out in the open sometime and it must be better not to wait.

Rebecca went for her diary and put them by the

cheeses. She had written about Tom being taken into custody. The only things for her to add to the history was Tom's side of the story, his views and what she hoped to achieve was to rationalize the present position before the good doctor had her say.

When she was clearing the kitchen table she relaxed a little but started to cry. Crying these days had become nearly as frequent as breathing. Tom did not see her as he was making their bed preparing the house and himself for the walk.

They walked in silence but hand in hand deep in their own thoughts.

Rebecca's first memories of Tom were wonderful. She knew of course that it was common to forget the bad days. Tom had always been such a caring and loving person. He still was, although he had changed. Rebecca could not blame Tom alone for this. She was burdened with the guilt herself that if she had not insisted on them going skating that fatal day, everything would have been as it had been between them, trusting, loving and no secrets kept from one another. Rebecca felt grief for the Tom she was missing. She felt grief for her feeling of lost marriage. She felt a sense of betrayal. She had been let down by Doctor Smith although Rebecca could not yet put her finger on why?. She had a nagging feeling that the doctor was not telling her all that she should know about Tom's condition.

Her nights had been filled with horror as sleep eluded her. She felt bitterness. She did not want to become an embittered old lady. She had no wish to be angry with anyone. Rebecca only asked for their "together life" to be back in order. She prayed for this to happen when sleep passed her by when she was lying wide awake in bed. She prayed for Tom continuously.

They got back and Tom had a cup of tea before he went to have a snooze. Rebecca brought her coffee into the garden to try to read but soon gave up and listened to the birds instead.

When the phone rang she was worried that it would wake Tom. It was James and all was forgiven.

Rebecca and James talked for a while.

James planned to come home to see them together with Gill in two weeks time. Gill was going down to her parents but perhaps they could all meet for lunch during that weekend.

They had to get Susan off their minds first. Gill had promised James to come with him to the funeral but no date had been fixed.

James had talked to Susan's parents. He had phoned them and given them his condolences.

Rebecca went into the kitchen. She put the kettle on to make some tea and put the casserole in the oven. She was pleased to have prepared their dinner earlier. Chicken, mushrooms and vegetables put together in an enameled dish. She would cook some rice to serve with it and make the usual fresh salad.

She turned round and went into the bedroom where Tom lay resting. He was awake and was looking at her. She thought that he had been crying.

'Did you have a relaxing sleep? You must have been shattered after all you have been through. How do you feel now? I have brought you a cup of tea.'

Tom sat up leaning on his elbow to be able to hold on to the cup and to have a sip.

'Thanks. I slept heavily as if I had been unconscious. I did feel faint and ready to drop ever since the police stopped me. You see I was convinced that one of them was the father of the twins and I was scared out of my wits.'

'No more secrets between us please. We must try to get our lives back together. We never had secrets from one another before and I have decided that we are not going to have any from now on either. You must agree, because I cannot face this on my own. We have to go through it together. Tom, I love you and don't want this kind of walking round in circles. I want you back here with me and that is in mind as well as in body.'

'I am sorry of what have put you through lately.' Tom said apologetically.

'I have made an appointment for you with Doctor Smith. We are going to see her next week.

'The News will be on soon and James phoned to tell us that there might be pictures of Susan and her boyfriend. The police had asked to borrow a photograph from Adam, her brother.'

Tom left the bed and dressed. He felt better but he was still in a state of shock. He was heavily burdened with guilt. How much suffering he had caused Rebecca by being selfish! How could he make this up to her? That she still loved him must be a miracle. He knew that he had never loved anyone as he loved Rebecca. She was worthy of a much better man than he was proving to be. He had dragged his own family into shame. The way he had been acting must have had a horrendous effect on Rebecca's and James' lives. They had been supportive when he came back home from the hospital. He had been told that Rebecca visited the hospital at least once a day when he was in the coma. She had bought Mozart for him to give him extra companionship. Tom could die for them. He knew that he had to solve his problems and rid his family of the worry he was creating. It centered around his recurring nightmare. He knew that if he could get on top of this black dream of his, he would understand things much better. Terrible thoughts worked in his mind. He was sure that he had never made love to Vallie so why did he see her on top of him as he made love to Rebecca? His problem with the twins would also be solved when he understood the meaning of his nightmare. Tom was convinced about this. He would unburden himself to Rebecca about these things and his thoughts.

On the News there was much about the murders. No more victims had been discovered. The police wanted to talk to the man by Susan's side in the photograph to be able to eliminate him as a suspect.

Rebecca and Tom sat in silence. In the end Rebecca said huskily that Susan had changed, although her choice of clothes was still far too sexy, too inviting and provocative.

Neither of them was particularly hungry when Rebecca served the dinner, but they did eat.

After their meal when they had cleared up the kitchen they decided to take Mozart for his evening walk. It was raining but it suited their moods

The sharp biting wind and the rain stung their faces. May had arrived, bringing with it a little more warmth but not today. They felt the gloom but Mozart was happy.

The trees were bending towards the walkers as if greeting them. The sky was black and there was no moon to be seen. The night was dark, wet and windy. It was not pleasant.

When they returned into the light of the kitchen Tom looked at his wife in pure admiration and love. Her hair glistened from the rain, her cheeks looked fresh and red from the wind. She was gorgeous.

They changed into their tracksuits after drying off and giving the dog a rub down. Tom opened the wine to let it breathe.

'It is a pity we haven't got one of these ceiling fans.' he commented.I remember on a holiday in Spain years ago, how I found you sitting on the hotel bed reading, and over your head were our trousers going round and round. You had put them on hangers and then attached them to the fan. I must say our trousers dried quickly.'

They sat down in front of the television. Rebecca made herself a cup of lovely hot coffee. They listened to the wind, now hurling around the corners of the house and the rain beating against the windows. The wind came down the chimney and made the coal fire hiss. They had made the correct choice in taking Mozart for his walk straight after dinner. They could not have gone out in this. It had turned worse. They had been lucky even if they had got wet. There was more wet and windy weather in store too. Climate change?

Soon the television was switched off, as neither of them had been able to concentrate. They listened to the wild weather. Rebecca decided it was time to have their talk. She served the wine, cheese and biscuits. She was thinking of everything that had happened to them and between them in the past week.

Sitting in the kitchen, telling each other what was

on their minds. Tom shook his head in disbelief and told her everything apart from the image of Vallie sometimes popping up in his mind, when he was making love to Rebecca. There were limits.

'Well', he said. 'You recall the red-haired woman that I call Vallie. I have been looking for her since I first met her. I was convinced that she was the key to my strange memories. As a matter of fact I still am. I was looking for her everywhere I went when I spotted the twin girls. I recognized them. My curiosity made me follow them. The girls look like Susan. I told you that Susan reminded me of someone else when I saw her photograph, remember?

Following them brought me into an area I felt I had been to before. When they turned into the gate of what I imagined to be their home I felt that I knew everything about the house. Vallie is their mother. I don't know anything about their father. I called at the house to confront Vallie and her daughters and asked kindly if they would answer some questions. They turned on me and more or less threw me out without revealing anything. They must have phoned the police and reported me as a mad stalker. Well, that's my story.'

Rebecca was shaken. 'You did act like a stalker, didn't you? I bet that's why they suspected you of being the serial killer. You darling stupid husband of mine! If you had told me, we could have gone together. Promise me that you won't ever do anything so stupid again. Promise that you'll confide in me before you plan to do anything rash. Please'! She beseeched him.

Rebecca told Tom about her note-books. They studied and discussed every detail of what she had written. They were going over old ground, but it was reassuring to discuss what had happened in the planned and relaxed atmosphere. Tensions were relieved by the cheese and the smooth Bordeaux. Tom's revelations fell into better perspective when recited without the tension of fear and accusation.

The warmth from the fire and the soothing effect of the alcohol was distinctly soporific.

They went to bed, desperately cuddling one another. It was not a time for making love, having so much on their minds.

The night was terrible. Tom's nightmare returned and he was ridden with guilt. He did not sleep, and woke up more tired than he had been when he went to bed the previous evening.

The noise from the wind and the rain lashing against the windows had also kept him awake. He had tried not to toss and turn. He knew that his restlessness disturbed her. It was lucky that they had bought this big bed some years ago. It was large enough for the pair of them not to remain in permanent contact, but movements could be sensed through the mattress and through the top sheet and the duvet. Perhaps if they had two simple duvets, it would be easier for Rebecca. As they would still be in the same bed, there would be no difficulty making their jigsaw as they snuggled up to one another. It would be for the best for them until he regained his relaxing sleep pattern and slept through the night.

Tom could not help returning to his thoughts of how much Rebecca had suffered because of him. She still did, especially after he had been such a fool. His guilt enveloped him like a heavy, tight overcoat. It was a huge burden on his shoulders. He had turned their lives into sour milk. Tom loved Rebecca more than words could express, and yet he had been utterly selfish. The outcome of his actions was not what he had hoped for, on the contrary. He did not know anything any longer. He was totally confused. What had he been thinking of following the twins and calling on Vallie and the girls? He admitted to himself that he had been stupid. He must have been out of his mind to act in the way he did and to scare the three women in that house. He had been curious like a gossipy woman and he loathed himself for his weakness.

Rebecca slept. She must be as tired as he was.

Tom awoke in a depressed mood. He not only pitied his wife and son, but he pitied himself too. Wasn't that truly pathetic? His thoughts took him along the path that the longer he was alive, the more problems he would create for his loved ones. The longer he went on living the life he was living at the moment, the closer he seemed to come to destroying his marriage and his family. He was ruining their "together life" at breakneck speed. Just look at how they had started to keep secrets from one another! He still kept one from Rebecca. How on earth could he get to the bottom of his problems. He always came back to this recurring dream. He tried not to think about it, at least during the daytime. He was consumed by thoughts and unanswered questions.

Lying here in bed next to Rebecca, his thoughts went back to Vallie and the twins. He returned to the questions he had put to them. He was bewildered and exasperated that they were reluctant to tell him the truth. Tom was certain that they did know one another but he had not succeeded in getting answers. He was fumbling around in the dark. He had made no progress with his investigations.

He had definitely recognized the house, garden and the area where Vallie lived. He must be recalling something which had happened a long time ago. Perhaps Vallie and the girls had forgotten about it. He hoped this was the case.

Tom shook his head and let out a sigh. He kept still listening to Rebecca's even breathing. He had obviously not disturbed her. She seemed to be sound asleep.

Having been taken into custody had upset him much more than he admitted to Rebecca and this was in spite of the friendly attitude of the older sergeant who led the interview. He felt ashamed of the way he had acted before he had been picked up.

Of course he knew that he had frightened the women whom he had followed and visited, although he had tried to reassure them that he was not going to hurt them. He did not understand what had made them scared. Obviously they must have considered him a threat, but what kind of threat? Did they really think that he was a wierdo?

Tom knew that he had to sleep more at night to function properly during the day. The thing he did not know was how to achieve a relaxing sleep, when he did not even dare to close his eyes. He was getting more and more depressed.

Their retirement plans were in the melting pot. He might not be allowed to travel abroad ever again. Although Rebecca had not said much when he had told her that he probably could not get insurance, surely she must be hugely disappointed. They had made so many plans for visits abroad in the near future. The fantastic cities they had talked about visiting now they had the time. How about their annual visit to Sweden and their friends? It was an enormous turnaround for their planning.

If he had not been kept alive after his accident, but he had been left to die, as he nearly had done, Rebecca would have been free to travel and free from a husband who "stalked" young girls.

It would have been better for her if he had not survived. She would have remembered the man he had been and the memories would have been kept untarnished and intact.

His last thoughts being centered on Doctor Smith, who had somehow saved his life but at what cost? He felt a profound animosity towards her. He was angry with her. What kind of life had she managed to keep him alive for? What she had done was obviously miraculous. Even Angus Anderson had said that she had saved his life.

Everything would be easier if only he could switch off his mind from working overtime for a night or two. If he only could manage to have a blank mind and a clear head to let him sleep through a few nights without his nightmare chasing him. If only....

Tom's eyes became heavy and he fell into a merciful slumber.

Rebecca had felt that Tom was awake, but did not want him to know, that sleep also eluded her. She wished to think things through. She was thinking about their discussion over the cheese and wine. Probably Tom had been doing the same. They had been awake and had been trying hard not to disturb the other. Rebecca loved Tom. She enjoyed his company. They did have lovely times together. She had to admit to herself that she did miss the old Tom, the man she married. Tom had changed since his accident, but was it only because of his recurring bad dream or had his personality changed? She could not tell. Tom still enjoyed the good things of life - although he now fancied fish and chips!

He had started to like some other television programmes. His choice of football and motor sport was annoying and bizarre. Perhaps she was not fair as he still liked to watch the programmes they had enjoyed before the accident, but he was obsessed with sport on television. He would never have considered watching any of these a few months ago.

Rebecca was sure that Tom loved her and James. He loved their home, their garden, to play golf and to read. He loved being with their old friends who kept telling her that they could not find any changes in Tom. They assured her that he was the good old Tom. They thought of him as their friend Tom. So was it just in her mind? Their friends did not know everything, did they? They would hopefully never hear about how he had been taken into custody. God forbid! Their good friend taken by police for "stalking" girls!? What would they think about that?

'Oh, poor poor Susan. What had you got yourself into? Why did this happen to you? How was it possible? My prayers go to you, your family and to the other victims as well. Poor girls.

What does James make of Susan's death? How does he feel, and if he feels more than horror, what does Gill make of it?' Rebecca wondered.

She was certain that Tom had not been stalking these two girls. It was absurd! He had followed them because he had recognized them. The only thing he had wanted had been to have a chat with them. Why had they not wanted anything to do with Tom? Had they thought that he was the serial killer? My god, if this had crossed their minds they must have been terrified. If only this Vallie could have told him the truth, none of this would have had happened. Rebecca wondered why she denied having met him before that day by the beach. So much unnecessary suffering through her being a stubborn woman. She disliked Vallie intensely although they had never met.

Rebecca knew where this family lived. Perhaps she should go there and try to talk some sense into these three women? Tom had said something about his recollection of Vallie being more evil than kind. Ever since he had seen Vallie, he had the feeling of being angry with her, but not with the two girls. It was too strange to understand.

Rebecca should not be thinking of this, especially not at night time. She needed to sleep to be able to cope the next day. She often felt like a zombie these days. What was it someone had told her when she was a little girl? It was something like "one hour's sleep before midnight is worth two hours after midnight". She never seamed to get any sleep before the early hours of the morning. Even these hours were often disturbed by Tom's restlessness.

His dream must be horrible for him to break out in a cold sweat – a sweat of pure fear. He sometimes screamed. He even smelled of fear. A sports car crashing into a huge tractor with a fork in front. Where on earth did this come from? What could it mean? So many unanswered questions, more and more of them piling up into an untidy heap.

She had to try to calm down .In order to do so she

told herself to let every single limb of her body go slack and relax one by one. Finally she started to count Tom's breathing. She often lost counting and had to start from scratch.

It was three o'clock when she woke up. It was Tom screaming that had almost scared her to death. Her heart nearly escaped out of her rib cage. They were suddenly jerked out of their sleep. His scream had been short, fearful and high pitched, although he uttered only the single word. "NO"!!

CHAPTER 22

The following morning she woke up to a glorious day. The wind had subsided and the rain had disappeared, simply vanished. Rebecca was awake early which surprised her. She watched a ray of the sun entering the bedroom through a gap between the drawn curtains. She noticed the sunbeam move along the floor, as the sun rose.

Tom stirred and Rebecca turned towards him. She looked at his face. He must have felt her eyes examining him, because he opened his eyes with a start. At first he seemed to be tense and lost, but as soon as his gaze focused, he gave her a smile and he bid her good morning with a soft touch and a kiss.

No words were necessary. They knew that the night had not been a good one for either of them.

She was pleased with herself that she had phoned her lady golfing friends and told them that she would not be able to play for another week or so. She had explained that she had far too much to do at the moment, and with James' ex girlfriend being one of the serial killer's victims there was so much happening around them.

Rebecca had said that it would hopefully be Tom's final visit to the hospital for his "check up" the following week. Rebecca missed her golfing friends and to play golf. She missed it much more than she had anticipated, but with paperwork and letters which had to be written the time would pass quickly. Rebecca had to finish reading the book in time for the next book group meeting too. This book was an easy read and also interesting. She had never heard of Victoria Hislop before someone had introduced her book "The Island" to the group. Rebecca had no idea about the leprosy colony on a Greek island as late as in the 1950's.

Apart from some time to read and write, she felt the need to spend some quality time with Tom before their marriage fell apart and vanished through the window. The threat was real unless they did something about it and quickly.

Rebecca asked Tom if he would like to invite Anna and Eric with Malcolm and Mary for dinner for the following evening. She thought that it would be a good idea for them to think of things other than the problems they were battling.

They enjoyed their breakfast with today's Times and some gorgeous sliced fresh navel oranges in their fruit salad. They were sitting on their terrace as it was warm enough. Global warming seemed to have made considerable change to their climate. Mozart loved this arrangement as well. He had been around the garden but was now resting on the paving by Rebecca's feet, lapping up the sunshine like a cat would have done.

Rebecca and Tom took their time over the papers enjoying the weather and the garden.

'I have always said, that when you do begin the morning by asking how the night has been, it must be a true sign of old age.' Rebecca said.

They smiled at this comment and nodded in unison like an ancient duo. They were obviously getting old.

Rebecca left the sunshine and went indoors to phone about the next evening's dinner party. It was a last minute call she knew, but it was worth a try. She returned to Tom telling him that all of their intended guests were delighted at the prospect of meeting for a meal.

Rebecca had talked a little longer with Anna and told her friend about Susan and James.

Back with Tom in the garden they talked about his appointment with the dreaded Doctor Smith. Neither of them was looking forward to it, but it had to be done. Perhaps she would be able to come up with some solutions for Tom's disturbed sleep.

Tom cleared the table and put everything into the dishwasher. They had decided to go to the beach for a walk and to let Mozart have a good run. Their picnic basket was going to be in use again.

Before they took off Rebecca took out the salmon from the big freezer. She planned to cook it for tomorrow's dinner. It would be served as the main course. The starter would be ham and melon. It was always popular and such an easy thing to prepare. After that, the cheese board and finally a lemon mousse together with a raspberry coulis and the coffee of course.

The traffic was not bad as they left for the beach after the school run was over.

Tom drove into the allocated car park and took the same space as the last time they had been there.

They looked at one another as they stepped out of the vehicle when they realized that their eyes had swept over the parked cars. Tom turned to Rebecca with a relieved smile and said 'Vallie is not here today, at least not yet.'

At first Rebecca had felt relaxed when she had noticed the absence of the specific silver car, but it was not long before she had her feelings reversed. She was disappointed. She would have loved to put Vallie against the wall. Rebecca would like to have been able to ask Vallie some questions. It would have been easier if they suddenly and accidentally met, so much easier to ask Vallie why she would not admit that she had met Tom before. Rebecca could not understand behavior like this any more than Tom could. If Rebecca did not bump into Vallie, she would have to go and pay her a visit, a prospect she did not relish.

Tom brought a bottle of water and their camera from the car. They left the basket in the boot for the time being. It was too heavy to carry around on a walk.

The sea reflected a variety of colours. Closest to the shore the water was mixed with sand and some sea weed. Then further out there was a strip, which was clear and turquoise, and closer to the horizon the water was the colour of lead. There was a light mist further out, but no clouds could be seen.

Rebecca and Tom walked hand in hand. There were other "doggie" people on the beach, retired oldies like themselves but also some people biking on the tarmac path stretching alongside the golden sand . Tom spun his wife around laughing happily into her eyes. Rebecca had to ask him what he had found so funny.

'I recalled a memory from the past, seeing these people on their bikes. Do you remember when you and I went to a beach when we were first going out together? I don't think that we had known one another for long, when I asked you to come with me for lunch which I had packed into my rucksack. You, on the other hand, had a folder with an essay tucked away in your basket attached to your handlebars. The front wheel of your bicycle went into a hole in the path and it made the basket jump, shedding its load. I can still see those sheets of paper flying around. Most of your essay was spread by the wind like the spoors from a kicked mushroom. I remember how we had to search everywhere for your papers. They had disappeared into gardens, hedges, under trees and into bushes. How lucky we were that it wasn't a stronger wind and that nothing ended up in the sea. Amazingly we did find every single part of your essay but, what a snowfall it was and how therapeutic it was putting the pages back into the correct order. Now it seems to be ages ago and funny. I think that was when I fell in love with you and decided that you were the woman for me.'

'It wasn't funny at the time.' Rebecca said. 'I was devastated. I thought that I had lost huge chunks of it. It must have looked hilarious with both of us crawling around picking up paper. Didn't I have a little cry? It had been such hard work writing that essay and I don't think I would have been able to rewrite it, not even any missing pages.'

The light by the sea had become extremely bright. Fortunately they had had the sense to bring their sunglasses. They noticed some strange looking people, some women more dressed for an evening out than a walk along the sand. One woman, probably oriental, had great difficulty walking wearing high heeled shoes. She was holding tightly on to her partner.

'Why doesn't she give up and take off her shoes? They will be ruined by the end of her walk? I wouldn't even consider walking on a floor indoors with shoes like those.' laughed Rebecca.

It looked absurd. The man was struggling to keep the woman upright and with a camera around his neck in typical Japanese fashion it must have been hard.

Mozart loved this place of freedom. He ran off in

front of Rebecca and Tom, stopped and waited for them to catch up, before he took off again or he came belting back to them. He got his fair share of exercise. Tom said that the dog ran for the entire week in one single day.

They retraced their tracks and were soon by the car to pick up the lunch basket.

Rebecca spread the blanket at the bottom of a sand dune to get some back support. They ate and listened to the soothing sound from the sea.

'The waves are like the movement the spectators make around a football pitch.' Tom said. 'One single viewer can't achieve this, but when a lot of them work together it looks amazing. The same happens to a wave of water. One drop of water makes no wave, but masses of tiny drops can, and when my eyes follow the waves on to the shore, they fold on top of one another. It is beautiful to watch.'

Rebecca nodded. She examined the heaving mass and thought how true it was. So many times the unity of the many parts was enthralling. A choir was a similar kind of togetherness. She sat deep in thoughts listening to the noise of the sea lapping against the shore. Tom's words 'A penny for your thoughts' brought her back. The light breeze was scented with the mix of salt and seaweed that had been thrown on to the beach by the tide. The seagulls were noisy but here in their natural environment they added to the pleasure of the relaxation. It was beautiful - pure bliss just to be there.

When the sun moved behind a cloud it became chilly. They gathered their belongings, whistled for Mozart, and started their retreat towards the car park. It was getting dark by the time they returned back home.

The dog well fed and watered went straight to his basket and fell asleep. He must have been exhausted.

Rebecca and Tom had a drink in front of television and watched the News before dinner was ready. James had left a message on the answering service. Tom talked to him to hear the latest news about Susan. Her boyfriend had been found. He was a man in his early thirties. A bit old for Susan, Rebecca thought. He had been held and was helping the police with their enquiries. It was not good that he had not come forward by himself but had been traced by the police. Nothing was said about him being the prime suspect for the murders on the News. Rebecca was upset and thought it strange as they had been so quick to announce that a suspect had been detained and was held for questioning when they detained Tom.

After dinner they sat and read. Rebecca had difficulty in concentrating on her book. Her thoughts went to Susan. In a strange way she felt sorry for the suspect. Something horrible must have happened to him at some stage in his life to trigger him to commit these awful crimes. She could not stop herself wondering what kind of home he came from. Were there caring parents suffering or had he not experienced love as a child?

In bed Tom fell instantly into a deep sleep but although Rebecca was tired she lay awake for a long time. She could hear the kitchen clock chime midnight before she had relaxed enough.

Rebecca had too much going on in her head. How she wished she could turn the clocks back! She would give anything for Tom's accident never to have happened. She longed for old times, times gone by. In her mind there were only two stages in her life, before Tom's fall and immediately afterwards. Now it seemed light years since they had been a happy normal married couple.

The unanswered questions which Rebecca turned over and over in her head were disturbing. So many unwanted things had happened, especially to Tom. He had always been a responsible and yet carefree man, but he had been turned into a tense football loving telly addict who had nightmares.

When she finally dropped off it was not for long. She was woken up by Tom having his dream. Sadly Rebecca had to admit that she was getting fed up with having her well needed sleep disturbed every night. She felt sorry for Tom but she was exhausted.

Night after night they went through the same procedure. "Fed up", was not the correct expression for her feelings, as she was not tired of being there for Tom. She was desperate to help him and to comfort him. The love she felt for him had never been deeper. Rebecca was determined to be there for him when he needed her. She was only "fed up" with the nightly disturbance. Rebecca did not believe that one could ever tire of helping a loved one.

Tom did not get enough sleep either. He looked wearied. It must be awful to be awakened each and every night by such hallucinations.

Rebecca went to the bathroom. She looked at herself in the mirror. What she saw did not please her. The gaze that met her was from a tired old woman. The wrinkles were multiplying. The cold white bathroom light made her look pale.

Rebecca took a few steps back, increasing the distance between herself and the mirror. She was examining the image staring back at her. She realized that by reducing the size of her reflection   what she saw was a younger looking person. She could no longer detect her wrinkles. Her skin looked more like a peach than a prune. Her weak, tired eye sight helped to blur the details and the reflection became more flattering.

She carefully slipped back into her side of their warm bed hoping to fall asleep again. In the twilight period between her being fully awake and asleep, she met her mother. Rebecca missed her although many years had passed since her mother had died. It was often Rebecca's thoughts went back to the older woman who had abruptly left this life and at too young an age. Rebecca wished for her to be there amongst them. She was in great need of motherly comfort and advice. On the 19th August this year her mother would have celebrated her 80th birthday.

Reflecting the smiling image of her mother, Rebecca passed the threshold into dreamland. She was far away and sound asleep in the early morning when Tom quietly left the bed. He tip-toed out of the room. He dressed and left the house together with Mozart for a short walk. It was a fresh morning, which looked promising.

Tom did not want to go far. He felt apprehensive. He was scared of meeting Vallie or the twins. He was ashamed. He could die of shame and from guilt when he thought of his behavior and its effect.

When the duo returned to the house, Rebecca was still asleep. Tom prepared breakfast and Rebecca woke up to the wonderful aroma of freshly made coffee. Tom sat down on the bed and asked her if she was ok.

'You didn't have a good night I know. I am sorry to disturb your nights. I am even looking forward to my appointment with "the wonderful and charming" Doctor Smith. I never thought I would be, but we are getting pretty desperate.' said Tom.

'Have you and Mozart been out already? asked Rebecca. I couldn't fall asleep last night. My mind was spinning and filled with thoughts. I was too tired. Talking about the doctor, I am cross with myself that I never asked to read your hospital journal before you were discharged. I feel that I ought to have studied it even if I might not have understood much of the medical jargon. I can't see how anything could possibly explain your nightmare though.'

'Darling, why bother getting upset about things undone? You did and still do, so much for me. How could what is written about my operation and the time in the coma be of any help? We can be pleased that they deliberately put me into the deep sleep. We must give them some credit for knowing what they were doing. Nevertheless, it would have helped if they had told you.'

Rebecca left the bed and went into the bathroom. When she spotted the lady in the mirror from a safe distance, she had to shake her head and give the image a big smile, saying to herself that there was more to this reflection than met her eyes.

She slipped into a soft blue denim skirt, only long enough to reach her knees. It went well with the white top she took out of the drawer. It was a golf shirt with a blue band around the edge of the collar and on the short sleeves. To be on the safe side she took out a blue cardigan. She swapped her bedroom slippers for a pair of espadrilles. They were bright red and made her feel mischievous. Her thoughts went to the film "The Red

Shoes" and she looked at her feet as if they were going to start dancing. She smiled to herself.

Tom served breakfast outside on the terrace. It was warm enough in the shelter of the wall, but not without her cardigan.

They talked about morning meals on balconies in the past. Their thoughts went specially to times they had spent near a miles long beach in the Algarve in Portugal close to the small fishing village of Alvor. It had been a warm early January. The days when they had not been playing golf, they used to walk along this enormous almost deserted beach. They had been dressed in shorts, sleeveless tops and hats. They used to walk for hours along that beach.

'Do you remember the names of the couple from Yorkshire we met several times on that beach? They were retired teachers I think.' Tom asked.

'You are thinking of the couple we discussed the Swedish crime writer Henning Mankell with, aren't you? I think they were called Celia and Tom.' Rebecca answered.

'That's right. It is lovely to meet new people when you are away from home. It is strange that you should mention them because the other day I came across the book they gave us.'

'I hope that we'll be able to go back there next January. I haven't given up on your travel insurance.. The friends we have there and the beautiful golf courses. I am longing for next year to arrive although I am aware that one shouldn't wish one's life away.' Rebecca told Tom.

'Let's hope for a clean bill of health and aim for a return visit. Perhaps Doctor Smith will come up trumps.'

It was a super morning to be able to sit in the sunshine and talk about good old times, one of the many bonuses of sharing a true love.

Anticipating dinner Rebecca put the salmon on a bed of rock salt, skin down, and placed it in the oven. She planned to serve it cold with a sauce made with caviar. Boiled potatoes and a green salad would make it a spring treat.

Tom set off down the Dell with Mozart. It was wonderful to be able to do a morning walk here without wearing wellie-boots.

The air was filled with the scent of early summer. In between the weathered foliage overhead the insects were dancing on the rays of sunlight. It did not only smell and sound like summer, but it was also beginning to look like the warmer season of the year had arrived. The bird song was a joy. Tom had to stop more than once to take it in. He was happy to be alive and this feeling stayed with him for the rest of the day, until the terrifying darkness descended upon him at night, heralding the return of the demons in his black dream.

When Mozart and Tom entered the house Tom put the kettle on and went in search of Rebecca. He knew she was not far away as he could hear the clatter of cutlery as she was laying the dining room table for tonight's event.

He embraced her from behind and nearly knocked her over in his enthusiasm. Rebecca saw that the spirit of joy was mirrored in Tom's eyes. She was relieved to see him full of life after the last days of pure emptiness when he seemed to be close to a break down. She asked him where he had taken the dog and reminded herself that the Dell was a place of magic. Here in front of her was the living proof of that.

'I do love this room. It is pure bliss and a treat to have a meal in here with friends. To really enjoy food you need a special space to eat it, and this dining room was made for such sheer delight.' Tom said.

They went into the garden with their coffee, and sat down holding hands admiring the birds which had taken possession of the several nesting boxes. There were bumble bees around the flower beds.

'I can hear and see the grass growing. It badly needs a cut. I think I'll do that before lunch. This weather is too good to waste away.'

When Rebecca was tidying up after their lunch and had switched the dishwasher on so that it could be emptied before the dinner plates had to go in, Tom kissed his wife on her neck and asked if she would like to come to bed with him in the afternoon. He needed a rest and thought that she probably needed to lie down for a while before their guests arrived.

Rebecca looked up into his eyes. She knew that they were not going to bed to sleep. She smiled into his face and off they went. Mozart was locked in the kitchen. Rebecca put a tray on top of the ready cooked salmon but she did not really think that he would touch it.

After their lovemaking, Tom fell into a light slumber. Rebecca though she was relaxed but could not sleep. She listened to the even breathing next to her and left. She was wearing her morning gown as she made herself a nice cup of coffee. She would bathe later. She went to sit outside but it had become chilly so she came in and closed the door.

The phone was buzzing. It was James telling her that he would like to call by on Sunday with Gill.

They were going to see Gill's parents during the

weekend and they could come for lunch on Sunday if it was convenient.

Tom will be thrilled, Rebecca thought.

Another lovely day would soon be near its end. Time passes so quickly.

They had a wonderful evening with champagne to start it off. Lovely pink sparkles get people going and help to break the ice. Not that they needed help to stimulate conversation. Talk comes easily with friends, but it was a good introduction. Rebecca and Tom, managed to have a few hours of relaxation in their wonderful company..

The afternoon spent together in bed had certainly helped them and it had been one of Rebecca's clever ideas to invite friends for dinner.

Anna came into the kitchen helping to clear up and for a quick chat. She wanted to know when Tom was due to see the doctor. They managed to have some girlie laughs with Mary who by then had joined them. Different cheeses were placed on the board, butter on the table and the biscuits in a basket.

Tom had produced a bottle of red wine and the evening went on. They talked about things they had done together in the past.

Nobody mentioned any travel plans. This subject was not touched upon although they did talk about golf. Anna and Mary asked Rebecca if she would like to join them and another friend for bridge.

'You played when you were young, didn't you? We are one short - please do say that you will. It is only one afternoon a week and you'll soon pick it up again. It'll be at my house on Thursday. You can let me know for sure after Monday.' Anna begged.

'I don't know, Anna. I am doing so much as it is, but it was lovely of you to think of me. Thanks anyway.'

'Of course she is going to you on Thursday.' Tom said. 'Rebecca darling, please, you will love it. Trust me, she will be with you on Thursday.' Tom answered Anna.

Eric asked if Tom would like a game of golf. Tom did not want to commit himself and make a date just yet. He said that he wanted to get the doctor's appointment over before making any plans. He admitted that he was nervous about Monday.

The guests left. It was not too late. Rebecca and Tom cleared the house and did the washing up before they went to bed. Tom told Rebecca that she should play golf the next morning, weather permitting.

'I would like you to play with your friends tomorrow, as we don't know what our commitments will be when we have seen our dear doctor friend.'

'If you will be fine on your own with Mozart I would love to get the fresh air and to see my friends at the club. Lets wait and decide in the morning. About bridge, you seem to be keen on getting me out of the house. Anything the matter that you are not telling me, Tom?' asked Rebecca.

Tom put his arms around her. He held her admiring her beautiful features. Her hair daintily framing her face. He smiled but was serious in a strange way. Rebecca could not put a finger on it, but he seemed sad. Rebecca asked him how he felt and he said that he was fine but tired and scared about Monday.

'What are you afraid of if you feel fine?' she persisted.

'Well, what is she going to come up with? You must admit that her behaviour has been odd.' complained Tom.

Rebecca and Tom let go of one another. The house was quiet after all the laughter. The silence felt like a blessing but how wonderful it was to have friends.

Rebecca could hear the breathing of the man next to her. Tom was not asleep either. He was thinking of Monday. If he was nervous now with several days to go, what on earth would he be like on the actual day? Rebecca turned over facing Tom's back. She started to stroke his body to make him relax.

CHAPTER 23

The sun was shining through the curtains when the alarm went off.

Tom let Mozart out into the garden. They would go for a walk after breakfast.

Rebecca was first in the bathroom, and then they sat down to have the first meal of the day. She phoned one of her friends to let her know that she would join them in an hour.

Tom kissed his wife goodbye as she left for her golf. He closed the gate behind her.

Tom told Mozart that he would tidy the kitchen and empty the dishwasher and then he would take him for a walk. He had no wish to go near ASDA. Rebecca had promised him she would take care of the shopping for the time being and after a week or so they would do it together.

She had not told Tom that she was planning to call on Vallie and the twins. She was going to try this afternoon or perhaps straight after golf. She was to "do a Tom", acting without letting anybody know. More secrets!

Tom was deep in thought as he went about the house. He was pleased that Rebecca had agreed to go to her golf this morning and that she was going to think about Anna's and Mary's proposal to join them for bridge.

He grabbed the lead from behind the door and with Mozart in tow, he left the locked and alarmed house and proceeded down the hill for the beloved Dell.

The birds were singing and the sound of running water from the little river ought to have been soothing for a tired mind and a poor soul, but Tom was walking with both hands deep inside his trouser pockets and did not take any notice. He neither heard nor saw the signs around him. He was sad. He knew that he had to appear to be happy when Rebecca could see him, when he was being observed. He had let her down. What could he do for her that nobody else could? He was not good enough for Rebecca.

Tom and the dog walked through the Dell and ended up in the village. He whistled for Mozart, and they turned round and walked back. Tom did not want to meet anybody. He chose to take the alternative route back on the other side of the river. They crossed the water and he stopped there, contemplating his fate and watching the stream passing under his feet.

Mozart had run off but had obviously given up and returned to Tom as he stood on the wooden bridge and sat down by his feet waiting expectantly. Every now and then he turned his head to watch his master. He was concerned.

In the end Tom smiled as he noticed the dog and with a sigh asked him what he thought his master ought to do, before retracing their walk home.

Rebecca on the other hand enjoyed the weather and the company of the other ladies. Her golf was not brilliant. She was not concentrating sufficiently to be able to score well. Her thoughts were with Tom and with Vallie.

Walking round the course she decided that she would not go to visit the twins and their mother as the girls would be at school and Vallie perhaps at work. No, she would go shopping and make the visit on Saturday morning instead, as it was more likely that the three women would be at home then.

One of her friends told Rebecca that she seemed to be a little distant – not really "with it" when they had their drinks after the game. Rebecca told them that Tom was going for this medical appointment first thing on Monday. She did not know why she was nervous about this meeting, but she was. She had an odd feeling about it. She said that Tom was apprehensive too.

She returned home. Tom had made a salad and prepared sardines on toast. He had remembered that Rebecca loved pickled beetroots with the sardines. He had put some on her plate.

They ate outside but were disturbed by a few wasps. A bit early for them, Rebecca thought.

It was time to try to observe them. Better keep an eye on them. This was the time to watch out for wasps nests. Tom followed her eyes and told her that it would be too early to notice wasps going in and out of spaces around the garden.

'There are not enough of them for us to be able to follow their flight. I agree that they seem to be early this year. We can't have had any real frost during the winter.'

They talked about golf and Tom's walk in the Dell but mostly about the garden. Rebecca announced that she was going to sit here in the sunshine and read during the afternoon. She would like to take full advantage of this gorgeous sunshine. Tom knew he would not be able to read a book. His concentration was not good enough. He would try to look through "The Week", which had just arrived with today's mail. If he could not relax, he would do some gardening.

Tom felt restless and pottered around the garden. He looked at what would be required to be done to the house. He noticed that the window frames on the summer house needed a fresh coat of paint and made a note of this and mentally noted that the pointing under the kitchen window required attention. He would do this during the weekend, weather permitting.

They had their meal in the kitchen before they moved into the snug to watch some golf on the television. After dinner Tom let Mozart out into the garden and stepped out on to the lawn himself to examine the sky. He could not detect any stars. He hoped that this did not mean that the weather was not going to be dry the next day. He wanted to have those windows painted. It was warm although it was late evening.

He went to bed and snuggled up to his wife. They once again made up a jigsaw of two well fitted pieces. Tom put his arms around Rebecca and his body felt warm and cosy against her back. He moved his arms and started to stroke her back with light movements. It was soothing for her tired body. She soon fell asleep.

Tom was restless, as he had been all day. He tried the trick of counting Rebecca's breathing but lost count several times without getting any closer to dreamland. He did not want his black dream to return and therefore he fought sleep. When he finally did fall into a slumber it was from pure exhaustion, and it was not long before he woke up with the usual start, the racing heartbeat and cold sweat. This time he managed to deal with it without waking Rebecca. Tom slid out of the bed to get a dry towel to put on the wet sheet.

When they woke up on Saturday morning, Tom listened for signs of the weather. There did not seem to be any wind or rain. He was pleased about this. He would be able to attend to the paintwork as planned.

Tom had started to go through his paper work. He

would try to finish that before Monday too. He wanted to be ready. If he had to leave Rebecca for any reason, he was going to make it as easy as he possibly could for her. He did not want to leave any mess behind. He had made enough mess in their lives lately.

There was no sunshine but it was dry. Tom enjoyed his weekly bacon and egg breakfast, and Rebecca had her usual fruit salad and two "lion cooked" eggs. They took their time at the table reading the paper and she doing the Su DoKu. Rebecca was toying with her decision to go and talk to Vallie and the girls. Neither Tom nor Rebecca let the other one into their respective thoughts.

Rebecca would realize that if she had told Tom about her plans it might have helped him but she could not have known that.

Rebecca said that she was going shopping, which was the truth. She did not tell him that she intended to go visiting. She should have told him.

Tom cleared the table and the kitchen and Rebecca went off in her little car. Mozart would get his walk when he had completed his chores hopefully before any rainfall.

Rebecca decided to go shopping first as she was not going to buy anything for the freezer. It would probably be wise to have that done before visiting Vallie. Rebecca was not looking forward to the confrontation but she felt she had to do it. After the visit she was planning she might be too upset to do anything.

Saturday morning at the supermarket was not too bad. It was early. Families had not arrived. The weather was not good enough to go for family outings. The shop felt deserted. Rebecca was pleased as she managed to obtain her shopping faster than usual. She packed the carrier bags into the boot and then off she went.

CHAPTER 24

Instead of going right on to the main road, Rebecca turned left and drove slowly until she noticed the corner house with the strange extension which Tom had talked about. It was an odd house, and she was surprised that she had not seen it before, but it was partly hidden. She turned off by this house and drove past. She knew that Vallie lived in No 13. Tom had told her so when he had revealed the story about his visit.

She drove up to the house with the correct number and there was a silver Honda parked in front of the gate. Rebecca had made some mental notes of what she would like to ask the three women if they would give her the chance and time to ask any questions. They might close their front door in her face as soon as they realized who she was.

Rebecca took a deep breath to steady her nerves before she left the security of her car. She went up to the wrought iron gate, which needed a coat of black paint. She opened it and the creak startled her. She closed it behind her and walked towards the front door following the gravel path. Rebecca knew that there was no turning back. Anyone in the building in front of her must have heard the visitor approaching.

Rebecca could hear the echo of the bell in the house as she pressed the button at the side of the door. She listened hard to detect any signs of life from the other side. She could hear someone moving. She was nervous but had calmed down a fraction after she had made her final decision to go through with this.

The door opened. In front of Rebecca stood a sturdy man with tattoos on the left forearm. Rebecca met the man with a smile and asked if "Vallie" was at home.

The man examined her closely. He turned his face into the house and shouted that **Val** had a visitor. However, he did not let Rebecca past through the door. He was holding it firmly and returned his gaze to look at the visitor. He was obviously suspicious but of what? She did not have the time to figure that out before a woman appeared by the door at his side. Rebecca was relieved by the appearance of this female face as she had felt as if the man had been undressing her with his hard gaze.

'Yes?' challenged the woman.

Rebecca saw the cold eyes in the red haired female's face but decided that she was not going to be affected by the glare.

'You wanted to see me I gather.'

The man left his place and walked back into the room. This allowed Rebecca to see a little more of the inside of the house but she only had eyes for the female in front of her and did not notice the big cat only a few feet away.

Rebecca once more asked to talk to "Vallie," although she had very clearly heard the man calling her "Val" and not "Vallie."

The woman still holding on to the door, not wanting to open it completely. She must have been a striking beauty once. Her hair had traces of red although it was turning a greyish colour. If she had a slimmer figure she would still have been a good looking woman. With her freckles and green eyes her colouring was stunning. Now however, her chin was set in a defiant mode which made her look hard and she was plump with double chins and a pale and lined face. Rebecca thought to herself that this woman would benefit from a mirror like the ones she had been told that could be found in Marks & Spencer's. A mirror that made you look slimmer.

'I am the woman you are looking for, but why do you call me "'Vallie?"'

Rebecca was surprised by this question. She answered that her husband Tom had told her that her nickname was "Vallie."

'If I am wrong I ask you for forgiveness. I know that the nickname "Val" is more common if your name is Valerie. Aren't you called "Vallie" then?'

She did not answer Rebecca's question. Vallie asked Rebecca another one instead.

'What do you want?'

Rebecca said that she would like to have a word.

'Please help me. I have come here without my husband's knowledge. He came to see you to ask you a few questions but you refused to answer him and put the police on to him instead. I am not here to tell you off but would like to clear up some misunderstandings. Please don't push me away before you have told me why you keep on telling him that you have never met. He is certain that you have.' pleaded Rebecca.

'I am telling you the truth when I repeat that I had never set eyes on your husband before he called out my name in that car park by the beach. How he knows about my nickname "Vallie" I haven't a clue. The only person who has ever called me that was my late husband.' said the woman.

'I am sorry to learn about your husband. We didn't know. Could it be that he knew my husband Tom? I mean my husband seems to know so much about you and your daughters. Am I correct when I assume that your daughters' father was your late husband?' asked Rebecca

'I don't know what this is about. My late husband, the father of the twins, is no longer with us. I don't want to talk about him and I certainly have no wish to upset the girls. We have a new life now, and what this could have to do with you, I don't know, and neither do I care for that matter.' replied the woman angrily.

Rebecca felt that she had to be careful. She did not want to have the front door slammed in her face. She looked into the other woman's eyes and asked her in a whisper when her late husband had died.

'What has this to do with you? Were you keen on him? Did you have an affair? Well??' asked the woman.

'No, your late husband and I probably never met. Please tell me.' begged Rebecca.

Vallie stared at the pleading woman at her front doorstep. She kept on looking at Rebecca for so long that Rebecca had to lower her eyes. Finally after what seemed to be hours of tense waiting she was told.

'He died in early January in a car crash.'

Rebecca had to hold her breath. She took in some air audibly. Even Vallie jerked at the sudden noise.

The two women looked into one another's eyes. They kept their gaze looked for a long time before Rebecca once again had to give way for the green hard glare.

'I am sorry.' whispered Rebecca.

'You must have read about his accident in the paper. The Evening News wrote about his death. Why is this so important to you?'

'I am sorry to have disturbed you. My husband was in hospital in January. I suppose the staff must have been talking about your late husband over Tom's head when he was unconscious.'

Rebecca stepped back almost falling over the cat in doing so. She turned her eyes to her feet and saw the big cat looking accusingly back at her. It was an indignant animal. Vallie told her off and said that she should be more careful as the cat was an old member of the family.

Rebecca said she was sorry and bent down to stroke the creature. She stood up and said thank you.

Rebecca turned round at the same time as she heard the door closing but not before she had heard Vallie voicing her irritation and that she hoped never to have to see her or her husband again.

'Let us get on with our lives and don't you dare try talking to my girls. They are still mourning their father. Leave us alone and don't come back.'

Rebecca had opened her mouth to say something but she had no time as the door slammed shut.

She traced her way back along the gravel path. She could feel angry eyes following her every step from behind the net curtains.

Rebecca opened the rusty and creaking wrought iron gate. She closed it behind her still without turning round. She walked slowly away towards her car and was relieved when the vehicle happily twinkled the lights in answer to her pressing the key to unlock the door.

Rebecca put on her seatbelt and drove off to turn the car round. She never glanced back at the house she had just left. She decided never ever to set foot near it again. Little did she know how soon she would feel the need to return. Little did she know!

Rebecca was in a state of agitated shock and could not sort out the thoughts going through in her head. She was pleased that she might have the solution to Tom's bad dream. How was she going to handle what she had found out? How was she going to talk to Tom about her visit? A visit paid behind his back?

Foolish of her not to have talked it through with him before she left? She had not thought that she would get any information, or had she? She cannot have. If she had thought that her visit would solve anything she would have let Tom know her plans.

What on earth had she been thinking of? If she had not thought that her visit would solve any problems, why did she go there?

The relief she had felt when she first had heard that a man had had a car crash at the same time as Tom was in hospital and that this occurrence must be connected to his dream, evaporated. The feeling of revelation was there, but the delight had soured. She felt stupid.

Back home Rebecca put a smile on her face and stepped out to open the gate. Mozart greeted her from the other side and insisted on being patted before she could drive the car into the driveway.

She was surprised but put it down to him having felt abandoned as Tom was occupied with his paint work. He turned round and came up to her, paintbrush in hand, to kiss her lightly on her cheek.

Rebecca had to smile. He looked like a little schoolboy who had done something which was not allowed. Tom had a patch of paint on his chin and the apron had not done too badly either.

'You have been a long time. There must have been a lot of customers in ASDA this morning. I had started to worry.

Could you please put the kettle on? I am dying for a cup of coffee. I have almost finished these windows.'

Rebecca was pleased that she had not been asked any questions. There had been in no need to invent answers. She had not realized how late it had become. The time for her had passed quickly and she had not thought up a story. She did not want to have to tell Tom anything at the moment. She would have to think it through and then talk to him.

Rebecca emptied the car and put everything away while waiting for the kettle to boil. She went to Tom and asked if he was ready to sit down. It would have to be indoors as there was no sunshine and it felt damp outside. Tom asked for another five minutes to clean up. Rebecca went indoors and suddenly she remembered something that Anna had said the other day and dialled her number.

'Anna, a short call. I have been asked for coffee for my hard working painter husband.

I remember you telling me recently that Tom's recurrent dream rang a bell with you. Could it have been that you read about a car crash in the paper in January? I have just been told about a man who died in a car crash. It was in the Evening News. Can you recall having read about it or heard about it?'

There was a pause before Anna replied ' Hang on a minute. I remember it clearly now you mentioned it. Why do you ask, Rebecca?'

Rebecca had to sit down. She was shivering.

'It is a long story, Anna. I'll explain later. I cannot remember having heard or read anything, but I was far too busy with Tom, but thanks for satisfying my curiosity.

I'll better make Tom that cup of coffee. I'll phone you on Monday after we have been to the doctor's.'

She hung up and went into the snug for the telephone directory. She made another phone call, this time to the library. Rebecca asked if they could find any newspaper articles written in January about a car-tractor accident. They would send it to her if they were successful.

The librarian seemed to be keen with the prospect of a challenge and promised to do his best.

Rebecca put the kettle on again and she made the promised coffee.

They sat in the kitchen enjoying the hot drink. Tom had come out from the shower and his hair was wet. He smelled lovely. Rebecca embraced him and had an extra sniff, taking in the sweetness of the lavender soap. He held her tight before sitting down at the table. The mail had arrived, a welcome distraction. She had an excuse to escape from having to talk about her morning's experiences. She needed to tell Tom but she would have to postpone the conversation until she had gathered her thoughts. She had not a clue how to raise the question but would hopefully think of something.

It was time for lunch. Rebecca had only agreed to have this cup of coffee to give herself an opportunity to sit down. She put the soup on the stove and boiled a couple of eggs.

Ever since her school days, she had loved spinach soup with egg halves in the dish to excite the green creamy liquid.

Once again they sat down at the kitchen table. It was a pity that there was no sunshine, but it was wonderful to sit informally in the kitchen and there would be many lovely sunny days to come.

They were lost deep in their own thoughts. Neither spoke. Rebecca wanted to talk. She had to break the news to Tom before Gill and James visited them after church tomorrow. She took a deep breath. Tom looked up at her and asked if she was all right and she grabbed the opportunity.

'Yes and no.'

'What is that supposed to mean? Something has been troubling you all morning so tell me please. What is on your mind?'

Rebecca reached out for his hand and held it tight on the table. She told him that she had been to see Vallie. He looked surprised and worried, but did not say much. The only words he managed to say came out in a whisper. He was obviously frightened of what he was about to hear. He only said 'Well?' and repeated the word twice as Rebecca was not quick enough to respond.

She looked at him and told him the full story how she had been left standing outside on the doorstep but that she had got some response from Vallie.

She told me that her late husband was killed in a car crash in January. I gained the impression that somehow she felt guilty. When I returned home I phoned Anna. I didn't tell her what I had been up to or what I had found out. It occurred to me that Anna once told me that your dream sounded somewhat familiar but she was unable to put her finger on why. When I told Anna about this man who had crashed his car into a tractor, I asked her if that rang a bell with her. What she told me is extraordinary. Now when I jogged her memory she remembered having read about the tragedy in the paper. Apparently it was all over the papers at the time. I didn't read the papers then, so I didn't see it. I was far too preoccupied with your fall and being in hospital at the brink of death. Anyway, what Anna could recall was that there had been a man who had been killed driving his sports car straight into a tractor. One reason why it had been so much about this accident was because the driver of the tractor was being charged with dangerous driving. That the man in the sports car had been speeding had not registered as being relevant. The tractor driver had been charged with culpable homicide because he was driving on the road with his front fork down. He hadn't bothered to fold it away as he was only going round the corner to his farm.

It occurs to me that there must have been a lot of talk about this in the hospital when you were there and although you were in a coma it could well have registered with you. I think it is possible that you are reliving the horror of what you must have heard. What do you think?'

Tom sat quietly trying to take it in, trying to understand what his wife had told him. He looked up and into her eyes before he answered.

'Thank you for going through this trouble for my sake, Rebecca. I am grateful to you.'

Rebecca opened her mouth to say something but was stopped midway.

'What you have told me could well be the explanation for my nightmare, I agree with you that it fits. I must admit that I am pleased that you went but I am hurt and surprised that you didn't tell me about your intentions before you left. I suppose that if you had let me know I would have begged you not to. I would have been worried sick and would have asked you to let me come with you. I don't know. I can't be angry with you after what I did without talking to you first. Look what happened to me when I tried! I was taken into custody. Let's look closely at these new revelations. I am thrilled that at last I think we seem to be getting somewhere.' Tom said.

Tom was pacing up and down the kitchen as he was talking. He stopped and looking down at her face went up to her and took her into his arms, telling her how much he loved her. He had tears in his eyes. The business they were discussing was serious. Tom wished they could have a drink but he wanted them to keep their minds clear. He longed for a whisky.

He took her hand in his and led her into the snug where they sat down to talk side by side. They left the kitchen as it was, the table cluttered with dirty dishes.

Tom was thrilled to have lifted the lid on the mystery surrounding the recurring nightmare. He asked Rebecca to tell him again what she had heard. He quietly listened and then he said that this showed how dangerous it might be to talk over somebody's head.

'Doctor Smith and the nurses did ask me to read and to talk to you.' said Rebecca. 'I was told that nobody could be certain whether a person in a coma would "hear" or not, but in case you would, they wanted me to keep on for you to perhaps learn to recognize my voice. I have a slight memory of the doctor telling me that if you heard my voice and felt my touch it could stir your subconscious. I wonder why she said that when later on we were told that you had been deliberately kept in a coma?'

'You didn't happened to find out more about Vallie, did you?' asked Tom. 'I mean where she works for instance? If she works at the hospital it might explain why I seem to know so much about her'

Did you see the twins?' asked Tom.

'No, I never met the girls, They might not have been at home. But a big man with tattoos on his arms opened the door and called for "**Val**" to come. I didn't like him or her for that matter but she must have been a beauty when she was younger.' answered Rebecca.

'Let's go for a walk.' Tom suggested. ' Mozart needs to move and some fresh air will do us good.'

They cleared the kitchen before picking up Mozart's lead.

Hand in hand they disappeared, following the dog down the lane. They had a lovely afternoon stroll into the trees.

It was a pity that the big noisy seagulls had found their way inland instead of settling down by the sea where they belonged. There was a big increase in the number of crows too, which were not even beautiful and with the magpies these unpleasant species seemed sadly to be taking over. Why they were not hunted down, Rebecca could not understand. They did after all live on small birds and their eggs.

Tom rescued her from the negative thoughts and pointed out that the couple of doves that they had had in their garden for several years were stunning. It was a shame that they had to leave their "visiting cards" on the patio and the garden furniture. Tom told Rebecca that he had been watching them the other day as the doves were taking turns in the bird bath.

She agreed that they were a pleasure to look at as long as there were just the one couple, but Rebecca reminded him that her favourite bird was the bullfinch, especially at mating time when their hallmark red breast was at its most radiant.

Tom brought a sugar lump out of his pocket and put

it on the ant hill which they passed on the side of an old tree stump. He had loved it when his father had taken him out for a walk and showed him how hard these small insects worked. The sugar was always covered with ants and he never failed to stop and admire their industry when passing on his return route. James had loved it too.

CHAPTER 25

When they returned, Tom collapsed in front of the television and switched on the rugby. Rebecca prepared the Sunday lunch for Gill, her parents and for James,s visit. It had been such a wonderful surprise when Gill phoned and asked if they could come too. She and James would like to introduce their parents to one another.

Rebecca and Tom were delighted.

She made some biscuits and an extra loaf of bread for the "children" to take back to St Andrews. While she was at the stove she decided to make a chicken pie for them to take away too. This felt therapeutic and took her mind off the noise emanating from the snug as Tom became involved in the attempts at goal scoring as the television took over.

Thinking of tomorrow's food, she had to make her mind up what to offer Tom for dinner. She decided to make one of her pasta dishes. That would be easy enough served with a fresh salad and a bottle of claret. Pasta with fresh tomatoes cooked with garlic in olive oil was one of their spaghetti favourites. It was a long time since she had given Tom this treat.

Tom's excitement increased in volume. She became curious herself and went through to the snug with his tea. Perhaps she would join him while the bread maker was doing its job and the biscuits were in the oven. She had brought the timer with her. She never relied on her memory.

By the time the alarm went off she had become interested in the match. It was exciting and intriguing watching Tom's reactions, although she did not understand the rules. To her it was just like a dirty heap of t-shirts and shorts running around like headless chickens.

Rebecca was pleased that she had put on the timer otherwise she would have burnt James' "goodies." She returned to the kitchen and took them out of the oven but quickly went back to the snug to follow the game. She did not want to miss Tom's enthusiasm. It was lovely to see him out of himself. She never thought that she would get hooked watching any sport apart from golf or some equestrian competition.

In the interval she fetched the telephone and dialled Anna's number from the kitchen. Rebecca told her about her morning's visit to the mysterious Vallie and explained the earlier inquiry about the accident with the tractor.

If Tom's dream could be explained it did not mean that everything else could. So many of his recent questions and remarks remained unanswered. However, learning of a parallel for parts of his dream had made her feel that they had come a long way. All they could do now, was to wait until Monday and the doctor's opinion. Rebecca told Anna how she dreaded this meeting and was unexplainedly filled with fear of the outcome.

By the time Rebecca had finished in the kitchen, it had started to rain. The weather forecast had been correct. Rebecca opened the back door for Mozart and stepped outside having slipped on her coat. The rain was a soft downpour. It was caressing her upturned face. She stood there taking it in. The sky was an even colour of silver lead. It looked like a velvet blanket. It was beautiful with the rain drops falling from the sky nourishing the vegetation. The weeping willow was at its best in weather like this. This was not going to be just a shower. It would probably continue for most of the evening.

Rebecca looked at the green grass and examined the few remaining daffodils and tulips bowing their heads. They seemed to be content soaking up the falling water. To follow one drop of rain slowly making its way down a flower petal was pure magic. The birds were quiet making only a few chirps as they searched for shelter. Rebecca felt like taking her shoes off to feel the damp grass touch the soles of her naked feet. She resisted. Ever practical she decided that she could not afford to catch a cold.

Back inside when it was "drinkies" time and Tom served her a dry martini, the rain pattered on the windows. They talked about the rugby. She tried to sound enthusiastic. She was grateful for this chance for him to escape from himself, which she desperately wanted to sustain.

After dinner they had to agree that the meal was utterly boring but wonderful. They let Mozart out into the wet garden. It was still raining.

They went to bed and although neither of them talked about it, they hoped that the revelation and explanation of the car accident would have released the tensions surrounding Tom's nightmare . Alas! They would soon become disappointed.

When they went to bed Tom was nervous. He had high hopes for an undisturbed night but at the same time he was scared. Before he fell asleep he thought of Rebecca and the trouble she had gone through for his sake. To go and pay Vallie a visit must have been a difficult thing for her to do. It must have been emotional and nerve wracking. He felt weaker and weaker, not in health but in his ability to cope.

Rebecca did not fall asleep directly either. She relived her morning's visit. She tried to remember every word that had been exchanged. She tried to visualize Vallie's body language. Such a complicated mess it had become. Although she had managed to get some answers there were many factors left to be resolved.

She finally fell asleep and now <u>she</u> was dreaming about a poor tractor driver, guilty of negligence, breaking the law and with a death on his conscience. Later she would feel much more sorry for him than for the speeding driver who had been killed.

Tom woke up. He was sitting up in the bed gasping for air. Rebecca tried to calm him down but it took her a long time to make him aware of her presence. The dream was there but it had turned into something different. He was not able to tell her in what way. It had been a more intense sensation of disaster, something that he had truly experienced, something happening to himself. He had felt the fork penetrating his body. The dream had become reality, still attacking their lives.

The weather the following morning was not good. It was not raining, but there was a wet mist. There was no wind but an anticipation that the wind was waiting round the corner. The weather forecast for Monday was awful, with rain and gale force winds.

Rebecca and Tom prepared themselves for church. At breakfast they talked about the night they had left behind. Both were devastated that the explanation about Tom's recurring nightmare had not helped to shut it out of Tom's subconscious mind. Rebecca had been confident that when he did know the truth about the event, which have been causing his problem, it would be gone for ever. Now she did not know what else they could do. They did not even know if doctor Smith would be able to help Tom.

It was cold. The temperature had fallen. Rebecca chose her navy blue suit and a white roll neck for church. The jumper was a thin one but it felt like a defeat to go back to woollies instead of a shirt. Tom looked dapper in his grey suit and his paisley bow tie.

In the church hall after the service they enjoyed the coffee and mingled with their friends. Anna and Eric were there and they managed to exchange a few words. They wished Tom all the best for his appointment on Monday morning.

Rebecca had laid the table the previous evening. She switched on the plate warmer immediately they returned from church. The guests arrived earlier than Rebecca had expected. She was pleased that she had prepared beforehand as much as she had. This meant that she could sit down with them for the drink, especially as it had to be champagne.

Rebecca and Tom were introduced to Gill's parents Helen and Gordon Walker. Tom went pale and thought that he would faint when he saw that Gill's father was The Police Superintendent. They had met before but under dreadful circumstances.

Tom wished he could disappear through the floor. He almost died of shame. Gill's father knew Tom's secret! How would Tom ever be able to live with this?

He felt distant but had to pretend that everything was fine as the youngsters announced that they had become engaged. James had proposed under a tree which Gill had confessed was her favourite spot, a tree she had climbed as a small child and on whose branches she used to sit and dream. The engagement was the reason why James had asked that they had lunch today. It was a happy occasion with much embracing.

Happy except for Tom. He managed to get his voice back but it was unsteady. His discomfort was panned off as emotion.

Gordon had given Tom a warm handshake and smile. He knew that the man he had been interviewing a few days earlier was James' father but Gordon looked straight into Tom's terrified eyes and gave him an extra warm and reassuring handshake.

James told them that he had been somewhat nervous as he had asked Gill's father for permission to marry his daughter but not nearly as nervous as he had been when he proposed. Gill's ring was much admired. It was made of white gold and had a row of diamonds all the way round the entire band. It was a beautiful eternity ring saying more than words could express. The happy couple said that they hoped they would get married the following year. It was a delight to see them being very much in love.

After lunch the conversation turned to Susan's boyfriend. James said that her brother had told him that he had been abused by an uncle as a teenager. He had no criminal record and his parents were devastated. They had never been told about the abuse of their son. All these disclosures had lead to the uncle's arrest too.

The date for Susan's funeral had been decided. It was to be a private affair with only the family present.

When the guests had left, Tom asked Rebecca if she wanted to come with him and Mozart for a short walk, or if she would rather stay at home and clear away the lunch party. Rebecca hesitated and then said that if Tom was going for a short walk she would stay and they could watch "Songs of Praise" together.

In the circumstances Tom was pleased to be on his own with his thoughts.

Rebecca was singing as she put the dishes away into the dishwasher. It was such good news and she had already started to think about what to wear for the wedding. Surely she would get an outfit and a new hat from McEwens of Perth specially for the occasion. However, her thoughts did not stop with the wedding bells. No, she was thinking and hoping for grandchildren. She had to laugh at herself. 'Stupid woman' she told herself aloud just as Tom and Mozart entered the kitchen.

Tom asked her what she had said but Rebecca only smiled and told him that she had been speaking to herself. He teased her that she was getting old.

Tom had been thinking a great deal about his son and daughter in law to be. His thoughts had been different from those of Rebecca. He was relieved that James had his life truly sorted out and would soon enter the haven of matrimony. He no longer had to worry about him. Rebecca was a different kettle of fish.

The wind had picked up. This was unusual as the winds usually slackened in the evenings. However, this spring it had been different.

They listened more than watched "The Songs of Praise"

Tom had decided not to have any more alcohol and was sitting there with his tomato juice but Rebecca had asked for a whiskey. She needed a relaxant to calm her down. She was beginning to fret.

'Let us enjoy this evening together. Tomorrow is

another day. Tomorrow bears its own problems and deals with its own worries. We have agreed on this so many times but it is worth repeating.' Rebecca said.

As it was going to be an early start the following morning, they decided to go to bed almost at sunset. Neither of them thought that they would manage to fall asleep directly and how right they were.

Rebecca was trying hard not to toss and turn. She could feel that Tom was awake too. His breathing was not deep and relaxed but uneven as it reflected his state of agitation. She thought about starting a conversation with him but changed her mind when she asked herself what could they talk about when they were fearful of tomorrow's meeting at the hospital? They had discussed Gill and James all evening. It had helped her at the time. For Tom it was another matter. He was filled by guilt and shame at the thought of his first meeting with Gill's father interrogating him at the station.

Rebecca could feel her heart beating at full speed and was finding it impossible to relax. She tried to clear her mind but counting sheep had no effect whatsoever. She started to count Tom's breathing but that had been fruitless. She even made a go of it in Swedish. The result of this had made her more uptight as she realized how much of her Swedish she had forgotten. She had started to think about her friends over the water and was longing to go and see them.

Tom did not wish to go to sleep. He wanted it to be Monday afternoon and to have this meeting over and done with. Little did he know how much he would wish for yesterday as the Beatles used to sing "Yesterday all my problems seemed so far away...."

He knew that Rebecca was awake but he could sense that she had fallen asleep around midnight. Tom did finally fall asleep as well but he had heard the clock in the kitchen chime three. He panicked then being desperate for much needed rest.

His thoughts went to James and he wished his son all the happiness in the world. Tom had tried hard to keep his mind on this. It had proved impossible. It was not long before he had the terror of his nightmare in his head. How could it be that he had to experience another poor man's death over and over? The fear was strong. It was such a real feeling and he could hear the screeching of brakes and metal of the car being penetrated by this huge fork. The terror was genuine. He was taking on the feeling of pure fear on behalf of someone else. The car meeting a tractor on a narrow country lane. Talk about being at the wrong place at the wrong time! If the sports car had not been speeding, the farmer would have reached his gate and nothing would have happened. The driver would be alive, the farmer working at his farm and Tom would not have heard people talking about the accident and would not be suffering from his dreadful dream.

When he finally fell asleep it was like falling into a swoon. He would be exhausted when the alarm would wake them up in a few hours time. The last thing which was on his mind was Gordon and the weather. He could hear the wind. The rain seemed to be running down the windows. He felt like touching Rebecca but thought better of it.

He prayed for good weather. A dry, bright day would make things look more cheerful and to make things easier for them.

PART THREE

The alarm woke Rebecca with a start. She went to the bathroom and dressed before she returned to the bedroom to wake up Tom. She knelt by his side of their bed and talked softly to him as she had done only a few months ago by his hospital bed. She stroked her hand over his chin and could feel and hear the bristles. Although Rebecca had tried to be careful Tom awoke with a jerk and his entire body became rigid. He gasped for air but calmed down when he heard her voice. He took her hand in his, holding it tight for a while and then gently kissed the back of her fingers, his lips lingering for some time. He looked up into her big eyes before he remembered he had to face the day. He took a deep breath, asking about the time and if she had been up long. He sat up, turned his body to let his legs hang down from the bed and his feet touch the carpet. He kept this posture for a second longer than usual. Unsteadily he stood up. He was tired. He could feel his body heavy with lack of sleep, but he had to get a grip on himself. As he was having his shower and shaving, he slowly woke up.

Rebecca prepared breakfast. She made a couple of cheese sandwiches and a flask of black coffee to take to the hospital. You never knew if the wait would be a long one.

The rain battered the poor flowers merciless. Rebecca wondered if they could feel it. If they were able to she felt sorry for them.

The wind of yesterday had disappeared. It was completely calm, with no movement apart from the raindrops bending down whatever came in their way.

Rebecca shivered. She felt lost. Her thoughts were everywhere and she had difficulty in concentrating. She desperately needed a clear mind. She hoped that Tom would be able to drive the car to the hospital. She hated to drive in rain like this.

Tom had let Mozart outside and it was a sodden dog that returned. Tom was quick to throw a towel around the dog to rub him down before he had any chance of trying to shake the water off in the kitchen. Poor Mozart, it was most unlikely that he would get a walk today.

Tom and Rebecca decided to leave early. There could be heavy traffic on the roads, and the weather would slow everything down. The spray from other vehicles was not going to help the visibility. What they did not want was to be late.

With the car loaded with sandwiches, coffee flask, a bottle of water, two bananas and todays news paper, they left their dog and home. At the last minute Rebecca had enclosed her note books of handwritten comments and thoughts about Tom after his accident. She did not know why she wanted to bring them but they might be of some importance.

As she closed the gate behind them looking up from underneath her umbrella, she could see Mozart standing on the other side of the kitchen glass panel. He was looking back at her. He was only visible as a pure dark shadow through the curtain of rain. Rebecca felt a pang in her heart. She knew that he did not want to be left alone and this made her feel worse.

Tom drove. The cup of tea that Rebecca had served him had made a difference. They travelled in silence. There were many cars on the road and Tom needed to pay attention.

Rebecca's mind was as confused as it had been since she went to bed. She had been thinking a lot about Vallie as a widow. She felt sad. Perhaps she ought to think more of the girls, who had lost their father. She felt uncomfortable with the whole business.

The windscreen wipers worked overtime. Drivers had put their lights on and the extra bright fog light at the back. Some stupid people could always be found, though luckily only a few, who did not use their heads and motored without any lights, like ghostly shadows. Tom had a red bus in front of him and he kept his distance well. The driver indicated when there were floods on the road and Tom did the same for the car behind him. They used the flashing warning lights.

When Rebecca and Tom reached the car park they drew a sigh of relief. Tom felt shaky and sat for a minute with the engine turned off. Rebecca looked at him and asked if he was all right. Tom turned to her and with a lop-sided smile told her he was as well as could be expected under these circumstances.

' We'll never be ready for this meeting, so lets get on with it. Bring the bag with you, please . I could do with a cup of coffee. We are half an hour early. How I wish it was over.' Tom said.

'Let's go for it.' sighed Rebecca.

Rebecca released the catch on the passenger door and opened the umbrella outside the car before she plucked up the courage to step outside. She waited for Tom. She picked up the bag and they rushed towards the entrance.

Tom went to the information desk and was told to go to reception. They were asked to take a seat in the waiting room. Rebecca was pleased that they had umbrellas with plastic tubes covering them when closed. The dripping water ran down into the container. A brilliant invention. They had bought these on their last visit to Madeira.

Tom took a few deep breaths and tried to calm his nerves whilst looking around the room. There were already people waiting. He hoped indeed that they were not there to see the same doctor.

Rebecca smiled towards a little old white haired lady who seemed to be on her own. It made Rebecca sad to see people in a hospital by themselves. This lady was wearing a fully pleated flower patterned skirt and a cardigan buttoned all the way up. At the top edge was a white lace collar. Perhaps she had crocheted it herself. The glass beaded necklace looked precious to its owner and was carried with pride. Her hair was thinning but permed with little compact hard curls. Her spectacles were large and horn-rimmed in a transparent frame. Her legs were covered by thick brown tights and the two narrow sticks ended up in heavy brown leather shoes. Perfect for this kind of weather. Rebecca found herself lost in childhood. This woman reminded her of her mother's cleaning lady. A kind carer she had been to Rebecca.

Rebecca served Tom the cup of coffee he had asked for. Rebecca did not fancy anything to drink but she was pleased that she had brought the bottle of water.

Tom was staring through the window and said something about the rain. Rebecca turned her eyes in the same direction telling Tom that it reminded her of the fishmonger's shop window at the time when she was only a child. There had been water streaming down the inside of the window to keep his fish display cool.

They tried to talk to keep calm and to make the time

to pass. Rebecca let her eyes sweep round the room. They were seven people waiting, mostly older men and women. She tried to listen to what Tom was saying but her attention was not there.

The little old lady Rebecca had noticed was called and disappeared, following a nurse out through one of the doors leading to corridors.

Tom started to walk restlessly around. He made a tour to the gents, then to the magazine rack before he stopped in front of the big window facing the view of parked cars.

It was still raining. The wind was picking up. He could see a single tree bending over in the prevailing wind. It did not look promising and for once he was happy to be indoors.

He turned and went back to the chair next to Rebecca. He told her about the weather getting worse.

His name was called and they rose to follow a female assistant or perhaps she was a nurse.

Rebecca and Tom were shown into a small room with only three chairs, a desk and a window. A single print on one of the walls was the only decoration. There were no curtains and it was painted in a friendly magnolia shade rather than the usual white or hospital green.

They were asked to take a seat. Doctor Smith would soon be with them. Rebecca reached out and took a firm hold of Tom's hand. They were in this position when the door opened and the doctor entered.

CHAPTER 26

Tom stood up to greet her. The woman took his hand and shook Rebecca's as she walked to the other side of the desk. Rebecca had a feeling that the doctor wanted to keep a distance and make sure that the two others in the room were aware of who was in charge.

Smiling she turned to Tom and asked how he was. She told him to tell her about his health. As Tom was talking about his good health, she stepped forward and asked him to remove his jacket so that she could take his blood pressure. She took a couple of blood samples telling him that he had a blood pressure of a seventeen year old. He looked well too, she added before returning to her position behind the desk. She asked Tom if he had suffered from headaches, nausea, lack of balance or problems with his vision. Tom told her that he had been fine on his bike. Then she turned to Rebecca and asked her to leave the room as she wished to speak to her husband on his own. Tom took hold of Rebecca's arm and asked to please keep her seat, telling the woman behind the desk, that if she had anything to tell him he would prefer it to be in the presence of his wife.

'She is part of my life and I wish her to stay'. He said firmly.

He had said this in a more determined tone than he had intended, and he could tell by the expression of the doctor's face that she had been taken by surprise and was far from pleased. She tried to persuade Tom that it was important for her to talk to him about his last months, about his time since he had left the hospital. They had much to discuss. Tom did not bat an eyelid and said that he wanted his wife to share everything the doctor had to say. He wanted her at his side particularly as she might be able to add to the conversation. He started to stand up and he knew he had won his case when he was asked to resume his seat.

The doctor watched them for a minute in silence then let out a big sigh and said

'Very well, as you wish, Mr Chaudler.'

Whilst Doctor Smith was talking, she did not look at Rebecca, only at Tom. Tom was asked about his memory. Did he have problems recalling things from the past?

Tom looked at Rebecca when he answered that his memory was good. He swallowed, took a deep breath and told the doctor that it seemed that his mind was in overdrive. His head was full of strange images that he found impossible to explain.

The doctor asked him to give her an illustration. Tom started off with his recurring nightmare which was ruining their lives. He was told to relate the entire dream in as much detail as he was able to recall.

While Tom was telling the story, Rebecca noticed how the doctor on the other side of the desk sometimes nodded and that her eyes grew bigger but she interpreted this to be from surprise rather than from horror.

Doctor Smith sounded a bit taken aback as she asked Tom about the other images he had mentioned. Tom told her about Vallie and the twins. However, he did not tell her how he had ended up in custody.

The detailed narration had taken some time. Doctor Smith pressed a button on her desk and a young girl entered the room. Rebecca and Tom were asked if they would like coffee or tea. They obviously still had some way to go.

The doctor was told the story of the cat, "the missing painting, and Tom's liking for fish and chips. His taste in programmes on television had changed, as had his vocabulary. He now used words he would never have dreamt of using before the operation. Rebecca held on to her books in the bag. She was ready to bring them forward if necessary.

The coffee and biscuits arrived and Doctor Smith left her place behind the desk. She stood up and turned to look out of the window. She was creating thinking time. Rebecca's heart became erratic as she felt panic. Why indeed did Doctor Smith need time? What on earth was she going to tell them? Rebecca was certain that what she was about to say was not going to be good news. Tom looked at Rebecca and she could sense that he was worried. They could not touch the coffee although Rebecca's mouth was as dry as dust.

Finally the doctor slowly turned to Tom. She cleared her voice, had a sip of her own tea and said that he must have heard about people having signed a paper to let their organs be of use after their death. Perhaps Tom had done this himself?

Rebecca could hardly stand the tension which was building up. The entire room seemed to vibrate. She thought that she would have to scream to get the doctor to tell them what she knew about Tom and his recovery. Rebecca let go of Tom's hand. She was clenching the bag in her lap. The silence that had followed the doctor's last question felt oppressive and the air was suddenly hot and clammy. All that could be heard was the wind and the rain, lashing against the window. And then suddenly Rebecca became completely calm. The tension she had felt a second ago had gone and been replaced by a sense of sadness. Not a feeling she could explain, but the rain probably contributed to her dramatic change of mood.

Doctor Smith smiled towards Tom when she told them how she had saved his life. She was the most clinical person Rebecca had ever met. She was completely devoid of any bedside manner. Her people skills were non existent. Obviously a brilliant surgeon – a master of her calling but when dealing with people she sounded like a humourless barrister for the prosecution. Obviously the woman by the window was proud of her skills. She became serious, her smile disappearing as she went on talking.

'You do realize Mr Chaudler that my team and I saved you from certain death. When you gave your permission for us to operate Mrs Chaudler, I made it clear that your husband was close to being brain dead and that in any attempt to preserve his life we were venturing into uncharted waters. The operation we performed took many hours, defied most of the rules and the outcome was unpredictable – saving your husband's life a gamble. Mrs Chaudler, which I am sure you are as delighted as we were that it paid off. Pioneering surgery saved your husband's life.

Whilst your were on life support following your admission Mr Chaudler, I was notified that another accident victim in an adjacent cubicle had just died. His chest, liver and spleen had been destroyed but his head was completely undamaged.

The man concerned carried organ donor papers and we were therefore able to match the two of you together.

The details would take hours to relate Mr Chaudler, but in short, your brain was damaged to the extent that life could not be preserved. The other victim was dead but his brain was untouched. We therefore took the opportunity; the only possible chance to save your life. We removed his brain and transplanted it into your body. No, more than that, we successfully brought you back to life with hope of a full recovery. We kept you in a coma for as long as we possibly could. During this time we tried to remove his memories and to install your own. We connected the two brains and I believe we were successful. It was a great relief when you regained consciousness and I realized that you had recollection of your own family and that speech, walking, thinking and all bodily functions had been restored. We had managed to give you back your life, Mr Chaudler. However, I am concerned to learn that we didn't erase the memory bank from the brain completely. You appear to have some recollection from the donor's memory.

Mr Chaudler, you are the first person in the whole world, who has undergone an entire brain transplant. You are the living evidence of successful pioneering surgery. You are unique in science and medicine.'

She looked at Tom and gave him a radiant smile. Tom felt numb. He felt weak and sick. He was in a state of shock. He stared at the proud woman standing in front of him. At first he did not speak, he did not move and the room went still. He was paralyzed and disgusted. The only part of him that moved were his lips. He quietly put a question to his "saviour". The only thing that could be heard apart from the wind and the rain was Tom's whispering voice as he turned to Rebecca.

'Did you know about this? Were you told or asked?'

'I am as shocked as you are Tom. I signed to give my permission for potentially life saving surgery but I had no idea - nobody ever gave me any details of the likely procedure.' Rebecca answered head down.

'You are alive Tom, for which I am eternally grateful, but the thought that you are not you is devastating.' Rebecca whispered, haltingly still head down.

Doctor Smith kept on standing behind her desk as if she might need shelter. Her smile had changed from one of unmitigated pride to one of astonishment at Tom's reaction. The change was obvious to Rebecca. The fact that Tom's reaction was unexpected made her even more furious.

''Who was this man?' Tom asked, his voice almost inaudible.

'I am sorry but I am not allowed to reveal his identity.' stated the doctor. 'I think you understand this.'

'No, I don't understand this. It is my life and I think I am entitled to know whose brain I am I using?'

Rebecca and Tom were pleased to have one another's support and to hold hands felt essential.

Tom regained his voice and looked up at the doctor, the woman he had never warmed to. His eyes were aflame and his words came out in staccato.

'If you will not tell us who this dead man was, at least let me know how he died. What happened to him?' he demanded.

'He was in a car crash. When you told me about your nightmare I knew I would have to let you know about the extent of the surgery you have undergone.' answered the doctor.

'Do you mean that you had no intention of telling

me, that I had been rescued from certain death because of another man's brain? Surely you cannot be serious?'

Rebecca noticed how Tom was clenching his fist. For a split second she thought that he would stand up and walk to the desk which separated them from the doctor. Rebecca was afraid that he was going to hit the woman.

Rebecca put her hand on Tom's arm to restrain him and he seemed to calm down a little.

'Well, I was of course going to let you know, but had hoped that the two of you would have showed some appreciation. You are alive, Mr Chaudler. You are the living proof that medical research has given us the means to be able to save a life where brain damage threatens. We have proved beyond doubt that it is possible to remove and replace a human brain. I would say that you, Mr Chaudler, are the proof of a medical miracle. You should be happy and proud. Remember that without this other tragic accident and the victim's authority to use his organs, you would not be here holding your wife's hand.'

Tom gave Rebecca's fingers a firm squeeze before putting another question.

'So what happens now? Will I have to live with another person's memories for the rest of my life?' Tom enquired.

'I am sorry that we failed in removing all the donor's personal memories. Mr Chaudler, you'll learn to live with this with time, I am sure.' The doctor said.

Tom rose to leave the room having pulled Rebecca up at his side when the woman on the other side of the desk gave them the final blow.

'Mr Chaudler, I have prepared a paper on the pioneering surgical success which I am in process of releasing for publication. In view of the importance of our research and its successful application we have arranged a press conference which will be on Monday at 10 here at the Royal. I have anticipated your willingness to attend. I am sure you will not let us down.'

Her smile was back. She was proud of the medical miracle she and her team had achieved.

Tom moved one foot towards the smiling face, but Rebecca pulled him back. He did not say one single word. He just turned round and made for the door, opened it and let his wife through, before he followed without turning round. Without closing the door, they left the doctor, the room and the building.

'Let's go home.' gasped Tom.

'Yes, let's get out of here and go home to Mozart. Are you fit to drive or are you still in a state of shock?'

Tom drove home through the torrential rain. Tension was not eased by the gusty wind which sometimes seemed to do its best to throw the car off the road. Tom held on to the steering wheel with both hands. His knuckles were white. Rebecca could not say if it was the difficulty of keeping the car on the road or with anger. He did not say a word on the way back. She could tell that he was rigid and she understood why.

Rebecca clenched her hands on her lap as if in prayer. Her body was stiff as a poker. She tried hard not to show Tom how close she was to tears. She did not want him to realize that she too was devastated.

Rebecca looked out through the window and seeing the force of the weather she thought that it was appropriate to her mood. She did not talk either. They were deep in thought and in shock. She wondered where his brain was taking him now.

Rebecca knew that she should be grateful to Doctor Smith for having saved Tom's life but now she was not sure?. Would she have felt differently about it if she had been informed before Tom's operation? She thought about this for only a split second. She was certain, that she would have agreed to anything to save Tom's life. Nevertheless she felt that it was despicable that she had not been informed of the details of the operation and that he was to be exhibited without consultation. What they had planned as proof of medical team's brilliance failed completely to consider any psychological consequences; had nothing to do with human feelings, but solely to exhibit the calculation of the frontier of medical science.

Rebecca would never ever trust this female 'leader of the pack'. This doctor had based her actions on purely technical aspects without thoughts of possible emotional consequence relating to the patient and his family. Consumed by her feelings, Rebecca could see why so many things fell into place with the answers to questions being revealed in such a devastatingly dramatic manner.

Why had she not explained to Rebecca why Tom had been kept in an induced comatose state? Why had she not told her about the scan? Why, why, questions still unanswered overwhelmed her.

Tom rushed out into the pouring rain to open the gate, came back and drove the car through on to the drive and stopped. Rebecca could see Mozart through the glass panels. He was waiting for them to join him. It was difficult to see him, and the image became even more blurred the longer she looked through the rain speckled glass.

Tom turned to Rebecca with the words 'I still adore you Rebecca even if I am not really me.'

'I love you too Tom.' Rebecca whispered.

Rebecca took out the keys and headed for the kitchen door. Tom went the other way to close the gate.

Mozart was let out. He was delirious to see them as always when they came back home.

Tom changed clothes. He was wet through. Rebecca waited for Mozart to return so that she could throw his towel over him and rub him down before she also changed.

Tom served them a stiff whiskey. She could do with some heat in her body and Tom needed the golden nectar to calm his shattered nerves.

He carried the drinks through to the snug and switched on the gas fire. He was cold but he soon realized the cold came from inside himself. The heat of the fire did not help. He was shivering.

Tom could not look at Rebecca. How could she love him now? How was it possible for her to deal with the fact that he was not himself?

As if Rebecca had been able to read his mind, his deepest thoughts, she turned towards Tom staring into the flames. The only sounds that could be heard were when each of them swallowed a mouthful of the blessed liquid, the wind lashing the rain against the windows and the fire hissing from the rain falling down the chimney.

Rebecca was the first to break the silence.

'Tom, I want you to know, that whichever brain you are using, I still love you. It is you, the entire Tom, and not a part of you, that I fell for. Tom, I am so happy to have you alive here with me that if Doctor Smith had revealed her intentions to me I would most definitely have agreed for her to go ahead. You are the most important person in the world to me, you and James. Don't you forget that.'

'Thank you for your comfort. I am confused. How I am going to feel about this whole thing in a day or two I don't know. At the moment I am empty, completely and utterly drained. I feel as if I have lost my identity. Rebecca, I am lost. I hear what you are trying to tell me and you are a gem darling, a real gem, but I cannot see myself as the person I was before we attended this morning's meeting. I am not the same. How can I ever be?' Tom said helplessly.

Rebecca moved her armchair closer to Tom, close enough for her to be able to rest her head on to his shoulder. She reached out for his hand and hold it in hers. She could no longer held back her tears. The barricade was broken. Her tears came down her cheeks like a torrential waterfall. She cried so hard that she started with hiccups. She could not contain her fear any longer. She was desperate, tired and hungry. She had held back on so much that had happened lately but now the floodgate had burst, which had been building up inside her.

Tom turned his eyes from the fire and looked at his wife's face on his shoulder. He wished he could cry too, but he was completely dry.

Even Mozart lifted his head from his front legs and paws. He wondered what was going on and tilted his head slightly. He was puzzled.

Tom put his glass on the side table and took his wife's face in his hands. He did not say anything. He just tried to soothe her, to calm her down. Tom kissed the tears away from her cheeks and then he finally broke too. Tears fell from his eyes, two wells of utter confusion. He continued stroking her hair. It was some time before she could stop her tears. She lifted up her lips to meet his. She told him how sorry she was about her selfish behaviour. She so wanted to be strong for his sake but it just came upon her. She simply could do nothing to stop it.

Tom dried their tears away with his handkerchief.

'I am pleased that you have been able to release your emotions, being a reaction to everything which has happened to you lately. You cannot keep on bottling things up for weeks on end. Mary told me that you needed to let your feelings surface. You were in severe need of opening up. Mary has been proved right. I have been trying to make you talk more about things happening around the two of us. I am not sorry that we had this cry. We are emotionally drained.'

Tom continued with some delicate questions.

'How much do we let our friends know? How do we tell James? What do we do now?'

'It is more what you feel you want people to know, I think. We are expected to phone Anna and Eric and to give Mary and Malcolm the news about the hospital visit. If we don't phone them today, they will think that you are not all right. The same applies to James. You are the one to take this decision, darling.' Rebecca said.

'This is going to be tricky. I would rather that nobody was told but this will not be possible if Doctor Smith is determined to publish her team's achievements. Don't you think that some of our friends will put two and two together? James, how I wished he could be kept in ignorance, but I simply cannot see how. Hell, what a mess. It'll be on television too. We must tell James.' Tom thought.

'I think I would prefer to phone our friends to tell

them that all the results are fine, as they actually were. We are then not telling any lies. I don't think that either of us are strong enough at the moment, to say more. I'll phone them while you make us lunch. I know neither of us want anything to eat but we have to try, Rebecca. We'll need the strength to get through the next few days. Do you agree that we shall not let people know just yet?. We have to give it a lot of thought. We have to get it right.'

Rebecca nodded. She could see no further than today. Tom was right. They needed more time and they had to be absolutely sure of how to handle this delicate situation.

'I'll try to keep the phone calls short and will tell them that we have just come back through this horrible weather and that lunch is on the table.' Tom said.

Tom stood up and grabbed Rebecca's hands and pulled her up. He enveloped her in a bear hug.

'Thank you for everything.'

Rebecca was speechless.

She went towards the kitchen while Tom dialled the number for Malcolm. He was going to save James for this evening as he would be studying this time of the day.

Their friends were pleased to hear from Tom and delighted to learn that the tests showed that he was in good health. Tom himself felt physically sick. He was not telling lies but he was not as cheerful as he pretended to be. On the contrary. He was far from happy. He had never liked playing games and he never felt happy telling half truths, and now he was treating his best friends in this way. What ever would they think when they found out what had really happened to him. He thought of himself as a false friend and father.

There was nothing wrong with the meal but they had to force themselves to put food into their mouths. They did not talk much as every effort went into forcing themselves to eat.

The weather was improving and by late afternoon it had stopped raining. The wind had eased too and when Tom put his nose outside the door, it felt pleasant and asked Rebecca if she would care for a walk.

They dressed in heavy shoes as it was bound to be muddy. Mozart jumped around them with joy as the three of them went through the gate.

Rebecca took hold of Tom's hand and looking forward to the fresh air, the thought crossed her mind that this was perhaps going to be the start of their new life?

Water was dripping and hanging on to the trees. The drops on the leaves were glistering. The bushes and plants were heavy with the fallen rain. It felt fresh and looked lush and clean and Rebecca stopped for a split second to take a deep breath. When she stopped Tom had to do the same as he was holding her hand. He let go but took her arm and they continued their walk arm in arm. Rebecca made Tom smell the rain. It was a delight to come out after the kind of weather they had experienced, but it was wet under foot with lots of leaves and twigs on the ground.

Rebecca noticed how quiet Tom was. Was what had happened lawful? Rebecca sighed and turned her eyes away from the trees and the woodland. She did not see anything. Her thoughts were with Tom walking in silence at her side. He had told her that he felt lost. How Tom would manage to 'bury' these memories which belonged not to him, but to somebody else whom he had never met, she did not know. They had to talk it through and decide what to do next.

Tom thought of the time of the year remembering that spring was supposed to bring hope. Everybody said "there is always a spring", when somebody felt low or when the winter weather was awful.

What hope was there for him? He had pinned his faith on the thought that to meet Vallie would help. What had that led to? It was the beginning of a complete disaster. He had pinned his hopes on the appointment with the doctor and had thought that today's meeting would solve everything. Ha, what a dream world he had been living in! It had only depressed him more and sent him even further down the scale of misery. He was feeling low, almost at the point of not caring about anything.

He put his hand on top of Rebecca's arm, which was locked into his own. He stared straight in front of him. He came to a halt as she sighed once more. Tom turned his head. He drowned in her moistened eyes and gathered strength and determination enough to grant her a warm smile before they continued their walk.

Mozart was loving every minute. Tom was pleased that there was at least one of them enjoying the afternoon. How wonderful it must be to be a dog. Tom looked at Mozart running around, tail high in the air, and he had to remember that some dogs were not this lucky. Mozart had had a troubled life before Rebecca found him and they had fallen for one another. Anybody could see that this dog was devoted to her. He was definitely Rebecca's dog. It was wonderful to watch.

They traced their way back home.

Tom looked up towards the sky and pointed out

some patches of blue sky. Tomorrow was another day but he found it almost impossible to look forward.

Rebecca filled Mozart's bowl with fresh water and his dinner was served.

Tom did his best to clean and dry the dog. Mozart was having difficulty in standing still. He had smelled his food. As soon as he possibly could he sneaked away from Tom and went for his bowl.

Tom could not settle down until he had phoned James. That was something that bothered him.

James was at Gill's place. They were going out for drinks with Sarah and Simon their best friends. James had kept his mobile on for his father to be able to reach him.

James was delighted to hear their good news. He was considering coming home for a short break on Saturday but he had to see how it was going to work out before making fixed plans.

'Look Tom,' Rebecca interrupted, 'We have got blue tits in the nesting box. The plum tree must be proud to accommodate a family. I hope that there are chicks.'

Tom turned to her and reminded her that they had to talk seriously about how to tackle their new situation. He could think of nothing else.

'We have to talk about what to do next, Rebecca. I am lost. I am unable to think straight. Have you had any thoughts? Have you any suggestions?'

Rebecca thought for a while. She could sense that she had to go easy. Tom was vulnerable and would be hurt if she was not careful. She looked at him and started to tell him what she thought that they had to do first of all.

'I suggest that we go and pay Vallie a visit. She ought

to hear what has happened. She will understand your visit to her and mine. How to go about this I don't know, but I think we owe this to her. We should tell her on her own without the twins being present. She will have to take the decision whether to explain to her daughters or not? We know that it is her late husband's past that you are living with. You have memories of her and of the twins from years past. Her late husband died in the car crash so graphically revealed in your nightmare.'

Tom listened to what she was saying. He kept silent for so long that Rebecca became worried. She thought that she had hurt Tom. She slowly turned her face towards him, trying to analyze his reaction.

Tom did not look at Rebecca but gazed straight ahead. He did not notice the squirrel crossing the path towards the plum tree. Rebecca saw it and got out of her chair, unlocking the glass panelled door which was enough to scare the animal away from the nesting box. She was grateful to have something to do. Her legs were filled with pins and needles. She had to stand up to restore the circulation.

Tom spoke and in so doing he hesitatingly turned towards her, now back sitting in her armchair.

His voice was trembling. For a split second Rebecca wondered if it was because of anger.

'Don't you think that it ought to be dealt with by Doctor Smith? She is the person responsible. She is the one taking pride in what she has done? Every time I think of her self seeking headline chasing attitude I get upset and furious. What did she think she was doing? I am torn between gratitude for her saving my life and her complete failure to think through the consequences of her actions.

Her personal ego has erased all ethical considerations. She is the one who should break the awful news to the surviving members of the dead man's family. How would you have reacted if it had been <u>my</u> brain which had been put into another man's head? Would you be pleased? I don't think so for a minute, not the brain with memories of you and James left intact? .

No Rebecca, it has to come from the doctor. She must inform Vallie and her family of the consequences of her actions – not us. Don't you see, Rebecca?' Tom asked.

'Yes, put that way I must say I do, but Doctor Smith doesn't know anything about our meetings with Vallie and her daughters. She doesn't know that Vallie is suffering. Don't you think that she should be told after all that has happened? She must be worried after our visits finding that you know so much about them? Wouldn't you have preferred to know the truth about such a mysterious couple and their revelations? Wouldn't you insist on knowing that part of your late husband is living in another person's body? How will she and her daughters ever be able to relax if they think that you or I might return to haunt them? I think that at least the wife should be told. Further more it will be us who will have to deal with the problem. Doctor Smith didn't even reveal to us who the dead man was. The only thing she was willing to let us know was that he died in a car crash. Do you know, I don't think she would have given you that information if it hadn't been for your disclosure of your recurring nightmare. She cannot have asked any one for permission to do what she has done. I was certainly not asked nor told, and if Vallie had been told she would have understood you when you tried to get information from her as to how it was possible for you to recognize her and the twins. No, I am sure she is ignorant of what has taken place.' Rebecca said.

'It is a complicated and delicate matter, Rebecca. I think we should forget about her and everything that has to do with her family. Please, let's leave it. The consequences of any involvement on our part are beyond comprehension, particularly when we are in such a turmoil ourselves. I know what you are saying and I do understand but I don't think I would have wanted to know. I certainly don't want James or anybody else to know about this either. We will have to face up to what we know and see what happens in the near future. How do you feel about me? I am no longer the person you married. In a way James will lose his father all over again if he finds out.' Tom said.

'I have told you that I married <u>you</u> the entire and complete person.' Rebecca reassured.

'I hear what you are trying to tell me, Rebecca, but think of the memories I carry with me that don't even belong to me. You have no part in those images and neither have I.'

'Tom, I have been married before, remember. I have many memories which you don't share with me, just as you must have memories of the life you were leading during the years before we were married.'

'Yes, but these new memories do not even belong to <u>me</u>. I can only repeat myself by telling you again how lost I am. I am no longer Tom. I am a mixture of Tom and somebody who obviously loved fish and chips, cats, football and motor sport, and whose wife liked to read 'Hello' and Ok magazines. There are two girls out there who are loved and missed by my so called "brain". How am I ever going to cope with this? How are <u>you</u> going to cope?' Tom said.

Tom shook his head in disbelief and sorrow. He wondered to himself how he could live through this. He was a walking disaster to himself, his family and friends but also to Vallie the wife of the "brain". He had let them down and now...?

Rebecca intervened to prevent a complete lapse into depression.

'Let's hope that the information given to us by the doctor explaining where your bad dream originates will scare away your night terrors.' Rebecca continued.

Tom left the snug to deal with their usual drinks.

Standing in the kitchen in front of the two glasses he had taken out of the cupboard, Tom had taken out a couple of ice cubes for Rebecca's drink but he stopped in his tracks on his way back to the freezer with the ice tray. He thought of what his wife had said earlier. He could see one single reason for her to want them to tell Vallie about what had happened to him. Rebecca must feel ashamed of him and how he had been acting. He understood her. He put his hands on the table top and bowed his head between his arms, sinking his forehead to his hands. He stood like this for a moment. The pain he felt was terrible even, brutal. Doctor Smith and her brilliant team had saved his life but what they had achieved was beginning to destroy him and his loved ones. If Vallie should find out how her late husband's brain had been used, her life would be destroyed too. How about James and Vallie's twin girls? No, he repeated to himself, Rebecca must be wrong, totally wrong.

He poured the drinks and took hold of the two

glasses, one in each hand and carried them through to the snug, where Rebecca was waiting.

'We have one huge problem, haven't we, Tom?'

'Yes, we have been given something we would never have asked for. How anyone can think herself as being above others and their feelings and reaction, I cannot grasp. I know that as a Christian I should be able to forgive, but I'll never be able to in this case. I'll not be able to forget either, which I invariably find more difficult anyway.'

'No, to forget will be impossible. This is something we'll have to learn to live with.' Rebecca answered in a whisper.

'We could discuss this matter for hours and still not find answers.'

Tom tried to change the subject once more.

'By the way, you are playing golf tomorrow with your lady friends aren't you? The prospect is for a lovely day according to the weather forecast,' he said. ' Mozart and I could go for a walk, and if you don't mind, I might have to be on my own with my thoughts for a couple of hours.'

Rebecca stood up from her armchair and kissed Tom on his forehead. She told him that she could understand him and said that if he changed his mind he just had to say so.

She dialled the number of one of her golfing friends and told her that she would probably play the following morning, if the course was open. She said that Tom's tests were fine. This was something that they had to get used to, people asking and them telling half the truth. Rebecca did not feel like playing golf but if Tom needed time on his own, she had to respect his wish.

They had a quiet meal. They had been more hungry than at lunchtime but still had to almost force themselves to eat. The desire for food was simply not there.

They had their coffee and glass of milk as usual, watching some mindless television to distract them from their problems

Tom took Mozart for a short walk. He was sick with tiredness. He was burnt out, completely shattered. He longed for their bed and to have the comfort of Rebecca next to him. As he did every night, he hoped that his nightmare would not recur, that he would be "cured."

CHAPTER 27

Tom and Rebecca woke up with a start as Tom cried out in his sleep. His black dream was back and now, that Tom knew that it was true and it did cause the driver's death, it had become even worse. Now he felt traumatized, recognizing that he in essence was the victim.

His body was dripping with perspiration. He was shivering and it was not just because of being wet, but from fear and dread. He started to weep like a child. His body glistening with the sweat, he sat with his legs dangling over the side of their bed. He could not stop the tears from falling down his cheeks and he was sobbing uncontrollably. Over and over he said how sorry he was to be like this. He felt ashamed and so, so sorry for Rebecca who had to deal with his problems.

'I am a man, for god's sake. I ought to be the strong one and not feel weak as a kitten, confused and bewildered, like a soldier back from the horror of war. Tom sobbed.

Rebecca sat on the bed holding him from behind, her head resting on his back, her arms around him trying to soothe and comfort him. She did not say anything, but kept on holding him tight. There they were, two naked bodies on an unmade bed. They looked like a Rodin sculpture.

It took a long time for Tom to gather himself together and become calmer. He stood up and went to the bathroom and although it was the middle of the night, he had to have a shower.

Rebecca changed the sheets and then dried Tom with a towel. She rubbed his back with loving care. She made him turn round to face her. He had difficulty looking at her. He was grateful for her love and attention.

They returned to bed and thankfully to sleep. She did not wake up until the alarm went off. It was time for Rebecca to get into her golfing clothes and to prepare the breakfast. She left Tom in bed sleeping.

The sun was shining. The difference in the weather from the previous day could not have been greater.

Rebecca kissed Tom and left a note for him on the kitchen table. She would come home for lunch and wished him a lovely morning, ending the note with love, kisses and a heart.

She was not happy leaving Tom, but he had asked to be on his own. She was pleased to have Mozart as company for him. She bent down and tapped him on his head and gave his ears a tussle.

Tom did not wake up until several hours later. He got out of bed remembering what had happened during the night. He examined himself in the bathroom mirror and once again had the feeling that it was not the right face meeting his gaze. He turned away but he now understood what the reflection in the glass meant. The face which he did see there was of course his own. It belonged to Tom, but the image he had expected must have been that of the dead man's. His brain carried around the wrong memory. How utterly ghastly. Tom did not know what to do. He wished he was dead and to be honest with himself, it was not the first time since his fall that he had had such thoughts.

He managed to eat the breakfast which Rebecca had prepared for him, although he had little appetite. He knew it would hurt her if he did not finish what she had made for him.

He asked the dog if he wanted to go for "walkies" and Mozart immediately jumped to his feet and off they went into the sunshine.

The sky was without clouds. The wind that had tormented them yesterday was gone. There was only a light breeze. Tom decided against taking the route down the Dell as it surely would be too muddy. They walked along the road and took the turning to walk through smaller roads on the other side of the main road. Tom did not feel like talking to people. He did not want to take Mozart through the village as he knew he would most likely meet friends there.

On the opposite side of the road he did not usually see anybody who would enquire about his well being.

He walked in a trance. He was lost, without purpose. His thoughts were far away and sometimes he could feel the dog coming up to him and lick his hand, to take a look at him his master who had suddenly stopped in his tracks. Mozart knew that there was something wrong. He could feel it. Tom bent down to talk to the dog before they went on along the pavement. Mozart was off the lead but he kept close to Tom as if protecting him.

Tom thought about Rebecca's suggestion that they ought to tell Vallie the truth. He was sure that his wife was wrong. It was probably the first time in their married life that their opinions had differed so much. If they did tell Vallie, how could he keep on living knowing that somebody apart from Rebecca knew the truth? To walk around with somebody else's liver, kidney or even heart, he thought was fine, but <u>not</u> their brain. Especially not a brain filled with someone else's memories still present. Further more there was this bloody nightmare which was a constant reminder of how the brain's previous owner had died. Tom realized that he would have to live with this for the rest of his life. His marriage was teetering on the brink of ruin and so was his life and the lives of those he loved. He knew inside that he could not continue this way, but what on earth could he do? He could picture no solution, not even on the distant horizon.

As they entered the back gate and his eyes caught the splendour of the garden and the house, he had to stop and catch his breath. His eyes filled with tears. He became sad. He sank into a bottomless depression. He had to leave this if ...

Rebecca would have to deal with selling this house and to move into a smaller property. They had often talked about down sizing but it had been all talk and nothing had come out of it. They should have been looking around for another villa and ought to have put this property on the market by now when the garden was at its best.

He had something else apart from nightmare, strange images in his mind. It did not take away his feelings about not being able to continue his life but for a moment he was somewhat sidetracked.

As soon as he entered the kitchen he switched on the kettle to make himself a cup of coffee and brought it outside, the mail in hand. He sat down facing the hot sun. He was no longer pale from having been ill and kept indoors.

He opened his mail to find an invitation from Doctor Smith to come to the hospital at 9 am for Friday morning's news conference. The occasion had been brought forward because of the holiday weekend. Her letter stated how much she was looking forward to seeing him.

Tom put the card on the table.

How could she fail to understand what she was doing to him and his family? He felt a frightening hatred of her welling up inside him.

The note was addressed to Mr T Chaudler so he did not have to show it to Rebecca, or did he? Was it unfair to hold this back from her? This frightful invitation made him furious.

There was another letter but this brown envelope was addressed to Mrs R Chaudler. It was in an handwriting that he didn't recognize. Tom turned it over in his hand but there was no sender marked. It had been posted in Edinburgh.

This brown envelope made him curious. He did not make a habit of opening mail addressed to Rebecca but this one was burning in his hands and gave him a strange feeling he was unable to resist. He knew he just had to know what was hiding inside.

He ripped it open with his index finger before he had a chance to change his mind. He could always pretend that he had opened it by mistake.

Tom pulled the two folded sheets of white paper from their protecting cocoon and opened them up one on top of the other. They were photocopies from a newspaper. The headline hit him like a thunderbolt. His body became rigid and he had difficulty breathing. The black ink etched into his eyes like tattoo needles. It hurt.

When his heartbeat finally settled down enough for him to read the article in his hands his mind had no difficulty in producing the image dramatically induced by the headline. This was about him and yet not about him.

"SPORTS CAR DRIVER KILLED IN HEAD ON COLLISION WITH TRACTOR!"

"The horrific collision on a remote country lane close to Edinburgh when the sports car apparently being driven at speed collided with the tractor driven by a farmer as he emerged from his farmyard with the fork lift on the tractor down as he was about to collect hay from his adjacent barn.

The tractor fork pierced the window of Mr Robert Simmons' car and his chest before lifting him out of his vehicle.

Mr Simmons died shortly after being admitted to hospital".

There it was. His recurrent nightmare described in words and as he read it he heard the metal against metal and felt the pain for a split second as the fork entered his chest. He was close to fainting and had to bend his head between his legs and to take a deep breath.

His memory recalled how he had grabbed the car keys after a quarrel with Vallie and in pure anger wheels spinning in the gravel of his drive the sports car had shot off at speed. He could visualize how close it had been to hitting one of the gateposts as he left the drive and the car went through the entrance and on to the road.

Tom draw his breath when he realized that if the car had smashed then, Robert would have been alive today, and he, Tom Chaudler, would not be sitting here now in his world of turmoil.

Tom shook his head trying to rationalize his thoughts from the chaotic rubble of mix-mash which was cascading through his mind. What a waste of a life and what an aftermath!

He could not come to terms with why his life had been spared at the cost of the twin's father. He felt the burden of another man's life heavy on his chest. He felt guilt as he read how Mr Robert Simmons had died from internal injuries.

The article concluded with a statement that the victim had been survived by his wife and twin daughters.

He turned his eyes to the second sheet which was a follow up of the accident revealing how the farmer had been prosecuted for dangerous driving and manslaughter although the sports car had been speeding.

Tom sat looking at the two sheets in his hands for a long time before he slowly and carefully folded them and put them back into the brown envelope. On top of the articles was a yellow label with a few words in handwriting which told him that the enclosures had been requested from the library by Rebecca. He had not noticed this when he first opened up the folded sheets.

He wondered when Rebecca had asked for these articles. Had she phoned before or after their appointment with Doctor Smith? Whenever, did it really matter?

Haunted by what he had read, Tom went to the bookshelf in the snug and took out "The Edinburgh District Road Map".

Finding the road where the accident had occurred he traced the route Robert Simmons would have taken to the place of his death.

The picture of the route interested him. The thought of Vallie and the twins haunted him. He had to see the girls again.

He patted Mozart apologizing for leaving him on his own.

Tom left the house, locked the door, opened the gate, entered his car and set off for the twins, leaving the back gate open.

He was calm as he drove the short distance to the bungalow, parked the car, opened the gate, walked up the path and rang the bell.

Nobody answered. He rang the bell three times but still no reply He peered through the window before he convinced himself that nobody was at home.

He looked around in despair and his imagination vividly recalled the scene as Robert Simmons left the house in rage, slamming the door behind him, storming into his sports car and driving off.

Tom left and picked up his car and drove away.

Without thinking he found himself on the same route that Robert Simmons must have been taken.

Curiosity, even excitement took over and he became consumed by the decision to drive the route himself.

Off he sped imagining the anger and the frustration that the father of the twins – his twins? Would have felt.

Entering through the village he turned right. He drove faster and faster passing the turning to the garden center and went straight ahead.

The road was straight but narrow. It passed farm fields and his speed increased. He was driving really fast now.

He did not notice the wildflowers growing on both sides.

He did not see how beautiful it was with the pink and silvery grass bellowing in the breeze making waves. He kept his eyes on the road enjoying the speed.

He tried to slow down for the oncoming bend, but panicked when he realized that he was not going to make the bend and applied the brakes too much. The car started to slide and he lost control just as the tractor was emerging.

As the points of the fork lift came towards him and the car which skidded across the road his last vision and his last utterance were encapsulated in a loud scream. 'VALLIE!!!!'

The flower patterned curtain bellowed in the warm breeze entering the open terrace door bringing sweet smell and sounds of promise of a future.

Spring had departed leaving the expected summer to take over.

About the Author

Amelie Bullough nee Renius, was born in Stockholm in 1946. She was brought up in Bofors in the centre of Sweden.

Amelie has a degree in History of Art and Architecture.

She has four sons living in Stockhom and Uppsala from her first marriage and lived most of her married life in Ornskoldsvik on the High Coast in N.E. of the country, where she worked at the library and in the reception of the local museum.

As an avid reader she formed a book group where she now lives and enjoys playing golf.

Amelie has always loved writing and has many pen friends around the world.

When she remarried in 1997 she moved to Colinton in Scotland.

"Playing God" is her first novel.